TWENTY TRILLION LEAGUES

UNDER THE SEA

Betterworld.

TWENTY TRILLION LEAGUES

UNDER THE SEA

• • • • • •

ADAM ROBERTS

ILLUSTRATED BY MAHENDRA SINGH

GOLLANCZ

LONDON

First published in Great Britain in 2014 by Gollancz
An imprint of the Orion Publishing Group
Orion House, 5 Upper St Martin's Lane,
London WC2H 9EA

An Hachette UK Company

A CIP catalogue record for this book
is available from the British Library

ISBN 978 0 575 13442 3

1 3 5 7 9 10 8 6 4 2

Typeset at The Spartan Press Ltd,
Lymington, Hants

Printed and bound by CPI Group (UK) Ltd,
Croydon, CR0 4YY

The Orion Publishing Group's policy is to use papers that are
natural, renewable and recyclable products and made from wood
grown in sustainable forests. The logging and manufacturing
processes are expected to conform to the environmental
regulations of the country of origin.

www.adamroberts.com
www.orionbooks.co.uk
www.gollancz.co.uk

They were the first
That ever burst
Into that silent sea ...

CREW OF THE *PLONGEUR*

Capitaine Adam Cloche

Lieutenant de vaisseau Pierre Boucher
Enseigne de vaisseau (de première classe) Jean Billiard-Fanon
Second-Maître Annick Le Petomain 'Le Banquier'
Matelot Alain de Chante
Matelot Denis Avocat
Matelot Jean Capot
Cook Herluin Pannier

Chief engineer: Eric Castor

Observer: Alain Lebret. Reporting to the Minister for National
  Defence, Charles de Gaulle.

The scientists: Mr Amanpreet Jhutti, Mr Dilraj Ghatwala

1

THE SINKING OF THE *PLONGEUR*

❦ ❦ ❦ ❦ ❦ ❦

On the 29th June, 1958, the submarine vessel *Plongeur* left the French port of Saint-Nazaire under the command of *Capitaine de vaisseau* Adam Cloche. The following day the *Plongeur* sank to the bottom of the ocean.

The submarine had travelled westward beyond the limit formed by the Atlantic continental shelf, and the depth of water at this place is considerably greater than three thousand metres. This can only mean that the submarine was lost with all hands. It is true, as some have pointed out, that the *Plongeur*'s design parameters – combining a plated-steel inner hull and a state-of-the-art 'atomic' propulsion system – enabled it to descend to unusual depths. But 'deep' in this context means only a maximum of one thousand metres or so. At three thousand metres the vessel would have been crushed to a mangled twist of metal. Even if the vessel had somehow managed to endure the unspeakable pressures of the profound deep, the sinking craft would, by this stage, have been dropping with such speed that the forward hull would have been cracked and shattered by collision with the rocky seafloor. And what else? Assume, if you choose, that they somehow, miraculously, survived the collision, and the *Plongeur* had settled onto the floor without shattering, and without being crushed by the abyssal pressures. What then? The melancholy truth is that the crew lacked the wherewithal to repair whatever malfunction in the main ballast tanks had brought about the disaster in the first place, and reascend. They would be condemned to a slow, coffined extinction. Better, perhaps, to be snuffed out in a single mighty crunch!

The *Plongeur* was an experimental vessel, powered by a new design of atomic pile, and boasting a number of innovative design features. Its very existence was a national top secret. Accordingly, its melancholy fate went entirely unreported in the French media. As far as the world was concerned, its captain was no-one; its crew nameless.

In these unlucky circumstances, perhaps it was a blessing that, despite its unusual size – for the *Plongeur* was one hundred and sixty feet long, and displaced two thousand four hundred tonnes – the vessel was carrying only a small crew. The more the glory for them, the less the loss for France. Captain Adam Cloche was a veteran of the Free French Navy during the Second World War, and a man so much at home in the salt, estranging medium of the sea that even his friends wondered if he had any kind of life at all on land – where else would he die, if not beneath the waves? It was his proper place. Directly under Cloche's command was Lieutenant Pierre Boucher, younger than his captain by a decade and a half, but an experienced sailor nonetheless. When he had been approached by the French Government to command this experimental submersible boat, Cloche had been permitted to choose any six officers and sailors. He personally approached Jean Billiard-Fanon to serve as *Enseigne de vaisseau*; and for Second Mate he recruited Annick Le Petomain, known to his friends as 'Le Banquier' for his skill at games of chance. Four Ordinary Seamen – Alain de Chante, Denis Avocat, Jean Capot and Herluin Pannier – were in turn recommended by Billiard-Fanon. But his request for a particular chief engineer – a certain Stefan Nevin of Calais, a veteran of the old war – was overruled by the powers that be. The new propulsion mechanism was top secret: for at its heart was an atomic pile, at that time a novelty in submarine power. An engineer with knowledge of such technologies, one Eric Castor, was assigned to the craft. More unusually still, two scientists from the team who had been developing the craft's new technologies were also to accompany the *Plongeur* on its maiden voyage. These were: Messieurs Amanpreet

Jhutti and Dilraj Ghatwala, Indian nationals both. Cloche did not pretend to be happy about this. Even if (he argued) there were some potential advantage in having the inventors of the experimental technologies on board during the maiden voyage, the benefit was surely offset by the disadvantage of cluttering up the craft with landlubbers – and foreigners to boot. Worst of all, from the captain's point of view, was the fact the presence on the *Plongeur* of an official 'Observer': Alain Lebret, reporting directly to the Ministry for National Defence. Cloche objected to the presence of these supernumeraries aboard his vessel; but his objections were overruled.

A crew of only nine was small for so large a craft, but the two-week voyage was expected to do no more than test the vessel's new technological capacities. And despite the skeleton crew, space was tight aboard the submarine. Although it was large, its engines took up a disproportionate amount of the vessel's central rear portions. Everything throughout was painted thickly with light blue paint, except for the engine itself which was painted red – it was strange, Cloche thought to himself, that there was no bare metal in the vessel anywhere to be seen. Still, it was certainly a well-*appointed* craft. Crew all had individual cabins, and a 'scientific room' was located fore, in which facilities for experimentation were laid out: a variety of technical accoutrements adorned this space. Most remarkable of all, a broad oval observation window was inset into the hull, and an observation chamber located below and fore of the bridge. When Captain Cloche was first shown round his new command, docked at Saint-Nazaire, he was – however much his imperturbable manner and large beard implied otherwise – especially dismayed to find this feature. 'It must,' he pointed out to the team who escorted him, 'represent a weak spot in the pressure-robustness of the hull! How can it not?' He was assured that steel plates, specially designed to lock together in an absolute seal, covered the six-foot-wide porthole when it was not being used for scientific observation. 'I have served in a dozen submarines,' Cloche said, shaking his head, 'and commanded three, and I have never seen anything like it. Is this a warship of the French navy – or is it a lakeside pleasure skiff?'

'May a warship not also have the capacity for observation and scientific enquiry?' returned the official.

'But – so *large* a porthole! The structure *must* be weaker at this place.'

'The tolerances of the *Plongeur* are far in advance of comparable vessels,' said the ministerial aide

'In point of fact, the shipyards of—' began a junior ministerial staffman.

The ministerial aide coughed loudly, and glowered at his subordinate. 'There is no need,' he said, brusquely, 'to trespass upon the official secrets of the Republic by speaking of specific locations.'

'Was the *Plongeur not* built here in the shipyards of Saint-Nazaire?' asked Cloche, amazed.

That the ministerial aide would not be drawn further on this matter suggested to the captain that the answer to his question was that Saint-Nazaire was not the site of construction. But if not here – then where?

Of course the *Plongeur* was top secret. Although two years had passed since the US Navy had included nuclear submarines in its fleet, and despite the fact that, of course, France *was* a nuclear power, the existence of this advanced prototype of a radically new sort of submarine was closely guarded. It sailed without fanfare or notice, and it vanished into the great deep in the same manner. Nobody save a few senior officials and technicians knew of the *Plongeur*'s existence; and few amongst that select group mourned its loss.

It sailed from Saint-Nazaire before dawn. Midmorning, it essayed submerging for the first time. For most of the day of the 29th it performed a set of pre-arranged manoeuvres; testing the underwater and surface fitnesses of the craft. Through the night of the 29th and through the early hours of the 30th June it sailed west-northwest, leaving behind it the coast of northern Spain. Its last transmission was received before dawn on the morning of the 30th: Captain Cloche reported that he was about to take the craft down to its maximum dive depth. In the event the *Plongeur* passed far below that supposed 'maximum'. No further transmissions were received.

2

THE CAPTAIN'S LAST SUPPER

❦ ❦ ❦ ❦ ❦ ❦

Almost as soon as the *Plongeur* was underway, Captain Cloche requested the presence of both Indian scientists in his cabin. The men entered a little awkwardly, unused to negotiating the confined spaces of the craft.

'Messieurs,' said Cloche, without further preliminary. 'There are few situations in which a robust chain-of-command matters as much as it does upon a submarine. We are not presently at war, but nevertheless. At one thousand metres below the surface of the sea, the slightest mistake is death. I trust I need not labour this point.'

'Indeed not, Captain,' said Amanpreet Jhutti.

'I have studied, as far as my capacity permits me, the operation of the engine that powers this craft. I do not pretend to understand it entirely. I do not need to. As captain, my study must in the first instance be *people*. I have confidence in my crew. But I will say frankly to you, messieurs, that I do not know you; and I do not know your Monsieur Lebret either. I appreciate that he has been posted here by the direct authority of the minister of National Defence; and I understand that he has been supervising your work...'

'Say, rather, *liaising*,' said Jhutti. He spoke French fluently, although with a slight accent.

The captain was not used to being interrupted. He cleared his throat, thunderously. 'So he is not, in effect, your superior officer?'

'Not at all,' said Ghatwala.

'I have no disobliging impulses as far as Monsieur Lebret is

6

concerned,' said the captain. 'But I do not know him, and cannot pretend to be happy that he has been parachuted into my crew at the last moment. I am prepared to tolerate the presence of you two, messieurs, since this experimental "atomic" drive is clearly beyond the technical capacity of ordinary naval engineers. But I must insist that you operate under *my* authority at all times. I request an assurance from you, in short, that there shall be no conflict between my orders and those of Monsieur Lebret.'

'We understand, Captain,' said Jhutti, gravely.

'Good. At any rate, I invite you all to join me for supper, this evening at seven. My *lieutenant de vaisseau* Monsieur Boucher will also be there. I suppose our Government "observer", Monsieur Lebret, will also attend.'

'You have no excess of love for your present Government I think, Captain,' said Jhutti.

'I avoid all political complications,' said Cloche, with a severe expression. 'Of whatever stripe. I only wish that political complications would similarly avoid me, and my work. But the presence of Monsieur Lebret suggests that this will not come to pass.'

'If it settles your mind at all, Captain,' said Jhutti, glancing briefly at his countryman, 'I do not believe that Lebret is here in a political capacity.'

'You know who his uncle is?'

'I do not.'

'Pierre Lebret, the very same. Through this relative, our "observer" has a personal relationship with the Minister of National Defence, de Gaulle.'

'I do not see—'

But the captain put up his hand, and shook his heavy head. 'Until this evening, messieurs.'

As the scientists turned to leave the cramped cabin, the captain spoke again. 'Since we have broached the subject of politics,' he said, 'you might gratify my curiosity on one subject.' Messieurs Jhutti and Ghatwala turned back to face him. 'You are Indian nationals. I commend the advances your nation has made – certain

7

advances in atomic technology. I can see why you might wish to develop these advances aboard a craft of a more advanced Western nation, rather than one of the as-yet rudimentary Indian navy. But I *am* curious why you brought your technological expertise to *my* nation? Would not the British Royal Navy have welcomed you enthusiastically?'

'Perhaps they would,' said Jhutti, drily.

'So?'

'Captain,' said Jhutti, again giving his compatriot a brief, queer look. 'You are, perhaps, aware of the reputation of Pierre Loti?'

'Loti? The sailor? Of course!'

'He *was* a celebrated naval officer,' agreed Jhutti. 'But also a writer of genius. Fifty years ago he published a book called *L'Inde sans les Anglais – India without the English*. Reading that book as a young man had – shall we say, a profound influence upon me.'

'Fifty years ago!' said the captain. He sniffed. 'Very well. I do not wish to initiate a political discussion. I care only for loyalty.'

'Loyalty,' said Jhutti, 'is a political word.'

But Cloche had turned his face away, pretending to busy himself with his log book. The men left the cabin.

The day was spent in simple manoeuvres; dives to a hundred feet or so, and resurfacings. Surfacing is more of a problem for submarines than many people realise; or to be precise, the problem is in surfacing *too rapidly*, for too eager a buoyancy can propel a submarine salmon-like into the air, to crash back down again. In such a circumstance the blow places unhealthy strains upon the superstructure, and can disarrange the pattern of hull plates, which in turn can provoke catastrophe when the vessel resubmerges. Indeed, after the loss of the *Plongeur*, the official enquiry specifically considered whether initial manoeuvres had caused any such flaw to appear in the skin or ballast tanks of the craft. But there was no evidence of anything out of the ordinary; and the last two messages received from Captain Cloche reported his perfect satisfaction with both the ongoing exercises and the health of his vessel.

Eventually the day's exercises were completed. Since the seas were calm – and since it is difficult for even the most sophisticated submarine to maintain horizontal trim whilst underwater – the *Plongeur* surfaced for the night. Tables were laid for the evening meal. The captain's nook, compact as a wall-set table in an underground café, was crowded. Cloche himself was there, of course; as well as Boucher, and the taciturn engineer Castor, and the two scientists Jhutti and Ghatwala. In addition, the government 'officer' Lebret was present. Matelot Pannier served the food.

'Eat as much as you can,' said Pannier, stacking empty soup bowls along his left arm whilst distributing the plates for the next course with his right. 'The torpedo racks are stuffed with grub.'

'With what, Monsieur Pannier?' asked the captain.

'Food, sir.'

'I gave no such order! Are you sure?'

'As eggs,' confirmed the cook.

'And you signed off on this?' gloomed Cloche, bunching his brows. 'Without my authority?'

The cook opened his eyes very wide, and wiped his chin with his white apron. But before he could answer, Monsieur Lebret spoke up.

'The space would otherwise be empty,' he said. 'Since we had no brief to carry weapons on a test mission, I authorised the arsenal spaces to be filled with extra supplies.'

The captain's face drew upon itself in contained fury. 'We will be at sea a mere two weeks, Monsieur,' he observed. 'Our complement of supplies will be more than sufficient.'

'It seemed to me, Captain,' said Lebret, affably, 'that useful ballast – such as tins and bottles – must be preferable to useless lumber.'

All eyes were on the captain. Everybody knew that this was a matter not of commissioning extra supplies, but rather of circumventing the authority of the captain. Perhaps Lebret hoped to sell this surplus requisitioned food through the black market upon the return to port.

'I am entitled,' Cloche said, in a soft voice, 'to know what is happening on *my* boat, M'sieur.'

Lebret met the captain's gaze without flinching. He was a man in his early forties, with a round, almost childlike face and a wispy beard like the hairs of a coconut sprouting from his chin and cheeks. But there was something olive-pit-hard about his eyes. 'Naturally,' he replied.

'It may be the *case*,' the captain said, his ire increasing incrementally with each word. 'That you are *unfamiliar* with the way things are ordered upon a vessel of the French navy. Permit me to inform you: the captain's authority is absolute, and must be consulted in every question, no matter how trivial. Do you understand this principle? More importantly do you *accept* it?'

'Like you,' said Lebret, 'I am accustomed to the exercise of authority, and have grown used to others deferring to me. Nevertheless, I am confident we will be able to maintain a détente during the short period we must spend together.'

This evasive answer, of course, caused the captain's ferocity to focus. 'No, M'sieur!' he said forcefully. 'No. Not *like me*. You may be accustomed to ordering others about, but your experience is not *like mine*. You did not fight for the Free French, risking death every day in the black waters of the winter Atlantic. You were not shipwrecked three times, clinging to wreckage in a sea of spilled oil amongst the corpses of your comrades!'

Lebret's eyebrows rose, but his expression settled almost at once back into its serenely insolent mask. 'Perhaps I understand your animosity, Captain Cloche. You have, I suppose, heard of my work for the Vichy administration?'

'I have heard the rumours,' said the captain, directing his attention to the food on his plate.

'Ah, but *rumours*,' said Lebret easily, 'may not be trusted. Appearances, you see, can trump reality. And since you claim familiarity with my past, captain, let me say: I know a great many things about *your* career, too. I may even be better placed to assess which of us has more truly served France.'

'You dare not compare our experiences!'

'I report directly to the chief of National Defence, de Gaulle himself. You think he would be happy having me working under him if he were not satisfied with my war record?'

'The ministry of National Defence,' Cloche returned, 'is under the joint command of Messieurs de Gaulle and Guillaumat. How do I know which of the two is your true master?'

Lebret pushed his plate away. 'My true master is France,' he replied, complacently.

'I insist,' the captain retorted instantly, 'that you agree to submit to my authority during this voyage!'

'I concede you *are* the captain of this vessel.'

Cloche glowered at the shoreman, his broad beard trembling as he chewed. But he said no more.

A gloomy mood settled over the table. Boucher, a red-faced, jolly-mouthed fellow whose small eyes were overroofed by a great white dome of bald forehead, tried to lighten the mood.

'So,' he said, perkily. 'Can anyone explain the why this atomic pile must be so large and heavy? It seems counterintuitive, since atoms themselves are the smallest of things!'

'Our pile is one of the smallest yet made,' replied Ghatwala. Then, looking at the ceiling, he added: 'I appreciate that you spoke in jest, Monsieur.'

'Top secret,' grumbled Castor. 'And more than half of what I knew about engines thrown in the incinerator!'

'That,' said Lebret, is one reason why we have the pleasure of Messieurs Jhutti and Ghatawala's company.'

Castor, the engineer, had a snouty, swarthy face; and a tendency to snuffle into his own sinuses. He glanced at the scientists, sitting awkwardly about the captain's narrow table, and scowled. 'There's *some* will hate a man for a black face,' he announced, to nobody in particular. 'But not I.' Something about the way he said this did not inspire confidence.

For several long seconds nobody spoke.

'Come!' said Lebret, suddenly, lifting his wine glass. 'We are sailing in open sea in the most advanced submarine France has yet seen! We have stolen a march on the USSR, on the British, even on the US Navy! Let us not sour the mood.'

Everyone at the table raised their glasses.

'Tomorrow,' said the captain. 'We shall take her down to a thousand metres, and see how well she stands the force of deep water.'

'I am confident,' said Amanpreet Jhutti, 'that she will surpass your expectations.'

'Speaking of rumours,' said Castor, although nobody had been. 'The chatter below decks is that this technology has been, shall we say, *appropriated* from the Russians.'

Jhutti shook his head, rapidly. 'Is this what the crew believe? Why would they think so?'

'Come, come,' said Castor. 'With any respect due to you, M'sieur, and so on, and so forth. But whoever heard of an Indian designing a submarine?'

'The inventor and captain of the *Nautilus*, Jules Verne's celebrated submarine, was an Indian,' observed Ghatwala.

Castor jerked in his seat and sat up straighter. 'By no means,' he snapped. 'A Pole.'

'I assure you, Monsieur,' Ghatwala began to say; but Castor spoke across him. 'Captain Nemo, the hero of a novel I know *very well* – written by a countryman of mine after all, and not yours – Captain Nemo was a *Polish* aristocrat.'

The Indians exchanged glances, and returned quietly to their meal.

'At any rate,' said Lebret, 'whilst the design of the atomic pile does owe a great deal to the input of these two talented Punjabis, the design of the submarine itself…' He broke off, and looked around. 'Well, shall we say – blueprints were discovered in Abdallabad. Despite their age, they specified a number of remarkable innovations in submarine design.' He lifted his glass of wine.

Lieutenant Boucher swallowed his mouthful. 'You don't say?' he said, perkily. 'Lucky for us that the *Indian* navy didn't seize those plans!'

'Lucky for us?' echoed Jhutti.

'For France, I mean.' He grinned. 'Now, don't get testy, M'sieur. I was born in Algeria. I have no problem thinking of a man with a black face as French – it doesn't disqualify him in *my* eyes.'

'I shall assume you intend no offensiveness in speaking this way,' said Jhutti, coolly.

'France is shattered,' declared Lebret, grandly. 'It has endured its greatest catastrophe, invasion and submission – and it *has* survived. Nevertheless we are barely piecing together our nation again. How many governments have we had in the last five years? Nine, is it? And the war is *thirteen* full years behind us now! Still we suffer.' He shook his head, took a slurp of wine and picked a cigarette case from his jacket pocket. 'The money for this project is not French, messieurs – the captain knows this already. The funding is, mostly, Swiss. This may in part explain his hostility.'

Cloche made a noise, halfway between a bark and a syllable of speech. He glowered at Lebret, who did not flinch.

'But,' said Boucher, startled, 'we *do* sail under the French flag!'

'Switzerland lacking seaports,' suggested Ghatwala, 'finds itself at a disadvantage, perhaps?'

'I talk of private money, not governmental funding,' said Lebret. 'May I smoke, captain?' he asked, pulling a cigarette case from his jacket pocket. 'My understanding of the technology involved in this manner of boat – incomplete though it is – leads me to believe that you can conjure air magically from the seawater itself, using the paring knife of atomic power. So perhaps you do not mind if we contaminate the breathable with a little fragrant tobacco?'

Captain Cloche was glowering at the official observer. 'Perhaps a cigarette,' he said eventually, 'will be a cork, to stop up your babbling mouth?'

Lebret laughed a gurgly laugh, clicking his lighter and dabbing a painterly touch of orange flame to the end of his cigarette. 'But discretion is my saint's day name, Captain! It is my very stock-in-trade! Of course, if you think I have said too much, I will happily hold my peace.'

The others continued eating, in silence, whilst Lebret sat back (as far as the confined space permitted him) and extruded limbs and tentacles of smoke from his mouth, as if a smoke-octopus lurked in his torso. Eventually the captain wiped his mouth with a napkin and spoke again.

'Messieurs,' he declared. 'Since our official observer has permitted the feline secret egress from its *sac*, I ought perhaps to say a little more. I am a Frenchman, first and last. I am a sailor, first and last. I do not concern myself with the doings of politicians and financiers, of businessmen and Jews and communists and capitalists. How the government of France were able to finance this splendid machine is not *my* business. Say the money *is* Swiss! Money is not our concern. Our concern is the sea. The sea is not persuaded by bankers' drafts and stocks of bullion; the sea respects nothing but the grit and willpower of dedicated seamen. And with that, messieurs, good night.'

The captain got creakily to his feet and withdrew to his cabin.

The *Plongeur* rode the tranquil sea that night, beneath the infinite spread of constellations; each star its own intricate world, gleaming white in the black ether. Waves caressed the flanks of the floating submarine with the tenderness violent beings sometimes bestow on a whim. Inside some men slept, and some served their turn on the night watch.

The dawn rose swiftly, as it does at sea. Captain Cloche took a last turn upon the deck of his conning tower. The wind was growing brisker, and myriad wavelets covered the surface of the water with dragon scales. The sky a pale blue. A few submarine-shaped white clouds clustered together near the western horizon.

'Prepare to dive!' Cloche announced, fitting his burly form through the small hatch and trotting down the metal ladder. Matelot Avocat followed him, drawing the hatch closed after him; shutting away – in fact – the last view of the wide sky any of that crew would ever see again.

3

THE DISASTER

❦ ❦ ❦ ❦ ❦ ❦

The crew took up their places and the engines powered up. Air was pumped from the two main floatation tanks and compressed into stainless steel cylinders; cold seawater flooded in to replace it. Le Petomain, sitting in the pilot's seat, steered the craft forward and downward, tipping the floor through twenty degrees, and causing the three observers – Lebret and the two scientists, none of whom were experienced in submarine operations – to skitter and slide on their feet, grasping at the grips depending from the ceilings to steady themselves.

The *Plongeur* dived.

The bridge of the craft was a low, angular place. Though built for a larger crew than presently manned the vessel, it nevertheless felt crowded. Electric lights, cradled in wire mesh, threw graph-grid patterns of shadow over the metal walls.

All eyes were on the depth metre – six sets of sliding numbers, marking out the tenths, the metres, the tens, hundreds and thousands, as the boat descended through the water.

The walls creaked, and sang. Loud, unpredictable popping noises resonated through along the central corridor of the craft. Ghatwala flinched at the first of these; but Lebret leaned back against the angled face of a locker and coolly lit a cigarette.

'One thousand metres, sir,' announced Le Banquier.

'Level out, M'sieur Le Petomain,' replied the captain.

The floor angled slowly back to the horizontal. The depth gauge hovered between nine hundred and ninety eight and nine hundred and ninety nine. 'Pressure one hundred kilograms per square centimetre.'

'Sounds a lot, doesn't it, Monsieur Lebret?' said the captain, without looking at his interlocutor. 'And indeed, if it were applied *unequally* upon steel even of the thickness of the hull of the *Plongeur*, it would punch through in a moment. Luckily for us, it is applied on all sides simultaneously.'

'Indeed,' drawled Lebret.

'What of the observation porthole – are the steel shutters holding up?'

'Very well, sir.'

'Sonar?'

'Nothing to report, Captain.'

'What do you say, messieurs?' announced the captain. 'Shall we try her lower?'

'You're sure that's a good idea, Captain?' Lebret asked.

'Ask the two messieurs standing to your left,' the captain returned, without looking at him. 'Take us down to one thousand five hundred metres.'

'Very good, sir.'

The vanes on the exterior of the vessel tilted, and more air was pumped from the main tanks; at the same time, the four smaller orientational tanks shifted ballast between them. The *Plongeur* tilted forward and resumed its descent.

Almost at once, disaster struck.

There was a cacophonous report, like a cannon firing. The whole vessel shook and trembled. An alarm sounded a flute-like, almost musical noise. The angle of the deck did not increase, but the boat began to fall much faster. Nobody on the bridge needed to look at the suddenly spinning numbers of the depth gauge – everybody registered the suddenly accelerating descent in their guts. 'Hey!' cried Lebret.

'Report!' demanded the captain.

'I don't know, sir,' said Le Banquier, looking frantically between the readouts of his various pieces of equipment. 'We're descending...'

'That much is obvious, sailor!' shouted the captain. 'Go aft, Capot! Avocat go to the stern. Find out what has happened.' The two crewmen hurried from the bridge.

'I'm trying to close the main ballast tanks, sir,' said Le Banquier. 'But the vents are not responding. Or perhaps they are. But either way – we are still going down.'

Metres fluttered past on the readout; tens adding to tens. The hundreds began to click round.

Abruptly Capot burst into the bridge from the stern of the vessel, sweat polishing bright patches upon his face. His eyes were wide, and for a moment he could not speak. 'The engines are fine,' he gasped. 'It must be the forward ballast tanks!' He ran through the bridge, heading fore; and Avocat followed after him.

The hull growled and coughed with the increasing pressure.

'Sir?' cried Le Banquier. 'I must report that the forward vanes are *stuck* in descent position.'

'What?' snapped the captain. 'The vanes themselves? Or have the control cables sheared?'

'I—I don't know, sir.'

'Well get forward and find out, man!'

Le Banquier scrambled clumsily from his seat and hurried down the forward corridor. The hull gave a great, shuddery moan, punctuated with rifle-shot cracks.

Nobody spoke. Of the remaining individuals inside the bridge, only Lebret could master even the appearance of unconcern. The scientists were gripping their leather ceiling handles tight; the captain brooded. One thousand five hundred metres flickered past on the depth gauge. Cloche drew a breath deep into his chest. 'So messieurs,' he said, addressing the Indians. 'We shall now see how far your design exceeds its safety margins.'

'May I go forward, captain?' asked Jhutti. 'To see if I can render assistance?'

'By all means.'

Jhutti made his way downslope and left the bridge along the corridor.

The silence was oppressive; but nobody broke it. For long

minutes the only sound was the strangely mournful hooting of the alarm, punctuated by the raucous gong-like clatterings made by the increasing weight of water pressure on the steel flanks of the *Plongeur*.

'How deep does the ocean go in these parts anyway?' asked Lebret.

'You ask an interesting question, sir,' replied the captain. 'In the open Atlantic, the seabed is between four and five thousand metres down – assuming that one does not disappear into one of the celebrated ocean trenches, some of which are ten thousand metres deep and more. But—' a drumroll of bangs and snaps clattered through the craft, and the captain stopped speaking. 'But,' he resumed, shortly, 'we were sailing *east* as we dived, and we have not moved far from the coast of France, so that we are in effect diving towards the mountain-slope of the continental shelf. As to its precise depth, it is hard to say. Somewhere between two and four thousand metres, I would guess.'

'Two thousand is fast approaching,' reported Ghatwala.

'And if we crash nose-first into the ocean floor,' Lebret said, insouciantly, 'I presume it is the end?'

'There's no chance of us settling gently onto a soft bed of sand,' said Cloche. 'If that is what you mean. No, if we hit the floor it will rupture the craft and we will die in moments. But, Monsieur, if that possibility scares you, I can assure you: the pressures at the abyssal depths will crush us in an instant, like an ogre's paw closing around an egg. Such a death will at least be quick!'

'Hardly a fairy-tale ending,' replied Lebret, distantly.

The depth gauge spun past two thousand metres.

The noises increased in volume and variety. A toccata of snapping and cracking noises marked the ever-increasing external pressure squeezing the hull. The whole submarine began to vibrate, and sway its massy snout in the water.

'Castor?' bellowed the captain, abruptly, shouting along the corridor. 'Report!'

When there was no reply, he called again, 'Monsieur! Tell me at once – *why* is my ship shaking her head like a melancholy-mad elephant?'

There were some indistinct voices from the front of the craft, and then Castor came clambering up the corridor. 'I've closed the ballast tanks by hand, but the pumps are struggling to pump air back in – the pressure's too high. Or else there's still some breach in the tanks. Or . . . I don't know! It ought to be working, but it is not.'

'Why are we shaking from side to side?'

'I don't—don't know, Captain.'

A growling noise swelled from the rear of the craft, overlaid by a wild percussion of cracks from the hull all around them, like a great quantity of pebbles hurled forcefully against a wall of metal.

'What about the vanes?'

'Won't budge, sir, I don't know why! They've seized, they've seized completely.'

'Captain,' came another voice. It was Billiard-Fanon, running through from the rear.

'What is it, *enseigne*?'

'The propellers are turning! The gearing has sheared – I can't turn them off, short of shutting down the entire engine.'

The skin above Cloche's beard whitened visibly. 'There must be a way to decouple the driveshaft!'

'Do I take it,' said Lebret, his insolent smoothness apparently unaffected by the disaster, 'that we are not only sinking, but actively *powering ourselves* into intolerable depths? Actively *hurrying* towards the rocky anvil that will shatter us to pieces?'

Billiard-Fanon scrambled back up the corridor to the engine room, gabbling 'Aye-sir! Aye-sir!' like a slogan. At the other extreme of the craft Castor's bestial face head popped through the doorway. 'The ballast tanks won't inflate, sir. They won't. There's—there's—'

'What is it, sailor?'

Castor spoke again in a smaller voice, 'There's nothing we can do, sir.'

The captain looked about, his brows ridged with wrinkles like beach sand at low tide. 'But this makes no sense! Three vital systems malfunctioning simultaneously – and on our first proper dive?'

'Ill luck,' noted Lebret, laconically.

'Luck? It *must* be sabotage!' roared the captain. 'It cannot be otherwise!'

'Well, Captain,' said Lebret with a weary sigh. 'If one of the crew has betrayed us, he is going to die along with everyone else. So justice will at least be done.'

The descent continued to tug insistently inside the guts of all the crew.

'There must be something we can do!' declared the captain.

The depth gauge spun past three thousand metres. At exactly that moment, by strange synchronicity, the whole length of the vessel began to moan, like a spirit in torment. The noise was a sinuously modulated organ note, an octave and a half below middle C: a weirdly vocalic, human-sounding din. Struggling back into his tipped-forward seat, Le Petomain wrestled the main controls.

'The ship itself sings our death chant,' said Dilraj Ghatwala, looking surprisingly calm. 'Under the circumstances …' he began, before drawing a silver cigarette case from the inside pocket of his tunic, and taking out a white tube.

The captain rubbed his face with his hand. Finally – an action nobody in any of his previous crews had ever seen him perform before – he crossed himself. 'Messieurs,' he announced, to the bridge. 'Our fate is sealed. We have, I fear, only short moments before inevitable extinction.'

He lifted the ship's microphone from its cradle, and addressed the entire craft. 'Messieurs, crewmen, comrades. Please assemble on the bridge, without delay.'

Replacing the microphone, he turned to Ghatwala, 'Sir, my pipe is in my cabin, and I do not believe I shall have time to retrieve it. May I trouble you for a cigarette, and a light?'

'By all means, Captain,' Ghatwala replied, in his heavily accented French. He fumbled one of the white, hyphen-shaped sticks from his case, and then struck a match to light it for Cloche. As the captain sat back, blowing out smoke, the bridge slowly filled with the entire complement of crew. Billiard-Fanon, his passage aided by the forward tilt of the craft, returned from the engine room. Alain de Chante led Avocat, Capot and Castor up from the front. Even Pannier emerged from the galley, wiping sweaty hands on his white apron.

'Monsieur Le Petomain,' the captain said, when everybody was assembled. 'Please silence the alarm.'

Though the chiming alarm-sound could hardly be heard over the Hadean groaning of the hull, Le Banquier did as he was ordered.

'Messieurs,' said Capitaine Cloche, drawing deeply on his cigarette and exhaling a spear of smoke. He spoke loudly, to be audible over the din. 'I regret to inform you all that disaster, swift and deadly as a serpent, has stung the *Plongeur*. We descend to inevitable death. You can all see for yourself, on the depth gauge, the terrible speed with which we are going down; you can hear for yourself the implacable, increasing forces pressing in upon us from every side. Truly did a great poet once write: *facilis descensus Averno*. As truly did he add: impossibility attends the return. We must ready ourselves!'

Every face was angled towards the captain; every ear strained to hear his words over the persistent metallic clanging noises.

'Soon one of two things will happen,' Cloche continued. 'Either we will strike the seabed in a collision that must rip open the stern; or else the sheer pressure of water will overwhelm the structural integrity of the *Plongeur*, crushing us all. In either case we will all die quickly, and cleanly, and so we shall surrender our spirits to the deep. Some of us here have been sailors all our lives; and fought not long ago through a long, bitter war, a conflict that could have taken our lives at any moment. Some of you' – and he nodded towards Lebret and the scientists – 'are not. In either case, messieurs, I suggest you direct your minds to whichever God commands your heart.'

He drew himself up in his chair, bracing himself against the angle with both feet, and looked about him, speaking still more loudly to be heard as the noises of the squeezed hull magnified and shrieked. 'I shall share with you all something I have told no other human being – not even my wife! It is this: *Death is an ocean*. I have always known that I would die beneath the surface of the sea. God created the earth not from void; but from the primal waters – you can read this truth, in the book of *Genesis*, at the very beginning of the Bible. *And the earth was void and empty, and darkness was upon the face of the deep; and the spirit of God moved over the waters.* What does this mean, messieurs? I am no theologian, but it seems clear enough to me. The deep waters *preceded* the creation of the universe. The deep waters preceded even God, perhaps. From the deeps came the cosmos; and we who are returning now into the deeps, to meet our final rest, will find a purer, more authentic death than those human beings fated to die upon the alienated land.'

He stopped speaking. All around the confined space of the bridge, faces looked harrowed, expressions clenched with fear. Only Lebret appeared calm in the face of his imminent demise.

Taking their cue from their captain, everybody – with the single exception of Billiard-Fanon, who did not smoke – brought out cigarettes, or borrowed some from others.

'Depth three thousand metres,' announced Le Banquier. 'Pressure three hundred and ten kilograms per square centimetre.'

'I'm astonished the hull has not already cracked,' said Jhutti, in a low voice. 'At the very least, the observation window should have caved-in.'

'Nothing on the sonar.'

'Nothing? Surely the seabed must be registering?'

'Nothing, Captain.'

'Is it working?'

'I—I don't know, Captain.'

Still the digits whirled.

'Comrades!' barked Castor, suddenly. 'I must unburden myself before I die. I married a woman called Marie in the town of Vésinet, in Alsace, before the war. Then in 1947 I married Antoinette Tronson in Marseille. Marie died of typhus a few years ago, but I had already married again – a widow called Emma Chassoux, who has a small dairy farm near the coast in Normandy. I planned to retire to that farm, messieurs. Antoinette has no idea of the existence of Emma, nor Emma of Antoinette.'

Nobody made any comment upon this confession of bigamy on behalf of the snout-faced engineer; for if none felt inclined to condemn, yet none felt authorised to forgive, his delinquency. The groaning of the hull increased in volume, and slid a semitone up in pitch. The entire structure of the sub was starting to vibrate, like a wine-glass rubbed around its rim by a wet finger.

A moment later young Avocat spoke up. 'I grew up on a farm,' he announced. 'Near Saint-Jean-les-Deux-Jumeaux, which is in Seine-et-Marne. When I was a boy, my cousin, Emmeline, died. I watched her die and I did nothing to help. She was epileptic, messieurs. One day she milked the cow. But she had a seizure, and her head became wedged in the milk jug, and she choked to death. I did nothing, except laugh at what seemed to me, as it was happening before my eyes, only an absurdity – a merely comic eventuality. I could say I thought she was deliberately acting the fool; or that I was simply overcome with the ridiculousness of this girl with her head in a jug – I no longer know the truth of it. By the time I realised how serious matters were it was too late.' He began to weep, tears clearing paths through the sweat upon his cheeks. 'I told the priest about it, and he absolved me, but I have never felt clean – I have never forgotten it. And I told no other human being, save my sainted mother who is dead now. I have told nobody else, until this moment!'

Billiard-Fanon, who was standing near the young sailor, patted his back reassuringly. 'God forgives you, young man,' he said, gruffly. 'God forgives.'

Avocat gulped like a frog once, twice, thrice, with sorrow, and buried his face in the crook of his arm.

Pannier coughed, and said. 'If it's death we're discussing,' he said, 'then I've my bit to add. I killed a man in the war. I killed many, of course, for it was war, and killing is the idiom of war. But this man was not a German. His name was Maheut, and he came from Saint-Andiol-Bouches-des-Rhône. I put a bullet in his back. I'm not sorry I shot him, for he was a bad man. But I regret that I did not shoot him in the front, like a man. There! I have spoken. I'm not going to say anything further about this matter, ever again.'

When nobody replied, and despite having declared that he would not say anything more, Pannier spoke again. His voice betrayed intense inner strain. 'I'm *not* sorry I killed him,' he said. 'He deserved to die, when round us both, men who deserved to live were being killed. He was a coward and a cheat. But sometimes I have dreams. Bad dreams. I don't know why it is so, for he was a wicked man. But sometimes I do. He was,' Pannier added, after another pause, as if this explained it, 'rich. I was poor.'

'We shall all be equally wealthy soon,' said Lebret.

After that nobody spoke.

When the time came, Le Banquier called out, 'Four thousand metres.'

De Chante gave a great, shouty laugh. 'What *is* the delay?' he cried. 'Our guilty consciences have confessed themselves. What is fate waiting for? Extreme unction?'

'It will be soon,' declared the captain. 'Is the sonar functioning?'

Le Petomain replied: 'the signal is going out, Captain. I think. But there's nothing coming back.'

'Another malfunction! The entire vessel is breaking down. No way of knowing when the collision shall occur.' He looked around the bridge. 'Perhaps there *will* be time for one last confession. Three things fail, simultaneously, catastrophically, *just* as we begin our first deep dive – it is *too much* to be a coincidence. I believe somebody here has sabotaged this craft! Somebody prepared to sacrifice his own life in order to destroy this vessel. Well … the sabotage has been successful. Nobody here will ever speak to another human being again. It will do you no harm. Whoever you are, confess!'

Not a word was spoken in reply to this; each one looked from face to face. Eventually the captain sighed – a resonant, thrumming sound, like a lion's purr.

'Whichever of you is behind this,' he announced, having to

shout to be heard, 'you disappoint me. Own your treachery! What harm can your confession do now? We shall all of us be folded into Death's bosom presently!'

Nobody spoke.

'So be it,' said Cloche, shaking his head slowly.

'Captain?' enquired Jhutti. 'May we—may we retire to our cabins? Since our individual extinction is assured, we would like prepare for it in the ways that our culture and religion stipulate.'

'Of course,' said the captain. The Indians struggled up the awkward slope and along the aft corridor.

'Captain?' asked Capot. 'Although it is hopeless, I think I would prefer to be busy. I would prefer not to meet my doom idle. May I go aft and attempt again to repair the driveshaft?'

'Of course,' said Cloche.

'And I will go fore and look again at the tanks,' declared Castor. 'With your permission, Captain. I don't pretend I will be able to fix things, but I would at least like to know *why* they failed. I would like to know it, before I die.'

'Everybody is excused. Go where you please, messieurs. Go to meet your dooms severally.'

Castor scurried down the sloping corridor and away from the bridge. Pannier repaired to the kitchen – to open a bottle of the captain's table wine (for, he thought to himself, it would add tragedy to tragedy to waste so fine a vintage). Le Banquier remained at the controls, though there was nothing he could do with them. But the other sailors dispersed throughout the craft. Only Lebret loitered, standing a little behind and to the left of the captain's chair.

The walls increased the intensity and tone of their vibrations: a step change. Several dials in the control panel popped their circular glass covers from their slots. One of the bolts that fixed the captain's chair to the floor worked loose and bounced upwards. A light bulb burst into a steam of glass fragments. 'Here it comes!' declared Cloche, and closed his eyes. 'It is the end!' But his words were inaudible, drowned out by the huge basso profundo roar of the metal fabric of the *Plongeur*, trembling on the extreme edge of collapsing under the inescapable weight of water.

4

AFTER THE DISASTER

❧ ❧ ❧ ❧ ❧ ❧

But the end did not come. Instead, and gradually, the shaking calmed, and the deep buzz of vibration quietened. It was a very long drawn out diminuendo, the noise and the shaking withdrawing itself incrementally until both had almost disappeared. Impossible to believe that the implacable wrath of the ocean was diminishing – it was quite against all the laws of physics.

'Monsieur Le Petomain,' said Captain Cloche. 'What has happened?'

'I—I cannot say, captain,' replied the astonished shipman.

'What is our depth?'

'Five thousand seven hundred metres, sir, and still descending.'

'Impossible! The ocean is not so deep! Not at our location, at any rate. We should long since have collided with the continental shelf.'

'Aye, sir.'

'Your instrumentation is faulty, sailor.'

'That may be, Captain,' conceded Le Petomain. 'Except that – well, we *are* still descending!'

There was no denying this. The *Plongeur* was still angled sharply forward; the downward motion, shuddery, a little uneven, but still unmistakably downwards, could still be felt in every solar plexus.

'Sonar?'

'Nothing, Captain.'

The captain pondered for a moment. 'The depth *is* consistent with both the rapidity of our descent and the length of time elapsed,' he announced. 'In which case – the only explanation is that we have fallen into some unmapped trench within the ocean floor.' But then, again like a lion, he shook his shaggy head; a gesture of immense force and emphasis. 'No!' he contradicted himself. 'These are not the south polar seas – or the middle of the Pacific! This is *a few score leagues west of the coast of France*! It is not possible that our oceanographic maps could have missed such a feature! I have sailed above and beneath the waves in these waters for two decades. There is no such trench!'

Lebret lowered himself into a seated position upon the sloping floor, his foot braced against a bulkhead. He lit a new cigarette. The smoke pooled about him like a caul. 'Quite apart from anything else,' he observed. 'Even if we had slipped inside some uncharted fissure, the pressure should have crushed us completely by now.'

'Six thousand metres,' announced Le Petomain. 'Hull pressure … is *decreasing*, sir. How can that be?'

'It cannot!' replied the captain. 'What is the reading?'

'Four hundred and seven kilograms per square centimetre, sir.'

'Quite impossible. That pressure gauge *must* be faulty, even if the *depth* gauge is correct. Indeed,' the captain added, as the idea started up in his head. 'It is likely that the pressure gauge *would* malfunction. The sensor is not designed to measure pressures of the intensity to which it has been exposed. The very thing it has been measuring would destroy it.'

'Sir!'

'Water pressure increases at approximately one hundred kilograms per square centimetre for every thousand metres one descends,' the captain said, as if speaking to himself. 'Accordingly we can calculate the approximate pressure that must obtain – if the depth gauge is indeed correct.'

'The calculation produces a number far in excess of the tolerances of our hull,' Lebret pointed out.

The captain shook his head again – a gesture of such exaggerated swing he might have been having a conniption fit. 'No!' he announced. 'It *cannot* be. You have kept something from me, Lebret. You and your damn blackface scientists from India, and your mysterious Jewish-Swiss finance. I don't care if de Gaulle himself vouched for your patriotism – *you* have kept something *from* me. I don't know what the *Plongeur*'s hull is made of, but it must be a material tougher than steel. Titanium is it? I have heard rumours that the Americans have built a bathysphere out of titanium, to lower into the Mariana trench. Is that it?'

'Take a moment, Captain,' said Lebret, carelessly. 'And think through what you are saying. You inspected the ship yourself, I presume, before you took her out of port. You went through her inside and out. Yes?'

'Of course,' conceded Cloche, reluctantly.

'You are saying you can't tell the difference between steel plates and some other metal?'

'That could hardly be,' said Cloche. 'Only I *did* note the newness and thickness of the paint that had been applied to all surfaces.'

'Quite apart from anything else,' Lebret said, shaking his head, 'there *is* no magic material that could preserve a teardrop-shaped cavity of air under the degrees of which we are speaking. Besides – the walls themselves shook and groaned as we descended. And now they are silent. You may believe the evidence of your own senses, I hope?'

The captain pulled on his beard with his right hand, deep in thought. After a moment, Le Petomain sang out: 'Seven thousand metres, sir! External pressure – according to the read-out, sir – is two hundred kilograms per square centimetre.'

'Impossible,' growled Cloche.

At that moment, Lieutenant Boucher and *Enseigne de vaisseau* Billiard-Fanon climbed back up the corridor and into the bridge. 'Sir?' asked the second-in-command. 'What has happened, sir?'

'The unexpected quiet is a little oppressive, no?' laughed Lebret, from his seated position – legs akimbo, bracing himself against the bar in the floor to prevent himself from slipping forward.

'Both the tanks still refuse to close,' announced Boucher, pulling himself alongside Le Petomain. 'But there is good news – if these pressure readings are correct.'

'How *can* they be?' snapped Billiard-Fanon, climbing up and checking the instrumentation himself. 'It's nonsense!'

'Sir?' said the lieutenant. 'Before, it would not have been possible to pump air back into the tanks, even if we *could* close them. The pressures were much too high – the pump could never have done the work, and the air itself would simply have compressed and liquefied, giving us no buoyancy. But if the pressures are falling at the rate this dial suggests – then soon it *would* be possible to refloat the tanks.'

'Assuming we can close them.'

'I know it seems impossible, sir. But if the pressure keeps falling there's even the chance that we could put a diver into the water. To have a look at the vents from the outside.'

'At *seven thousand metres* below the surface?' scoffed Cloche. 'Don't talk nonsense. A man in a diving suit would be squashed to jelly in an instant!'

'But, sir, the pressure gauge reads...'

'I don't care what it reads! Would you trust that gauge with *your* life, sailor? I can feel in my bowels that we are still descending – that we've been descending without intermission – and accordingly there's no way that instrument can be wrong! So, we have gone down and down. It follows, as the night the day, by all that is immutable in the laws of physics, that the pressure must be approaching a thousand kilograms per square centimetre.'

The lieutenant did not contradict his captain, but his face betrayed disagreement.

'Seven thousand five hundred metres,' announced Le Petomain.

'It is,' declared the captain. 'It is—' But he could not find in his vocabulary the word that expressed what it was.

'To have prepared for inevitable catastrophic extinction,' observed Lebret, lighting yet another cigarette. 'And then for it simply to evaporate into mystery. It is anticlimactic. Is it not?' And he laughed.

5

THE IMPOSSIBLE DEPTHS

ʕ ʕ ʕ ʕ ʕ ʕ

The captain called a general muster. By the time the entire complement of crew had reassembled in the bridge (with the exception of Pannier, who was discovered dead drunk and passed out in the kitchen), the depth gauge showed a depth of nine thousand metres. The pressure sensors, at the same time, registered a pressure of only eighty kilograms per square centimetre – a lesser weight upon the hull than had obtained before the disaster had struck.

The crew discussed the impossibility of this; but there was nowhere for the discussion to go except round and round. The bottom line was that most of the crew believed the impossibly low pressure reading – it was consistent, after all, with the absence of compression noises from the hull. Some refused to believe it, on the equally reasonable grounds that a depth of nearly a full kilometre must necessarily, by the laws of physics, entail a pressure much greater than the dial showed. This was an unavoidable fact of nature.

A breeze had started up in the cabin; gentle but persistent – it blew at the trouser legs and jacket flaps, and agitated them. Lebret wondered aloud whether it derived from a steeped temperature differential between the outside water and the warmer innards of the craft. It seemed a trivial matter. Men tugged their tunics down, and smoothed their fluttering trouser legs.

Then, Monsieur Ghatwala suggested a means of testing the pressure gauge reading. The *Plongeur* possessed the capacity to generate its own air by breaking down seawater into its constituent elements of hydrogen and oxygen. To this end small catalyst tanks existed, one on each side of the craft, with systolic hoses connecting them to the open water. 'Open these,' Jhutti suggested, 'and circulate the water. If the external pressures are truly as manageable as the dials suggest, that operation should proceed without a hitch. But if the pressures are what they *should* be at a depth of almost,' he swallowed before uttering the number, 'ten thousand metres, then opening the tanks will cause them to crumple.'

'To crumple,' said Castor, 'explosively! That might cause significant damage to the *Plongeur*.'

The captain considered this.

'Captain,' put in Jhutti. 'I might simply note that at a depth of nine and a half thousand metres the *Plongeur* should *long since* have been crushed to a mass of metal. Nobody has dived to such depths! Not in the history of mankind! And I, who know the design parameters of this craft better than any, know that it was not designed for such a thing. Opening the catalytic tanks is a very small risk, when set against the simple impossibility of our being alive at all.'

Cloche nodded a single nod. 'Do it,' he ordered.

The tanks were opened. Water circulated, and the atomic pile began its work of recharging the ship's onboard oxygen supply. Everything happened without a hitch.

'Extraordinary,' the captain breathed.

'It merely confirms the evidence of our own ears,' was Lebret's opinion. 'When the pressure built up, the metal walls of our oceanic coffin shook and wailed. That they have ceased their unpleasant music proves the pressure to have reduced.'

'But *how?*' Boucher demanded, banging the side of a bank of instruments with his fist. 'It is wholly against the laws of physics!'

'It is,' confirmed Jhutti. 'I can see no explanation for it. None at all.'

The dial reached the limit of its measurement: 9999.9 metres flashed briefly before the disks all turned as one and a depth of 0000.0 was recorded. There was a collective gasp.

Slowly, Le Petomain reached inside his tunic, and brought out a pearl-inset handle, the size and shape of a razor shell. The slightest pressure of his thumb flicked the blade of this knife into play, and – looking momentarily at his captain – he brought it down and carved a small nick onto the metallic top edge of his instrument panel. As he folded the knife away he spoke to the entire room. 'I wonder,' he said, 'whether that is the last time we will go, as the phrase has it, "round the clock".'

Since their collective extinction was apparently not as imminent as they had previously assumed, the captain declared that they should return to their posts and attempt again to repair whatever damage had precipitated the disaster in the first place. 'Monsieur Castor,' he said. 'Take Capot and Avocat and try once again to restore the propeller to our control. Monsieur Chatallah, perhaps you would accompany my chief engineer?'

'Ghatwala,' said Ghatwala.

The captain did not acknowledge this correction. 'I suppose it *will* be necessary to close down the engine altogether. I presume your assistance in doing so, and in restarting the device, will prove invaluable.'

'The engine is not designed to be switched off mid-voyage,' said Ghatwala. 'I say so only to warn you, Captain. We can turn it off; but there are no guarantees we can turn it on again. And without the engine …'

'I appreciate the consequences of being without the engine, Monsieur. No power, therefore no air. I have confidence in your ability to restart the atomic pile. We have twelve hours of battery power. I trust you can perform the operation within that time frame?'

'We shall try, Captain,' said Ghatwala.

'Good. Billiard-Fanon and de Chante – please try once again to close the ballast tanks. If we can fill them again with air, then I will be well pleased. The vanes must also be unfrozen, and returned to my control.'

'Aye, sir!'

'Aye, sir!'

'Monsieur Jhutti. You and I will undertake a survey of the whole craft. If you would be so kind? Your specialist knowledge will prove useful to me.'

'Of course.'

'Messieurs,' announced the captain, standing. 'I do not know what has happened to us. But we are still alive! And as long as our hearts are beating, and our lungs drawing breath, we may set our collective will and intelligence against this pitiless environment.'

'Perhaps I should accompany you as well, Captain?' said Lebret, hauling himself awkwardly to his feet.

'There is no need,' the captain replied.

'As you wish,' Lebret said, indifferently. 'There is, of course, one explanation for our present situation that nobody has offered.'

'And what is that?' asked the captain, with a sarcastic edge to his voice.

'We all *expected* to die,' said Lebret. 'Perhaps we did. You said yourself, captain, that death is an infinite ocean. Who's to say that we are not now voyaging through precisely that body of water? Perhaps the afterlife – *our* afterlife, I mean – will be a Flying Dutchman eternity of traversing these black submarine waters.' He looked around the bridge. The faces of several of the crew had fallen. That of Le Banquier in particular looked horror-struck.

For a moment even the captain looked alarmed at this thought. But then he struck his broad chest with his heavy fist, and boomed out. 'Nonsense! *I still live*! Look at you all—idiots! You think *you* are whimpering shades? You're still breathing, aren't you? Still sweating and farting? Ghosts? Nonsense! You are living men – living Frenchmen! You ought to act accordingly.'

'Sir!' barked the crew, automatically.

'Monsieur Lebret,' the captain said. 'I have changed my mind. It would be a good idea for you to accompany us after all.' And as the crew vacated the bridge – all save Le Petomain, who remained at the controls – Cloche took Lebret by his arm. 'I'll thank you *not* to undermine the morale of my crew, M'sieur,' he said, in a tight voice.

'Captain,' said Lebret, extracting his arm from the older man's grasp, 'you can rest assured—I will not.'

The captain declared that he wanted to ascend into the conning tower, and take a look through the periscope. 'I don't expect to see anything but darkness,' he admitted. 'But still.'

This presented a problem, however. As he started to unscrew the ceiling hatch above the bridge, water began leaking into the bridge. It did not spurt, which was a good sign. Rather it poured as steam might, making a shimmering semi-circular pattern under the electric lights.

The captain stopped unscrewing the hatch, but neither did he close it up entirely. The water continued coming out, in an agitated mist. 'It's cold!' Cloche declared, as the water swirled about his head. 'If the con is flooded, and we are at the depths the instruments suggest – why then the pressure ought to have shot this hatch like a cannonball from a gun as soon as I began to turn it. On the other hand, if the pressure has reduced to the levels the gauge says, it ought to be possible to repair any leaks in the con.'

'What do you suggest, Captain?' asked Jhutti. He was staring at the strange behaviour of the water, billowing in chill clouds.

'De Chante!' Cloche bellowed. 'Come here – and bring a tool box!'

The mate appeared a moment later, clambering up the sloping corridor. 'One,' said the captain. 'Two. Three!'

He unscrewed the hatch and let it bang downwards, fully open. A quantity of water fell through the hole, falling not as a shower but rather, it seemed, as a single bundle, almost like a transparent sack filled with brine and attached to the underside of the hatch. It splashed through the grid in the floor of the bridge and drained through into the bilges. But something had whipped up the internal breeze, and droplets sprayed all about, wetting everybody. It was very cold. Gasping at the chill, de Chante climbed up the ladder, his toolbox hooked over his elbow like a flower-seller's basket. 'Captain, it's ...' he began to say. More water, a great chunk of it, fell through the hatch. There was a bang, perhaps the sound of de Chante falling over, and more water came down. The whole bridge was being sprayed, water blowing in every direction.

The fall of water diminished. From above came the sound of plangent metallic clangs.

'Can you fix it?' the captain called up.

And a moment later, the reply, 'Done, sir! The plates had been a little bent, but I've forced them back down.'

Indeed, the flow of water diminished, and eventually resolved itself into a series of heavy droplets. De Chante came down the ladder; he was of course soaked. 'Good work, sailor,' said his Captain. 'Go and change into dry clothes.'

The captain, Jhutti and Lebret climbed up into the con. Water ran along the walls, and droplets of spray, supported by a gust of air coming up through the hatch, swam in the air. The three men were soon thoroughly wet.

Cloche did not extend the periscope. He put his eyes to the viewer and swivelled it about. There was nothing to see. 'Perfectly black in every direction,' he noted. 'Perhaps that is as one might expect.'

Lebret took a turn after Cloche, and finally Jhutti. But there was really nothing to see except blackness. In his wet clothes, and in the chill of the little space, Jhutti was shivering. 'Captain,' he said. 'One thing occurs to me. It makes no sense; but I can think of no other explanation for our ... I apologise, my French is not providing me with the correct word.'

'Our predicament,' said Lebret.

'Our situation,' corrected Cloche. 'Your explanation, Monsieur Jhutti?'

'We have descended *below* the level of the seabed – that much is clear. Even the deepest portions of the Atlantic do not ... descend to ten thousand metres. Even the deepest Pacific trenches do not go down so far! Only one ... possibility explains these things. We must have passed below the earth's crust.'

'Yet we are still floating in water,' Lebret pointed out.

'The precise composition of the interior of the globe has yet to be established. It is certainly the case,' Jhutti went on, hugging himself and even hopping on the spot to warm himself, 'that seismographic evidence points to it being molten magma, mantled over by solid rock. But who knows what reservoirs of water lie within that substratum? The only explanation that fits the facts is that we have somehow slipped into such a hidden reservoir of water.'

'With respect, Monsieur,' said Lebret. 'I dispute your assertion that such a theorem explains all the facts. Even if we accept that there are bulbs of water, hidden within the rock of the earth's mantle, and connected to the oceans by uncharted chimneys – a circumstance no scientist or geologist has ever supported – nonetheless, the water pressure *within* such spaces would be immense. As immense as at the bottom of the Mariana trench!' He then added something in Punjabi, speaking fluently and rapidly.

'I did not realise,' said the captain, eyeing him, 'that you spoke Indian.'

'Do you not?' replied Lebret, drily.

Cloche scowled.

'Captain, I agree it sounds unlikely,' said Jhutti. 'But – what if a crust of rock had sealed away a reservoir of water – the reservoir itself having previously existed at regular water pressures? We have somehow fallen inside. Perhaps ... perhaps our descent coincided with that crust of rock falling away. If that were the case, then perhaps the much higher pressure water at the bottom of the Atlantic would *wash* into the relatively low-pressure cavity, and equally likely that (being in the vicinity) we would be flushed through too, like flotsam being rinsed down a plughole as the bath empties.'

'If that is what has happened,' Lebret returned, 'then – and depending upon the size of this notional cavity of yours – the water pressure will rise steadily, and quickly. Eventually we will be crushed.' Lebret ground his cigarette into the metal floor of the con with his boot. 'If it will not disarrange you, my eminent friend, I shall retain my scepticism.'

'You have another explanation?' asked Jhutti, shivering.

'It seems to me,' said Lebret, 'unlikely that a reservoir of any size could exist in such proximity to the enormous pressures of the water at the bottom of the Atlantic. If the crust were thin enough to crumble, it would have done so long ago. Are we to believe it is simply a matter of coincidence that this rock doorway you posit opened just as we approached? No, sir.' He shook his head, and added something in Punjabi. Then he reverted to French, 'Also, we must consider our orientation. We began our dive some small distance west of the French coast, and facing east. We should have crashed – as the captain here predicted we *would* crash – into the flank of the continental shelf. That would place your speculative underground sea beneath France, would it not? Under the *Pays des Gasgogne*. Which is to say – beneath one of the most thoroughly studied geological areas on the globe. Can we believe that a few kilometres directly underneath France there is a subterranean ocean that no scientist has yet noticed? That is hard to credit.'

'I repeat my question, my friend,' said the shivering Indian. 'What alternative explanation can you offer?'

Lebret smiled and shook his head. 'I have no idea,' he said. 'It is a pure mystery. Isn't that exciting?'

'Messieurs,' said the captain. 'I propose we change into dry clothes. I intend to tour the ship, and I would like you to accompany me. As to your theories of oceans beneath the land – they are, I fear, what my grandmother used to call *les sottises*. There must be some other explanation.'

'At any rate,' opined Lebret, 'this gives is the opportunity to explore whatever new realm it is we have entered.'

'I am not interested in that,' barked Cloche. 'Our job is to get back to port – and only that.'

'Come!' wheedled Lebret. 'We might discover whole new continents down here, and claim them for France!'

41

'No,' boomed Cloche, striking the metal wall with his fist. 'That is not our mission!'

'But...' Lebret began to say.

'No!' Cloche cut him off, again. Lebret flushed pink with a sudden anger; but a moment later his composure reasserted itself, and the colour drained from his face.

The three men descended, and closed the hatch to the con. It took only minutes for them to change their clothes, and place the wet gear in one of the ventilated airing cupboards with which the aft corridor was supplied.

Cloche led the way into the rear of the craft. They came first of all into a cluttered space – silver-steel cabinets lining the wall, pipes and cables snaking like metal creepers over the ceiling and wall. Beyond that the corridor split like the forks of a Y, passing either side of the central engine. The pile itself was painted red. Sheets of close laid wire were pinned to its wainscot like corduroy; and silver panels were bolted at regular intervals along its flank. It was humming audibly. The breeze was even stronger here; as the captain approached, a sheet of paper blew from a work surface and squirled up towards the ceiling. Two floor panels were up, and the very top of Capot's ruddy head of hair was visible poking out of the hole.

'Holloa!' boomed the captain.

There was the sound of motion below. 'Captain!' cried Castor, climbing high enough for his doggish face to appear over the lip. 'I've been looking at ways of decoupling the drive shaft without stopping the engine – but it's spinning full pelt! We are going to have to shut the reactor down.'

Ghatwala's head poked up as well. 'Captain, I repeat – the device is not designed to be switched off and on like a diesel engine. Turning it off involves withdrawing a number of the uranium-oxide lances upon which the reaction depends. Only when enough have been withdrawn will the engine shut down. More worrying, reinserting them risks chain-reaction.'

'What do you think, *Monsieur* Castor?' the captain asked.

'I can't see any other way of getting into the workings and seeing why the driveshaft gears have fused – let alone separating them,' said Castor, wiping his forehead on the meat of his forearm. 'But, see, I'm used to regular engines which – as *Monsieur Visage-noir* here says – can be simply shut down. Oh, I've done my homework on these atomic piles, of course, and I'll say only this: The US Navy have been running their USS *Nautilus*, their atomic sub, for three years. And in all that time the engine has only ever been shut off in dock.'

'This is correct,' confirmed Ghatwala.

'It is a balance of risk, Captain Cloche,' declared Lebret. 'If Monsieur Jhutti is correct in his speculation, then we are plunging rapidly towards what must be the rocky floor of a brine-filled subterranean cavern. If so, then there is a *hypothetical* risk that we will all die. On the other hand – tampering with the pile introduces a *real* risk that we will all die.'

'The reactor circulates water at extremely high pressures and temperatures,' said Jhutti. 'I cannot recommend tampering with it.'

The captain brooded. 'I must have command of my sub returned to me,' he announced. 'There is a risk, yes of course – but we are all as good as dead anyway! Castor, proceed.'

'Captain—'

Cloche roared. 'I have *made* my decision. You *shall* respect my authority.'

Castor wiped his hands on his trousers, paused just long enough for the delay to register as insubordination, and replied, 'Yes, Captain.'

With Jhutti and Ghatwala supervising his every movement, Castor withdrew the reaction mass from the centre of the pile. The lights throughout the vessel flickered and dimmed as battery power took up the slack. The hum of the engines died, and the propellers ceased churning the water.

'Good,' declared the captain. 'Now get in there and find out why the driveshaft has seized!'

He came back down the sloping corridor, awkwardly, and into the bridge. In the uncanny quiet, Le Petomain looked round. Two large, distinct beads of sweat, like glass tadpoles, were visible upon his forehead. 'Captain!'

'The props are stilled,' announced the captain. 'Our rate of descent must have diminished.'

'No change, my Captain!'

Cloche said nothing: he made his way to the instrument panel, and saw for himself. They were descending at exactly the same rate as they had been without the action of the propellers. 'That can't be! With the tanks open, of course we will still descend – but we are,' and he made a quick calculation in his head, 'we are dropping at *greater* than terminal velocity in water!'

'I know, sir. I can't explain it.'

'We are surrounded by water – are we not?'

'We are, sir. We've sampled it – it's in the catalytic tanks.'

'Then,' announced the captain, 'we are simply falling too fast. Faster than physics can explain – or allow!'

Ghatwala was helping Castor examine the main propeller drive-pole. The other crew were at their posts. Jhutti, feeling at a loose end, came through to the mess. It was deserted, except for Lieutenant Boucher, who was enjoying a quiet smoke. He offered the scientist a cigarette.

'Gladly,' said Jhutti. He seated himself next to the lieutenant at the table.

'So. Do you believe this theory that the earth is hollow and filled with water?' the lieutenant asked Amanpreet Jhutti, as both filled their lungs with particulate tobacco.

'It goes against everything modern science has established concerning our globe,' was Jhutti's opinion.

'Indeed! Well one thing occurs to me – we are still descending, at something approaching a metre a second. If this continues we will soon have descended deeper than the earth's diameter. Then we shall know – unless, perhaps, we suddenly pop into sunlight and air, off the coast of New Zealand! Surfacing upside down, our propeller still churning!' Boucher laughed; and even the sober Jhutti smiled.

44

'Not a very likely circumstance,' the scientist said.

'Of course I know that,' said Boucher. 'Only – are any of the things that have occurred to us *likely*? Would you like to lay a wager with me, Monsieur Scientist, as to whether our adventure will end with us simply surfacing in some antipodean sea?'

'I do not gamble, I am afraid,' said Jhutti.

'Like Einstein's God,' said Boucher, beaming again. 'But, you know – I think it was you, but perhaps it was your colleague – somebody mentioned Jules Verne earlier.'

This mention of the celebrated author's name seemed almost to startle Jhutti. 'What of him?'

'Only, Monsieur, that in addition to writing his famous story of submarine adventure, Verne also wrote a story about a journey towards the centre of the earth. Perhaps you know it?'

'Of course I do,' said Jhutti.

'Then you'll recall what filled the globe in Verne's narrative? A great ocean! A vast primal sea, swimming with dinosaurs and pteric fish!' Boucher laughed again. 'Could it be that we have somehow slipped out of reality altogether, and into the imagination of Monsieur Jules Verne?'

The lieutenant was, of course, joking; but Jhutti, peering at the glowing end of his cigarette, appeared to be taking the idea seriously.

'A dead man's imagination,' he said, in a dull voice. 'Monsieur Lebret suggested that we had indeed all died, and were now voyaging through the unforgiving medium of human mortality. Is your idea more outrageous than his?'

'Oh, I did not mean to be taken literally!' said Boucher, smacking the flat of his hand upon the metal surface of the table and barking with laughter. 'Sailing inside Verne's head? No man has a skull so capacious!'

Jhutti smiled, but only weakly. 'Though I have dedicated my life to material science, yet I still live with the insights of my mother-civilisation in my heart. One thing we Indians understand, that too many Westerners have yet to grasp, is that "reality" is not so simple or straightforward as it is sometimes thought to be. Reality, in truth is … what is the word? Reality is *ironic*. In a deep sense.'

'No mysticism, my Hindu friend,' laughed Boucher, draining his coffee. 'We need practical solutions to our problems.'

'And who is to say that mysticism is not practical?' returned Jhutti, smiling.

After three hours work, Castor re-emerged from beneath the metal floor of the engine room, his face grimed. 'There's nothing wrong with the shaft,' he gasped. 'I don't know why the gearbox seized up. I can't find a reason.'

'There must *be* a reason,' insisted the captain.

'Without doubt,' agreed Castor, hauling himself upon his elbow. 'But I can't work it out. Neither can the black-faced gentleman you sent to assist me.' Given the amount of black engine grease smeared over Castor's own face, this racist descriptor was, to say nothing else, imprecise. 'The problem must have been in the gearing; but why they should seize up – I simply don't understand it.'

'Will the system work correctly if we restart it?' Cloche wanted to know.

Castor shrugged his shoulders after the manner only Frenchman are properly capable of. He plunged his face into a large white flannel, and rubbed as if he wished to erase his own features.

'Well,' Cloche declared. 'We must have power. Monsieur Ghatwala—can you restart this bomb-like motor?'

'With the assistance of my tovarisch, Jhutti, I can,' was Ghatwala's answer. He went off to retrieve Jhutti and begin the delicate procedure.

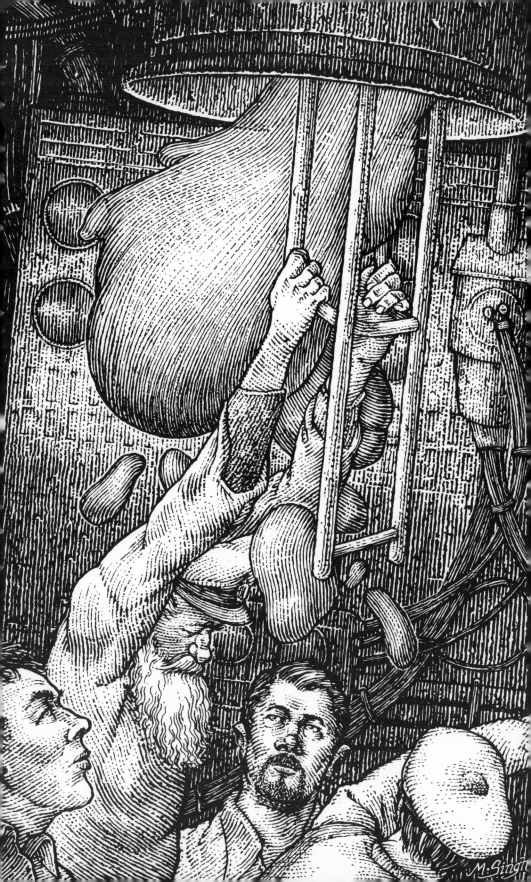

6

THE INFINITE OCEAN

❧ ❧ ❧ ❧ ❧ ❧

Jhutti and Ghatwala, acting together, and proceeding with a ponderous caution that, perhaps counterintuitively, actually infected the rest of the crew with fear, re-inserted the reaction mass into the atomic pile. The temperature inside the engine rose perilously high, but then settled back within operational parameters.

The engines restarted. The propellers were once again under the pilot's control.

But this did little good. With or without propeller motion, the *Plongeur* sank at a too-precipitous speed. Reversing the props, hoping to draw the vessel backwards and upwards, or at the least to *arrest* the velocitous downward trajectory, had no effect at all. 'Even if we were dead weight in the water,' Le Petomain grumbled, 'we shouldn't be sinking *this* fast.'

They all knew it to be true.

For three days and nights the *Plongeur* descended. The crew passed through a period of collective elation at having escaped what had been, after all, inevitable death in that initial catastrophic descent. But this did not last long, and it was succeeded by a period of gloom. They were still alive, true; but they were confined, helpless and unable to see how, or even if, they might ever return to their homes. For twenty-four hours the captain considered whether to risk sending out a diver into the unknown waters. During that time, the depth gauge passed its limit no fewer than nine times. The crew watched with fascination, and then horror, and finally with boredom as the numbers continued their relentless accumulation.

Odd things were happening inside the vessel, though, and these only served to make the crew nervous and unhappy. The talk was of *haunting*. The talk was of the spirits of the discontented dead. The captain scoffed noisily and publicly when these rumours were reported to him. 'In the middle of the twentieth century?' he demanded. 'To talk of ghosts and goblins? Absurd!' But the sailors continued their agitated chatter. The consensus was – something supernatural was at play.

For instance, the strange breezes and drafts all about the *Plongeur* did not abate. Air blew up hard and cold from the floor for no evident reason – the bottoms of the sailors' trouser legs were often inflated and even lifted a little way up the calves of their legs. Jackets shifted weirdly about the wearer's torso. Or, sometimes, the air would blow downwards from the ceilings and along the walls. There was nothing dangerous or harmful about these breezes, but that did not stop them from being profoundly unnerving. 'There is nowhere for this air to be blowing *from*,' growled Billiard-Fanon. 'You! Indian Monsieur! You're a scientist – can you explain it?'

'It is puzzling,' said Jhutti, shaking his head. 'It must, as Monsieur Lebret noted, have to do with the differential of temperature between…'

'*Can* you explain? Yes or no!'

'No, Monsieur. I regret to say.'

Sometimes the air would gust violently – loose papers would be blown hard from a desk and slap against the ceiling of the room. They would then fall back down, but in a more slow and leisurely fashion than one might expect. Cups held in the hand would suddenly fly out, and clang against the wall. The breeze would whip coffee from mugs and spatter it in fat droplets upon the sides of the room. Sailors took to fitting lids to their cups and drinking through the aperture of a prised-back side in order to defeat this *poltergeist*.

'Poltergeist,' said Avocat. 'Or poltergeists? Plural? They seem to be everywhere!'

'I have books in my quarters,' said Monsieur Jhutti. 'They just flew from the shelf! They literally flew! They fluttered about the ceiling like trapped birds! I was forced to lock them in my seaman's trunk.'

'We are haunted,' said Billiard-Fanon, in a sepulchral voice. 'We must pray – we must pray to the God of justice, the enemy of Satan.'

'Come!' said Lebret, shaking his head and smoking another cigarette. 'Do you genuinely believe a submarine can be *haunted*? I have never read a ghost story set aboard a submarine! We are not a Gothic mansion, after all!'

'I don't know *why* nobody has written such a story,' said Billiard-Fanon, shivering. 'Our vessel is as big as a house, is it not? People die aboard submarines, do they not? Why might they not come back and haunt it? We need a priest, to exorcise the *Plongeur*!'

'*You* were the one, Monsieur Lebret,' observed Lieutenant Boucher, 'who suggested we were all dead.'

'You think *we* are haunting *ourselves*?' asked Lebret. 'Come come! How could that be?'

'I had to put my chest upside down,' said Le Petomain. He looked around. 'My sea chest. Where I store my stuff. The lid kept flying open. Just the lid. I don't understand it – I don't pretend to understand it. The chest itself sits firm on the floor, but the lid keeps banging open. As if the poltergeist wants to rummage through my things. So I turned it upside down, and now it sits still and calm.'

'An evil spirit,' said Billiard-Fanon, with a preacher's vibrato. 'It need not be the spirit of a dead man. It could be a devil.'

'Nonsense, nonsense,' insisted Lebret, shaking his head. 'This is a new realm! An entirely new ocean! The English poetess Joan Keats talks of Balboa laying eyes for the first time upon the Pacific ocean with wonder and admiration! We are the new Balboas – and all you can do is fret like schoolchildren about ghost stories?'

'The sooner we can get home,' was Billiard-Fanon's surly reply, 'the better.'

*

50

There seemed no obvious explanation for these small-scale mysteries – sharp breezes that blew up from nowhere to splash coffee out of cups or slap the captain's cap off his head and playfully roll it along the ceiling until its choleric owner grabbed it and wedged it back upon his head.

Nor was this all. They did what they could to discover more about the surrounding medium. Samples of water were drawn from the catalytic tanks and examined. Plain, unsalinated, pure water – clear and without contaminant of any kind, as far as they could see. Lebret, in a gesture the others considered rash, drank a mouthful; he appeared to suffer no ill effects.

'*Fresh* water!' said the captain, shaking his head in bewilderment. 'Not even brine! Yet more mystery!'

'At any rate it shows,' Boucher said, 'that we are no longer in the Atlantic – for that ocean is salt.'

'As if such a thing needed showing,' grumbled Lebret. 'As if anybody could doubt it! Come Captain – we have discovered a *new* ocean! Let us name it – we can call it after you. *La Cloche Mer.*'

The captain snapped his teeth together. 'No!' he growled. 'I'll not play such games. We are not here to explore. Our job is to return to France – nothing more.'

'But we must explore a little deeper,' suggested Lebret. 'Who knows what riches lie just a few fathoms below us...'

'Stop it, M'sieur!' Cloche ordered him. 'Once and for all – no.'

Sonar returned nothing. From time to time the captain would climb into the con and peer through the periscope – but nothing could be seen save perfect blackness. 'We might be floating in outer space,' he observed; 'were it not that we can feel ourselves descending.'

'And that we are able to circulate water from our immediate environment through our catalytic tanks,' Boucher noted.

'A good thing too,' Cloche agreed. 'Or we would suffocate in days.'

The captain invited his lieutenant, Lebret, Castor and the two scientists to the bridge to discuss what they ought to do. Le Petomain was again in the pilot's chair.

'I have been revolving whether I ought to send out a diver,' Cloche announced. 'Of course, I have no desire to send a man to *certain* death. We have no real knowledge of where we are, or what dangers there might be. We are moving through a sunless sea, of the kind the poet hymned – I forget his name.'

Lebret gave voice to what everybody in the vessel was thinking. 'We have been working on the assumption that we are sinking through some subterranean ocean. But messieurs – we are at an approximate depth of *ninety thousand kilometres*. The earth itself is no more than thirteen thousand kilometres in diameter.'

Boucher was shaking his head, but Lebret pressed on, 'Any idea that we somehow slipped through a fissure in the ocean bed and into a body of water contained within the earth is surely exploded by our continuing descent.'

'It cannot *be*,' growled Cloche, from the captain's chair, his right hand gripping his own beard as if thereby holding on to logical reality itself. 'Are we caught in some … circular current? Are we rolling round and round?'

'It is hard to see how that can be, Captain,' said Lebret. 'We would hardly feel the descent in the vertical plane, the way we do.'

'No, no,' countered Boucher. 'Let us not entirely abandon Occam's razor! The possible, no matter how unlikely, is always to be preferred to the impossible, however appealing. Our depth gauge does not measure absolute depth, after all.'

'I am not sure I know what "absolute depth" means, anyway,' said Jhutti.

'If modern science is wrong, and our globe *is* truly filled with water,' Boucher pressed, '—and if we have somehow made our way to that interior ocean, well it would not be a stationary mass, would it? The earth turns, and its diurnal spin would twist any interior body of liquid into a permanent, three-dimensional whirlpool. Rather than simply plunging directly down, perhaps we have rather been following a spiral, down through the fluid gyre?'

'An ingenious theory,' admitted Jhutti. 'Although an unlikely one. Our motion has continued with a downward vector without interruption. Were we caught in a vortex, there would be palpable shearing vectors, motions to the side. Quite apart from the fundamental unlikelihood of any such inner whirlpool of water going undetected by modern science.'

'There must be *some* explanation,' insisted the captain.

'Indeed there must,' agreed Lebret. 'I have no desire to contradict the lieutenant, but it seems to me that even a spiral descent must come to an end long before a hundred thousand kilometres.'

'So?'

'So, we must address the possibility that ours is ... is no longer a terrestrial location.'

The six other men on the bridge looked from one to the other; several shook their heads. 'Impossible,' declared Boucher. 'Permit me to invoke Occam's razor once more. Any possible explanation must, even if unlikely, be possible.'

'I do not pretend to be able to explain how the transition occurred – or where we now find ourselves. But I am emboldened to go further in my speculations.'

'Please do, Monsieur Lebret,' instructed the captain.

'I suggest we have slipped from our material dimension into another.'

'Another *dimension*?' snapped Cloche. 'Meaningless pseudo-babble! Explain yourself.'

'There is one datum I can adduce, I believe,' said Lebret, scratching his beard with his left hand and manoeuvring a cigarette out of its case with his left, 'to support my theory. The pressure! Let us agree, for the sake of argument, to trust our instrumentations, and agree that we have passed through a continuous column of water – for surely we *are* surrounded by water, and have been this whole time – to a "depth" of one hundred thousand kilometres. Were such a prodigious depth possible in any terrestrial location, the pressures at the bottom would be ... quite unimaginable! Millions of tonnes per square centimetre, enough to crush the water itself into a supersolid. Probably enough to crush the atoms into a nuclear furnace. We ought, according to everything we

53

know of the physical sciences, we ought to be sailing through the heart of a burning star, not an ocean! Whatever else is happening to us in our strange voyage, it is not that!'

'Then what, Monsieur?'

'Indulge me, my friends,' said Lebret. 'Imagine that we *have* passed through some ... portal. Imagine that we have moved from the finite Atlantic into an infinite ocean. A body of water literally without limit.'

The others considered this bizarre suggestion. 'This is your earlier theory ... that we have passed from life to death?' demanded Cloche.

'By no means,' said Lebret, an uncharacteristically sombre expression on his face. 'I consider our plight material, not spiritual. But I ask you – if we imagine a body of water infinite in extent in all directions – what would the water pressure be within it?'

It was such a strange, and unexpected question, that at first nobody offered to answer it. Eventually, however, Jhutti stirred himself.

'A strange speculation! I would say,' Jhutti said, speaking slowly as if working it out as he went along, 'that at every point an infinite quantity of water would press down. That, in brief, were such a body of water to exist (and I do not concede for a moment that it ever could) then the water pressure within it would be ... infinite too. Water could not exist under such a circumstance. Indeed, *matter* could not exist like that, in any form.'

'With all respect due to your eminence and intellectual capacity, I cannot agree,' said Lebret, smiling. He then said something rapidly in Punjabi, before going on in French. 'Water at the bottom of the Mariana trench is crushed by the *weight* of water, not its mass. Weight is a function of gravity. I am not proposing a vast planet surrounded by a vast ocean – an oceanic Jupiter, or something of that sort. Such a thing would not fit the circumstances in which we find ourselves.'

'Jupiter – or say rather *Neptune*,' murmured Ghatwala.

'No – I am proposing an *infinite* ocean. Imagine it! In such a location there would be no place in which the pressure could *build*

54

up, for there would be nowhere for the mass of water to *bear down upon*. Do you see?'

'I am not sure,' said Jhutti. 'An infinite ocean strikes me as a rank impossibility. Where would all the water in such a place *come from*?'

'Well – if it comes to that,' returned Lebret. 'We might ask – where does all the matter in our actual universe "come from"?'

'These are questions beyond observational science,' said Jhutti, a little primly.

'In which case...' drawled Lebret, complacently.

But Jhutti was not finished. 'Even if I accepted so outrageous a supposition as your *infinite universe of water*,' he said. 'I do not believe the medium would remain uniformly dissipated. Surely it would coalesce into innumerable gravitational centres?'

'Perhaps not,' said Lebret. 'For such a cosmos would be governed not by the simple gravitational mechanics of agglomerative matter, but by the infinitely more subtle and complex equations of fluid dynamics – and (since our measurements confirm that the temperature of the fluid is as high as 4°C) Brownian motion. Any whirlpool or tourbillon would be as likely to disaggregate as aggregate the medium.'

'No—no—' Jhutti said. 'You do not give enough credit to the inescapable, agglomerative powers of gravity itself.'

'I might wish, Monsieur,' said Pierre Boucher, scratching the pockmarked lunar expanse of his great white brow, 'that you talk in ordinary French...'

'I repeat,' said Jhutti, 'that the existence of such an entity – an infinite universe comprised wholly of water – is mere supposition. There is certainly no evidence that we have *entered into* such a place. How could we have done so? By what means?'

'Say rather,' said Lebret, 'by what portal? For as to the existence of some sort of portal, at least, we must all agree. In the world with which we are familiar, our rapid descent should have terminated in the ocean floor. It did not. Logically, therefore, we somehow passed *through* – or beyond, or behind, or in some other dimensional relation *to* – that brute physical reality.'

'I have another objection to Monsieur Lebret's ingenious theory,' put in Dilraj Ghatwala. 'For we are all of us standing upon the deck of this bridge, under the influence of gravity. How could that be, in the bizarre universe you suggest?'

'Ah!' said Lebret, seemingly pleased. 'That, Monsieur, is a *very* good point! And I concede without blushing that I am not certain of the answer. But I can at least think of a number of ways in which it can be explained. Some portal – I make no apology for reusing the word – had granted us egress. Presumably it has also allowed in a quantity of water. The release of water, at the immense pressures of the Atlantic bottom, into a vast reservoir of water at what are evidently much lower pressures must perforce have been after the manner of a great *jet*. What if the *Plongeur* were rolled about, and what we perceive as gravity is in fact the *acceleration* imparted to us by the force of this spout? Or what if – more fancifully – the portal has somehow allowed in *gravity itself* from our world?'

'Preposterous!' exclaimed the usually polite Jhutti, unable to contain himself further. 'Gravity is not a fluid, to be released like a stream from a water pistol! And we could hardly have experienced an acceleration of one gravity continually, smoothly, without turbulence or interruption for *three days straight*! If we had, then by now we would be travelling at ...' he performed a rapid mental calculation, '... at nearing one hundred and fifty thousand metres per second!'

But Lebret lost none of his good humour. 'Good points, all,' he conceded. 'In which case, there must another explanation! One thing only is certain – *we need to explore*. We must continue our journey through this strange new medium, and not return too precipitously to France.'

'Enough,' said the captain. 'None of this helps me make the decisions required by command. Shall I send a seaman out in a suit, and hope he can fix the ballast tank intakes? I *must* regain control of my own ship! That is the most important thing. Everything else is secondary.'

'Indeed, sir' said Boucher, smartly.

'Very well,' said Cloche. 'Let me make plain, gentlemen, my broader strategy: regain control of my vessel, in order to retrace our trajectory. Into whatever bizarre place we have sunk, it must be possible to return the way we came.'

'You are the captain,' Lebret observed.

'Thank you for noticing, Monsieur Lebret!' returned Cloche, sarcastically.

'I would only note, sir,' Lebret added, with the slightest hint of insolent emphasis on the honorific, 'that if my hypothesis is correct, then ascent or descent will be equally fruitless. The chance of finding the precise point at which we passed from the mundane ocean to this strange new location – if it *be* infinite – is mathematically: zero. We can never again return home. We shall sail these endless, unlit waters until our food gives out and we starve – or until we grow insane with confinement and kill one another.' He smiled a weird little smile.

'Sir,' said the captain, with asperity. 'For the second time upon this voyage I am compelled to rebuke you for pessimism. Morale is as important in maintaining the good running of a ship as discipline – and both are more vital than any amount of technological know-how or fanciful theorising! I must *insist* you refrain from giving voice to sentiments liable to depress and discourage the crew.'

'But we must be realistic, Captain,' said Lebret. 'And plan for every eventuality. Let us try and find a refuge in this new place, and not yearn hopelessly after the return home.'

The captain snapped, 'You are dismissed, sir! Please return to your cabin!'

Languidly, Lebret complied.

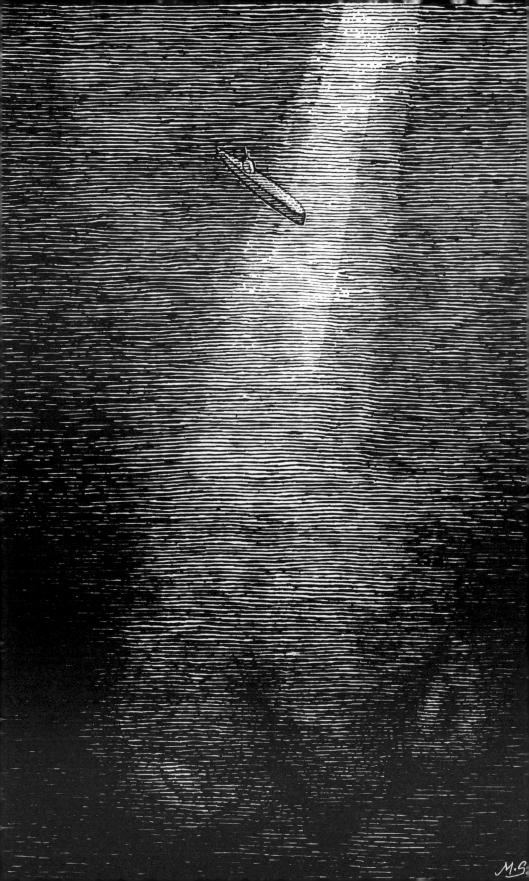

7

LEAVING THE *PLONGEUR*

❦ ❦ ❦ ❦ ❦ ❦

Cloche summoned de Chante, Avocat and Capot to the bridge and asked for volunteers; but none of the three men came forward. 'Come, come!' chided Cloche. 'You don't want me to ask Pannier, surely?'

'He's drunk,' said Capot, running fingers through his greasy, rust-coloured hair. 'And Castor is chief engineer, too important to risk on such an undertaking – I see. You've gathered the three of us because we are the most dispensable; and you don't know what hell-monsters lurk in the water outside.'

'Monsieur!'

'We all know, Captain – we all know what's happened. We've been sucked alive into Satan's hell, and you're looking for a volunteer to swim out and meet the demons.'

The captain stood up from his chair. 'Sailor!' he said, sternly. 'I am undecided as to whether I shall shoot you for insubordination or lock you in the brig!'

Capot had gone white. 'Might as well shoot me, Captain,' he returned. 'We're all doomed to a drawn-out death sailing through this godless cess-pit for evermore. I'd rather get it out of the way.' His voice was level, but his hands were visibly trembling.

Cloche slowly unbuttoned the flap on his holster and brought out his pistol. He levelled this at Capot's head. 'Sailor,' he said. 'You may have given up hope, but I have not. And luckily for you it is *my* will that matters. Lieutenant! Lock Matelot Capot in the brig. Avocat!'

'Captain?'

'Suit up. Get Castor to help you. You're going outside to take a look at the ballast tank intakes, and see what must be done to fix them.'

'Yes, sir.'

'I want my vessel brought back under my control!'

Boucher led Capot away, and Cloche re-holstered his weapon. 'Messieurs,' he announced. 'We have drifted, and sunk, for long enough. It is time to take charge of our destiny!'

Below the observation deck (the steel shutters still closed upon the oval porthole), down a blue-painted metal ladder, was a compact chamber from which, via an airlock, egress from the vessel could be effected. This space contained two cupboards, in each of which hung a thick, rubber diving suit and tanks of compressed air.

Down into this place climbed de Chante, Avocat and Lebret. Matters did not get off to a good start: de Chante opened one cupboard, and one of the vessel's freak breezes blew suddenly up, making the empty arms of the suit flap and thrash, as if warning Avocat away. The motion was so unexpected that Avocat yelped in fear and recoiled flinching.

He rebuked himself for his foolishness. Lebret and de Chante dragged the heavy rubber outfit from its space, and wrangled it down as Avocat clambered inside. Sensing that his nerves were jangled, Lebret attempted to keep the diver's spirits up. 'Have no fear, Monsieur,' he said, lighting them both a cigarette. 'You are certainly safer in *this* ocean – whatever it is, and wherever we are – than you would be in the South Seas or the Mediterranean. There will be no sharks to trouble us here.'

'You think so, M'sieur?'

'I am certain. We know the water is not excessively cold; we know that it is ordinary water – we are breathing it, after all. I have even tasted it! The sonar shows nothing – no shoals of strange fish, no leviathans. It is a huge swimming pool, nothing more.'

'I hope you're right, sir.'

Avocat's helmet was fixed around his skull, the light embedded above his faceplate switched on and the air supply checked and double-checked. Finally, a yard-long spanner and a long-handled hammer were strapped to each leg, and he was helped through into the airlock. The door closed with a chunky sound, and the handle spun through two complete revolutions. Through the little window, no broader than a handspan, it was possible to see the water swirl in until the entire chamber was full.

The exterior hatch swung open and Avocat ventured into the unknown.

De Chante remained below; Lebret climbed back up and joined Castor and Cloche in the forward hull where the main ballast tanks were located. 'If we can only get air back in our ballast tanks,' growled the captain, 'then it won't matter that regaining the control of the propeller seems to have been no use in arresting our descent. We can begin to *ascend*, retrace our path.'

'There's also the question of the vanes, Captain,' said Boucher.

'The vanes, yes,' grumbled Cloche. 'But ballast tanks first! A submarine without functioning tanks is just an iron bar dropped in the water.'

They waited. Distant clanging and knocking could be heard.

'There!' said Lebret, putting his head on one side like a dog. 'Avocat has reached the inlets. He is effecting repairs!' A series of distant, muffled noises of metallic percussion could be heard.

Suddenly the whole vessel shook, rotating a metre to the left. Then it rolled back through to right itself. Some mechanical arrangement of the vessel's workings audibly caught, and with a whir of motors the vent on the starboard ballast tank began to close. 'I'm inflating the tanks now, Captain,' cried Le Petomain.

The men in the slant space began spontaneously to cheer.

The downwards angle of the deck began to right itself. In moments, the slope of the decks reduced considerably. The vessel was not perfectly horizontal, but the angle was agreeably reduced.

'It is done!' cried Cloche, uncharacteristic delight distorting his face. 'Once the vanes are sorted, we will have full control of our craft and can arrest this interminable descent! We can turn our trajectory about, and return to the surface!'

Lebret shook his head, slowly, with a sly smile on his face – as if to say that the captain's optimism was sadly misplaced.

The banging stopped. 'Is our descent slowing?' Cloche demanded.

'A little, sir,' said Le Petomain.

'Assemble the men in the mess!' ordered Cloche. 'Get Pannier to bring out some bottles! We must celebrate!'

'We *are* still descending, though, sir...' Le Petomain said.

But Cloche appeared not to hear. 'Once the *vanes* are repaired,' he announced, 'we shall start our ascent. And if Avocat could repair the main tank vents so easily, then the vanes should be a simple matter!'

'Sir—' Le Petomain said again.

'A drink!' Cloche bellowed. 'Celebration! Soon we shall return home, my comrades!'

Boucher hurried along the now-horizontal corridor and went through to the kitchen. He found Pannier immediately – once again dead drunk, slumped unconscious on his knees with his face on the seat of a chair, in a parody of prayer. The lieutenant didn't waste time tutting; he rummaged through the stores until he found two bottles, and a corkscrew, and came back through to the mess.

From below climbed de Chante, and Avocat in his rubber suit, shinily wet. The diver was the only man not grinning.

'Bravo Avocat!' yelled somebody.

But the diver merely shook his head.

'Cheer up man,' instructed Cloche. 'You have done a great thing!' He pulled on a cork and it emerged from the bottleneck with a gloopy noise. But he was clumsy, and spilled a portion of the wine – a freak breeze caught the droplets and spattered them upwards at the ceiling. Cloche, cursing, put his thumb over the top.

'I'm sorry, Captain,' said Avocat, glumly.

'No matter! Most of the bottle remains!'

Avocat shook his head again. 'I don't mean the wine.' The breeze

63

was certainly flowing vigorously around the cabin (although, oddly, it did not chill the skin). But when Avocat lifted his arm to rub his face, droplets were lifted from the wet rubber and flew about the space.

The diver stood to attention. 'Captain – I'm sorry,' he announced, stiffly, 'sorry to have failed to complete my mission. I have let you down!'

'Don't be absurd!' barked Cloche, his brow crumpling. 'What are you saying? Nonsense!'

'My captain,' said Avocat, looking crushed. 'I didn't *get* to the vents—'

'What? What?'

'I dared not venture out! I dared not let go my hold on the lip of the airlock! The waters—the waters are treacherous.'

Cloche's expression grew fierce. 'What on earth are you talking about man? The vents have closed!'

'They have?' Avocat looked confused. 'I don't—I don't understand. *I* did not leave the airlock.'

'You're saying you *didn't* fix the ballast vents?'

'No, Captain.'

'But we heard you banging away!'

'That,' said de Chante, in an awkward voice, 'was Monsieur Avocat banging the door of the airlock with his spanner. He was ... keen to come back inside.'

'You never *left* the airlock?' thundered Cloche.

'I *intended* to swim out, Captain. I promise you, I did. But no sooner did I put my legs out, a whirlpool seized me.'

Cloche closed his eyes, and opened them again, as if he expected to see Avocat no longer there, vanished like a chimera. 'This is a poor joke, sailor,' he glowered.

'I am not joking, my Captain! It sucked at my legs – I could feel the *pull* of the water. The dark. I was there, a cone of light no bigger than a baseball bat spilling from my helmet, in ... all this dark. And the whirlpool was pulling me down—down to hell!'

'You're imagining things, man!' put in Boucher. He uncorked the second bottle, took a swig and passed it to the dripping man.

'There's nothing out there – a whirlpool would have registered on the ship's sensors.'

'I felt it! It was horribly strong,' Avocat insisted, shuddering. 'It must be this current that is pulling the entire vessel downwards! That is how we are descending as fast as we are.'

'Nonsense! When we fully inflate the ballasts we will start to rise ...' boomed the captain.

'Monsieur,' noted the practical-minded Ghatwala addressing Avocat. 'I must respectfully agree with these officers, that what you are saying makes no sense. If there were a current pulling the ship down it would pull you down at the same rate. You would not feel it. And in point of fact, if the ship were being sucked down a whirlpool we would be spun round and round. We would feel that!'

'If not a whirlpool,' said Avocat, growing angry, 'then some linear current – but strong! Strong, like a creature pulling at my legs. I could feel it *pulling* at my legs.'

Ghatwala possessed a mind supple and fast-thinking, but so perfectly logical that it found it difficult comprehending the slower, less rational mentition of other people. He spoke again, in a level voice. 'In that case – assuming there were some purely vertical force dragging you down – it would also act upon the entire vessel. There would be no perceptual difference from your point of view. You could not feel such a current.'

Avocat shrieked. 'I know what I felt! It almost sucked me away! I had to hang on to the bottom of the lock-door, grasping desperately as it pulled at my legs! I only just got back inside the airlock!'

There was an awkward pause. Castor took a noisy glug from one of the open bottles of wine.

'If you *didn't* go, then how did the ballast vents get fixed?' asked Lebret.

'I don't know!' And he began to weep.

'Get a grip on yourself, sailor,' the captain insisted. 'It won't do you any good being hysterical like this. You'll need to keep a level head when you go out again.'

Avocat's reaction was immediate. 'Go out again? No!' he cried, his eyes round as oranges. 'Sir – send me out again and you'll be sending me to my death. Don't, I beg of you!'

The captain's lined face clenched into its more habitual expression of displeasure. 'What's this babyishness? The vanes, sailor! You must address the vanes.'

'Please sir,' said Avocat. He was quivering with fear now, shaking droplets of water onto the floor. The pleading expression in his eyes gave his round face a childlike quality. 'Please don't send me out.'

'Nonsense!' barked Cloche.

'I beg of you, sir,' said Avocat, stepping towards his Captain, and holding his hands out.

De Chante spoke up. 'I'll go, Captain. It's my turn anyway.'

'No,' said the captain. 'Avocat is already suited-up. I don't want to waste more time. And above all, I will not nurture *cowardice* amongst my crew!'

The mention of cowardice had the effect of a slap to the face. Avocat straightened up and took a step backwards.

'Captain Cloche,' said Lebret, attempting a mollifying tone.

But the captain's temper – never a moderate or even thing – had compressed itself into the hardest mode of fury. Like a great mass of snow poised on a mountain flank, finally shaken free by a tremor, his rage came thundering down upon his crewman.

'*Will* you go back in the water, sailor?' he shouted, his hand groping for his pistol. In his anger he omitted to unbutton the holster, so his elderly fingers fumbled fruitlessly at the leather flap. Without giving Avocat time to reply, he continued. 'You can join your fellow mutineer in the brig. Boucher! Boucher!'

'Captain!'

'Take him away. And you—' he turned on Lebret. 'Keep your collaborationist chatter to yourself, sir, or I'll have you locked in the brig as well.'

The mood of elation had evaporated. Boucher was holding the open wine bottle by its neck. He passed it across to Castor, put his hand on Avocat's shoulder, and followed him out of the mess, clambering awkwardly up the still-sloping corridor.

'You, sailor,' the captain spluttered, pointing at de Chante. 'Whatever your name is. Go along too. Wring that miserable coward out of the wetsuit, and put it on yourself. Your orders: to dive for'ard, and do what you can to unjam the front vanes.'

De Chante had gone very white. 'No, sir,' he said.

Cloche's skin went redder, throwing his white beard into remarkable contrast. He stared hard at de Chante, then turned his head to look down at his flank. With deliberation he coordinated his fingers to unbutton the flap.

'No?'

'Not on these terms, sir.'

'On these … *terms?*'

'Captain, I had already offered to take Avocat's place.' De Chante spoke rapidly. 'There was no need to send him to the brig. He is no coward, Captain. He is my friend, and calling him a coward is unconscionable. To call a Frenchman such a thing is to—'

The captain's pistol was directly in de Chante's face. 'Another word,' hissed Cloche, 'and I shall make an example of you.'

Nobody spoke.

'I repeat my order,' said Cloche. 'You will then either follow it, or die – here and now. Do you understand?'

De Chante nodded slowly.

'Very well. Boucher – the celebrations are … Boucher? Boucher! Where *is* my lieutenant?'

'He is locking up Avocat,' said Lebret in a mild voice.

Cloche glared at him. 'These celebrations have proved *premature*,' he declared. 'Pannier will return these bottles of wine to the store – Pannier? Pannier! And meanwhile, de, de, this sailor here will venture outside the *Plongeur* and, and, and restore control to the forward vanes. And – Pannier!' he bellowed. 'Where *is* the man?'

The others in the mess swapped uncertain glances. Billiard-Fanon evidently considered it his duty to inform the captain.

'Captain, I regret to inform you—'

'What?'

'Pannier is,' said the ensign, nervously. 'Pannier is—'

'Drunk,' said Lebret, in a voice so loud that Billiard-Fanon jumped, like a man pinched. 'Dead drunk, in fact. By which I mean insensible.'

For a moment nothing happened. The time felt weirdly suspended. Cloche glared at Lebret. Everybody waited to see what would happen next.

Then the captain took in a deep breath, held it, and released it. Slowly he replaced his pistol in its holster. 'The crew of the *Plongeur*,' he said, speaking distinctly, but directing his words into the space between Lebret and Jhutti. 'The crew of the *Plongeur* has disgraced me. The crew has disgraced France. With God's help and my leadership we *shall* return to Saint-Nazaire. And when we do, I shall report you all to the authorities for dishonourable discharge from the French navy, and imprisonment or execution depending on the degree of the mutiny. Messieurs—' He swivelled his gaze to the two Punjabi scientists, '—are not sworn-in members of the Navy of France, and I exclude you from my disapprobation. Nevertheless, I expect you to respect my authority and follow my orders.' He sighed heavily. 'I am going to my cabin,' he announced. Then, slowly, he pulled his way along the sloping floor of the bridge, and up the corridor.

For long minutes, nobody spoke. It was clear that some profound violence had been enacted upon the structures of authority in the submarine. Something had broken.

De Chante sat down. 'The captain has gone mad,' he breathed.

'Sailor!' snapped Billiard-Fanon. 'Be quiet! To say such a thing is tantamount to mutiny.'

'Even if it's *true*?' retorted the white-faced de Chante. He pulled a cigarette case from his shirt pocket, an action that made plain how much his hand was trembling.

'You have your orders, sailor,' Billiard-Fanon said. But his voice lacked certainty.

Boucher came half-stepping, half-tumbling down the slope and into the bridge. He was carrying the sodden wetsuit, draped over one arm. He saw at once that something was wrong. 'Where's the captain?' he asked.

'The captain has retired to his cabin,' replied Billiard-Fanon.

'Things flip-flopped rather suddenly,' drawled Lebret, 'in terms of the – shall we say, the captain's mood.'

'He... he left us with orders,' Billiard-Fanon insisted.

'Well, follow them!' said Boucher. But the expression on Billiard-Fanon's face clearly disconcerted him. 'I mean – what *were* the orders?'

'He said de Chante was to go out, try to fix the vanes,' said Billiard-Fanon.

'Yes, I heard that. Avocat has removed the suit – here it is...'

'The captain *also* said,' Lebret interrupted him, 'that the entire crew, save only the two Indians, can expect to be court-martialled when we return to Saint-Nazaire.'.

'He said that?' returned Boucher, his cigar-shaped eyebrows floating up his brow.

'It was unclear whether his words applied to me or not,' Lebret added. 'I presume they did.'

'He has lost his mind,' said de Chante, emboldened by the uncertain mood of the group.

'Sailor – I shan't warn you again,' said Billiard-Fanon. 'Keep your tongue behind the fence of your teeth.'

'The fact that the captain believes we *can* return to Saint-Nazaire,' said Lebret, 'rather supports de Chante's assessment of his mental state.'

Boucher rubbed his face. 'What *has* happened here? Moments ago the entire crew was cheering with delight – and now we're in despair? Come! The captain is right – we *can* return home. Of course we can. More than that – we will! Let's—let's.' He looked around; for he was unused to and uncomfortable with, command. 'Let us try refloating the tanks, and... no, wait. We must first free up the vanes. De Chante – into your suit, please!'

With a sigh, de Chante took hold of the suit, and clambered down the ladder to the airlock chamber. Billiard-Fanon went after him. 'I'll help him into his, into his...' And before he pulled himself through the doorway he added. 'Monsieur Lebret, and Monsieur Indian – would you be so kind as to carry Pannier through to his cabin. I suppose we must, ah, *remove him* from the sources of his temptation.'

8

THE CRACK

❦ ❦ ❦ ❦ ❦ ❦

The two men manhandled the cook's unconscious body out of the kitchen with some difficulty. Lugging him along the corridor involved banging his flopping limbs awkwardly against the walls and the floor. Eventually they bundled him into his cabin, and shut the door on him.

As they returned, Lebret noted. 'Soon enough de Chante will sort out the vanes and we'll have a more-or-less functioning submarine. It's just a question of waiting. I think I shall have some coffee. Would you join me?'

'By all means.'

They made their way together into the empty mess hall. A steel urn was set into a rotating bracket in the wall. From this, Lebret poured coffee into two steel mugs. The fluid sloshed weirdly; he fitted lids over the top of each before handing one to Jhutti.

'I wonder if you agree with me,' Lebret said, looking slyly at the engineer, 'that we ought to *explore* this new territory? Wherever we are, whatever this place is. I mean of course – once the vessel is fully repaired. Wouldn't it be a foolishness simply to flee back to France. We must go a little deeper yet, surely! Who knows what's down there.'

Jhutti did not answer this directly. Instead, seating himself opposite Lebret, he asked, 'So, M'sieur. Tell me truly. Do *you* think the diver experienced an actual whirlpool current?'

Lebret shook his head slowly. 'As to that – your compatriot's points *seemed* irrefutable. Yet, isn't it more likely that Monsieur

72

Avocat suffered a momentary psychological breakdown? Some terror gripped his muscles and he found himself unable to swim out?'

'I suppose that sounds more plausible,' agreed Jhutti. 'Still, there must surely *be* whirlpools and strange currents within your infinite ocean? If that is truly where we are.'

'I suppose so – as to the currents, I mean.'

'Tell me, my friend. Do you *actually* believe,' Jhutti pressed, 'that we have slipped from our natural dimension into such a place?'

'We passed through something,' said Lebret. 'That is one thing of which we can be sure. And so we have travelled *into* something.'

'But through what did we pass?'

For some moments it appeared that Lebret was not going to answer. Then he breathed deeply. 'I shall tell you what I suspect, my friend. There is a poem,' he said, his voice slipping down a semitone. 'A poem by the Irish Romantic poet, Alfred De Neeson. It is called "The Crack".'

In a singsong voice he recited the English words:

Below the thunders of the upper deep;
Far, far beneath in the abysmal sea,
Its ancient, dreamless, uninvaded sleep,
The Crack, it sleepeth: faintest sunlights flee
About its shadowy sides; above it swell
Huge sponges of millennial growth and height;
And far away into the sickly light,
From many a wondrous grot and secret cell
Unnumbered and enormous polypi
Winnow with giant arms the slumbering green.
There hath it lain for ages and will lie
Swallowing huge sea-worms in its sleep,
Until the latter fire shall heat the deep;
Then once by man and angels to be seen,
Roaring he shall swallow all the seas, and die.

'My English,' said Jhutti, in Punjabi, 'is not wholly competent to grasp such flowery turns. This is a poem about…?'

'It is a hymn, a sonnet, a lyric!' said Lebret, with more feeling than precision. 'The Vikings possess an ancient myth, the oldest amongst their many legends. It is that the world was born from the chasm – the crack, as Neeson calls it here – and that at the end of time it is this crack that will swallow the world. It is a mighty valley at the bottom of the deepest ocean, but unlike other ocean trenches it descends forever – without end. There is an analogue in Greek mythology – the *Chasm* is the prison in which the rebellious Titans are imprisoned.'

'And you think we have sunk into this legendary space?'

'Legends are rarely invented out of nothing, my friend,' said Lebret, gravely. 'They are invariably based upon facts, race-memories, primordial truths. Often distorted and embellished of course, but at their core is always a truth.'

'This crack, or chasm – you believe it to be a literal feature of the world?'

'Literal,' said Lebret, a more characteristically ironic gleam entering his eye, 'is a very dull and materialist word for a Hindu to use – don't you think?'

'I am trained in Western material science, after all,' Jhutti replied, smiling. Then, in a low voice he added, 'Cloche will never agree to use his vessel to explore this new ocean. Never. He wishes to go home, and nothing else.'

'I fear you are right,' agreed Lebret. 'But perhaps he can be persuaded? The possibilities, for science I mean… they are unprecedented!'

'Does he seem to you the type of man who can be persuaded? Of anything?'

'No,' Lebret conceded, wearily.

The two sat in silence for a long time.

'Surely de Chante must have finished working on the vanes?' said Lebret. 'Let us go and see what the situation is.' And so they walked along the shallowly-angled corridor and through into the bridge.

9

THE LIGHT

♥ ♥ ♥ ♥ ♥ ♥

But there was no sign of the diver. Fifteen minutes became twenty, and Boucher's agitation grew. 'I'm getting,' he complained, bunching his hands into fists and unflexing them again, 'these *spasms* in my hands. Is anybody else getting that?'

'Where is our diver?' asked Lebret.

'Nobody knows.'

Half an hour passed.

'Spasms in my hands,' the lieutenant complained, vaguely. 'And where's de Chante? Where has he *got* to? He should be back by now. Are the forward vanes working now?'

'No, Lieutenant.'

'He's gone,' said Lebret.

'Hush!' pleaded Boucher, making alternate starfish and ball shapes with his hands. 'Don't say so!'

'Gone,' repeated Lebret. 'It's true.'

'There must be some way we can see what he's up to – does he show up on the sonar?'

'I'm not sure the sonar's even working, Lieutenant,' reported Le Petomain. 'It has returned only blankness since we began our dive. But even if it *is* working, a diver swimming close about the hull wouldn't show up on it – unless he passed directly in front of the sensor, perhaps.'

'I'll have a look through the periscope,' Boucher announced. 'Somebody go down to the observation room – open the shutters and see what you can see.'

76

'I'll go,' said Billiard-Fanon. He stomped, scowling, down the corridor.

Boucher clambered up into the con. They heard the miniature whir of a servo, as the periscope deployed and began to rotate. 'It's dark,' he called, a little superfluously. 'But de Chante has a light on his helmet, doesn't he? I should at least be able to see that.'

They waited.

'He must be beneath the vessel. Le Petomain,' Boucher called down through the open hatch, shortly. 'There's nothing up here – I ask you to roll the ship a little, and also to pitch her back and forth, so I can see more.

'The vanes are stuck, Lieutenant,' the pilot replied. 'I can pitch by shifting air in the ballast tanks, but the manoeuvres will be a little stiff; and rolling the vessel is beyond me.'

'Let's start by pitching forward a little.'

Slowly, the *Plongeur's* whale-shaped nose dipped forward in the water; and the men in the observation chamber braced themselves. The walls of the vessel groaned mildly. The floors slanted forward once more.

For a moment there was nothing. Then, abruptly, there was a clatter from below, and Billiard-Fanon clambered up the hill and into the bridge. His big face was sweating.

'Light!' he cried. 'Below us – light!'

'What?'

'I didn't see to begin with,' said the ensign, gruffly. 'It's not visible when the ship is lying flat. I opened the shutters, turned the lights off and smoked a cigarette. Nothing to see. But then – the vessel pitched forward, and...'

'You saw de Chante's light?'

'What?' Puzzlement gave Billiard-Fanon's long, jowly face an idiot look.

'De Chante,' said Castor. 'You saw his helmet light?'

'There's no sign of *him*. I'm talking about *the light*! God has not abandoned us! Come and see!'

Billiard-Fanon led Lebret, Jhutti, Ghatwala and Castor down

77

into the observation chamber. The angle of the corridor meant that they had to pick their way with some care.

'There!' said Billiard-Fanon, triumphantly.

At first – nothing. But then, slowly, unmistakeably, a mauve-blue gleam was nebulously but unmistakeably visible at the bottom of the viewing portal.

'Light,' breathed Billiard-Fanon.

'We can all see that, I presume,' said Lebret. 'Yes? That rules out the notion of hallucination. There is *something* shining down there.'

'But what?' asked Castor.

The light possessed some strange aspect – a deathly, or more precisely a life-in-deathly quality to the hue. A chill blue. An antithetical blue – purple-black and uneasy.

'We must inform the captain,' said Billiard-Fanon.

'Yes,' said Lebret. 'I think we must. When he sees this, he will understand – understand that we must go further down and investigate!'

Boucher tapped gingerly at the door of Cloche's cabin and went inside. Four minutes later he re-emerged. The captain followed him. The old man had not, by the look of him, been sleeping. Indeed, his beard appeared even more massy and spread-out than before – almost as wide as his broad chest, covering three of the four brass buttons on his jacket, as thick as a beaver's tail. Cloche had fixed it to his shirt with a tie-pin – of all things. Cloche's eyes were fixed, stern, the signals of a set and implacable will. 'My lieutenant says there is a light in the water.'

'Indeed, Captain!'

'Messieurs,' he said. 'I am *also* told that we have lost de Chante – lost at sea. Is it so?'

'It appears so, Captain.'

'A brave sailor,' Cloche growled. He seemed to have forgotten that only hours earlier he had called the fellow a coward. Nor did he seem unduly distressed by the loss of one of his crew. 'Did he fix the vanes first?'

'No, Captain.'

Cloche tutted. 'A malfunction with his apparatus,' he said. 'Clumsiness? An accident? Or perhaps there truly *are* dangerous currents in this sea. It is a great shame. And what of this light you say is below us?'

'It is, I think, distant. Blue-white.'

'Well! Well! Show me!'

Boucher led Cloche down to the observation chamber, with a half dozen others following behind. The captain peered through the broad porthole at the weird, vague illumination. 'Very pretty,' he announced. 'And?'

Nobody said anything for several long seconds.

'Perhaps we ought to investigate, Captain,' said Jhutti, eventually.

'Just so,' agreed Lebret. 'We *must* descend further, and see what is causing this light.'

'No,' said the captain, without hesitation. He pointed a finger at Boucher. 'I gave orders that we were to ascend. Why have we not done so?'

'The forward vanes remain to be fixed,' said the lieutenant, in a tremulous voice.

'If they cannot be fixed, then we must ascend without their help. Fill the ballast tanks fully with air. Angle the propellers. The ascent might not be as smooth as we would like, but ascent is the order.'

At these words, Lebret laid a hand on the captain's arm. Cloche glowered at him, and he removed the hand. Lebret smiled with his usual supercilious insouciance.

'Surely, Captain,' he drawled. 'Surely we could spare a *few* hours – to descend a little deeper through this strange medium, and discover the cause of this light? Science would honour you as its discoverer...'

'I am not interested in the accolades of Science,' replied the captain, abruptly. 'Science can conduct its own investigations. I am interested only in returning my command to port.'

'But to have come so far – to within touching distance of a mystery hitherto unsuspected by...'

'*When* we have returned to the surface,' interrupted the captain, forcefully, 'I shall submit a full report. I have no doubt that the French Academy of Science will sponsor a – properly equipped – scientific expedition. It will surely be a simple matter to retrace our steps. But this – Monsieur Lebret – *this* – messieurs all – is not *our* business.'

He took hold of his magnificent, immense beard with two hands, and gave it a mighty tug – as if, by this emphatic physical gesture to forestall any and all disagreement.

Lebret, though, persisted. 'No, Captain, I must register my disagreement. After everything we have been through – to miss this opportunity? It would be like a nineteenth-century explorer travelling through immense hardship to within two hundred yards of the North Pole and then giving up and going home.'

Cloche turned his steel eye towards Lebret. 'You must *register your disagreement*, must you Monsieur?' he said, in a level, voice. 'Consider it registered. Consider it simultaneously disregarded. We return – as soon as the vanes are fixed.'

'Monsieur Captain . . .'

'No, Monsieur! No! The *Plongeur* suffered triple malfunctions simultaneously . . . either through sabotage, or perhaps through some design flaw. It is not safe, *not* a safe vessel to embark upon further exploration. We must return to port, sir. I order it.'

Lebret persisted. 'What if the light and de Chante's disappearance are connected? What if he is *down* there? Ought we not at least to investigate?'

'Monsieur,' said the captain, addressing himself to Lebret. 'Speak again, so as to contradict my order, and I shall confine you to your cabin. Monsieur de Chante is dead. He is a hero of France, and shall be honoured – *when* we return to port.'

The scientist in Ghatwala spoke up for Lebret's suggestion. 'One hour, Captain!' he pleaded. 'Delay the ascent by one hour – to give us time at least to *observe* this phenomenon!'

'And to give de Chante a little more time to return to the airlock,' put in Boucher. 'If he is able.'

Cloche glared at them, one after the other. 'I sniff *insubordination*,' he said, in a steady voice.

'No sir!' Boucher yelped. 'We follow your orders, sir! It is only a question of whether we do so immediately, or whether you can permit us one hour to prepare for...'

'*Half* an hour,' said Cloche, thunderously. 'That is all!'

10

AN INTERVIEW WITH CAPTAIN CLOCHE

❦ ❦ ❦ ❦ ❦ ❦

The captain returned to his cabin. The Indian scientists retrieved such scientific instrumentation as they had in their cabins, and returned to the observation chamber. Le Petomain was in the pilot's seat and Boucher in the captain's chair. With de Chante gone, and Avocat and Pannier locked into their cabins, the boat felt deserted.

Lebret lit another cigarette and loitered for a while in the bridge. According to the depth gauge, augmented by the notches in the panel, the submarine had sunk to something approaching 100,000 kilometres (it was hard to be precise). 'A remarkable depth!' he murmured.

Le Petomain ignored him.

Behind the hum of the functioning submarine – the whirr of the propellers, the hum of the electrics – a distant moaning noise could just about be heard. It rose and fell.

'Do *you* believe, Lieutenant,' Lebret asked, offhandedly, 'that we will be able simply to retrace our steps and return home? Even if we could locate whichever portal granted us entrance in all this vast quantity of alien water – and even supposing it permitted us to go back through – then the sudden pressure differential would surely tear us to shreds...'

'Monsieur,' Boucher interrupted him. 'Please do not continue speaking. You cannot persuade me to listen to you. The captain has given his orders, and I intend to follow them.'

'Commendable loyalty,' said Lebret. 'I'm sure.' His tone of voice was not wholly respectful.

The background moaning noise rose in intensity, and Lebret suddenly realised what was causing it. It was Pannier, locked in his cabin, crying aloud his complaints. 'Be quiet!' bellowed Boucher.

The moaning ceased. But shortly the cook began banging at the inside of his door.

'What does that old soak want?' growled Le Petomain.

'I'll try to quieten him down,' said Lebret.

He made his way along into the corridor behind the Bridge to Pannier's door. Pannier presumably heard somebody moving outside his cabin, for he redoubled the force of his hammering. There Lebret stood, waiting for a pause in the noise. Eventually he called out, 'Monsieur, please cease this clamour! It will do you no good.'

'Let me out.' Pannier's voice sounded muffled, by the door, or by drink, or by both.

'No, Monsieur,' said Lebret.

'Is it you, Monsieur Observer? Monsieur Vichy? I can't expect comradeship from you, I suppose! Well, if you won't let me out, at least fetch me a bottle from the kitchen. One bottle!'

'I don't think so, Monsieur.'

'Come! You can't stand on your honour to refuse me – you have none.' The words were slightly slurred. 'We're all going to die – you can't expect a man to face that fate *sober*? I'll strike a deal with you, Monsieur Vichy – fetch me a bottle and I'll stop banging and shouting. But leave me here to sober up and by the sacred colour blue I'll bash this door off its hinges! I swear it.'

'Monsieur,' Lebret began, wearily. There was motion behind him, and he looked away from Pannier's door to see Captain Cloche approaching.

'Pannier,' boomed the captain. 'Be quiet! You are in enough trouble already – silence your mutinous racket. I am giving you a direct order.'

Without waiting for a reply he turned and moved ponderously back up the sloping corridor. Lebret danced after him.

'Captain!' he called. 'Captain – might I have a word?'

Cloche's broad back disappeared into the captain's cabin; but he did not close the door behind him, and Lebret – tentatively – followed him inside.

The captain's cabin was a sparely furnished, blue room. The captain sat himself heavily on the edge of his bunk, and looked up at Lebret. 'Yes, Monsieur?' he said. The inner lining of his eyes was red; the eyes themselves exhausted, lunar, distant.

Bang! Bang! Bang! came with clattering regularity from Pannier's room.

'You look tired, Captain,' Lebret said, a little stab of compassion starting up in his breast.

Cloche said nothing at first; but then he sighed. 'You have not come here to discuss whether I am tired or not, Monsieur.'

'No, Captain' Lebret agreed. 'I have not.'

'I believe you have come to try and persuade me to take the *Plongeur* further down, to sink us deeper into these strange waters, so as to investigate this faint light.'

'That is exactly why I am here, Captain,' Lebret agreed. He tried a smile.

'I won't do it,' said Cloche, simply. 'That's all.'

Lebret took a breath, and began to say, 'An opportunity for scientific discovery of quite literally unprecedented...' But his heart was not in it, and his sentence petered out.

'We have never served together before, Monsieur, you and I,' said Cloche, with a certain smugness. 'But I think you understand me well enough to know that I am not a man to go back on a decision, once I have made it.'

'No,' said Lebret, mournfully. 'Of course, you understand that the journey back might kill us all!'

'It might,' conceded the captain. 'De Chante is dead already. Better, then, to die attempting to get home, rather than to throw our lives away chasing some blue-light chimera. Let us at least be men. Warriors of France. Not kittens distracted by... by a spot of sunlight on, ah!, on the floor reflected by... eh, by a shaving

86

mirror.' He looked pleased with himself, in a severe sort of way, with this metaphor.

Outside, Pannier's banging had fallen into a regular rhythm. The captain shook his head. 'I may have to shoot that drunkard,' he growled.

It was evident to Lebret that there was no changing the captain's mind. He dressed his face in a smile – an unconvincing expression, even for him. 'Good-day Captain,' he said. He turned to leave the cabin, but instead of stepping out into the corridor he shut the captain's door.

'Monsieur?' said Cloche. 'There is more you wish to say? Rest assured, you will not change my mind.'

'The blue light, Captain. What if it is the *sky*?'

Cloche looked dully at him. 'What?'

'I am serious. The blue colour of the sky! What if, by ordering the *Plongeur* to ascend, you were actually taking us *away* from the surface?'

Suddenly the captain laughed – one, two, three bark-like noises. 'This is your latest surreal theory, Monsieur? First you claimed we had all died and gone to a watery heaven. Then you said we had entered an infinite sea! Now you are saying that all that has happened is that we have flopped upside down?' *Ha! Ha!* Cloche's laugh was a peculiar thing – machinic, perfectly empty of warmth. 'If it is so, wouldn't we all be standing upon the ceiling?' he asked.

'Captain, listen for a moment, permit me to ...' said Lebret, fishing through the pockets of his trousers.

Thud, thud, thud went Pannier's fist against his door. Then he paused; then he banged again. *Thud, thud, thud.*

Cloche's strange smile fell away. 'You really believe it, don't you? You are insane, Monsieur. I see it now – insane.'

'Ah!' said Lebret, finding what he was looking for in his left pocket. He pulled it out. It was a small pistol – a tiny gun, looking rather like a cigarette lighter with a spout.

Cloche saw at once what it was. 'Oho!' he snorted. 'You think to intimidate me with that lady's pistoletta?'

'What choice do you leave me, Captain?'

Cloche's sneer fell away. Without getting to his feet, he reached his right hand round to his left hip where his own, much more substantial weapon was holstered.

But the flap of his holster was, as always, buttoned up. It was this that gave Lebret time to act.

He did so without haste. With an almost leisurely motion, he stepped over to where Cloche was sitting. As he came, he held out his left, empty hand, keeping the right, with the gun in it, pointed at the floor. The cabin was small; it took only two steps to cross the floor.

What occurred next happened rapidly. Lebret slipped his left hand out and up, underneath Cloche's beard, grasping his throat. His hand looked small, almost feminine; but the effect on the captain of its grip upon his windpipe was pronounced. His eyes popped open. His own right hand gave up its fumbling at the flap of his holster, and seized Lebret's left wrist.

Thud, thud, thud went Pannier, striking the inside of his own door.

The captain's left hand joined his right, clutching at Lebret's arm; but even with both he was unable to dislodge Lebret's grip. The slightness of the fellow's frame belied what was, evidently, a considerable muscular strength in his arm.

Lebret and Cloche locked eyes. Cloche's lips parted. A hiss emerged; a gasping and rasping sound.

Then – *thud, thud, thud* went Pannier, out in the corridor.

Lebret brought up his pistol. Even a small gun, like his, would make an unmissably loud report in the close confines of the *Plongeur*, and the closer confines of the captain's cabin.

Lebret looked past the captain to the pillow at the head of his bunk, to muffle the gunshot. It was out of reach. To get it, Lebret would have to relinquish his grasp – and that would allow Cloche to retrieve his own weapon. The captain's eyes followed Lebret's gaze. He choked, rasped, and kicked out with his leg. His cheeks and brow were dark.

Lebret met the captain's bulging gaze. With a rapid twisting motion he rolled his gun up in Cloche's long white beard, twisting

88

it over once, and over again, until it was swaddled in the old man's face hair. The tip of the little barrel rested against the underside of the captain's chin.

Cloche's eyes widened again as he felt the metal touch him. He gave another convulsive kick with his right leg, and tried wriggling his whole body away from his assailant's hold. It did no good.

Lebret was waiting, his head slightly inclined. In his eye was the same perfect blankness you see in a heron's eye, as it holds the fish against the unflinching riverside rock, drowning its prey in air. And then—

Thud, thud, thud went Pannier. And tucked in the middle, another sound, almost exactly timed to coincide with the middle *thud*: a sharper-edged cracking sound.

Cloche's head twitched upward. A thread of scarlet was picked out, suddenly, in the white of the left eye.

The force drained from his double grip on Lebret's arm. The other man released his hold on Cloche's throat, and brushed the captain's hands away. They fell, nerveless, to flop against the mattress.

Lebret began to untangle his right hand, as if unpacking a present from a mess of white packing straw. He brought out two things: his small pistol in his hand, but also a long thread of grey wool. Lebret regarded this. It wasn't wool – it was an upwards trailing thread of smoke.

It took a moment for Lebret to understand. He snatched his hand away at almost exactly the same time that the smoke kindled into a flash of flame, and the whole beard began to burn. A potent reek of singed hair filled the cabin. Flame tickled upwards.

Lebret stepped back.

Cloche's body slumped slowly backwards, the back of his head striking the wall, his spine bowing out. His entire beard was alight now, myriad little orange-white flames shimmering across his chest and black smoke gushing upwards. This veil did not obscure the sight of the old man's cheeks blackening and blistering.

Lebret pocketed his pistol, opened the captain's door, checked the corridor and stepped into it. He had just reached his own door and opened it when the sound of a klaxon split the air.

He put one foot inside his room, in time to be able to make it look as though he was stepping *out* of his cabin – drawing the door shut behind him – as Le Petomain and Billiard-Fanon hurried into the corridor.

'Fire alarm!' called Billiard-Fanon.

'Is *that* what it is?' replied Lebret coolly. 'I did wonder.'

'Smoke – seeping around the captain's door!' cried Le Banquier.

'Is it locked? Is the door locked?' Billiard-Fanon demanded.

But Le Petomain had already opened the door. He recoiled as a billow of foul-smelling smoke burlied out. Then he covered his mouth with the crook of his arm, and dived in. Billiard-Fanon followed, and Lebret came to stand at the door.

'Shall I fetch water?' Lebret called. He could see what was happening inside the cabin – Le Petomain hauling the blanket from the captain's bunk and wrapping it around the burning skull.

The alarm sounded, a hammer-drill din. Pannier's banging at the door redoubled in intensity.

Le Petomain wrestled the captain from his bunk and onto the floor so as to be able to fold the blanket the whole way around. But it was all too obvious that Cloche was dead.

Coughing, Le Petomain piled the rest of the blanket about the site of the fire. The flames were stifled, but smoke filled the room. Billiard-Fanon was weeping, either at the shock and tragedy of his captain's death, or else from the stinging, foul smoke.

The alarm stopped abruptly, leaving only Pannier's rhythmic thumping at his cabin door. Boucher emerged into the corridor. 'Where's the fire?'

Lebret gestured into Cloche's cabin. 'Too late, I fear,' he added, as the lieutenant peered around the door.

'Good God!' he exclaimed. 'What happened?'

'I don't know,' gasped Billiard-Fanon, rubbing his eyes on the sleeves of his shirt.

'He—he caught fire,' said Le Petomain, between coughs. 'He was on his bunk, and somehow – he caught fire!'

'But how?' demanded Boucher.

'Spontaneous human combustion!' said the ensign, in a scared voice. 'I read about it in a novel – an English novel. A devilish thing!'

'Unlikely,' observed Lebret, drily.

Le Petomain stepped out of the cabin. His face was streaked with smuts, and his eyes were watering. 'He was on his bunk. Did he—did he light a cigarette, and fall asleep? Did his cigarette fall into his beard and set it alight?'

'It must be that,' said Boucher.

Thud-thud, thud-thud, thud-thud went Pannier.

'It must be that,' the lieutenant repeated. 'What a tragic accident!'

'Are you sure he is dead?' asked Lebret.

Le Petomain looked at the prone figure, his head wrapped in blanket. 'Do you want me to … look? To check? I have been trained in First Aid.'

'I will do it,' said Boucher. 'I'm—God of the depths, I suppose I'm in command now! It's my duty.'

Thud-thud, thud-thud, thud-thud went Pannier. Boucher hollered, 'Be quiet, Pannier!'

The banging stopped. 'What's happening?' came Pannier's voice. He sounded less drunk, although it was hard to tell through the door. 'I heard the fire alarm.'

'There's been an … accident,' said Billiard-Fanon. 'God, first de Chante and now this! There's a curse – upon this boat, a *curse* …'

'Such talk,' Lebret offered, 'is surely not helpful.'

'What's going *on?*' cried Pannier, inside his cabin.

'The fire's out now, don't worry,' Boucher called to the imprisoned cook. He turned his head away, took a deep breath, and then stepped into the captain's berth. Going down onto his haunches beside Cloche's body, he picked away the blanket. Scorched sheets, blue on one side and carbonised black on the other, came away in yard-wide flakes and flapped about the room. The last of the blanket unfolded in a great scorched crumple to reveal the top of Cloche's captain's jacket (weirdly untouched by flame) and the charcoal lump that had once been his head. Soot and smut swirled through the smoky air.

With a heave of his right arm Boucher turned the corpse over. Yellow teeth glinted in a scowl of black ashes. 'Yes, gentlemen,' said the lieutenant, standing up. 'I think it's fair to say – he is dead.'

Castor had appeared in the corridor. 'What is it?'

'The captain is dead,' said Boucher, stepping back out from the scorched cabin.

'He fell asleep in his bunk smoking a cigarette!' said Billiard-Fanon, excitedly. 'He set fire to his beard – burnt his whole head!'

'Dead?' called Pannier, from inside his cabin. 'How? What's that? What's happened?'

'No!' said Castor, his face falling.

'He *cannot* be,' said Pannier.

'He was a hero of the Republic!' said Castor, in a desolated voice. 'One of the finest naval officers France ever had! To die – like that? It's … appalling.'

'It is certainly that,' said Lebret.

'I can't believe it!' announced Boucher. 'He set his *beard* on fire?'

'Hard to credit,' agreed Lebret. 'Yet, here we are.' He brought out his own silver cigarette case, and flipped it open; but then he noticed Boucher glowering at him. 'Oh,' he said, nodding. He folded away the case. 'Insensitive of me – in the circumstances.'

11

COUNCIL OF WAR

❧ ❧ ❧ ❧ ❧ ❧

The first order of business was to tidy away the captain's body. Castor fetched a tarpaulin from the storeroom, and carefully wrapped Cloche's corpse in it. Then, since there was nowhere better to stow it, he laid it back on its couch, and shut the door.

'Isn't burial at sea the usual procedure?' Lebret drawled.

'I refuse to kick Captain Cloche's body out of the airlock, like so much rubbish,' said Boucher. 'Especially as we are not sailing the waters of any known ocean.'

'I take the force of what you say,' Lebret agreed. 'Only – the captain's cabin is no refrigerator. Shortly the body will start to decay.'

'We are only four days into our,' Boucher returned, stumbling over the correct word. 'Our,' he said, casting about, 'our extraordinary voyage – a mere four days. We must hope that this means we are no more than four days away from home.'

'Hope is a splendid thing,' was Lebret's opinion.

The next thing was that Boucher decided to release Capot and Avocat from the brig. The situation was explained to them, and they were both visibly shaken to hear of Cloche's death. Pannier began banging again at the inside of his door, like an ape in a cage. 'If we let him out,' Billiard-Fanon noted, 'we won't be able to keep him from the bottle.'

'Let him sober up a little longer,' Boucher agreed. 'Everybody else: please join me in the mess. We must discuss the situation in which we find ourselves.'

94

With Pannier still locked up, and the captain dead, only nine men gathered in the mess. The mood was as you would expect it to be.

'I'm in command now,' said Boucher. 'I'm not happy about that fact, but this is the way things are. And I *will* say this. Naturally we are all shocked by the horrible eventuality of the captain's accidental demise. But there will be time to mourn correctly later – now is not the time to sink into depression.'

'Sink,' repeated Lebret in a low voice, smiling, as if the lieutenant had said something amusing. He looked around at the dour faces of the others, and breathed noisily in through his nose.

'Our duty is to follow the captain's last orders,' went on Boucher, neither rebuking Lebret, nor meeting his eye. 'He instructed us to repair the *Plongeur*, and to return home.'

'An excellent idea!' said Lebret in a loud voice. 'Surely we are unanimous in our desire to return home.' He looked around the mess. 'The captain was quite correct to say that we are not equipped, even if we were in a fit state of repair, to explore this strange new realm into which we have – somehow – strayed.'

'Moniseur Lebret,' said Boucher, in a weak voice. 'May I be permitted to …?'

'Please, Lieutenant. I am seeking only to support your authority, as the new commanding officer of this vessel. More, I may have been the last person with whom the captain spoke, before he had his … unfortunate accident.'

'You?'

'Yes, yes. He and I exchanged words in the corridor, before he went into his cabin and I to mine.'

'Why was he in the *corridor*?' snapped Billiard-Fanon.

'I believe he had stepped out to order Pannier to cease his banging and yelling. I was in the corridor for the same reason.'

'And what,' Billiard-Fanon asked, with a degree of hostility, 'did he say to you?'

'He asked my opinion on the best way to *get* home.'

'He asked your opinion?' scoffed the ensign.

'Indeed. It is possible,' Lebret went on, reaching into his own jacket pocket to retrieve his cigarette case, 'that he retired to his bunk precisely to contemplate the best way forward.' He raised the case to his face, occluding it, and when he lowered it he had plucked out a cigarette with his mouth. His left hand was ready with the lighter. Nobody objected.

'What is there to contemplate?' demanded Castor, in a rough voice. 'We mend the vanes, pump air fully into the tanks and float back up. We came here by sinking down, we go home by rising up.'

'That would be one possible route,' agreed Lebret, surrounding his head with spectral wraps of white smoke. 'But there is another. Two ways home. The question – the question we must all now ponder – is: which is the less dangerous of the two?'

'What *other* route?' asked Lieutenant Boucher.

'Let me say this,' said Lebret, folding his arms with his smoking cigarette tucked in-between the little-finger and ring-finger of his left hand. 'We must all acknowledge that we have passed through some crack in reality – some portal, some undersea gateway. We are no longer upon the earth.'

'That is,' growled Billiard-Fanon, 'bizarre! Impossible to conceive of it.'

'I do not pretend, messieurs,' Lebret went on, 'that I can entirely explain it. But certain features cannot be ignored. Clearly we are in a vast body of water, wheresoever we are. We know nothing about the portal by which we entered – what size it is, whether it permits only one-way traffic, and so on. Imagine that we spend three days floating upwards. Very well. Now ask yourself this – what are the chances we will locate exactly the right spot in an infinite ocean of dark water? And even if we happened to chance upon it – where would we re-emerge, in the earth? Why, at the bottom of the Atlantic! Descending slowly through those terrestrial waters, the pressure gradually building, almost crushed us! To return from these lesser pressures to those massive ones, abruptly, would certainly destroy us!'

'We survived coming down,' Billiard-Fanon pointed out. 'We can survive going back up.'

'But coming down the pressure *gradually* increased before

96

suddenly relenting,' said Lebret. 'To return the same way would be to suddenly apply the pressures of the bottom of the Atlantic to our already battered vessel. It would destroy us.'

'You have not yet said, Monsieur,' pointed Le Petomain, 'what our second route might be.'

'I am not certain there *is* one,' conceded Lebret. 'But consider this – how can there *be* light, seemingly below us? What could possibly be shining, down there?'

Nobody answered at first. Finally Boucher said: 'it is a mystery, I agree. But surely we all agree with Captain Cloche's words – that it is not our business to investigate. Let the Institute of Marine Science send a specially prepared craft to follow our tracks – *when* we are home.'

Lebret held up his cigarette, like a miniature baton. 'Permit me, Lieutenant,' he said. '*How we get home* is precisely the question we are discussing. With your permission, I will enumerate the possibilities – the light *could* be a phosphorescent phenomena, of a sort not previously encountered. Or it could, I suppose, be an artificial light source – created by the lamps of other sub oceanic vessels, or structures. Although I feel the range and extent of the brightness makes this unlikely. Or there is another possible explanation – and this is what made our esteemed captain pause for thought. It could be *the sky*.'

'Pff!' snorted Castor.

'Attend,' said Lebret, severely. 'For what I shall say next, though complex, is of the utmost significance for our predicament. Among the many things we must explain is this one – how can the water pressure around us be so low? Evidently we are surrounded by a vast body of fluid! We have sunk through thousands of kilometres of water, so we are deeper than any earthly ocean. The pressure should, by now, be so immense as to crush us to shards. Why does it not? Because – perhaps – we are now in an infinite ocean!'

'You must explain further,' said Lieutenant Boucher.

'Think of it as an analogue of the cosmos with which we are familiar: of infinite extent but filled almost entirely with empty space. What if there were *another* cosmos, likewise infinite, but filled instead with water?'

'A strange hypothesis,' said Boucher. 'Although I concede that much that has happened over these last few days has *been* strange.'

'Exactly! I ask – what would the pressure be inside an infinite ocean of water? Perhaps it would itself be infinite – or perhaps it would be zero, since any number divided by infinity (and the equations for water pressure require us to divide by the size of the body of water) must be as near zero as makes no odds. But how could the pressure be zero? We are, after all, surrounded by water molecules.' He put his cigarette to his lips, breathed in, and pushed out a large, misty lozenge of smoke before going on. 'I believe the pressure would be merely the *standard* pressure of the medium, its mass rather than its weight. Now, what follows? If we are *within* an infinite body of water?'

'Monsieur,' said Billiard-Fanon. 'This is the realm of Alice in Wonderland, I think.'

'Very well said!' laughed Lebret. 'Precisely so! Walking backwards to go forwards, running as fast as you can to stay still – the *geometry* of an infinite ocean, its *topography*, would embody strange features. Perhaps to rise up towards the sky we must – peculiar though it sounds – sink down? Perhaps the light we can see apparently below us *is* the sky, shining through the intervening waters?'

'But if the water we are in is infinite…'

'Infinite, yet co-existent with the infinite universe from which we have come! Two such infinites would interpenetrate themselves. Perhaps we passed through one such overlap – and perhaps the light we can see below is another such. The skies of the Oceanus Australis! Descend to it, and we can emerge once again in our home world!'

Everybody was silent for a while. 'It sounds – insane,' Boucher offered, in a tentative voice.

'I agree,' said Lebret, expansively. 'But perhaps it is the truth nonetheless! Monsieur Ghatwala,' he gestured with his cigarette in the direction of the scientist, who was sitting holding a cup of coffee in both hands, 'you are scientifically trained. Is anything

I have said incompatible with the dimensions of an infinite geometry.'

Ghatwala looked surprised to be invoked as an authority; but he said, 'No, no, I suppose not.'

'So?' prompted the lieutenant.

'I offer this only *as* a suggestion,' said Lebret, stubbing his cigarette out. 'And as a tribute to the honoured memory of our captain. Of course the final decision must be yours, Lieutenant. We could attempt to retrace our path, and float upwards for many days. Or we could spend a few hours descending towards the light, to determine whether it truly is a more direct route to the surface. If it is not – well then, we have lost only some few hours, and can inflate the tanks and go backwards. But if it *is*! Think only of that!'

12

THE LIGHT BELOW

There was some desultory discussion of the plausibility of Lebret's account; and some toing and froing about the best course of action. But with the implacable stubbornness of Cloche removed, Lebret was much better able to manipulate the mood of the group. Besides, as he himself insisted – his request *was* reasonable. After such an epic, impossible descent, what were a few more hundred leagues downward?

It looked for a while as if Boucher were going to put it to the vote. Billiard-Fanon, however, cut across this. 'The decision must be yours, sir,' he insisted. 'There's no place for voting on a naval vessel!' Boucher's authority was fragile enough without inviting the contempt of the men via spurious appeals to democracy.

'Then,' said Boucher, sounding flustered, 'let us go down a little further, and see what these lights *are*. Yes, we shall see if Monsieur Lebret's bizarre theory is correct. I am willing to spend another day on that mission. But if the lights merely are some form of phosphorescence, then we shall immediately re-fill the tanks and ascend.'

'It may be,' suggested Lebret, 'that the light has something to do with Seaman de Chante's ... disappearance.'

'He must at least have made it to the ballast tanks,' was Castor's opinion. 'We have functioning vents, at any rate.'

'But the tanks became functional before he went out,' said Billiard-Fanon. 'I believe it was coincidence.'

'There are many oddities here,' agreed Boucher. 'I mean, about the functioning of the ship, never mind the world outside. When we return,' – for that seductive idiom of hope had started to percolate into the general conversation aboard the ship – 'an official investigation will be able clear them up.'

He sat himself tentatively in the captain's chair. Le Petomain was pilot. Lebret, the two scientists and Billiard-Fanon were at the observation porthole. The remaining crew were at their posts at various places in the craft.

Once again, the *Plongeur* tipped forwards to dive down through the waters.

Down they went.

At first the light was indistinct – a vague, blue glimmer. After two hours it was possible to discern an area of more focused light, away to the left. Lebret suggested Boucher come down to the observation chamber and see for himself.

'Lieutenant,' said Lebret. 'We ought to steer towards where the light is brightest.'

'Very well,' agreed Boucher. He passed co-ordinates to Le Petomain, through the speaking tube, and the *Plongeur* reoriented itself in its descent. The brightness swung round to occupy the exact centre of the observation porthole.

'What *is* it?' Jhutti asked. 'It is too localised to be the whole sky.'

'I do not know what it is,' said Lebret, looking forward as if hypnotised. 'But soon we shall find out!'

The colour subtly changed, very slowly. The light was now a slightly greener shade of cyan. Brightness was evident in a wide spread up ahead, but it was now certainly most intense in a circular patch.

'Might it be a *clump* of phosphorescence?' asked Jhutti, leaning forward.

'Or an entrance, as if to a tunnel? A cave mouth through which sunlight is shining?' suggested Ghatwala.

'A portal, perhaps,' said Boucher, with wonder in his voice. 'Just as you said, Monsieur Lebret. If it is some manner of gateway, how can we determine whether it is safe to pass through it? Where will it take us?'

Lebret was silent, staring intently at the brightness below them.

Slowly the descent continued. Another forty thousand metres rolled past on the depth gauge. Boucher returned to the bridge; went aft to check on the engines, and finally returned to the observation porthole. Lebret, the scientists and Billiard-Fanon were all gazing at the slowly strengthening light, as if rapt.

'I have read accounts of people at the moment of death,' said Lebret, as Boucher took a seat beside him, 'in which they talk of a circle of light, hypnotising them and compelling them to move towards it. Do you think this such a phenomenon?'

'Are we not yet dead, then, Monsieur?' Boucher asked, trying to humour but sounding only strained and anxious.

Everybody was silent for a while.

'What gives it that *colour*?' asked Ghatwala. The light was now a deep glaucous-blue, magenta tinged with green.

'Algae?' suggested Jhutti. 'If we are approaching a source of sunlight then we might also expect to encounter manifestations of life. Blue-green krill, seaweed, anything that can make use of the energy of the light.'

'And perhaps fish,' agreed Ghatwala, 'that feed upon the vegetation.'

They sank deeper through that mysterious sea. The light strengthened. It was evident now that a central circle, or sphere, was the source of the light.

'The sonar!' announced Le Petomain, excitedly. 'At last – it is returning something – an image.'

'I thought you said it was broken?' said Boucher. 'No matter – that's excellent news! What does it report?'

'Lieutenant, it's a—it's a *dome*. Or perhaps it is the prow of something. Something enormous. And there's a lot of noise, perhaps a fleet of little craft – or a shoal of fish, I think.'

'The prow?' repeated Boucher. 'You mean – another vessel?'

'Look!' exclaimed Lebret. 'There *are* things moving!'

Everybody strained forward. Tiny rice grain-shaped objects, dark blue against the light, *were* swirling around the source. 'Exactly as I said!' said Ghatwala. 'Fish!'

'Monsieur Lebret,' said Boucher. 'I must congratulate you on your intimation! Surely we are approaching the surface, howsoever unconventionally... for surely fish cannot shoal like this in the deep depths, but only at the surface.'

'The surface,' agreed Lebret. 'Or *a* surface.'

'Lieutenant?' It was Le Petomain's voice, reedy through the communication pipe. 'The external temperature has risen quite markedly.'

'Getting warmer!' said Boucher. He looked pleased. 'It all makes a sense. Except only that we are apparently *de*scending, when we ought to be *a*scending, it makes sense! The pressure increased when we went sank through the Atlantic; it reduced again as we passed into this mirror ocean. The temperature went down, now it comes back up. It got darker, now it gets lighter. It can only mean we *are* returning!'

'Praise the Lord!' cried Billiard-Fanon.

The more they descended, the larger and brighter everything was. The circle of blue-green brightness was now, very obviously, a distinct thing, the cause of, but differentiated from, the more diffuse brightness all around them. The indistinct shapes of the swimming creatures – whatever they were – began to acquire definition – more like octopi than ordinary fish, for they trailed tentacles behind them as they moved.

'It's warm,' observed Jhutti. The air inside the observation chamber was palpably hotter.

'It is,' agreed Boucher. He picked up the communication pipe. 'Le Petomain?'

'Lieutenant?'

'What is the external temperature reading?'

'37°, Lieutenant.'

'What? How can it be so high? A few hours ago it was 4°C!'

'I'm sorry, Lieutenant Boucher,' replied the pilot. 'I must report it is 37°.'

'Something is wrong,' said Jhutti. 'That is much too hot.'

'I am unpleasantly reminded,' put in Billiard-Fanon, in a gruff voice, 'of the story of the frog placed in cold water which is slowly heated up. The frog,' he added, perhaps superfluously, 'fooled by the slow increments of temperature increase, and not realising his danger, does not leap from the pot, and so dies.'

'How can it *be* so hot?' Boucher repeated.

'Le Petomain,' said the lieutenant, speaking into the tube. 'What do the instruments say? How can it be so hot, suddenly?'

'I don't know, Lieutenant.'

'What about the sonar?'

'Something is jutting out, the source of the light and the heat. But there are so many of these strange fish swimming about it is interfering with the signal. Too much noise.'

'*Jutting out*, you say?' asked Boucher.

'Yes, Lieutenant.'

'Like the peak of an undersea volcano? That would explain both the heat and light.'

'It would be consistent with the data,' said Jhutti, in a grave voice. 'What if we *are* finally approaching the bottom of this impossible ocean?' He scratched his beard. 'I can't explain the lack of pressure – but what if we are looking at some kind of volcanic eruption through the ocean bed? It would explain how there is light *and* heat at this great depth.'

Lebret shook his head. 'Monsieur, consider the colour! Observe it! Magma would surely be red!'

'I cannot explain the colour,' conceded Jhutti.

'No, no,' said Boucher, fretfully. 'We cannot risk getting closer.'

Disappointment was palpable. The prospect of a quick passage back to normality had possessed everyone; to have that suddenly snatched away lowered morale.

'We simply cannot descend any further, given the increase in temperature,' Boucher said. 'To go lower would be to cook ourselves. And besides, if the seabed is approaching, we must avoid a collision. Time to go back *up*, I think.' He gave the order, and the *Plongeur* stopped descending.

Not even Lebret challenged this. The two scientists begged an hour to observe what they could of the peculiar phenomenon, and it was agreed that a short period would be given over to the collection of whatever scientific data could be gleaned from the circumstance.

Jhutti and Ghatwala had left their camera down in the observation window. They went back down; and Boucher angled the submarine in the water so as to bring the light source – whatever it might be – into better view. In ones and twos the whole crew came down to take a look for themselves. Lebret, smoking, scowled through the glass.

'Another crack in the seabed, perhaps, Monsieur?' Jhutti suggested, to him. 'A circular vent, through which is pouring ... what?'

'It cannot be lava,' was all Lebret would say.

'But,' Jhutti pressed. 'The lieutenant is surely right to be cautious. If the external temperature became too high, it might provoke further malfunction ...'

'Look!' Lebret interrupted him. 'We have, at any rate, attracted the attention of the local fish.'

It was true – a number of the creatures had broken off from their circling trajectories around the light, and were coming towards the *Plongeur*. As they approached their shape became easier to make out. Crewmen crowded into the observation chamber to look at them.

'We are surely the first ever to clap eyes upon these forms of life!' Lebret declared. 'There are dozens of Nobel prizes in science to be claimed if we could capture one!'

'They look like,' said Boucher, in an awed tone, 'like men!'

'Are they *mermen*?' asked Avocat. 'Have we passed from reality into a realm of legend and myth?'

'Hardly that,' observed Lebret. 'It is surely nothing more than a freak of parallel evolution. Their flippers or ... tentacles, or whatever they are, merely *resemble* limbs.'

'They are certainly unlike any kind of cuttlefish hitherto observed,' was Ghatwala's opinion.

The creatures possessed skinny torsos, from which two front and two rear fins (or perhaps they were fat tentacles) trailed; and their bullet-shaped heads protruded necklessly from their bodies. They were of a silvery-blue or blue-white colour, as fish tend to be; their eyes were black saucers and their mouths gaped on under-jaws shaped like a Norman arch. Yet despite all these obviously piscine qualities, there *was* something uncannily human-looking about them – something to do with their undulating passage through the water, some freakish reminiscence of mankind about their arrangement of body, head and limbs.

Yet the most distinctive thing about them had no human analogue. From their 'shoulders' sprouted two great seaweed-like appendages – five or six times as long as their actual bodies, branching and bifurcating into a foliage-like complexity away from their bodies. As the creatures swam and circled about the observation porthole these great doubled bunches folded, and swirled, following after like two great crinkled capes.

'Gills?' suggested Jhutti.

Lebret seemed to have recovered his spirits. He was right up against the glass. 'Marvellous!' he breathed. 'Exceptional! The cape-things *must* be gills. There was no oxygen in the higher, black water – but down here, with a source of light and heat and blue-green algae, there must be some.'

'*External* gills, though?' said Ghatwala. 'And of such prodigious size?'

'It suggests that such oxygen is here is in low concentration.'

'They're certainly fascinated by *us*!' Lebret noted. 'And why not? They've surely never seen anything like it in their lives.'

'Visited by the great metal whale!' laughed Boucher.

'Perhaps they will worship us as a god, as the South Sea Islanders did Captain Cook?' Billiard-Fanon suggested.

'Did the South Sea Islanders not murder Cook?' said Ghatwala.

'That was afterwards. And anyway,' said Boucher. 'They are but fish. They clearly do not possess the intelligence to...'

There was a loud *thump*. One of the fishmen had thrust itself up, suddenly, close against the glass of the observation porthole. The collision was not accidental. The creature grasped the slight bulge of glass with two forward flippers – lined with suckers like the holes in Swiss cheese – and battened his large mouth against it. The overlong lower jaw was clearly capable of being extended and retracted, and its shape adjusted to the contour of glass. A fat, black tongue, covered in rasping protrusions, slithered up from the beast's throat and licked horribly over the outside of the window.

Lebret had recoiled from the glass at the impact, but he now stepped forward again. The black eyes of the monster swivelled, following him. 'He's watching me,' he observed.

More thumps and bangs were audible, at various points along the metal hull of the vessel. Castor and Capot hurried from the observation room.

'What are they doing? Is it trying to bite through the glass?' asked Boucher.

'I think we should move away, Lieutenant,' said Jhutti.

The creature affixed to the observation window was still rubbing its black tongue against the surface. Then, abruptly, everything inside dimmed. It took a moment for the people inside to see why – the creature had brought its two huge cloak-gills round and draped them across the glass.

Ghatwala took another photograph, and cursed the light. 'Where are the flashbulbs stored?' he asked.

'Lieutenant,' said Billiard-Fanon. 'I concur with the Indian gentleman. I suggest we ascend immediately, and try to shake off these ...'

There was a horrible crunching sound; the metal fabric of the *Plongeur* shook and thrummed like a gong.

'They're ripping us to pieces!' yelled Boucher. He leapt up, and made to run up the sloping floor and out of the observation chamber. But he was too hasty; his footing was not sure, and he fell, knocking his forehead against the bottom lip of the hatchway.

'Lieutenant!' cried Billiard-Fanon, leaping to the fallen officer. He turned Boucher over – a smile-shaped cut had been grooved into the man's forehead, and blood was flowing freely from it. He groaned, still alive, but close to insensibility. 'Avocat! Help me move the lieutenant.'

There was another terrible wrenching, shuddering noise; like metal being cut by giant scissors.

'What is going on?'

'They want to eat us!' cried Ghatwala.

'What creature eats metal? No – no – I believe it's our air,' said Lebret. 'Our air. They're greedy for our air!'

The whole of the *Plongeur* shook, leaned through twenty degrees, and tilted further forward. The men inside the observation chamber tumbled and fell, scrambled back to their feet.

Lebret leapt over the supine form of the lieutenant, and scrabbled up the steeply sloping corridor, hauling himself physically into the bridge. 'Le Petomain,' he called. 'Release *air* – open the forward vents and release air.'

'Where's the lieutenant?' the pilot demanded.

'It's life-or-death man! Do as I say!'

But Le Petomain hesitated.

Jhutti and Ghatwala were just behind him, pulling themselves up into the bridge. 'What is on your mind, Monsieur?'

'You said yourself – oxygen levels down here must be very low. They can smell it in us! They want it! They have somehow intuited that we're full of it. I don't know how. But they can never have experienced the stuff in gaseous form. They cannot know how reactive the stuff is. They're moths to the flame … well, *let the flame burn them*, and shake them off the *Plongeur*. Sailor – do as I say!'

The pilot looked from the scientists to Lebret and back again.

Suddenly the whole craft shuddered violently, and the three standing men fell to their knees. A cacophonous din resounded through the air.

'Too late—' shouted Le Petomain. 'Too late – they've pulled the port vent clear off—'

'I must *see*,' said Lebret.

He slid on his rear down the sloping corridor, past Billiard-Fanon and Avocat who were endeavouring, with only limited success, to haul the unconscious lieutenant up the shuddering, bucking vessel.

The observation porthole was free again; the sea-beast that had been battened there had gone. Great constellations of bubbles flushed past the glass, not only floating upwards, but disseminating in every direction. The mermen-creatures were twisting and struggling, their gill-cloaks tangling about them. They contorted in agony – or in ecstasy, it was impossible to tell.

The whole vessel tilted once again, and bubbles flew past the glass. Lebret's could feel in his stomach that they were sinking.

He could hear the shouting from the bridge as Le Petomain expelled the remaining water from the one remaining functioning ballast tank, attempting to compensate for the loss of air in the other. The whole structure of the *Plongeur* shuddered. The white-noise of the air pumps cut cleanly through the other various noises – the groaning of the metal, the clangs and bangs, the weird subsonic groaning or moaning side.

But the port tank was full of water, and filling the starboard tank with air made the whole vessel pendulum and swing, as if suspended from its front-right. Lebret was thrown against the wall of the observation chamber. Avocat came tumbling back through the hatch, head over heels.

The craft pendulumed round, bringing the observation porthole up. For a moment it hung there, and Lebret got a glimpse of a swarm of mermen. It looked like the feeding frenzy of a school of sharks, jerking and massing around the globular structures of the released air. The bubbles spread and roiled, but – crazily – did not rise through the water. Hundreds of the strange-looking cuttlemen darted at the bubbles, only to flinch sharply away.

Then, still sinking, the *Plongeur* swung back around its own hinge of partial buoyancy and Lebret and Avocat were rattled around the observation chamber. By wedging his feet against the place where one of the room's seats was bolted to the floor and grasping at the walls with both hands, Lebret was able to prevent himself being thrown through the air. Avocat was not so lucky – he cried out in pain as he was slammed hard against the wall a few yards to the right of Lebret.

The light – bright and blue-white and evidently hot – came into view below them. Then the whole craft swung further about, the light slipped away right, and the swarm of mermen about the released air was visible again. The frenzy was further away now, a pattern of pulse and flow like sardines being pursued by a swordfish.

'Brace!' came Le Petomain's voice. 'Brace!'

The *Plongeur* began to swing back, and a sound loud as a cannon report was added to the other clangs and drones. It was the vent to the starboard tank giving way. The vessel vomited out a giant bladderwrack mass of bubbling air, and fell hard away down.

Robbed of all buoyancy, the *Plongeur* was falling now, nose down – directly towards the source of heat and light.

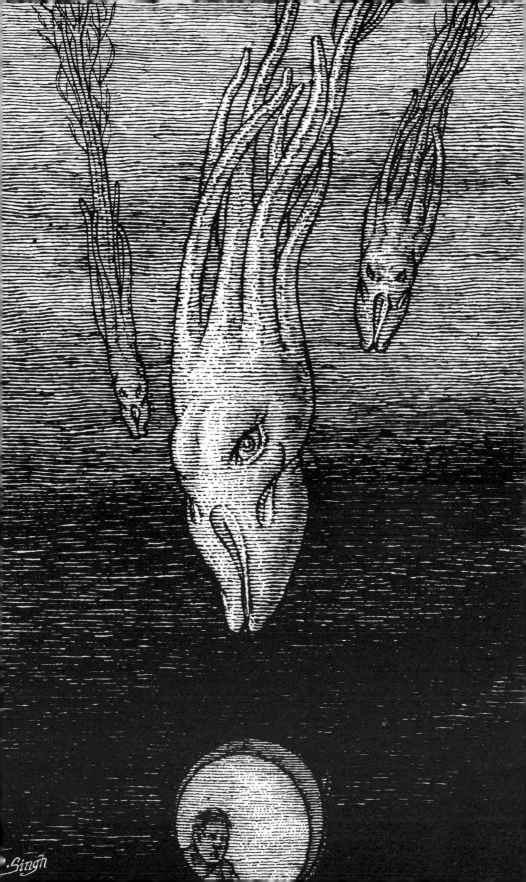

13

SUB OCEANIC SUN

✦ ✦ ✦ ✦ ✦ ✦

An alarm began to sound. After several ear-splitting seconds, somebody on the bridge shut it off. The whole craft rocked sickeningly, its metal flanks groaning under the torsion like a whale in mournful song.

Lebret made his way across the obstacle course that the observation room had become towards Avocat. 'Are you alright?'

'My arm!' cried the sailor. 'Broken!' His face behind his beard was the white of cooked fish flesh.

'Let me see,' said Lebret.

'I *heard* the bone snap,' Avocat gasped. 'Like a stick burning in a fire!'

Lebret tried to pull the sailor's jacket off, as the *Plongeur* swayed and fell, but Avocat's yelps of pain dissuaded him. 'Give me a belt to bite upon at least, Monsieur, for pity of the Virgin Mother!' he cried out. 'Or fetch me some brandy!'

The shouts of other men could be heard far away in other portions of the submarine. 'Why didn't those air bubbles float away?' Lebret muttered to himself, unsnaking his belt from his trouser loops. 'What's the *nature* of this strange place?'

'We're going *down*,' moaned Avocat. 'I can feel it in my spine and guts – Christ have mercy. We'll all die! Oh, Christ have mercy!'

'Le Petomain!' boomed a voice, from the bridge, echoing through the speaking tube. 'Straighten her out!' It was a moment before Lebret recognised it as Castor's.

'I'm trying, chief!' called back the pilot.

Lebret gave Avocat the belt, and the sailor fixed it between his teeth. The ends thrashed and flailed in the air like a snake. Then, as the vessel rocked back on its swing, Lebret wrenched the man's jacket off him and quickly rolled back the shirtsleeve. The wound was revealed – a bad fracture. A triangle of bone broke the skin like a shark's-fin poking above the surface of the sea. There was a great deal of bruising, with only a few trickles of blood. Under the electric light of the observation room these looked dark green and black.

Lebret, despite himself, quailed at the sight. 'Shall I try and reset the bone?' he asked.

'What are you asking *me* for, Vichy?' muttered Avocat, speaking without relinquishing his teeth's grip on the belt. He was staring furiously at a spot on the ceiling. 'I daren't even *look* at the thing. Don't you know first aid?'

'Only what they told us in basic training,' said Lebret. He was fumbling for a cigarette with automatic hand. 'Maybe it would be better to leave it alone?'

'Oh Christ it hurts,' Avocat hissed.

A series of yells and shouts were audible from above: the words indistinct, but the mood of panic unmistakeable. 'What's going on?'

Then, louder than the background cacophony, came Castor's voice again. 'We're taking on water!' he boomed.

Avocat laughed a joyless little laugh. 'I think the ocean will soon render your rudimentary knowledge of first aid irrelevant. May I have one?'

'Eh?'

Avocat nodded at the cigarette case Lebret was holding in his hand.

'A dying man, a cigarette,' said Avocat. 'I apologise for the cliché.'

Lebret fitted one into the sailor's mouth, and held out his lighter to ignite it. As he did so, he noticed that his hand cast two, equally distinct shadows. One was from the room's electric light; the other was cast by light streaming brightly through the observation portal itself.

The circle of light was twice the size it had formerly been. 'We're falling towards it,' Lebret said. 'Even though we're taking on water, I believe that hot light – whatever it is – will end us, before the ocean has a chance to drown us.'

'Doubly doomed,' laughed Avocat.

'I can't believe we're about to die!' said Lebret, shaking his head. 'It seems so ... unfair.'

Avocat cradled his broken arm in his lap, and sucked hungrily on his cigarette. 'A pitiful end,' he agreed.

'I'm going up the ladder to see if I can be of assistance,' Lebret declared. 'I will return.'

'Then bring me something to drink,' said the sailor. 'And I don't mean water – we'll all have our fill of water very soon now. I mean something for the pain. Brandy!'

Lebret took one last look through the observation porthole at the incandescing circle of white-blue light, twice the size of the sun in earthly skies. Its heat was palpable, literally so. When Lebret put his hand on the wall to steady himself, picking his way across the quaking space, he could feel the metal beneath the paint – warm as human flesh.

He got up the sloping corridor with some difficulty, and found Le Petomain in the pilot's seat. Billiard-Fanon, water flying from him, was peering at the temperature gauge. 'Can I help?' he asked.

Billiard-Fanon glared at him. 'Unless you can perform miracles, Monsieur,' he said. 'Then no, you cannot help. The temperature is rising at such a rate that we will all be baked to death within minutes.'

'The cuttlemen wrenched our forward vanes clean away,' gasped Le Petomain. 'Far as I can tell, at any rate. We've *no* control! The port ballast tank is wrecked, the water can't be expelled. The starboard is holding, but there's been damage at various places, and we're taking on water.'

'Hot water!' growled Billiard-Fanon. 'I've just come from there – it's scalding the men who are trying to fix the leaks.'

'It's a matter of minutes,' said Le Petomain. 'I can't steer us away, and we're falling directly into that – into whatever *that* is.'

'Avocat has broken his arm,' Lebret reported. Since this felt like trivial news after what Le Petomain and Billiard-Fanon had said, Lebret added: 'a bad break – the bone has punctured the skin.'

'So?'

'I said I'd fetch him some alcohol – for the pain,' Lebret said.

'Be my guest,' said Billiard-Fanon. 'Just get out of my face. It's your fault we're even *down* here.'

Lebret clambered up and out of the bridge. As he struggled round the corner into the kitchen, he heard Pannier knocking at his door, and saying in a piteously sober-sounding voice. 'Monsieur? Monsieur? Whoever you are – let me out! I can hear what's going on – don't leave me to drown in my cabin like a cat in a bag!'

'I haven't the key,' said Lebret. He coughed, and wiped his brow – oily with sweat. It was much hotter now.

'Monsieur Collaborator-Vichy? It's you? *Get* the key! I beg of you!'

'I'll come back,' Lebret promised.

There was a shudder, a great groan of metal, and the whole of the vessel tipped more steeply forward. The floors were now at forty degrees. Lebret almost lost his balance, nearly plunging straight back through the bridge – but he held on, scrabbled into the kitchen, and sat for a moment in the coign of floor and wall. Items were piled, higgledy-piggledy into the V of the space, a heap of steel cans shifting like shingle as the *Plongeur* continued its slow swing. Lighter cardboard packets bounced through the air. A cupboard door had burst its lock, and swayed in time to the vessel's motion like a blue flag being waved.

Lebret laid his hand upon an unbroken bottle of rum, pulled the cork, took a fiery swig, and stuffed it into his jacket pocket. The air was uncomfortably hot, now.

Lebret made his way out of the kitchen and down the corridor back into the bridge like descending a ladder. Billiard-Fanon was in the captain's chair.

'Where's Le Petomain?'

'I sent him fore,' growled the ensign. 'All hands to staunch the leaks. Though we'll soon be cooked like a side of ham in an oven—'

'And you—?'

'Boucher is in his cabin, strapped to his bed, quite unconscious. He cracked his head hard against the side when the vessel was bouncing about. The captain is dead. *I'm* in command now. I choose to meet my death in the proper place.'

Lebret picked a path down and across the bridge, and half-climbed, half-slipped down into the observation room. The circle of hot sub oceanic light was now so large that it filled more than half the window. Detail was nebulously visible in its disc: swirling patterns moving in tight tourbillons, like a pattern of writhing white bubbles against the background of blue-white glare. From time to time shadows, small and indistinct, danced across the disc of light: left-right, right-left – presumably marking the passage of cuttlemen.

'I've brought you some rum,' Lebret announced.

Avocat did not reply. Lebret could see that he had passed out, presumably with the pain. The sailor was sprawled into the crook of floor and wall, his legs tucked underneath him. His head was turned a little to the side. The cigarette in his lips had burned to a slug of ash that was lying across his cheek. Lebret brushed this away and saw that it had left a puckered patch of burned skin beneath it. 'That's not good,' he muttered, leaning forward to see if the fellow was still breathing. The background cacophony made it hard to hear, but when he slipped a hand beneath the man's shirt he could feel the heart beating.

The arm, however, did not look good. It was swollen, nearly twice as fat as its fellow limb. A blue-black colour had spread across the skin.

Lebret looked again at the growing circle of white heat, through the porthole. He removed his own jacket – it was oppressively hot, now – and took another drink of the scalding rum. 'I should take advantage of the fact that you are unconscious to set the arm, I suppose,' he said, to the unresponsive body of Avocat. 'Although it seems a fruitless gesture, in the circumstances. Still…'

He got hold of the arm, holding it above the wrist with his left hand and grasping the elbow with his right. His fingers sank unpleasantly into the puffed-up flesh. Then, wincing, he pulled the break apart. Avocat moaned and shifted, but did not wake. Lebret put more pressure upon his grip, pulling the wrist towards him and pushing the elbow-end of the forearm away. The beak of bone disappeared beneath the skin; a little black blood flowed through the cut and then stopped.

He manipulated the two ends of bone, feeling them grind and catch against each other. Avocat's body twitched, and he moaned, as if in the middle of a nightmare.

Never having done this sort of thing before, Lebret wasn't sure what he was feeling for. Ought the two ends-of-bone to click together, like a buckle connecting? If so, Lebret was not succeeding. He shifted the two sections of the arm again, like an inexperienced driver grindingly shifting the gears of a car. Then, abruptly disgusted by the procedure, he let go.

The finger marks, where he had grasped Avocat's swollen flesh, were printed pale against the darkened skin. He watched, sweating, as bruising flowed back under the puffed skin and began to erase them.

The whole arm looked monstrous – three times the proper size, now; lumpy and distorted as if with elephantiasis. 'I ought to release the pressure,' Lebret muttered to himself. 'Ought I? Or ought I to let well alone?'

He brought out his penknife, and flicked open the blade. It shone, reflecting the weird brightness of the sub oceanic sun. Every action seemed equally irrelevant. Locating what he looked like the place of greatest swelling, near the crook of Avocat's elbow, Lebret jabbed the end of the knife in.

The result was not as he expected. A jet of black-red liquid flew halfway across the room. Blood splashed up along Lebret's arm, and he recoiled. Then, scrambling back to the unconscious man, he slipped and tumbled. 'No,' he gasped. 'Oh no!'

The spurt of blood throbbed and shook in air, but did not diminish in the force of its flow. It began to pool at the bottom of the observation chamber, sloshing as the *Plongeur* continued its heavy, slow sway.

Using his knife, Lebret cut away the sleeve of Avocat's shirt. By the time he was finished the cloth was blood-soaked and slippery, which made it harder to tie into a tourniquet. Lebret hands, greasy with blood, kept losing grip. Worse, the swelling in the arm made it impossible to get the tourniquet to dig deep enough into the flesh to stem the flow.

The yelling from the other parts of the ship crescendoed and diminuendoed against the various other noises. Lebret sat back, despairing of his efforts. Avocat's lifeblood was draining into the V of wall-and-floor.

Then something strange happened. Lebret could feel the motion of descent in his belly; but with a nauseous shift in his gut he had the sense – only momentarily – that he was upside-down on the ceiling. He blinked, and blinked again; and his senses reoriented themselves. He was tucked into the space between floor and wall in a forward-tipped submarine as it sank through impossible waters.

His shadow moved against the wall. Looking out, he saw the great disk of hot white light shifting. It slid to the side of the window, and then it slid out of sight altogether.

The porthole threw a bright patch of oval light upon the wall of the observation room; and then slid it smoothly along and up. Like a searchlight beam the light picked out Avocat's motionless body and passed on.

Lebret gasped. It took him a moment to understand that the sensation in his gut meant they were still sinking straight down. They had not steered past the light; the light itself – whatever it was – had moved.

'Billiard-Fanon!' he called, his voice catching in his throat. He tried again with more force: 'Billiard-Fanon! Ensign! Are we saved?'

There was a pause, and then the ensign's voice returned, 'What?'

'We are no longer sinking towards the sub oceanic sun!' Lebret hollered. 'Did you steer us past it?'

'What? *I've* no control. What are you saying?'

'Check the sonar! Or come down here and see,' Lebret suggested.

For several minutes Billiard-Fanon neither replied nor complied. But eventually he could be heard clangingly making his way down the linking corridor. His legs appeared, and then he did. 'What's going on?'

'The light – whatever it is,' Lebret gasped. 'It was right there, in the window. Then it just ... slid away. We're no longer headed towards it.'

'I don't understand,' said Billiard-Fanon. 'I made no change to our trajectory. I've not been able to!'

'In that case,' said Lebret, 'then the obstacle has moved itself out of our way. Or has *been* moved.'

'Impossible!'

'Only look!' said Lebret. Now that the direct light of the sub oceanic sun was no longer blinding them, they could see that the waters all around them was swarming with wriggling cuttlemen. They filled the waters in the middle distances in their thousands; writhing and coiling in shifting flows like starlings massing in autumnal skies. Some few were closer by, and one slipped quicksilver past the window, no more than a few yards distant.

'What have you *done*?' cried Billiard-Fanon.

'Me? I haven't done it – I don't know how it has happened. But at least we won't be scorched to death. Now all we need do is staunch the leaks in ...'

'Not *that*!' Billiard-Fanon snapped. '*This*.'

The ensign was pointing at the body of Avocat. 'What?' said Lebret. 'Yes. He fell badly when the *Plongeur* started sinking. His arm is broken, I'm sorry to say.'

'The blood!' Billiard-Fanon said. He scrambled over to the body.

'His arm was horribly swollen,' said Lebret, feeling dazed. He still had his penknife in his hand. 'It was *three* times the proper size. At least that big. I thought I ought to relieve the pressure.'

'So you *severed an artery*? What were you thinking? Look at this blood!'

'I,' Lebret began. 'I didn't mean.' It occurred to him that he ought to have lied – said that it was splintered bone that had severed the artery, and that he had done nothing but try to staunch the accidental wound. But it was too late for that now. He folded his penknife. 'The accidental...' he started again. 'I mean that in my attempts to...'

'He's dead,' noted Billiard-Fanon.

'I was trying to help him,' said Lebret.

'You *killed* him,' said Billiard-Fanon, accusingly. '*You* brought us down here – *you* persuaded us all that we should descend to this hell-zone. And now you've stabbed Avocat to death!'

'I was trying,' Lebret repeated, in a stumbling voice, 'to help him.'

'You're under arrest, Monsieur Lebret,' said Billiard-Fanon, getting uneasily to his feet. 'You're confined to your cabin. You've proved a real Jonah on this voyage, Monsieur; but this – this is too much! Murderer!'

'An unfortunate accident,' Lebret mumbled. 'I assure you...'

'Stop! Cease! I don't have time for this now,' snapped Billiard-Fanon. 'We need to take advantage of our good fortune – the fact that we're no longer falling into that volcanic vent. We need to repair as much of the ship as we can. But this is not over, Monsieur! No longer falling into the vent... but we may still crash into the ocean floor at any moment.'

'It was no vent, Ensign,' said Lebret – his excitement overcoming his fear. 'Look! A sun – a veritable sun. Burning beneath the waters, like a magnesium flare. Or perhaps a sub oceanic comet – for it *has* moved out of our way.'

'I'm sick to my stomach!' yelled Billiard-Fanon, 'of your *fantasy stories*! I don't care! I don't care!' He was holding something in his right hand, and Lebret saw what it was. The captain's pistol. 'Confine yourself to your cabin, Monsieur, or I shall shoot you here and be done with it!'

Lebret put his left hand in front of him. 'Ensign,' he said. 'I beg of you. I intended to *help* Monsieur Avocat, not harm him. I brought him rum! Look – I fixed a tourniquet to his damaged arm. You can see—'

'You think I give a damn for your *intentions*? To your cabin!'

The entire situation resolved itself, with the sudden clarity of revelation, inside Lebret's head. Boucher was unconscious and so Billiard-Fanon commanded the ship – and Billiard-Fanon hated him. He thought him a murderer!

This was intolerable. He must act. The stakes were too high.

He pictured the course of action in an unbroken series of images. First: he would distract Billiard-Fanon somehow, jump upon him – and kill him with the penknife. Then to cover his tracks; would take the pistol and shoot the... no, *first* he would clamber up to the hatchway. He would close it most of the way, leaving just enough space to aim the pistol around. Shoot the window – and close the hatch before the water, flooding in, spilled through into the corridor. He could then tell the rest of the crew any story he chose; there would be nobody to contradict him.

He looked Billiard-Fanon straight in the eye. 'Ensign—' he began to say.

Something failed in his resolve; something stuttered in his head. He had, it might not be too fanciful to say, a small seizure, a blankness deep inside his head. He heard a whispered voice saying *the water loves you*, and he knew the truth of it. The water loved all of them utterly. It wanted nothing more than to embrace them with its myriad limbs and press its mouth to their mouths. But although those four words formed in Lebret's brain, *the water loves you*, he knew that they had not been spoken by any person in that shaking, swaying room – least of all by Billiard-Fanon. The ensign was a knot of hard land, deep beneath this infinite ocean; no man was made of less fluidity – the look of his eyes was stone, and his thoughts were desert air and absolute certainty. And he hated Lebret. And he would shoot Lebret, given only the flimsiest of excuse.

Where had the strange whisper come from? Lebret looked

behind him, and nearly fell as the *Plongeur* swayed through again. There was nobody there. 'I'm going mad,' he said, in a low tone.

'What was that?' snapped Billiard-Fanon, still holding his gun.

'I'm—' Lebret began to say. Suddenly there were *faces* at the observation porthole – cuttlefolk, crowding round again. Each head was shaped with the smooth pale perfection of a peeled clove of garlic; their eyes were fathomless. They slapped their fins against the glass, and sucked voraciously at it with hideous mouths. Their gills billowed out behind them, huge folded and pleated membranes. 'Look! Ensign – look at the window!' cried Lebret.

Billiard-Fanon looked round.

This was Lebret's distraction. He could have acted at this moment; lunged at Billiard-Fanon, taken his chances against the gun with his own little knife.

He didn't move.

'Ugh!' cried Billiard-Fanon. 'The brutes!'

'I believe,' Lebret suggested, 'that we passed so close to the sub oceanic sun that we were in a zone of water too hot for them. But that now we are sinking through cooler water, and so they are swarming around us again.' said Lebret.

Billiard-Fanon scrambled to the window. 'They're all over the ship!'

'They'll damage us further – we must get rid of them.'

'How?'

Picking his way clumsily down, Lebret reached the observation porthole. 'Start the propellers,' he said. 'Push on *downwards* – they seem to cluster around the light of this, this whatever-it-is. If we accelerate away from it they may drop off.'

'Accelerate downward?'

'We are hardly in a position to accelerate in any other direction,' said Lebret. He pressed his face to the glass, straining to see past the obstructing figures latched to its outside. The wormlike writhing bodies of the cuttlefolk were clinging leechlike all about the forward bulb of the *Plongeur* – a hideous sight. Three were battened upon the glass of the observation window itself. Lebret could clearly hear the sound their teeth made, scraping and scratching against the outside of the safety glass.

'Start the propellers,' he urged, again. 'Or these beasts will break the vessel apart.'

He felt a metal rod jab him in the side. The pistol, of course. Billiard-Fanon brought his face closer. 'Maybe I'll take your advice on this, Vichy-man,' he hissed. 'But I've not forgotten that it was *taking your advice* that has brought us to this watery circle of Dante-hell in the first place.'

'Ensign, please, you must listen when I say...'

'And I'll not soon forget that you killed Avocat. *Why* did you do that? What did you hope to gain?'

'I didn't kill him—'

'You are arrested, Monsieur Lebret. Climb up in front of me; I'll lock you in your cabin.'

'We can't afford to waste time with such nonsense!'

'If you prefer I can simply shoot a bullet into your skull here and now?'

Lebret did not doubt the man's sincerity. 'Very well, Ensign,' he said. 'I shall take myself off to my cabin.'

As he starting the awkward climb up the corridor, using what impromptu handholds and footholds he could, Lebret heard Billiard-Fanon close behind him, shouting at the top of his voice. 'Le Banquier! Le Banquier! Start the props – push us faster downwards before these sea monsters tear us to pieces!'

14

CONFINEMENT

❦ ❦ ❦ ❦ ❦ ❦

Castor was in the bridge, naked to the waist and wet. Red patches on his arms and stomach showed where scalding water had burned him. 'I need more men—' he gasped. 'Those creatures are outside again – breaches are...'

'You shall *have* more men,' said Billiard-Fanon. 'But start the props, for Christ's sake, and hurry us away from these monsters!'

'The water is scalding – and it won't play fair!'

'What?'

'Flies about,' said Castor, enigmatically. 'Like it's possessed. What about him?' The chief nodded at Lebret. '*He* could help... I wouldn't weep to see him scalded.'

'I'm locking him up. He killed Avocat.'

Castor's face darkened. 'You Vichy swine!'

'There's been a misunderstanding...' Lebret began to say.

'Props, Banquier!' Billiard-Fanon called to Le Petomain, who was climbing into the sloping pilot's seat. 'We need to dive as fast as possible – try to shake off these leeches.'

'If not him,' said Castor, 'then release Pannier, to come help us. He must have sobered up by now – I need every hand I can get.'

'Alright, I will. In fact, *you* can go in Pannier's cabin, you Vichy murderer. I don't have time to search *your* cabin for – I don't know what treacherous things you've hidden in there.'

Everybody felt the kick of added acceleration as the propellers started up.

Billiard-Fanon shoved Lebret up into the aft corridor. The

ensign opened Pannier's cabin door. The cook tumbled out, looking blanched and chastened; a fiercely unpleasant smell followed him. 'You!' he gasped, seeing Lebret. 'You said you'd come back for me! You never did!'

'Monsieur,' said Lebret, struggling to regain his composure. 'You see that Ensign Billiard-Fanon has a gun on me? I am his prisoner, and my actions are not my own.'

But the cook was not to be mollified. 'You left me to die! Like a kitten drowning in a sack! You left me to die!'

'Monsieur, I beg of you ...'

'You *promised* you'd come back,' Pannier repeated. 'You abandoned me.'

'Stop this,' snarled Billiard-Fanon. 'Pannier: go forward with Castor – we need to staunch the leaks down there and *you* can help, you old drunk. As for *you*, Monsieur Vichy – into Pannier's cabin.'

Lebret, as he squeezed past Pannier, could not mistake the look of pure hatred upon the cook's face. He made one last appeal. 'Messieurs – as Engineer Castor says, we need every last hand ... why not permit me to—'

The door slammed in his face.

There was nothing for Lebret to do now. He looked about his new prison. Pannier had left it none too clean. A small metal toilet was set into the corner; but this appeared to be blocked – or else the cook had not bothered to flush it – and the various upendings, rollings and reorientations of the *Plongeur* had spilled its noisome contents to slop along the impromptu trench made by the angle of wall and floor. Worse, the shaking of the vessel, or perhaps the weird poltergeist breeze, had spread the noisome matter all the way up the wall and floor, even to the ceiling. It was hard to see where a man could sit without becoming defiled.

Some of the cook's few personal items had been shaken out of the room's cupboard to lie in filth, caught in corners and niches. There were two books wedged in the space underneath the bunk, both soiled – one, Lebret could see without picking it up, a Bible. There was little else in the room.

Lebret, with one foot awkwardly on either side of the gutter made by the tipped-forward orientation of the room, made his way to the bunk. It was not possible to sit or lie on this, at the angle the *Plongeur* was current at, even with the bed frame's wooden lip. But underneath the bunk was Pannier's trunk. Lebret loosed the catch that held it in place, and it tumbled out. With a little manoeuvring he got it to bridge the gutter, thereby making a clean place to sit in amongst all the smeared filth. Then he sat himself upon this object, with his back leaning against the sloping wall, and smoked another cigarette. Globs of filth were being blown about the space, and there was no way to avoid being dirtied by them; but he made the best he could of his situation.

For a while he simply sat, and let his mind empty. The noises of the submarine blended into a strange melange – the creakings and groaning of the metal structure, the whirr of the propellers, the shouts and yells of men, muffled and indistinct. The roll of the boat was less pronounced now.

It was, he thought, a little cooler now.

He dozed. He woke again after an indeterminate time, almost shaken from his perch by a great sideways lurch of the craft. Clutching the sides of his makeshift bench, he listened – did the shouts of the men sound more desperate? Had there been a fatal breach in the fabric of the submarine?

'There's no way to know,' he muttered to himself, fishing his cigarette case from his jacket. There were three smokes left inside. He had two cartons in his cabin; but that was no good to him. 'Ah well,' he announced, to the empty air. 'If the vessel is about to fill with water, I might as well enjoy these. And Billiard-Fanon is probably going to shoot me anyway, even if we survive.'

He smoked one cigarette, listening. The noises were hard to decipher.

The passivity of his situation, whilst not pleasant, was bearable. It was not the first time he had had to wait, powerlessly, to see how things turned out.

Things seemed to have quietened down. He dozed, woke and dozed again. To stretch his legs he clambered around the awkward metal V Pannier's cabin now was. He demonstrated to his own satisfaction that the toilet flush still operated, and then he stripped the cook's bedding and used it to wipe away at least some of the revolting matter smeared about the sloping walls and floor, afterwards stowing the soiled blanket and sheet in a cupboard. This gave him the opportunity to examine Pannier's two books. The Bible was well-thumbed, with passages underlined and incomprehensible annotations squidged, microscopically, into the narrow margins. Though the text was in French, the inside front cover bore an English name ('Godfrey Smithson'). The other book was a copy of Jules Verne's *Captain Hatteras*. Lebret leafed idly through this for a while. But it did not hold his attention.

He waited.

After a while there came a knock at the door. 'Alain?' It was Ghatwala

'Dilraj!' cried Lebret, scrambling over to the door. 'What is going on? Are we all about to die?'

'Not today, my friend. Tomorrow – who knows?'

'Did they empty the starboard tank?' Lebret asked, in Punjabi. 'I felt a great shock, and then the vessel settled into a more balanced yaw – though we're obviously still pitched pretty steeply.'

Ghatwala replied in the same tongue. 'The fish people tore the vent open – I saw it from the observation room. It was a horrible sight! The air hurt them, yet they clustered around it. Surely they are dumb animals?'

'Perhaps, my friend, but have you never seen human beings acting in a mob-frenzy? Have you never seen a religious rite that tipped people over the edge? Did you not see footage of the rock-and-roll music concerts they have in America?'

'At any rate,' said Ghatwala. 'We have left the underwater sun behind us. You can no longer see it from the observation portal – but if you climb into the con and look through the periscope it makes a fine sight.'

'How does it work, do you think?'

'The periscope?'

'The sub oceanic sun, idiot!' Lebret lapsed back into French.

'Does it burn with radioactive fusion, as does the sun around which earth orbits? It cannot. It cannot – the surface of our sun is four thousand degrees centigrade! – such a temperature would surely have vaporised trillions of cubic kilometres of water in every direction.'

'It would depend upon the length of time this sub oceanic sun has been shining,' agreed Ghatwala. 'But I doubt its surface temperature, though hot, was equivalent to our sun's – it is much smaller, for one thing – no bigger than an asteroid. I tend to think it was a sphere shining at a few hundred degrees, creating a skin of superheated steam about it that in turn generated layers of boiling water, and hot water.'

'But eventually it *will* heat up the whole ocean.'

'If the ocean is genuinely infinite, as you suspect, that would take an infinite amount of time. But, yes; the fact that we have passed from cold to hot water in only a few days of descent – the fact that the water only a few thousands of kilometres away from this sub oceanic sun remains at 4°C – suggests that it is young. I need more concrete data to be able to estimate *how* young.'

'Young enough to have been set here by – you know who?'

'How could *he* do such a thing! Even he?'

'I do not know, my friend. Yet this sun is evidently close, relatively speaking, to our point of entry. Is that coincidence?'

'You are forgetting, Alain,' Ghatwala countered, speaking again in Punjabi, 'the population of cuttlefolk. There is a limited but functioning ecological system in place – algae photosynthesise and release oxygen which the cuttlefolk breathe – and presumably there are other fish and shrimp and so on feeding on the algae for the cuttlefolk to eat.'

'Has it evolved, this ecological system?' Lebret asked. 'Or was it created to go along with the sun? Set up from scratch, as it were?'

'My point is that whilst *he* might be able to manufacture an artificial sun – though with what raw materials or tools I can't imagine – nevertheless it beggars belief that he could established all these creatures. He is not the God of the Book of Genesis, after all!'

'Might they have migrated from elsewhere?'

'Perhaps, my friend. Certainly the existence of elsewhere – of other sub oceanic suns, I mean – would explain the fact of one here. Would it not? Perhaps they are very numerous, and our running into one is not such a coincidence.'

'Good points, comrade,' said Lebret. 'But something far stranger is going on here, I think. I watched the air escaping from the tanks – I saw it from the observation portal. The bubbles did not rise, my friend. They did nothing but bulge out – until the cuttlefolk thrashed into them, and cut the mass of air into myriad smaller bubbles and shapes. Even then they simply roiled about.'

'If this is truly an infinite universe of water,' replied the scientist, 'then you would not expect anything different. Of course the environment would be weightless. Like outer space.'

'You are missing my point,' chided Lebret. 'I am standing on a surface, and so are you. Something is exerting a downward force upon us. But if we are subject to gravity, then why are the bubbles not? And how *could* we be subject to gravity, if we have come to that place we both suspected? How can we be descending? There is no down in space!'

'I do not know,' said Ghatwala. 'It does not appear to make sense. You are correct, of course. The bubbles' actions confirms the pressure readings – if we were actually descending through a body of water under the influence of gravity, then the water pressure would rise in direct proportion to our depth. And we would long since have been crushed to death.'

'Are we in a dream?' Lebret asked. 'Might we actually *be* dead and in some afterlife?'

'How could we test either supposition?' the scientist asked, with characteristic practical-mindedness. 'What conceivable experiment could we design to falsify such a claim?'

'Dilraj,' said Lebret, shortly. 'Can you let me out of here? Can you lay your hands on a key to this door?'

'What would be the point, Alain? Boucher is still unconscious, and Billiard-Fanon nurses a furious hatred of you in his breast.

And he still has the captain's old gun. If he saw you walking about the *Plongeur*, he'd likely shoot you on sight.'

'Yes,' conceded Lebret, sadly. 'I suppose you're right.'

After a short pause, Ghatwala asked, 'Alain – what happened with Avocat?'

Lebret tutted loudly. 'Poor Avocat! Most unfortunate. He broke his arm. It swelled to horrible proportions. I was trying to release the pressure, but I unfortunately cut an artery.'

'Billiard-Fanon says you murdered him.'

'Why would I do such a thing?'

'And the captain?'

Lebret was silent for a long time. Then he said, 'I was going to tell you about that, my friend. Events crowded it out.'

'Not an accident?'

'He was implacable! He was going to take us back up, hoping to find a way to the Atlantic again. There was no reasoning with him. He couldn't be made to understand that we *must* descend – and since he could not be made to understand ...' he stopped, half-shocked to hear himself talk so.

'Still, Alain!' Ghatwala said, in a shocked voice. 'Murder!'

'Too much at stake, Dilraj. Too much! You, at least, understand *that*. I don't ask you to endorse what I have done. But we've come so far!'

'I fear Billiard-Fanon intends to convene a short-order court-martial,' said Ghatwala, in a low voice. 'Though they think Cloche's death an accident, they hold you directly responsible for Avocat's. Ironic!'

'Perhaps tempers will cool.'

'Or perhaps,' said Ghatwala, earnestly. 'We should tell them *what's really going on.*'

Lebret didn't say anything for a while; then he said. 'Have you spoken to Jhutti?'

'Without consulting you first? Or course not!'

'Listen. If it comes to a trial ...' Lebret began to say. But a sudden clatter outside, and raised French voices, interrupted him.

Something banged hard against the door, and a man – was it Ghatwala? – yelled in pain.

'What's going on?' demanded Lebret.

Another brief series of bangs, and more voices. 'Pannier?' It was Billiard-Fanon's voice. 'Pannier, what are you doing?'

'I overheard them,' Pannier's crowed. 'This black man and the Vichy feller – through that door – they were *whispering treason together.*'

Lebret found it intensely frustrating that he couldn't see what was happening. 'What have you done to Ghatwala?' he yelled, slapping his palm on the door. 'You beast! What have you done?'

There was the jingly sound of keys being fumbled, and the door opened with a squeak. There was Billiard-Fanon, his long nose and his small eyes and his hoggishly bristling jowls. He had the captain's pistol in his right hand. 'Out of there,' he announced. 'Now! Justice awaits.'

Lebret stumbled into the corridor, catching sight of Ghatwala. The scientist was perched like a bird in the tipped-forward open door frame of the adjoining cabin. With his left hand he was holding onto the wall, with his right he was clutching his mouth. His beard was bloody. 'What did you do?'

Pannier's leer was not a pleasant sight. 'I socked him in the jaw.'

'Into the mess, everybody,' announced Billiard-Fanon. 'We need to sort this whole business out, once and for all! Traitors and murderers and worst of all – unbelievers!'

15

COURT MARTIAL

• • • • • •

The bolted down benches and tables of the mess hall gave the remaining crew of the *Plongeur* copious handholds and vantages points; although the steep forward angle gave the gathering a surreal feeling. Billiard-Fanon, at gunpoint, made Lebret, Ghatwala and Jhutti – this latter blinking and looking about himself confusedly – sit in the angle of the room's forward wall and floor. This had the effect of positioning the rest of the crew, above them, looking severely down. 'I've searched everywhere for handcuffs,' growled Billiard Fanon. 'Can't find any.'

'There's no need for handcuffs,' said Jhutti, nervously. 'Surely!'

The ensign scowled.

Lebret looked about him – Castor wore his jacket over his shoulders. Visible beneath, on his naked torso, were several bandage patches, covering the burns on his skin. Capot looked half asleep. Water dribbled from the clothing of most of them.

Billiard-Fanon lit a cigarette, and breathed deeply in. 'Let's fill everybody in,' announced. 'The captain is dead, and since the lieutenant is, unfortunately, still unconscious, authority devolves to …' he pointed at himself. 'Me. I wasn't expecting this, and can't say I enjoy it. But someone needs to pull this bucket together, and get us home. And that means we all have to *haul the same line*, and to do so *at the same time*. You understand what I mean?'

'How bad is the lieutenant?' asked Castor, rubbing the end of his snout-nose so vigorously it looked as though he wanted to pull it off altogether.

'We rolled him in a blanket and left him in the little valley made by wall and floor,' said Castor. 'Anyway. Let's sum up. Good news first. We *were* falling into something hot and bright. An underwater volcano mouth, I was initially told.'

'It was an underwater sun!' Lebret called out. 'Can't you see? Can't you understand what that *means*?'

To Billiard-Fanon's right a number of steel mugs dangled in a sloping line from hooks on the wall. The ensign plucked one of these and threw it, hard and straight, at Lebret. He tried to duck his head away, but his motion came a fraction too late, and the cup cracked off the side of his forehead with a distinct *ping* noise. It clattered against the wall, and bounced once again off the floor before coming to rest. Lebret put a finger up to his head; it came away bloody.

'*Or*,' Billiard-Fanon said, shifting the captain's pistol from his left jacket pocket to his right, for no other reason than to show it off. 'Or an underwater sun. Like it matters! At any rate, we have avoided collision with it.'

'We did not move. It moved out of *our* way,' said Jhutti. 'It may have been … alive. I think the light was … a *thinking creature*.'

Billiard-Fanon reached for another tin mug, from the line of hooks, but Jhutti held up both hands. 'I am merely speculating, sir! There's no need to stone *me* to death, Ensign Billiard-Fanon.'

'Whatever *it* was,' said Billiard-Fanon, twirling the mug around his forefinger, 'it is behind us now. Or above us. But here's the thing: swimming about the light was a crowd of sea monsters – the cuttlefolk, somebody called them, can't remember whom. They attacked us. Seems they craved our oxygen. *You* were saying, I believe Monsieur Je-ti, that you thought it was a mating ritual.'

'A hypothesis only,' said Jhutti, looking cautiously upwards at Billiard-Fanon and the projectile he was still holding in his hand. 'I speculated that in a relatively low-oxygen environment, the – *cuttlefolk*, if that is what we are calling them – the cuttlefolk would lead relatively torpid lives. Perhaps their breeding cycles are tuned to take advantage of, let us say, periodic algae blooms, that …'

Billiard-Fanon threw his second mug. His aim was not so good with this one, and it bounced noisily but harmlessly, between the floor and wall to Jhutti's right. But it shut him up.

'I don't care!' Billiard-Fanon barked. 'I don't care about your impious science and explanations and all that baggage! Those animals – they ripped the vanes off the *Plongeur*! They ripped open our main flotation tanks! They caused a dozen leaks in the vessel! Well, thanks to Monsieur Castor here, we've fixed the leaks. Although he got himself badly burned. He is a true hero!'

'The tanks are useless, though,' said Castor, in a sour voice. 'Ruined. Hopeless.'

'The one good thing is that we've sunk past the cuttlefolk. They've dropped away, like leeches under the hot end of a cigarette. So, not all bad. Not enough oxygen, or something – I don't care why. But here's the *not* good part; we can't go back up. That was the captain's last order, and I wish we could follow it, but we can't. So, let's go down. We'll see what turns up. Now!' he said, with sudden force. 'Monsieur Pannier. *You* have something to report?'

Pannier was holding an open bottle by its neck. Most of the wine inside had gone, but he did not sound drunk. 'What? Yes, yes, yes. I happened to chance upon the Indian gentleman, whose name I can't remember if I ever knew it...'

'Ghatwala,' said Ghatwala.

'The *Indian gentleman*,' Pannier said, pointedly. '*And* the Vichy feller, Monsieur Lebret. They were having a little secret conversation through the locked door of Lebret's cell. Gabbling away in Indian, too; not in honest French. I've never seen a more suspicious scene, messieurs! Now, we already know Lebret is a treacherous collaborationist swine; the sort of man who'd promise to come back for a comrade and then leave him to die – leave him to drown in his cabin like a cat in a bag! As for the other gentleman, well, I don't hold anything against him *personally*. I'm not the sort of man who thinks that a black skin stops a feller from being a proper Frenchman, or anything like that. Although the gentleman *isn't* French, is he? And now I happen upon the two of them, together. Whispering treason, they were.'

'You said we were speaking Punjabi!' Lebret objected. 'How

do you know *what* we were saying? Or are you claiming you can speak Punjabi?'

Lebret grabbed a third steel mug from a hook, fumbled and dropped it. It bounced harmlessly down the wall. 'Be quiet!' he snapped. 'Second item! As some of you know – Monsieur Lebret stabbed Matelot Avocat to death, a few hours ago.'

'I did not!' blurted Lebret.

'Be quiet! You deny that you stabbed him?'

Lebret rubbed his knuckles into his eyes. 'But...'

'You deny that he *died*, and that this death occurred *after* you stabbed him?'

'I was trying to relieve the pressure in his...'

'Open *and* shut,' crowed Pannier. 'If only submarines came equipped with a guillotine!'

'Let me state my case!' Lebret demanded, growing angry. 'The accused is permitted to state his case, in any court of law! You see, it was like this... poor Monsieur Avocat fell down and broke his arm. A very bad break. His arm swelled up, like a, like a... I thought only to relieve the pressure! By terrible misfortune I nicked an artery and...'

'Bung him in the airlock,' Pannier interrupted. 'Fill it with water. See how *he* likes being left alone, in a cabin, or – er, airlock – waiting to drown. Like a cat in a bag! Like a *cat*!'

Lebret tried to make appeal to the other sailors. 'This is absurd! You can't possibly believe this!'

'Believe it?' snarled Billiard-Fanon. 'This is a jury of your peers, Monsieur. We believe what the *evidence* tells us to believe.'

'Put him in a torpedo tube and shoot him out!' cried Pannier. A couple of sailors laughed. Billiard-Fanon, looking about him, seemed pleased at this notion. 'Good idea! Set an example!'

'Insanity!' cried Lebret. '*Why* would I kill Monsieur Avocat?'

'You tell us, M'sieur! You tell us!' snapped Billiard-Fanon. 'You'd better start explaining things, you Vichy monster.'

'You have to concede it looks bad for you, Monsieur,' said Le Petomain. 'Why *did* you do what you did?'

'I was trying to help!' said Lebret. He glanced from face to face;

but the mood of the group was shifting unpredictably. He could see that Billiard-Fanon was giving these men a point of certainty to grasp in amongst all the estrangement and fear. That this point of certainty enabled them to vent their anxiety as violence only made it more effective. His guilt or innocence was equally beside the point. A terrified and confused group of men; they were close to mob hysteria.

'If *he* won't talk,' said Pannier. 'Maybe his Indian friend will?'

'All eyes turned to Ghatwala. His chin, crusted with dried blood, moved and he spoke, his words emerging stickily. 'I do not understand,' he said, 'why you call Monsieur Lebret, Vichy. He was no collaborator – surely you see that? He was working under cover.'

'Balls!' cried Billiard-Fanon.

'He was personally chosen for this present mission by de Gaulle, in the latter's capacity as Minister of Defence. You think de Gaulle would choose a former collaborationist?'

'Shut him up,' Billiard-Fanon ordered. Pannier leaned down and slapped the scientist on the back of his head. 'Skin for skin,' the ensign said, holding the weighty pistol in his hands, as if contemplating what to do with it. 'Skin for skin, all that a man hath he will give for his life. You can only expect them to lie – right?'

'But we're telling the truth,' insisted Lebret.

With surprising gracefulness Billiard-Fanon jumped down from his eminence, to stand in the V made by the room's tipped-up floor and wall, right next to Lebret. 'I think Monsieur Pannier made a most interesting suggestion,' he announced, aiming the captain's pistol at Lebret's chest. 'I say we let him lie down – in the torpedo tube! Fire him out into the waters, to explain his crimes to the cuttlefolk!'

Pannier cheered, a solitary cry. But Lebret could see, looking about him, that the other crewmen were nodding.

'This is no justice,' said Ghatwala, in a thick voice. 'This is no proper *trial*.'

'Say another word,' Billiard-Fanon told him, 'and you will join your conspirator in the torpedo tube. I suppose a heathen will drown as quick as a Christian, out there – always assuming you *are* a Christian, Monsieur Lebret.'

Lebret felt a heady sense of incipient hysteria. He almost laughed. 'I'm a dialectical materialist,' he returned.

'Some kind of Protestant, eh?'

'Should we not,' said Capot, tentatively, 'should we not at least wait for the lieutenant to wake up, before … er, sentence is passed?'

'What for?' snarled Pannier.

'And what if he *doesn't* wake up?' was Billiard-Fanon's question. 'A ship needs discipline. At the moment, I *am* that discipline. I'm in charge – anybody want to challenge my authority?'

Capot said nothing.

'You'd better think,' Billiard-Fanon said, turning to Lebret again, 'of clearing your soul. Before you meet your God, you know.'

'Alright, alright,' said Lebret. He was sweating profusely. 'There is more to this situation than I have admitted … than I have said. I've not shared this with you all before because … well – because I was *ordered* to keep it to myself, actually.' He glanced up at Ghatwala, as if considering whether to include him in what he had to say. But he went on, 'Several of you have speculated why I am here. In fact, I am working directly for the Secret Services of France. I received my commission directly from de Gaulle – as was said. I was no more a collaborationist during the last war than any of you.'

'A pretty fiction,' said Billiard-Fanon. 'Carry on – your lies only make it clearer I've made the right decision in condemning you to death.'

'These are not lies,' said Lebret, fiercely. He brought a cigarette out of his case – his last, he thought grimly – but his hands were trembling visibly. He fumbled the little white tube, dropped it. Another of the vessel's weird poltergeist-like breezes sprung up from nowhere and blew the cigarette away, away towards the far wall. Lebret watched it go forlornly, as if his last hope went with it.

'So,' Pannier prompted. 'You are not a Vichy traitor, you're a heroic undercover spy? Is that what you were saying?'

'Remember when the *Plongeur* first sank?' Lebret asked, putting his now empty cigarette case back into his jacket pocket. 'And for a terrifying half-hour we all thought we would die at any moment? I recall that *you* confessed, Monsieur Pannier, to murdering a man.'

Pannier's eyes narrowed. 'A typically low and treacherous move, Lebret,' he returned, 'to bring that up. A moment of crisis! What about poor Avocat, and his cousin drowning in milk? You want to taunt *him* about that, now that he's dead?'

'My point is this. We *didn't* die,' Lebret continued. 'That's so amazing a circumstance that perhaps we've forgotten it! We ought to be have been crushed by the pressure, or dashed against the seabed. Instead we have passed into a new realm – who can doubt it?'

Billiard-Fanon lowered the pistol. 'You know more about this than you've said,' he accused. 'Spit it out! Have you known all along?'

'We didn't know! Which is to say, we didn't know *for certain*,' said Lebret. 'But there was ... shall we say *reason to believe* that some manner of passage was possible from our cosmos of vacuum and hydrogen into, well, into what we see. A cosmos of water. Nor are we the first to have travelled this way.'

'Not the first?' gasped Jhutti.

'How likely is it that we would have been the first? If we could enter this realm, then others could have done so before us.' Once again Lebret's eyes met Ghatwala's, but he snatched his glance away as if fearing to incriminate the other man. 'But there were many imponderables. Anyway you must believe me when I say that – that neither I nor the powers for which I work – powers, I might add, dedicated to tapping this resource for the greater glory of France – that neither they nor I had any idea that we would detect an entrance to a portal upon the *maiden* voyage of ...'

'Stop,' said Le Petomain. 'Wait. You knew that we would pass into this terrible place?'

'I didn't know,' said Lebret.

'But the people you work for knew – or suspected. Why didn't they tell us?'

'It is … complicated,' said Lebret, rubbing his eyes. Suddenly he felt terribly weary.

'Did Captain Cloche know?'

'He did not.'

'Why would the Navy do such a thing? Send a ship out to explore an underwater tunnel to a new dimension, without telling the captain or crew that's what they were doing?'

'It doesn't make sense,' agreed Billiard-Fanon, scowling.

'You misunderstand the nature of our … knowledge,' said Lebret. 'And do I need to remind you how volatile French politics has been over the last few years? To say nothing of the … extraordinary and … well, intrinsically questionable nature of the information we had received.' Once more Lebret was unable to prevent his glance searching out Ghatwala.

'Is this what you've been conspiring about, you and he?' Billiard-Fanon demanded, pointing the pistol at Ghatwala. Pannier, sitting next to the scientist, flinched away, and – a little sheepishly – Billiard-Fanon brought the aim of the gun back round to Lebret.

'The little I know about this new realm …' Lebret began to say.

'*This* is why,' Billiard-Fanon interrupted him. 'This is why you were so insistent we keep diving down – when the captain wanted to refloat the tanks and go back up, towards home. You tricked us into diving deeper! And here we are … descending through watery hell.'

'As I say,' Lebret repeated, trying to assert a degree of control over the exchange, 'I don't know everything about this place. But I am certain that going back *up* would be a wild goose chase. I know we have to keep going *down*.'

'What choice do we have?' yelled Pannier. 'You've doomed us all!'

There was general, vocal agreement to this proposition.

'We're not doomed—' Lebret began to say. But Billiard-Fanon cut him off.

'You still haven't said why you killed Avocat. Not content to wait for us all to die, you've decided to go about the vessel killing us one at a time?'

145

'No—no—'

'Are you murdering to a purpose?' Billiard-Fanon demanded. 'Or are you simply insane – a maniac?'

'I'll say it again, I don't know why you won't believe me. Monsieur Avocat hurt his arm, and I was trying to help! It's the truth!'

Billiard-Fanon took a step towards Lebret. 'You're innocent, you say?'

'Yes!'

'Look me in the eye, Monsieur Lebret,' demanded Billiard-Fanon. 'Look me right in the eye, and say "I am innocent of murder". Say it, and I'll know whether you're telling the truth.'

The walls of the *Plongeur* shuddered and groaned, and the boat rolled a little. Everyone in the mess twitched, and gripped more tightly onto whatever they were holding. Lebret looked about him. A bank of hostile faces. His eye snagged on a number of oddities – there was his cigarette, stuck somehow to the ceiling. There, too, were various pieces of detritus and rubbish, discarded food, papers, littered about the ceiling. He wondered, idly, what was sticking them up there. Presumably they were wet, and the water was acting as some kind of glue. He listened – there were roiling, watery sounds distantly visible – and he heard, in his imagination, the sound of the ocean speaking to him as it had done before: *the water loves you utterly, yearns to embrace you with all its limbs and press its mouth to your mouth.* He tried to focus. Billiard-Fanon was leaning in towards him.

He locked his gaze with the ensign, and began to speak. But as the words emerged, there flashed upon Lebret's inner eye a vivid image of the scowling captain, struggling with him upon his bunk. He recalled the feeling of the small pistol discharging his hands, and the abrupt stiffening and twitching backwards.

'I am innocent of murder,' he said.

Billiard-Fanon nodded slowly, and stepped back. 'He's lying,' he said, and then, once again, for the benefit of the assembled audience, 'He's lying!'

'Of course he is,' growled Pannier. 'Does anyone doubt it?'

16

SENTENCE

ʘ ʘ ʘ ʘ ʘ ʘ

Lebret took a breath. 'Listen to me, everybody,' he said, in a loud voice. 'Is this truly what you choose? This insanity? I am the only person on board the *Plongeur* who can ensure we all get back safe to port. Only I!'

This announcement had a gratifying effect. Nobody contradicted it; and as Lebret cast his gaze about he could see on the face of several of the sailors that they believed him.

'And what assurances can you provide,' Billiard-Fanon demanded, 'that you can truly do this thing?'

'I do not pretend to be a saint,' said Lebret. 'But I am no *traitor* – and most of all I *am* the only person who even begins to understand the nature of the place in which we find ourselves. I say only this: let me help you. Hold off your trial and sentence until we are docked again. Then, by all means, stand me before a court martial, convened upon French soil and presided over by a French judge, to arraign me for what I have done. But until that time *you need me* – you need me alive.'

'He has a point,' muttered Capot. 'Does he? Does he have a point?'

'If you believe him,' countered Le Petomain.

'And why should we believe him?' snarled Pannier. 'He's the kind of treacherous dog would promise to rescue a comrade from a drowning room and then abandon him to his fate.'

Sensing an advantage, however slim, Lebret pressed, 'I do not ask you to like, or even trust me. Judge me by how effectively I can guide you through this place. Because,' he repeated, playing his trump card again, 'only I have any idea of what we're dealing with.'

'You didn't help when the cuttlefolk attacked our vessel!' Pannier called.

'I don't pretend to know everything,' Lebret agreed. 'But I know something. Which is more than any of you can say!'

'No,' said Billiard-Fanon, shaking his head. 'No, I don't trust you, Monsieur. Put ourselves in your hands? Who's to say you won't navigate the *Plongeur* straight into the heart of one of these undersea suns, and kill us all?'

'I know how to get us home...' Lebret insisted.

'At least let's discuss this,' suggested Le Petomain. 'Put him back in his cell, and *test* what he says. Get him to explain this place, whatever it is, and test what he says against observations. That way we can ascertain how useful he will be to us.'

Capot and Jhutti nodded at this. Pannier stared at the wall in disgust. Billiard-Fanon seemed to ponder the variables. Then he straightened his spine. 'No,' he said. 'I'm in charge now. I have passed sentence.'

He lifted the pistol, and pointed it at Lebret's head.

'Wait!' Lebret cried, his mouth wide, his eyes bulging.

Billiard-Fanon pulled the trigger and shot Lebret in the mouth.

Lebret's head snapped backward in a splash of vivid red. He lurched, flying back, hitting the angled wall with a thud.

In the enclosed space the retort of the pistol's blast was ear-stunningly loud. It left a residual tinnitus whine in the hearing of those present. Ghatwala shrieked in surprise. Pannier grinned. Billiard-Fanon flipped his left hand up to grab at the punchy recoil of the weapon, and stop the gun jumping out of his hands.

There was a loud gong-like chime, and a serpentine hissing sound.

Billiard-Fanon yelled with joy. 'Rejoice not against me, O mine enemy!' he cried.

'You've breached the hull!' shouted Le Petomain, in horror.

The look of triumph froze on the ensign's face. He looked round

– it was true. The bullet had pierced not only Lebret's head and the wall of the mess, but the outer hull of the *Plongeur* too. A thin spike of water protruded in through the gap, spraying droplets in every direction. Everybody stared at it, horrified. The water died away. There was a gulping sound, and the jet started up again. A thick mist of water roiled around the mess.

'What have you *done?*' Le Petomain shrieked.

'Plug it!' yelled Castor.

Capot began to clamber down from his vantage towards the point of the breach, but Billiard-Fanon was closest. He stepped awkwardly over Lebret's body and tried to scrabble up the sloping wall to where the hole was. But the wall was slippery-wet, and he made no progress.

Capot got to him. 'Tiny little pinhole,' Billiard-Fanon announced, in a loud, brittle voice. 'A strip of chewing gum would block it… give me a leg-up, Capot.'

'It's gone straight through the outer hull,' yelled Castor.

Billiard-Fanon was lifted closer towards the breach. It was alternately spurting out water and sucking back, almost as if alive and breathing – or at least sputtering. 'It's,' he said, bringing his eye up to it.

Then something quite unexpected happened. A claw poked through the hole, and pulled upwards, tearing the metal as easily as if it had been paper.

Billiard-Fanon yelled with sheer terror, and fell from Capot's supporting hold. He banged his spine against the edge of one of the angled tables, rolled off, and fell into the V of wall-and-floor next to Lebret's body. He was screaming 'the devil, the devil!'

'What was it?' yelled Pannier.

'I didn't see—'

'The breach,' Castor boomed. 'It's a rip – it's a tear—'

'The devils! They're outside, trying to get in!' howled Billiard-Fanon, writhing in the metal cleft.

Le Petomain was already clambering up to the mess hatch. 'Out of here,' he called. 'Everybody! Before the whole panel gives way and this space floods completely.'

The other sailors needed no further encouragement. Even Castor, who was calling out 'We can mend it!' nevertheless scrabbled up the sloping floor and out through the hatch.

'The water is scorching me!' screamed Billiard-Fanon, struggling to get to his knees, his face contorted with terror – or pain. His eyes were tight shut. 'It's the *opposite* of holy water! The unholy water – that burns me! Burns me! The devils!'

The water was certainly swirling about the space as if possessed; although none of the other men remarked upon its heat. But the uncanny motion of the fluid filled their hearts with fear.

Le Petomain had already leapt through the hatch, and away from there. Pannier bundled Ghatwala through and Jhutti was not far behind.

'Don't leave me!' Billiard-Fanon yelled. 'Capot – I hurt my back when I fell.'

Water was surging into the mess now, through the enlarged breach. It flew around in a diabolic frenzy like a monsoon rainstorm. The claw, or beak, was no longer visible – if it had ever been there. But whether the claw had been a real phenomenon or a hallucination, something non-human had certainly expanded the hole.

Capot put his shoulder under Billiard-Fanon's armpit, and helped the ensign to his feet. Together they used the bolted-down tables and chairs as a stairway to climb up towards the hatch. Jhutti on the far side, was leaning through, his arm out. 'Come on! Come on!' he called.

'The devils,' Billiard-Fanon wept, struggling upward. 'They're all about the ship! They want to break in! A cursed vessel, a haunted vessel… we must pray to God! Let us pray!'

'I pray you to shut up,' grunted Capot, shrugging the ensign's body through the hatch. He climbed up after and through. Jhutti slammed the hatch door shut, and spun the wheel to lock it.

They were all wet. Billiard-Fanon lay on his back, sodden, moaning. 'The devils, the devils!'

'What were you *thinking*?' Le Petomain shouted at him.

'Discharging your pistol inside the vessel like that? What were you *thinking?*'

But Billiard-Fanon was laughing, now; and there was a maniac in the laugh.

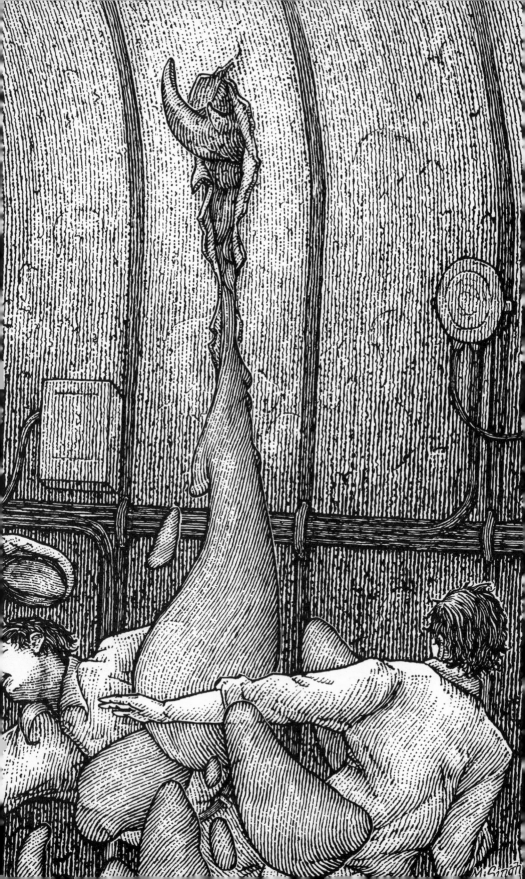

17

WHO'S IN COMMAND?

💧 💧 💧 💧 💧 💧

They all struggled through to the bridge. The entire vessel shook and rolled suddenly, spinning ninety-degrees and more. Everybody lost their footing and fell. 'The devils!' yelled Billiard-Fanon, as the seven men tumbled and fell against the sides. 'They spin us and roll us – but they cannot snatch our souls!'

'Take the gun away from him!' Jhutti urged Le Petomain. 'He has lost his mind.'

The *Plongeur* bucked, abruptly, and all seven men fell again. As they struggled to get back to their feet Le Banquier glanced over at Billiard-Fanon. The latter read his intent. 'No you don't, Monsieur pilot. *I* am in command and I won't stand for any insubordination!' He brought the gun up. Ghatwala yelled out in alarm.

The *Plongeur* rolled yet again, and the seven men tumbled and sprawled. Several of them shouted in pain. The fabric of the vessel trembled and made terrifying hooting and keening noises. Grinning, Billiard-Fanon picked himself from the mass of bodies. 'They are all about us – the devils are all about us!' He aimed the gun at Le Petomain, as if to shoot him, but just at that moment the *Plongeur* shook with an earthquake motion, and rolled again – back again. Everybody fell. Billiard-Fanon's arm struck the edge of a bank of equipment and he yelped. The pistol fell from his hand.

'Though I walk through the valley of death ...' howled Billiard-Fanon. 'Rejoice not against me, o mine enemy!' He lurched towards where the gun had fallen, but the *Plongeur* rolled again, and the gun clattered chimingly upon the metal of the bridge's control panels.

The vessel shook once more, but then – finally – it settled, having rolled through a quarter-turn. The walls were now the floor, the seats and controls of the bridge projecting from the wall.

Everybody picked themselves up. Billiard-Fanon was clutching his wrist and grinning. 'So,' he said. 'Monsieur Indian. Now *you* have the pistol.'

Jhutti was holding the gun.

'You have lost your mind, Monsieur,' he said. 'You cannot be trusted with this weapon.'

'Jhutti,' said Le Petomain. 'Give *me* the gun.'

Jhutti looked at the pilot. His expression was not calm. 'He shot Lebret! In cold blood! Billiard-Fanon shot Monsieur Lebret in the face!'

Billiard-Fanon laughed. 'Lebret was a devil. Literally so! Did you see his master, the father of lies, poke his dinosaur fingernail in at the bullet hole and rip the panel? Satan seeking to reclaim the body of his son.'

Jhutti addressed the ensign directly. 'Why shoot him?'

'His head must have been made of paper!' Billiard-Fanon exclaimed. 'The bullet went straight through – as if his skull were not there. It went straight through and punctured the skin of the submarine. Did anybody else see that? I expected the bullet to lodge in the man's skull, but his skull must have been made of soft cheese.'

'It *was* a reckless action, Jean,' said Le Petomain, sorrowfully. 'It endangered us all.'

'Nonsense!' boomed Billiard-Fanon. 'I *saved* us all! That man – say rather, that devil, Lebret – he was the cause of all our woes. He was the Jonah. We've got rid of him. Now we will be well.'

'The mess is flooded!' growled Castor. 'We have no access to the forward portion of the *Plongeur* at all!'

'So what?' laughed the ensign. 'We have the bridge, and our cabins. The engines are still working, which means that we still have air to breathe.' He looked around at the other men. 'There

155

was nothing fore, anyway. The ballast tanks are ripped. What else? The torpedo tubes? We don't need them!'

'The food,' said Capot. 'What are we going to eat?'

Billiard-Fanon laughed. 'Have faith, and the Lord will provide! We can throw a fishing line out through the airlock, and try a bit of native calamari.' He was rubbing his wrist, back and forth. 'You're missing the larger picture, messieurs! Food? Jesus lasted forty days in the wilderness without food, tormented by devils the entire time! God has seen fit to test us. Do you think we're not in a wilderness? A wilderness of water! And can you not see the devils that torment us? There is only one way to survive this situation, and it is faith. Faith!'

'Forty days without food,' said Capot, in a grim voice.

'Ensign Billiard-Fanon,' said Le Petomain. 'I am relieving you of command. Monsieur Jhutti, please give me the gun.'

But the scientist did not relinquish the pistol.

'Hey!' said Castor. 'Why should *you* assume command? I'm the engineer! I outrank you.'

'You do not,' said Le Petomain. 'And besides, Lieutenant Boucher may regain consciousness at any moment. As pilot, I...'

'I am chief engineer! I *outrank* you,' Castor repeated.

'A self-confessed bigamist,' Le Petomain began.

Castor clapped his hands together. 'What has that got to do with anything? What has that got to do with anything – down here?'

'I am assuming command of the *Plongeur*,' Le Petomain repeated.

'Monsieur Indian,' said Castor, stepping forward. 'I request you give me the gun.'

'Oh what does it matter who has the gun?!' shouted Pannier. 'What does it matter? We've no flotation; we've no food or drink; we're tumbling through an alien sea, completely out of control! Command? Command is a chimera! We're all going to die. We were all always going to die.' He kicked at the wall. 'Cut off from the galley! No drink at all!' he repeated. 'Not even a single glass to ease the terror of mortality!'

'We could, perhaps,' suggested Capot, whose mind was also

clearly running along similar grooves, 'use the remaining diving suit? We lost one suit when de Chante ... was taken, but we have another.'

'Taken!' repeated Le Petomain. 'You've no proof that's what happened to poor de Chante! None of us know what happened to him!'

'At any rate, there *is* another diving suit, down below. One of us could get into that, and retrieve some food and drink from the kitchen.'

'It's ...' said Le Petomain. 'It's possible, I suppose. But it would be a desperate strategy. How would we gain access? The mess is flooded now – if we opened the hatch, we risk inundating the bridge as well.'

'Perhaps a diver could swim out and round. The breach in the wall is large enough to allow a diver in, I think?'

Billiard-Fanon had sat himself down and was kissing his wrist and repeating the Lord's Prayer. But upon hearing this he spoke up. 'Satan himself is out there. Good luck swimming through that! You wondered what happened to Monsieur de Chante? Now you know! The devil snatched him to his scaly bosom.'

Castor took another step towards Jhutti. 'I repeat my request, Monsieur, that you give me the pistol. I am now the ranking officer.'

'I think,' said Jhutti, backing off, 'it would be better if I held on to this gun. I have no interest in whether Monsieur Castor or Monsieur Le Petomain has precedence, in terms of the chain of command. Consider me a neutral party. At any rate, this gun has caused enough damage, I feel.'

'Don't let him have it!' chirruped Billiard-Fanon, with a lopsided grin. 'He's not even a Christian! It will anger God if he has it!'

'Capot,' said Le Petomain. 'Please go aft and check on the lieutenant. He will have been thrown around by the tossing and bucking of the submarine. Go and see if he is alright.'

'Capot,' said Castor, standing taller. 'Capot – wait.' When the sailor hesitated, the engineer said, 'Yes, on second thoughts, go. Go and have a look-see, check on Monsieur Boucher.'

Castor looked from pilot to engineer and back. Then, without a word, he climbed up and along the wall, manoeuvred himself with some difficulty through the hatch and went aft.

'Perhaps,' suggested Jhutti, fitting the pistol into a pocket in his tunic, 'you could agree to share command?'

'As if it matters!' laughed Billiard-Fanon. 'We must *pray*, brothers! Prayer is all that will save us now. God is testing us.'

'Jean,' said Le Petomain. 'You have acted recklessly, and endangered the ship. You should not have discharged that pistol inside the submarine.'

'Come! That little hole in the skin would have been perfectly mendable,' said Billiard-Fanon. 'It wasn't my little bullet that did the damage! My little bullet of justice. It was the finger of Satan, poking through that hole – ripping the skin of the submarine like cotton!'

'I think you ought to go back to your cabin, Jean,' said Le Petomain. 'If you want to pray – well then, pray there. Prayer can't do any harm, I suppose.'

'Are you locking me up, Annick?' asked Billiard-Fanon, looking up with a lopsided grin. 'Are you trying to *contain* me?'

'He's right,' Castor said. 'I agree. You're a liability, Monsieur. You have proved that.'

Capot poked his head through the sideways-lying hatch. 'The lieutenant is conscious,' he announced.

Le Petomain, Castor and Jhutti made their way, awkwardly, through the hatchway and up the slant, rolled-about corridor. Boucher was sitting on what had once been the wall of his cabin. Le Petomain and Castor squeezed through into his cabin.

The lieutenant's first words were, 'Clearly we are still descending. What depth have we reached, Monsieur Le Petomain?'

'We have been around the clock more times than anybody has been able to count, Lieutenant,' reported the pilot. 'Many hundreds of thousands of kilometres of "depth" I would say – soon we will approach a million.'

'Kilometres?' repeated Boucher. 'Why not leagues? And besides, surely you mean "metres". Do not attach a keel to the metre. It's bad seamanship.' Then he laughed a weirdly high-pitched, childish laugh,

Le Petomain looked at Castor uncertainly. 'I regret to report, Lieutenant,' he went on, 'that not only have we lost the ability to refloat the main ballast tanks, but there has been a breach in the wall of the mess.'

'That's what Capot just told me,' said Boucher. He pressed the heel of his hand against his forehead. 'I feel awful, really bad. A headache like ... a headache like—' He looked up, suddenly startled. 'Wait – who are you?'

'I am Le Petomain,' said Le Petomain.

'I know *that*,' snapped Boucher. 'How did the mess get flooded?'

'A firearm was discharged inside the vessel, Lieutenant,' said Jhutti.

'That's a damn foolish way to celebrate Christmas Day!' said Boucher. 'Who did it? Was it you, Monsieur?'

'No!' replied Jhutti, startled.

'It was Billiard-Fanon,' said Castor. 'The fool's gone God crazy.'

'Well,' said Boucher, vaguely. 'We're all under a lot of strain. You should probably tell the captain, though. He'll want to know that there's a hole in the skin of his vessel.'

'The captain is dead, Lieutenant,' said Le Petomain, in a tentative voice.

Boucher buckled up his brow and stared at his own feet. But whatever he saw there only seemed to inflame his anger. 'I know that,' he said, darkly. Then he started shouting, 'You think I don't know *that*? Of course I know that! Oh Christ, we'll need to organise a burial at sea, I hate those. Surface! We can't do it submerged, we'll have to come to the surface. *Yes*, that's an order! Look – look – pilot. Pilot. Monsieur ...'

'Le Petomain?' suggested Le Petomain.

'Exactly! I am in command, because the captain is dead.'

'Yes, Lieutenant.'

'In which case my orders are – take us back into port. Take us back to Saint-Nazaire.'

There was an awkward silence . 'Lieutenant,' said Castor, tentatively, 'that may be …'

'Those are my orders, goddammit!' Boucher sounded querulous rather than furious, but he would brook no disagreement. 'Follow my orders! Obedience, Monsieur, obedience. The captain is very keen on obedience. Don't make me tell him you disobeyed me.'

'But …'

'Orders! And turn the vessel around – I mean, bring it about, so that I can lie properly on my couch. I'm not comfortable crouched here hallways between wall and ceiling.'

'We cannot necessarily control the …' Castor began.

'What? What's that? Speak up, man! Damnable *ringing* in my ears.' Boucher tapped two forefingers at both his ear holes. 'Horrible ringing noise.'

'We have suffered a number of malfunctions,' said Le Petomain, speaking loudly and clearly. 'That make it impossible to bring the vessel into a proper orientation.'

'What? Really? Oh well. They'll be able to fix that, back at Saint-Nazaire.'

'Lieutenant …?'

But Boucher's temper sizzled again. 'You have your orders, messieurs! You have your orders! Now leave me alone. Leave me alone.'

There was little point in staying. The three men extricated themselves from the cabin. 'Well,' said Le Petomain, when they were all out in the corridor. 'What do we do now?'

'Get along,' said Castor. 'As best we can. I'll go and see how the engines are bearing up, under all this abuse.'

'Very well. I'll go back to the bridge.'

Castor clambered up, and disappeared from view. Le Petomain and Jhutti started the harder business of climbing down the slanting mineshaft that the corridor had become. Before they reached the bottom, Capot's face appeared in the hatchway. 'It's another light, Annick,' he said. 'Come and see.'

18

THE DEMONS OF THE SEA

❡ ❡ ❡ ❡ ❡ ❡

Now that the submarine had been rolled about through ninety-degrees, getting to the observation chamber was easier – a shuffle along rather than a ladder-climb down. 'Turn the interior light off,' Le Petomain instructed.

Jhutti complied. An eerie blue glow of filled the chamber. 'Another sub oceanic sun, I presume,' said the pilot. 'Will we fall into it, as we did before? Get ourselves boiled like potatoes in a pot?'

'I think we're already missing it,' said Capot. 'Look.'

Shuffling along, they peered in at the corner of the observation porthole – the circle of blue-white brightness was clearly visible, half obscured by the body of the submarine. There was motion in the lit water too. 'More cuttlefolk?' suggested Le Petomain.

'I don't know,' said Jhutti. 'These look larger, I think. Although I would not be surprised if there are not cuttlefolk as well. But that – is *that* – some sort of whale?'

One of the swimming creatures was clearly very much larger than the others.

'Maybe a whale, doubtless of some new genus. Cetology would love to classify it. At any rate, they are a long way away from us at the moment.'

'I can count,' Jhutti began to say, leaning further to peer round. 'One, two, three whales ... and if we look over there ...'

There was a clunk – the pistol he had tucked into his tunic had fallen from it. Le Petomain pounced, rather ponderously, and laid his right hand upon it. Jhutti looked up and met his gaze. They said nothing. The pilot tucked the weapon into the top of his trousers, and turned his attention back to the view.

'How many of these sub oceanic suns do you think there are, Monsieur Jhutti?' Le Petomain asked, shortly. 'An infinite number?'

'I can only hope not, Monsieur Le Petomain,' replied the scientist, in a weary voice.

'Why so?'

'Because if the recently deceased Monsieur Lebret *is* correct and we have entered a parallel dimension of infinite water – well then, what does our fate hold, except to fall forever until we all starve? Or all go mad, and murder each other?'

'But if we are in an infinite ocean, why would we be *falling* at all?'

'A very good question, M'sieur.'

'Monsieur Jhutti,' said Le Petomain. 'I must ask you this question. It seems clear the late Lebret and your compatriot, Monsieur Ghatwala, were – as the phrase goes – in cahoots.'

'I do not understand what this phrase means,' said Jhutti, stiffly.

Le Petomain sat back. 'You can guess its meaning from the context, I think. Conspiring together. By his own admission, before he died, Lebret said—'

'Before he was *murdered*, you mean,' Jhutti said.

'By his own admission,' Le Petomain went on doggedly, 'Lebret was some sort of spy. He was plotting something. Entering this strange place was his intention. He was, I think, looking for something down here. Certainly, he lied to us, and kept things *from* us.'

'It certainly appears that way,' conceded Jhutti.

'But Monsieur Ghatwala was also involved this business! And so I have to ask you – what do you know of it?'

'Nothing, Monsieur,' said Jhutti, with dignity.

'Truly?'

'Indeed. I was recruited because of my expertise with the atomic pile. Before I joined this mission, I had never before exchanged two words with Dilraj – with Monsieur Ghatwala, I mean. Just because we happen to come from the same part of the world does not mean that we are co-conspirators. If that were a general principle, I might as well suspect you of plotting something with Lebret! For are you not both Frenchmen?'

Le Petomain considered this. 'Very well, Monsieur,' he said, eventually. 'I believe you. But if Lebret *did* have something particular in mind – if he was looking for *something*, then I would like to know what it was.'

'As would I.'

'Well,' said Capot, who had been listening to this exchange, 'Lebret was certainly very excited by the light. He thought the light was the end of our journey. The lengths he went to, trying to convince us to continue descending when the captain gave the order to ascend! There must be something special about the light.'

Le Petomain nodded again. 'Perhaps these lights do hold the answer to our predicament. If only Billiard-Fanon hadn't shot him, Lebret could have answered our questions! Well – we must make the best of it, not the worst. We must see what can be done with this crippled craft.'

The three men crawled back along and up to the bridge. There they found Billiard-Fanon laughing and chatting with Pannier. The cook was already more than half-drunk; and a bottle of rum was being passed between the two men. The ensign was holding it, with his thumb over the top. Castor was there too – watching, but not intervening. 'Where did that bottle come from?'

'I was keeping it in my trunk,' said Billiard-Fanon. 'For emergencies.'

'I thought I *said*,' Le Petomain announced, severely, 'that Ensign Billiard-Fanon was to be confined to his cabin!'

Billiard-Fanon chuckled. 'Come along, Annick,' he replied. 'Don't act as if you're the ranking officer! Why should I follow *your* orders?'

'Because,' said Le Petomain, bringing out the weapon, 'I have the pistol!'

Billiard-Fanon made a play-face of concern and respect, elaborately bunching up his brows and making an 'o' of his mouth.

Then he laughed, and waved the sloshy bottle in his direction. 'Relax, Annick! You aren't going to shoot me! Look what happened the last time that gun was discharged inside this vessel!'

'Castor, what are you playing at? Just standing there? Jean has lost it – he's had a nervous collapse. He's a danger to us all!'

'Maybe,' said Castor. 'But maybe I'm not taking orders from *you*.'

'Remove him to his cabin!'

Castor shook his head.

'Go on, give *me* the gun, Annick,' said Billiard-Fanon, in a slurred, coaxing voice . 'I'm the person who is really in charge here.'

'You? Indeed not. For one thing, the lieutenant is now awake!' said Le Petomain. 'For another – nobody is going to follow *you*, Jean! We're in a dire spot. Nobody will follow a madman!'

'Madman,' echoed Billiard-Fanon, looking hurt. 'I'm the only sane person here! I'm the only one who truly understands what has happened to us.'

'He's right,' was Pannier's opinion.

'You're drunk, again,' Le Petomain told Pannier in a scornful voice. 'Again! Come along, Herluin! We all need to work together, if we're to survive! What use will you be to us drunk?'

'It's a sacred rite of the Roman Catholic church!' Pannier returned, crossly. 'It's holy – wine is. But rum too, I'm thinking. It's all the same family. Holy family. We're surrounded by demons, man! You should listen to Jean. He knows his what-what.'

'Castor,' said Le Petomain. 'Will you assist me in locking Monsieur Billiard-Fanon up?'

Castor took a step forward, although without great conviction. But Billiard-Fanon put his left hand out, like a policeman stopping traffic, and spoke, 'Wait a moment. I am in command, not Annick. I am in command and I can prove it.'

Le Petomain aimed the pistol at the ensign's head. 'I'm willing to bet your skull is thicker than Lebret's was. I'm willing to bet – if I shoot, you'll stop the bullet very nicely.'

Billiard-Fanon ignored him. 'Listen, Capot – listen to what I have to say... wait, what's your first name?'

Capot looked around. 'It's Jean, too,' he said.

'Jean, a fine name! Listen, from one Jean to another. You're a young man. You haven't been through some of the experiences us older sailors have. You haven't come face-to-face with the prince of evil before. But I say to you – I can *prove* that I'm the only one who truly understands what's going on!'

Capot looked at Le Petomain. 'Go on, then,' this latter said, lowering the gun. 'Prove it.'

Billiard-Fanon was grinning broadly. With his free hand, he reached inside his shirt. 'I served on the *Terreur*,' he said. 'Perhaps you've heard of it? All but seven of its crew were killed. I survived, with a chunk of the hull stuck into my thigh. The doctors took it out, and I had this –' he lifted out a pendant cross, fashioned from dull grey metal '– made from it. A reminder! God saved my life, that day. He saved me for a purpose.'

'A cross,' said Le Petomain. 'Very pious. I don't see what it proves, though.'

'You're not looking! The truth has been staring us in the face, for days now – but we simply refuse to see it! This cross is Christ's symbol. See how it dangles from the chain?'

'Exactly as you'd expect.'

'Quite! It obeys the laws of physics – God's laws. Now, this rum …' He looked at the bottle in his right hand. 'Whatever Pannier says, rum is not a holy drink. Drunkenness is devilish. Does this rum obey the laws of physics?'

He took his thumb from the top of the bottle and gave it a shake. A great gloopy shape of transparent liquid spilled out and sailed upwards, deforming a little as it went. It struck what had been the wall, and was now the ceiling, and broke into a number of smaller pearls and ball-bearings. 'We've all been seeing this, for days now – and ignoring it!' cried Billiard-Fanon, suddenly inspired with a preacher's force and rhetoric. 'We've been ignoring it because it doesn't fit the materialist mind-set we've been used to cultivate! But the truth is – the place we are in now is not governed by any materialist or scientific logic!'

'Some crazy something,' said Le Petomain. 'Magnetism, or a freak gust of air, or... something.'

'The Devil!' boomed Billiard-Fanon. 'Man alive, give *up* this irritable groping after fact and science, it won't save us here! You need to understand... we are in a *spiritual* realm now. Outside, we are beset by actual demons. Prayer is what we need. What we need is not to fix the nuts-and-bolts of this submarine. What we need is to exorcise the waters around us!'

With impeccable timing, a series of bangs and knocks chimed from the *Plongeur*'s hull. Everybody jumped, except Billiard-Fanon – who laughed again. 'You cling to materialism and science,' he said, making a general address to everyone in the room. 'But in your hearts you know that I am telling the truth. That gun, Annick? That gun won't help you. God is your shield, and the Holy Ghost your weapon.'

Le Petomain listened. 'That came from the airlock,' he said. 'Capot – go and see what was banging.'

'What?' said Capot, startled.

'It's inside, I'm sure of it. Somebody's banging about down there. It's not devils, man! Get a grip – the ensign's mumbo-jumbo is just a fairy-story to scare children! Maybe it's the lieutenant.'

'The lieutenant?'

'You spoke to him – you know his concussion has left him a little confused. I don't want him doing something he'd regret, like thinking he needs to go out in a diving suit.'

'The lieutenant,' said Castor, speaking up. 'How could he have got down to the airlock? We'd have noticed him, going past.'

'I don't know. But somebody's there! Go and see, Capot.' Another bang sounded, and then another. 'That's definitely *inside*. Go on!'

With some reluctance, Capot scrambled along the now-horizontal passage that formerly led down to the airlock chamber and the submarine's one remaining diving suit.

'Jean,' Le Petomain asked. 'Where's Ghatwala?'

'You weren't impressed by my miracle, Annick?' chuckled the

ensign. 'You deny the proof? Too much a banker, I fear – too much a numbers and figures man.'

'Where is Ghatwala?' Le Petomain repeated.

'In his cabin,' said Castor, in strange voice.

'At supper,' said Billiard-Fanon. 'How does that go? "Not where he eats, but where he is eaten"?' He laughed again. 'Racine has his moments, sure, but you can't beat Shakespeare for the really grisly stuff.'

The realisation dawned on Le Petomain. He shook his head.

'Oh no!' murmured Jhutti.

Billiard-Fanon's mobile face hardened. '*You* need to get a grip, Annick! *You* don't seem to grasp the seriousness of the situation we are in! He was a heathen, a pagan, a devil worshipper – and a traitor, conspiring with Lebret! We must purge ourselves of unbelief and devil-worship if we are to exorcise the waters around us!'

'You're mad!' Le Petomain breathed. He could feel tears filling his eyes. 'Quite mad! It's brute murder, nothing else.' He looked at Castor. 'How could you let him *do* such a thing?'

Castor only shrugged. Pannier snatched the bottle out of Billiard-Fanon's hand, and put its neck into his mouth. The ensign snarled at him like a dog, looked around the bridge, and settled a smile back upon his face. 'We must be pure,' he said. 'Ah! Monsieur Jean Capot!'

Capot was back – white as blancmange and with a strange look in his eye.

'Well?' Le Petomain demanded?

Capot looked at him, but said nothing.

'Never mind,' Le Petomain said. 'Monsieur Capot – Ensign Billiard-Fanon has become murderously insane. He will kill all of us, unless we restrain him. You and I – we must overpower him, and lock him in his cabin.'

The young sailor looked at him, or rather seemed to look *through* him. Then he nodded, very slowly. 'I understand,' he said.

Le Petomain aimed the pistol at Billiard-Fanon once again. 'I think you and I, Capot, are the only two left aboard this vessel still sane,' he said.

'I'm sorry for it,' said Capot. Then he punched Le Petomain hard, on the jaw. The pilot stumbled and started to fall; Capot leapt immediately upon him, grabbing his arm and wrenching the pistol from his grip.

Le Petomain fell hard against the wall, and cried out. 'What are you doing?' He wriggled ignominiously for a moment, and then hauled himself back to his feet, clutching his chin in both hands. 'What are you *doing*?'

Capot had hurt his right hand with the blow; that was obvious. He held it limp at his side. But with his *left* hand he passed the pistol over to Billiard-Fanon. 'The ensign is right,' he said, in a colourless voice. 'Ours is a spiritual problem. Our souls are in danger of damnation.'

'What's got into you! You *wrenched* my jaw! I can feel it in at the hinge, under my ear!'

'I'm sorry,' was all Capot would say. 'But the ensign is right.'

'What did you see, lad?' Billiard-Fanon asked, genially, passing the pistol from hand to hand. 'Tell us *exactly* what you saw in the airlock.'

'I didn't get there,' said Capot. 'Because I saw—'

'Saw what?'

'A ghost,' said Capot.

'Don't be absurd!' fumed Le Petomain, rubbing the side of his face. 'What ghost?'

'The ghost of Monsieur Lebret,' said Capot.

'He was unrighteous,' said Billiard-Fanon in a resonant voice, nodding as if this information confirmed everything he has said. 'His spirit cannot find rest!'

'How did you know it was him?' asked Castor.

'It was him,' said Capot. 'I recognised him at once. The wound was in his head, where you shot him, Ensign. When he opened his mouth to speak, blood poured out like a scarf of scarlet. His beard was ruby and glistening with the blood. He was wet, all wet with blood.'

'His spirit bears the stain of the innocent blood of others that he spilled!'

'Then he spoke to me.' Capot shuddered, his skin like a horse's flank twitching under the irritation of midges.

'What did he *say*, lad?' asked Billiard-Fanon, not unkindly.

'He said we should all get out. He said a monster was coming greater than the most terrible of earthly leviathans. He said we must all get out.'

19

THE SHIELD OF FAITH

❦ ❦ ❦ ❦ ❦ ❦

Billiard-Fanon's authority was sealed by this apparition. Capot was convinced that they were facing a spiritual test; Pannier, his voice slurred now with drink, swore that he would follow the ensign 'to the ends of the earth – or the ends of this endless ocean, if needs be.'

'You'd follow anyone who gives you a drink,' cried Le Petomain, moving his bruised jaw gingerly from side to side. 'Castor! You must see – he is insane!'

'I'm an engineer,' was Castor's reply. 'I believe in the laws that make machines work. But we've seen some things … we've all seen some things aboard this vessel that science cannot explain. I say – well, I say Billiard-Fanon's explanation makes the greatest sense of any I have heard.'

'Makes sense?' snapped Le Petomain. 'What sense?'

'The ghost, Monsieur?' Castor pressed. 'The poltergeist who keeps throwing our belongings about? The sea-devils outside? You cannot explain all this in material terms.'

Billiard-Fanon spoke up: 'You were so kind as to suggest I should be confined to my cabin,' he said. 'Well, I am now in a position to return the favour. Capot, Castor – take him off.'

'And I, Monsieur?' demanded Jhutti, straightening his back, and speaking with as much dignity as he could muster. 'Will you kill me too, because I happen not to worship the same gods you worship?'

Billiard-Fanon put his head on one side. 'The taciturn Indian,' he said. 'What to do with you? Well, nobody is beyond God's grace, Monsieur. I suggest you too spend a little time in your cabin, like a monk in his cell. I suggest you contemplate the nature of the threat we all face.'

Capot took hold of Le Petomain's elbow, but the pilot shook himself free. 'You've killed us all, sailor,' he said. 'Giving this madman the pistol – it's doomed us all.'

'*You* didn't see him,' said Capot, in a bleak voice. 'The ghost. I saw the ghost with my own two eyes. The *Plongeur* is haunted.'

'We're all doomed,' repeated Le Petomain in a low voice. Finally he permitted himself to be led off the bridge, bent double, and away along the aft corridor. Jhutti went too.

Soon enough Capot returned. 'I looked in on the lieutenant,' he said. 'He's sleeping.'

'We four will suffice!' declared Billiard-Fanon, with a gleam in his eye. 'Four Christian Frenchmen! On us, and our faith, depends the future of this vessel. Prayer, and belief, and the power of Christ are our best protection! Let us pray!'

The ensign tucked his pistol into the belt of his trousers. Pannier belched and started to laugh; but when the ensign looked severely upon him his face fell, like a child who has been rebuked. Billiard-Fanon joined hands with Castor on his left and Pannier on his right; Pannier took Capot's hand, and Capot completed the circle with Billiard-Fanon.

'Ensign,' said Capot. 'I was in the observation chamber with Le Petomain and the Indian, and we saw another of the great underwater lights, shining. Ensign – what *are* the lights?'

Billiard-Fanon answered immediately, with complete conviction. 'The lights,' he said, 'are the light of God shining through into this benighted, devilish ocean. That is why the Satan-fish swarm and school around them in such numbers; they are trying to block out the light. But if we pray hard enough, God will guide this stricken vessel *into* the light, and through that mystic portal we will come home again. We came close before, but we were not then worthy. But we have purged our number of the ungodly since then!'

Capot dropped his gaze; and Pannier looked impressed, in a

drunken kind of way. But Castor retained enough of an engineer's natural scepticism to ask, 'How do you know?'

'Because,' Billiard-Fanon replied, serenely, 'God has told me.'

The engineer sucked in his lower lip, and plopped it out again. 'For real?'

'He is pleased that we have purged the *Plongeur* of the unrighteous,' Billiard-Fanon reported. 'With prayer and supplication we can reach him – He is speaking to me, right now, and He tells me so. Do everything I tell you to do and He may still save us!'

Young Capot shut his eyes, and his face assumed a fervent expression. 'I believe!' he announced.

'Sure,' agreed Pannier. 'The spirit is moving within me, whatever.'

'Let us pray!' said Billiard-Fanon. And as he began, the others mumblingly joined on, 'Our father, who art in heaven . . .'

Le Petomain sat with his back against the surface that had once been the floor of his cabin and rubbed his face. He worked his jaw around the tender spot where it connected to his skull, just underneath his ear. 'The world has gone mad,' he muttered to himself.

Time passed. It was impossible to gauge how long. The metal fabric of the submarine creaked intermittently, and the descent continued without abatement. At one point Le Petomain heard the sound of hymn-singing, muffled to incoherence by the intervening walls.

He waited as patiently as he could. 'This,' he told himself, 'will not end well.' His stomach growled hungrily, but he knew there was nothing he could do about that.

After a while, the door was opened and Pannier was there. 'The holy one wants to see you,' he announced.

'The holy one?'

Pannier grimaced, as if to acknowledge the absurdity of it. But what he said was, 'He's taking it *very* seriously, I should warn you. Don't mock him. And young Capot is a true believer. Seeing that ghost has turned his head.'

'And you, Herluin? Are you a true believer?'

'I believe prayer is as likely to do as any good as anything else – more so than engineering. To tell you the truth: I believe we'll all be dead in a few days whatever we do. And I tell you what else.' He grinned. 'The holy one actively encourages the use of wine sacramentally in worship.'

'The wine is all in the flooded mess, surely?'

'I've a few bottles, squirreled away in other places,' Pannier admitted. 'And if it comes to it, I may go for a little recreational diving to recover the rest. We've still got one suit left, after all. Anyway – come along. The holy one wants to have a word.'

Pannier led Le Petomain back to the bridge, where Billiard-Fanon was sitting on the side of the rotated-about captain's chair, like a throne. Capot was squatting beside him, like a faithful hound. 'Where's Castor?' Le Petomain asked.

'Castor is having another look at the engines,' Billiard-Fanon replied, in a heightened 'serene' voice.

'I'm pleased to hear he hasn't been executed as a heretic, at any rate,' said Le Petomain, sarcastically.

Billiard-Fanon looked at him. 'I have every reason to believe that Monsieur Castor is a good and faithful servant.'

Le Petomain straightened his spine. 'I'm supposed to call you the holy one, it seems?'

'We prayed together, we four. The holy spirit entered into me. Calling me the holy one has nothing to do with my merit, or eminence. It is acknowledging the glory of God. Surely you can see that?' He lifted the pistol from his lap, took the stock in both hands, and aimed the barrel at Le Petomain's chest.

'Shoot,' said the latter, calmly. 'Go ahead. We're all doomed anyway. Might as well get it out of the way.'

'But we are *not* doomed. There is a road out of death, and into light – and it is me,' said Billiard-Fanon. 'Science won't save us, but faith will. *I* am the shield of faith – the Holy Spirit has vouchsafed to me that it is only my presence upon the *Plongeur* that is keeping the aquatic devils from overwhelming us and feeding upon our very souls.'

'You may believe what you wish, Monsieur,' replied Le Petomain, with dignity. 'It is no concern of mine.'

'If I asked my disciple here to pull out your tongue,' said Billiard-Fanon, his voice betraying irritation for the first time. 'He would.' He dropped the pistol back into his lap, and patted Capot on his head. 'But I am merciful, because the Holy Spirit that flows *through* me is merciful.'

'Look, Jean,' said Le Petomain, wearily. 'You can believe what you like. Young Capot, there, and Pannier – that old soak – even Castor, with cogwheels where a human heart should be. All of you! Believe what you like, but leave me out of it. Shoot me, if you wish. Or send me back to my cabin.'

Billiard-Fanon shook his head. 'I am sorry to hear this,' he said. 'You have given up hope. But hope, who is Jesus Christ and Lord of the universe, has not given up *you*. I have been given a vision of how we can return home. Follow me, and provided only that you have enough faith in your heart we will end this day – this very day – back in the harbour at Saint-Nazaire!'

Le Petomain sighed. 'Jean, I only ...' he began to say.

'No!' interrupted Billiard-Fanon. 'You have a devil of despair inside you. We shall cast him out – because your despair would poison the ceremony.'

'Ceremony?'

'God has given me a vision. The world is fourfold, the tetragrammaton! YHWH, the holy name of God – four letters! – the Christian trinity *plus* mankind, folded into the bosom of the divine, three plus one is *four*. I am the holy one, the shield of faith, preserving the vessel from the devils outside. But I am the head. The vision is unambiguous. I must have *four* disciples, all praying in the correct way, for the grace of God to lift us out of this hell.'

'Capot, Castor and Pannier make three,' said Le Petomain. 'I see. So get the lieutenant to be your fourth.'

'Lieutenant Boucher is ... not responsive,' said Billiard-Fanon. 'He is not competent to ... to be allowed out of his cabin.'

Le Petomain shook his head. 'Poor fellow,' he said. 'Well – what about Jhutti?'

'A pagan!' retorted Billiard-Fanon, in a shocked voice. 'A heathen? Hardly! No, my friend. It must be you. You must be the fourth.'

'Capot, Castor, Pannier and me – an unlikely group of monks, I must say. So – what? We four say the Lord's prayer backwards and it magics the *Plongeur* back to port.'

Billiard-Fanon sighed. 'Such weakness of faith! No wonder God is testing us. Well, *Second-Mate* Annick Le Petomain, known to some as Le Banquier, and erstwhile pilot of this vessel. I am the way, the truth and the light, and I shall help you.'

Pannier's face appeared suddenly over Le Petomain's shoulder. The reek of rum was unmistakeable. 'Happy to assist, holy one,' he leered, grabbing the pilot's two elbows and crushing them together behind his back.

'Sometimes,' said Billiard-Fanon, getting to his feet and taking hold of the pistol by its barrel, 'Satan must be chastised with a rod!'

'It is clear,' gasped Le Petomain, his arms twisted painfully behind him. 'That you are insane. Insane!'

'The madness of faith is a very different thing from the madness of Enlightenment Reason,' said Billiard-Fanon in a level voice as he raised the pistol. 'The latter breeds monsters; but the former releases the mind from its material manacles and brings you closer to God.'

The butt of the pistol came down upon Le Petomain's skull with the sound of somebody knocking at a door.

20

THE FATE OF LEBRET

✦ ✦ ✦ ✦ ✦ ✦

Attend. It is needful that we pause at this point in our narrative, and move backwards in time a little way – to return ourselves to Lebret, in the flooding mess, immediately after he had been shot in the mouth by Billiard-Fanon. Lebret was not unconscious for very long.

The *Plongeur* rolled, and water sprayed and swirled all through the mess.

He woke abruptly, and cried out; although his voice was inaudible against the maelstrom roar of water and wind, of the clatter of metal. The whole submarine rolled on its side.

As a door on its hinges so he in his bed,
Turns his side and his shoulders and his heavy head.

His jaw was broken. He could feel it. The pain in his face, on the right side, was fierce and persistent, and when he touched it, it roared. The vessel rolled once again, and shook him from his back onto his front. The water was warm. He wiped a hand over his eyes to clear his vision from the spray, but it was all around him. There was no escaping it. His hand came away red. He was bleeding from the mouth.

What had happened?

A flash of memory – Billiard-Fanon's expression as he raised the captain's pistol and aimed it. He *had* fired. *He shot me,* Lebret thought. I should be dead. But the fact that the hard pain in his jaw was so unremitting rather persuaded him that he was still alive. He tried to steady himself on all fours, and reached a finger inside his mouth. Everything felt unnaturally slippery. He half-expected to discover a bullet, lodged in his soft palate, but there was nothing here. His tongue lolled against the digit; he felt it against the finger but not in the tongue itself. How could his mouth simultaneously be numb *and* in such pain?

The *Plongeur* rolled again, and Lebret was slammed against one of the inner struts. 'Ah!' he gasped. Something fell from his mouth – a tooth, or part of one – and pinged noisily off the wall. He felt inside his mouth again. On the bottom, to the right, where once he had possessed a neat row of white teeth, now there was a broken battlement. An exposed nerve screeched when he poked it – the pain was so intense it nearly made him vomit.

One tooth had been completely removed; the one next to it sheared off. 'Oh God,' he groaned.

He got onto all fours as the vessel rolled and swayed, and spat great blobs of blood and sputum onto the floor. His tooth raged, unremittingly, and inside his jaw a different sort of pain nested, fiery and less specifically focused.

He looked about him. There was a gap in the wall, roughly triangular in shape and large as a tea-tray. Some water was spraying in through this, but – weirdly – the ocean outside seemed almost to form some kind of skin. Its flow and ripples were visible through the rent.

Lebret looked to the hatch that led through to the bridge. Shut. He got to his feet, acting almost on instinct, thinking to stumble across to it. But the pain in his jaw sang inside his skull. *And then what?* he asked himself. *Get through to the bridge – and have Billiard-Fanon shoot you again?*

The whole ship shook. It was fantastic – the ensign had shot him in the mouth, and the bullet had ricocheted off his teeth, to pierce the skin of the submarine! What odds of such an occurrence? Lebret would not have believed it possible, if there were not such intense pain bunched in at his jaw.

The white noise of gushing and swirling water surrounded him.

He looked again at the breach in the side of the vessel. How had a single bullet-hole mutated into such a large gap? It was impossible.

And as he looked, he saw what Billiard-Fanon had seen – a talon. More than a single claw, a bunch of three, reaching in through the gap – a monster's paw, groping in at the space. The skin of it was profoundly purple in colour, and the claws themselves a pale green. It scooped at the air and drew a bubble out, wrenching back more of the *Plongeur's* plating in the process, widening the hole.

Just for a moment – no longer – Lebret's terror blotted out his pain.

Then his senses returned, or at least some of them. His mouth flared and throbbed in agony. 'Oxygen,' he gasped, spitting out red pearls and blobs with the words. 'The creature is scooping the—'

The vessel rolled again, with a great metallic groan, and Lebret was thrown hard on his back. He cried out with the impact. The agony in his face made him sob like a child.

The hole in the side of the vessel was now as wide as a manhole. By all rights, water ought to be flowing in – the whole mess ought to be flooded. And some water *was* coming in, spraying and swirling to join the crazy internal monsoon. But the bulk was being held out, as if by an invisible force field. Through the shimmery window formed against this breach, Lebret saw something move – something indistinct, and large, slithering by.

'Worry later,' Lebret told himself, although it was painful to move his jaw. Globules of blood scattered from his mouth to join the larger swirl. 'Get out now.'

Something was giving him a moment of grace, but the mess would eventually flood entirely. If he got through the hatch and into the bridge, he would have to confront Billiard-Fanon again. But there was the other hatch, that led forward. There wasn't much there, but at the moment it seemed a preferable direction. *I'll need to fix this tooth – or kill the nerve*, he thought. *This pain will drive me out of my wits.*

He thought – alcohol. Would he have time to snatch a bottle from the kitchen before getting away?

Lebret got to his feet, unsteadily. The pain in his jaw scorched his senses, and made it hard to coordinate his actions. The hatch through to the kitchen was not as solid as the main hatchways that separated the successive chambers running the length of the *Plongeur* – but perhaps it would hold? Should he sequester himself in there? But that thought was chased down hard by a *why?* What good would it do, prolonging his life by some hours, or even days – to cling on to life in agony – only to die in the end?

What to do?

The thought of a drink decided him – to take at least the edge off his raging jaw. He started towards the kitchen, fighting through the swirling internal rainstorm, his legs sloshing through an increasing depth of water.

Then the world turned upside down – the vessel rolled through a half-turn and Lebret's legs swooped round and over his head. He cried out, a single syllable, and fell – plummeted straight down.

His body was configured in an L-shape, legs straight and torso at ninety-degrees. He was in that rather awkward posture when he thumped against the wall – or floor – of the vessel. His head went straight through the breach, like a diver, into the water. But his gut thumped against the edge, and his legs clattered painfully against the internal wall.

Lebret felt a conflict of orientations. He felt as if he were simultaneously lying – from the waist down – prone on the floor, and – from the waist up – he felt as if he were hanging upside down in a pool. Then the *Plongeur* shuddered, and began to roll back.

And with that Lebret slipped all the way through, and out into the ocean.

Instinctively he grabbed at the lip of the hole, and his hands held on. His legs came out into the water, and his whole body swung about. Then he was smacked against the external curve of the *Plongeur*'s steel plating, and he let go. Worse, the collision knocked the breath from his lungs. Bubbles fled from his mouth.

The water was neither cold nor hot, and the sea was not black around him. He was aware of a faint blue-white glimmer all around him. Something vast moved in the corner of his eye. *Focus*, he told himself. *If I don't get back in through the gap, I will drown here.*

The pain helped him; it refused to release its clamp upon his jaw, and this in turn stopped him drifting away. He did not wish to drown. That was a fact solid enough to cling to.

He drew his knees up and lifted himself unsteadily. It was easier to see through this salt-less sea than in ordinary brine, but still the vision was hard to process. A great wraith-like, silvery-white shape was interposed between himself and the breach in the flank of the *Plongeur*. It looked so entirely like a ghost that it took Lebret a moment to recognise it for what it was – air! A great *blob* of air, a metre across, somehow not rushing towards the surface as an air bubble would do in a terrestrial ocean, but instead balancing itself and forming a slowly morphing protoplasmic shape upon the external surface of the submarine.

Lebret's empty lungs spasmed. He pushed himself forward. His head passed from water to air, and he sucked in a huge breath; but then he was down again, on his stomach, and back in water.

Fighting the rising panic, Lebret struggled to his knees. The silvery twisting bulbous shape of the air bubble had moved a few yards away from the side of the *Plongeur*. Looking up, he saw his own face, slightly distorted, as if in a funfair mirror, in the side of the bubble. It was a strange sight – his hair floating in the water, trails and tendrils of blood dribbling from his mouth.

Breathe. He must breathe. He got to his feet, and his head broke through once again.

He panted. Gulped more air.

For the briefest moment he was conscious of the strangeness of his situation. He was standing on the *outside* of a submerged submarine. His legs were in the water, yet his head was inside a giant air-bubble. The walls of his temporary air-cell bulged and trembled, and that made it hard to see through them, but he could just about make out the long grey-black flank of the submarine (upon which he was standing) stretching away before and behind him. He brought both his hands out of the water and into the bubble to wipe his eyes. He looked again. He had to get back inside the *Plongeur*. The breach must be nearby.

How his jaw hurt!

Then he saw it – a fold of metal plating, and the dark, irregularly spaced gap. Lebret emptied his lungs then took a deep breath, readying himself to scramble – somehow – across to that gap; to pull himself back inside and hope that he could get through the forward hatch before he drowned. He readied himself.

At that exactly moment, the leviathan – for whatever manner of beast it *was* swimming around, it was a being of prodigious size – knocked him down. It swept round the curve of the *Plongeur's* hull, and stuck out a gigantic clawed-flipper. Even as he flew backwards, Lebret had the presence of mind to think: the creature seeks only to dissipate the oxygen! He is not interested in *me*. But what if it weren't true? I am bleeding into the water. What if these beasts are like terrestrial sharks? Would they devour me? Would my oxygen rich haemoglobin drive them wild?

He had more immediate concerns, though. The leviathan's vast flipper caught him in the chest and face, and as it knocked the larger air bubble into a million spherical fragments it also pushed him down. He skidded on the curving metal floor, scrabbled to regain his grip. But it was no good. He was falling – sliding round the curving flank of the *Plongeur*. Something was sucking him down – the vortex that had tried to claim Avocat and had in fact claimed de Chante! If he fell *off* the submarine, he would be dead in moments.

He hauled himself over onto his front with a slam and slapped at the hull with his empty hands. This did little to slow his precipitous slide, and he knew he must soon fall entirely off. At the edge of his vision he saw the belly of the leviathan rearing up, and caught a glimpse – did he? – of a pyramidic head, and two, gigantic, nightmarish human eyes, with whites and pupils, peering down at him. Then he felt the curve of the hull go vertical underneath him, and he was falling free.

His right hand struck some jut or prop, and grasped it. His shoulder complained, but he clung on, and his body executed a slow, underwater monkey-swing. His left hand reached for the hold, and found it – the airlock hatch. He pulled himself up, set his feet against the side of the hull, and tried to turn it.

It was stiff, and he could hardly gain purchase, but his life depended on the effort, so he pulled again. It turned, turned a little more, and the hatch opened a sliver.

This was enough. He pressed himself through, like a letter going through a slot, and broke through into air.

Gasping, heaving air into his lungs, he pulled the exterior hatch shut behind him. Once again the weird physics of this place had somehow prevented the air in the airlock from simply flooding out, or the water rushing in. There was a spatter mist of water, like rain, swirling through the confined space, but he could breathe – thank Providence, he could breathe! Had the chamber flooded, as it would have done in any terrestrial ocean, he would surely have drowned before he could have opened the inner door. As it was, he collapsed against the side of the space (which was, on account of the orientation of the vessel, below him) and lay for a while simply recovering his breath. His heart was thumping in his chest; the pulse throbbed in his jaw, and this accentuated the pain in his jaw with every throb.

He felt his own face, gingerly. Perhaps the jaw was not actually broken, but it had certainly suffered a potent trauma. The hinge-joint felt tender, and by touch alone Lebret could tell that the right side of his face was much more swollen than the left. The teeth were a different matter; the raw nerve squealed with pain every time he breathed in. The pain would presumably fade, eventually, if only because the nerve had died; but Lebret wondered if it were possible to speed that process up. How does one kill a nerve? Could he, perhaps, reach in and *pinch* it dead? The very thought made him shake with revulsion. Once again he felt his gorge rise.

Still, he thought, *I'm alive. Against all the odds, and the best efforts of Billiard-Fanon, I am still alive.*

He had to decide what to do next. Certainly he couldn't lurk in this intermediary space between ocean and the submarine's interior – quite apart from anything else, the air would soon be used up. But going back into the *Plongeur* remained an unappealing prospect. He could go inside, crawl through to the bridge – but Billiard-Fanon would surely only shoot him again. For a minute or so he pondered the likelihood that Billiard-Fanon had been disarmed and locked in his cabin. Maybe the crew had seen the ensign for the lunatic he was. Perhaps Lebret, were he to reappear, would be greeted joyously, clapped on his shoulder, asked to repeat his incredible story – perhaps given treatment, painkillers, a shot of whisky. This thought made him giddy with hope, but he dismissed it. Illusory. He had to be realistic. Billiard-Fanon had the gun. He was quite mad enough to shoot anybody who challenged him.

No. Going back into the *Plongeur* was not an option. But what else could he do?

His jaw twinged and flared. There was, he decided, only one other possibility. There remained a single diving suit, just on the other side of the inner airlock door. He could take this, swim back along to the breach in the side of the *Plongeur*, and back into the mess. It would be completely flooded by now, of course; but he ought to be able to open the forward hatch and get into the dry forward compartments – if the crazy physics of this place still obtained, he could do so without necessarily letting in too much water. He could get access to the food and drink stowed in the torpedo tubes. And then? Well, then he would have to consider his position.

The pain inside his skull swelled savagely, and slowly fell away from that dolorous intensity. He swore. His thoughts reverted to the strange leviathan that was swimming about the *Plongeur*, and whose gigantic talon had presumably ripped the gigantic hole in the hull. Presumably it was after oxygen, as the cuttlefolk had been. But what if it wanted more? Was it alone? Then, thinking further, Lebret's thoughts went back to de Chante. What *had* happened to that brave sailor, on his dive to repair the ballast tanks? Had there been some cousin of this leviathan, this alien whale, that had noticed him swimming and had snapped him into its jaws?

Then the whole crazy unreality of the situation he was in fell

187

upon Lebret's mind like a landslide. He had started this voyage with only the vaguest intimations that there was anything beneath – or more strictly speaking, *beyond* – the Atlantic. Now he was confronted with the appalling reality of those suspicions. The message had been true. And yet, the truth had been more than he could possibly have imagined, and had cost lives. 'Including mine, more or less,' he said aloud, spitting blood. The strange thing was: water droplets from his body rolled through the air in the small space as if blown by a breeze, but his blood fell fell slowly downward.

The pain brought him back – well, not 'to earth', but to whatever the equivalent was in that place. He had to think practically.

The only illumination in the airlock space came through the little window set in the internal door. It took Lebret a deal of fumbling about, all the while struggling to ignore the debilitating pain in his face, before he found the release catch. Once it was sprung, he was able to spin the wheel and open the door. He tumbled through into the larger chamber.

Awkwardly he got to his feet. It took him longer than it ought to understand why the room looked wrong, and why he could not locate the cupboard with the diving suit inside it. The whole space had been rotated through ninety-degrees (of course!). The cupboard was part of the floor rather than part of the wall.

Pain stabbed through him. It throbbed, coming and going, but the going was never far enough, and the coming excruciating. Lebret shut his eyes and waited. Finally the agony in his mouth abated, even if only a little. When he opened his eyes, Capot was standing in front of him.

Lebret was surprised to see him; but, judging by the colour of the sailor's face, not as surprised as Capot was. 'What—what?' the young man gasped.

'Get out,' said Lebret, without thinking. Blood spattered from his mouth when he spoke. 'You should get out.'

'Why?'

A cold anger swelled inside Lebret. 'Have you seen what is swimming through the waters outside the *Plongeur*?' His words were rendered somewhat indistinct by the swelling in the side of his face, and the slick lubrication of blood inside his mouth. 'Leviathan, larger than earthly whales. Will it swallow us all, whole? Billiard-Fanon called me a Jonah. I suggest he consult the *relevant Biblical passage!*' These last few words were little more than incomprehensible splutters, but they galvanised the terrified-looking Capot. He turned and fled the small space.

He will go and warn Billiard-Fanon, Lebret thought, with a sinking heart. I must work quickly.

He tried to ignore the swelling-withdrawing-swelling agony in his jaw, and brought out the diving suit. Its cold rubbery weight – still wet from its previous wearer – gave it a most unpleasant, flayed-amphibian quality. Lebret's own clothes were sodden; he removed his shoes, and peeled his socks off with an audible smacking sound. Then he took off his trousers, sweater and shirt and rolled them into a bundle around his shoes. He was shivering, but the cold was not unbearable. The sub oceanic sun must have heated the water to a reasonable temperature. He tied the bundle of clothes to the back of the suit with one of its straps, and then pulled the clammy fabric over his legs. It squeaked, as if in pain. With some difficulty he got his arms and body into it. Finally there was the helmet. Lebret examined it – the design was a little different to the rebreathers he'd been trained on during the war – it had been that long since he'd swum underwater. This design was a full face mask that left his head bare at the back. On the side it said, in small letters, *Air Liquide*. 'Necessity,' he told himself, 'is the best drill instructor.' He fitted the miniature rubber anvil mouthpiece between his lips, fiddled with the tank, and breathed in.

He would only need it for the ten minutes it would take him to scramble over the top of the sub, into the now-flooded mess, and through into the forward compartments of the *Plongeur*. As to what he would do then – well, he would deal with that problem when it presented itself. It did not do to think too far into the future. After all, there almost certainly *was* no far future for anybody on the *Plongeur*.

He had to hurry. Cabot must have informed Billiard-Fanon of his presence aboard by now. He was surprised the ensign hadn't come hurrying straight over with his pistol out to finish what he had started.

Lebret fitted himself clumsily back through the airlock, water spraying up through the opening. He pulled the door shut behind him. The outer door opened easily enough, and he squeezed himself out. The added pressure of the water upon his jaw caused the pain to flare. The spike in agony was sharp enough to make him lose concentration; his grip on the edge of the door loosened, and the current – or whatever it was – snatched at his body. Adrenaline skittered through him, and he gripped tight at the lip of metal of the airlock door.

His heart was thudding, but the pain was a little less now. Manoeuvring himself awkwardly he got his feet on the ledge. It did feel, crazily, as if he were standing on a ledge at the top of a tower-block. By all rights, and every law of physics, he ought to be able just to launch himself into the water and swim where he wanted to go. But the invisible sucking current tugged palpably at his legs. Fear gripped him. His teeth sang with pain. Awkwardly, and clinging to the fabric of the submarine, he reached up and put his hand into the intake valve for the airlock chamber.

Pulling himself up was hard, but he was able to bring his left foot high enough up to slip it into the crevice, and from *there* he could push himself up to a place where the slope of the submarine's hull was less precipitous. He stopped. A powerful twinge rang through his injured jaw, resonating inside his skull. He could feel the action of the water as he swished his arm through it; the resistance and fluidity of it. Only minutes earlier, he had been immersed in it, and nearly drowned. Yet now, inside his suit, it felt as if he were standing on a high curving roof in air; as if the slightest misstep and he could fall. Impossible!

'Not the first impossible thing,' he thought to himself. 'Maybe I need to believe – believe and I will be able to swim.'

He centred himself as best he could, tried to concentrate on what he was doing despite the pain he was in, and resumed clambering his way up the C-curve. At one point he slipped back a little, but was able to scrabble back up. Eventually, breathing with hisses and clicks, he got to the top of the metal hill. The blue-white light of the sub oceanic sun was bright enough to cast a fuzzy grey shadow. The leviathan seemed to have departed. But, no – looking up, he could still see it – or see *them* – three of the huge beasts. The bubbles, catching the light and glinting like stars against the blacker upper water. The leviathans turned and threaded the faintly glittery zone, like sharks trying to catch sardines.

Lebret breathed out. Bubbles twisted around his faceplate and neck like slugs. Why didn't they go flying buoyantly upwards? He himself felt the downward tug so forcefully; they ought by the same logic to have sped away upwards. He couldn't say why they didn't. He had to wave his hand to clear the mirror-shapes from his line of sight.

But at last he could see the breach in the side of the vessel. Stepping carefully, he started towards it. There were strange tinny pinging sounds inside his ears. His jaw ached terribly.

A shadow passed over him. Looking round he saw that one of the leviathans was looming up at him. Perhaps it had been lurking behind the far side of the *Plongeur*, or maybe it had darted down from the school above them. But Lebret could see what had excited the beast – the trail of air bubbles, stubbornly refusing to zip up and away. The bubbles *were* rising, but much too slowly, and the effect was to lay a sloping trail of bubbles down towards him. Like a line of breadcrumbs.

Lebret quickened his pace, walking across the 'roof' of the *Plongeur*'s external hull, but it was not easy moving through water, and the effort made him breathe more heavily, which in turn squeezed more pain out of his broken mouth. The next thing he knew, his feet were sliding over the metal of the hull. Somebody had punched him in the small of his back. He went over – lying flat, face down, and swooshing feet-first onwards. The great flank of the leviathan swept past him.

The beast's flipper caught him a second time. With a powerful throb of pain in his jaw, Lebret spun upside down. He saw the long grey arc of the *Plongeur*'s hull passing away from him, and then he felt the tug in his gut as he started to fall.

A beat too late he understood what was happening. Trying to ignore the agony in his face, he thrashed his arms and legs as forcefully as he could – if only he could swim hard enough, surely he could reach the submarine. But the dark-grey wall of metal slipped past, and disappeared above him, and he was sinking hard into the depths.

21

THE CHILDRANHA

For long minutes Lebret surrendered himself to impotent rage – despair and the physical pain fuelling pure *outrage* at the cosmic injustice of it all. He had been so close to getting back inside the *Plongeur*! If fate wanted him dead, why hadn't Billiard-Fanon's bullet simply knocked out his brains? Why survive that assault by a freak chance, and struggle against circumstance and the odds to come within metres of safety... only to have it snatched away at the last moment? For Fate to toy with him, in such a manner – it was too unfair.

But pain is a very wearying thing, and soon enough he ran out of the energy he needed to rage at his circumstance. The emotion that followed rage was a kind of exhausted acceptance. Looking about him, he saw that he was falling directly towards the sub oceanic sun. The water was already warmer around him; he could feel it. Well, he thought to himself; soon I shall be boiled alive like a lobster. Perhaps not a pleasant way to go, but at least it will put a stop to this raging jaw.

With acceptance came a sort of peace, for struggle is a draining thing, and there was a speck of comfort in the thought that it would all soon end. But this was contaminated by the irritation that he would die without solving the mystery that had brought him here. 'It seems I shall not now get to the bottom of it all,' he said aloud inside his mask. Then, although it hurt to move his jaw, he laughed at the idiom. There was no seabed to *this* ocean.

He craned his neck. The *Plongeur* was far above him now,

a black hyphen of metal. The leviathans were distantly visible, swimming about it.

Directly 'below' him was the sun, now too bright to look at directly. If it is drawing me down with its gravity, he thought, then why is it not drawing the *Plongeur* too? We ought to be falling at the same rate. But, then again, if gravity operated at all in this strange liquid place, then the hundreds of thousands of kilometres of water above him ought to be creating enough pressure to squash him to the size of a sugar-lump. None of it made sense; and soon he would die. Which meant that it would *never* make sense. For some reason this struck him as funny, and he laughed a strangulated, hissing sort of laugh.

He was pleasantly warm, now; like a man in a hot bath. Soon, he knew, it would become scorching.

For a long time he simply sank through the waters. He lost the sense that he was in motion, as if he were simply hanging motionless in the fluid medium. But he knew he was descending. From time to time he would look into the depths below him; each time the sub oceanic sun was unmistakeably larger.

The passage of time became complicated, hard to parse. Breaths, heartbeats, motion. The throb in his wounded jaw. What did all mean? We descend all the time, and the bottom of the ocean is called death.

There was motion in the water below him. Soon enough this motion was all around him. Cuttlefolk? No – these creatures were small. The cuttlefolk, with their great trailing capes of external gills, were man-sized; these were smaller. Child-sized. Shoals swarmed below him, but an arc of the creatures was swimming towards him. They were too far away for Lebret to make out details about their physique; but then – abruptly – they were almost upon him, and he caught a glimpse of wide-mouths, and zig-zag teeth, and snapping jaws. They were upon him, in a feeding frenzy. But the most disturbing thing about them was that these alarming-looking befanged mouths were set in faces that had the round blandness of children's faces.

There were five, six, seven of them – Lebret was too startled to be able to count, as they circled and snapped and darted at him. But they looked horribly like children in shape and size. Except for the teeth. He felt a mantrap seize upon his leg, a row of diamond teeth sharp digging through the fabric of the diving suit. Another was at his hand – he flapped the arm, frantically. A third lunged at his face, black eyes and small-snout horribly reminiscent of a child's moon face. He cried out – he couldn't help himself. Panic possessed him. Bubbles spooled from his regulator, and bulged into the space between himself and the giant piranha-like childfish. The air made the creature reel back, twisting frantically as if stung.

Enough of Lebret's presence of mind remained for him to grasp what had happened. It was the same effect air bubbles had had upon the cuttlefolk – they craved it, but at the same time it burnt them. These children-piranha must be related beasts.

One of the creatures was tearing at the pack of rolled up clothes on his back; Lebret could feel the sharp little tugs. Another was biting at his shoulder. Teeth ripped through the suit and punctured his skin.

Cupping both hands together, Lebret scooped some air back and did his best to fling it over his shoulder. The fish immediately relinquished its bite. He brought up his leg – there were two of the childranha-things fixed on his flesh like dogs with a bone – he waved bubbles down towards them. They opened their jaws and spun away as if shot.

The next minute Lebret had sunk below the level of the swarming monsters. He gasped. Looking up he could see a great knot of the beasts darting into and flinching away from the nest of bubbles he had left behind him. Blood was leaking through the punctures in his leg of his suit, but the ribbons of black-red stayed swirling alongside him, unlike the bubbles, that rose slowly up – or rather, that stayed in the water whilst *he* sank down.

He was holding his breath. To exhale would be to emit a necklace of bubbles about him and draw the childranha upon him again. But he couldn't hold his breath indefinitely! And, looking below him – the sub oceanic sun much larger, brighter and hotter below his feet – he saw a great mass of the things, like insects swarming.

Being boiled alive was horrible enough; but the thought of being torn into lumps of flesh by these monsters was incomparably worse. He ran his hands up and down his suit, and found a small knife inside a pocket on his thigh. It seemed a pitifully insignificant weapon against such numbers of sharp-toothed monsters.

As he sank further towards the seething mass of them, he saw the carcass of a leviathan, floating at an angle. The childranha were feeding upon it, great waves of the creatures breaking upon its flanks, tearing chunks and darting away. What looked like convection patterns flowed through the swarm. Lebret could even see shudders pass along the massive, fleshy flanks of the beast as the monsters collided with it and ripped mouthfuls away.

Was this, Lebret wondered, good news for him? Perhaps the beasts would be so caught up in their feeding frenzy that he could slip past them unnoticed (to – he added, with a rueful inner voice – fall into the sun instead of being eaten alive – only very marginally the better of two horrible fates). Or perhaps the presence of such a large meal, surely a rare occurrence in the life-cycle of the creatures, would have driven them into an ecstasy of violence, and any morsel that passed would be shredded? For all he knew, the childranha were peaceful sluggish fish most of the time, and it was only the presence of this whale-sized feast that had roiled them up.

It was fruitless to wonder. Another spasm of pain passed through his jaw. He would find out soon enough. And then, because Lebret had been trained to think dialectically, he found himself arguing the contrary position. Might it not be better for the fish to get him? Clearly it would be painful to be torn to pieces, but it would be over quickly – and was he not already in pain? On the other hand, if he escaped the fish, there was every chance that his death would be as protracted and horrible as a witch being burnt alive at the stake.

Something swam past him, several metres below; and at almost exactly the same time a shape lurched towards his face.

He glimpsed twin zig-zag lines of teeth, and two close-set dolls' eyes, and then he slashed out with the knife.

The blade struck home, and the creature danced away; but the impact knocked the knife from his hand. He cursed aloud, and looked down to watch the metal blade sinking through the water below him. It wasn't there. Almost too late he looked up – there was the knife, floating very slowly upwards. He reached out and grabbed it, missed his grip, tried again and took hold of it.

He examined the blade, holding it close to his face-plate. Definitely metal. It clearly *was* falling; but equally it wasn't falling quite as quickly as he was himself. But why should it fall through the water less rapidly than he, with his lungs full of buoyant air? It was nonsensical. This was an Alice-in-Wonderland dimension.

Suddenly Lebret began to laugh. It was all absurd, simply absurd! Below his boots, the leviathan carcass was growing larger. The granulated waves crashing against its side and recoiling were acquiring definition, resolving into the great clusters of individual flesh-eating fish that they were.

'En garde!' Lebret cried in his best 'Three Musketeers' manner, ignoring the pain in his jaw. 'Have at you!' He brandished the small knife.

A flag fluttered slowly below him, black against the blue-white light. It coiled away, folded up to became almost invisible; then it unfurled again. It seemed to be floating up towards him; but, Lebret knew, that was in illusion – it was actually hanging in the water as he sank towards it. He came within ten metres of it before he saw it for what it was.

It was a ripped and opened-out stretch of the fabric out of which diving suits were made.

There was no mistaking it. Lebret knew it instantly for what it was; and what it meant. De Chant had passed this way, encountered the childranha, and then had been pulled out of his suit and devoured.

'Well,' Lebret said. 'So now I know!'

He was heading towards the largest concentration of the beasts. It would soon be over.

The stretch of ruined wetsuit folded and unfolded slowly in the eddies caused by the massed motion of the fish below.

Lebret drew a deep breath into his lungs, and tried to centre himself. He had been many things in his life, including spy; but he had also once been a soldier. And one great virtue of being trained as a soldier is that it teaches you how best to meet death. The best way to meet death is: *fighting*.

One moment Lebret was sinking through the clear, bright-lit water, and the chaos of the childranha feeding frenzy was below him. The next he plunged, boot-first, right into the midst of it. It was not possible to select individual targets. He swung his knife about him in a rapid series of arcs.

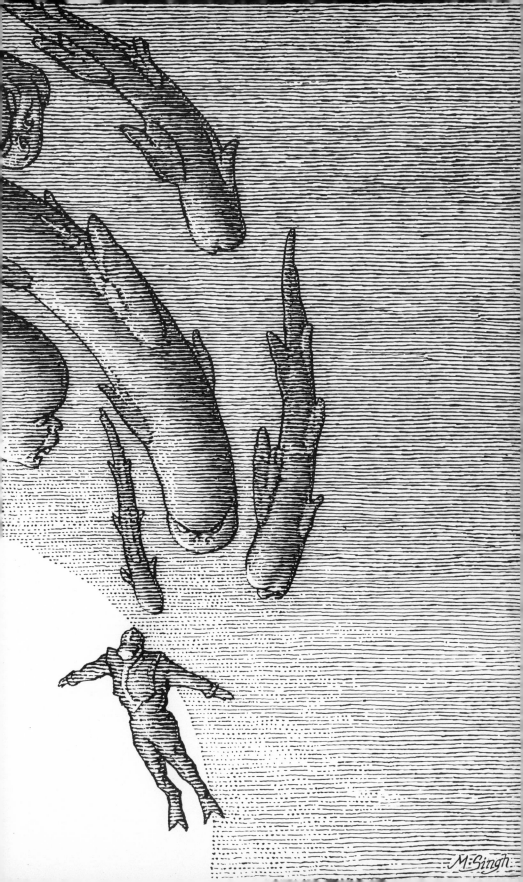

22

THE FATHOMLESS DEPTHS

❛ ❛ ❛ ❛ ❛ ❛

The light from the sun was extinguished. Lebret entered the vale of shadow. He felt motion all around him as turbulence in the water, and as myriad bumps and knocks. The wave of childranha surged past him, swimming as one towards the leviathan. Lebret felt a dozen sharp points of pain, and lashed out as well as he could with his knife. But they were all over him – biting through his suit at his legs and arms, at his neck and stomach.

There was a powerful and sudden pain in his left calf. He drew his legs up to his chest so as to able to bring his knife within reach, and cut down at the beast that was biting there. The blade slid easily into its flesh, and the creature released its bite, but the damage was done – a chunk of leg-meat bitten away. The intensity of the pain surprised Lebret. He would not have said that he had become *accustomed* to the pain in his jaw, and his skull still rang with acute physical suffering; but this new hurt was savage enough to drown out even that.

It roused him. He thrashed left and right, up and down with his little knife, yelling. With the cry a great caul of air was released from his regulator, and the childranha at his neck and chest reeled away with muscular twists of their tails. With his right hand he stabbed down over and again, and with his left hand he scooped and waved as much of the air downwards as he could.

All around him the light was dappled by the throng of fish in motion. It was loud in his ears, the flutter and drum-roll noise.

He was buffeted. New points of pain stabbed in at him, on his shoulder blade, on his arm, on his left foot.

And then, as suddenly as he had entered the school, he dropped below it. The fish swarmed above him, a shimmering dark ceiling of living creatures an arm's length above – and then ten metres above him – and then twenty. One beast remained, its teeth sunk agonisingly into Lebret's left foot. Gasping, he stabbed at it, cutting it in several places before it let go to lollop off through the water, upwards, to join its fellows.

Lebret hardly had time to take stock. He could still breathe, that was one thing – it was a miracle none of the monsters had severed his air-line. But he ached in a dozen places, and his left leg was the site, at calf and foot, of two raging foci of pain that rivalled his broken jaw in their intensity.

The water around him was now very hot. He was sweating inside the face-plate; and his suit, now shredded and tattered, offered little protection against the scalding water. At least it was – evidently – too hot for the childranha; although that was meagre enough comfort. The sub oceanic sun was large and very bright, directly below him. There was no doubt that he was falling directly towards it.

'Should I pray?' he said aloud. Thoughts of his first communion returned to him – childhood Sundays in church, the old familiar words. But that would be a betrayal of the dialectical materialism that had subsequently converted him. And even the superstitious core of his mind, the part that rationality and maturity can never quite eradicate – even that remnant of his childish belief could not accept that the God of Abraham and Jesus was present *down here*. Wherever *here* was, he had travelled very far from the sites holy to that Deity. Maybe he should pray to a new god? Some alien Neptune?

But how would he know which was the true suboceanic power?

Lebret grew still hotter. He became aware that he was very thirsty, and then he considered how strange to be so thirsty whilst surrounded by water. 'But a man cannot drink brine,' he muttered to himself, his jaw creaking and sparking with pain as he moved it. Then he remembered – this was no terrestrial ocean – this was another body of water altogether, and not salty. He *could* drink it, if he wished to. All he needed to do was remove his face-plate; but if he did that, then he would drown. And anyway, this water was too hot. What he wanted was a cold glass, with ice-cubes in it. Or a beer! A cold beer, transparent pimples of moisture on the outside of the bottle, that little exhalation of visible gas, like breath, when the lid was prised off.

His eyes were closing of their own accord. He had to will himself to keep them open. But why was he bothering to do that? There was nothing to see, now, but brightness. His mouth was dry, although his face was runny with sweat.

And then he became aware of a new sensation, deep in his gut. It was like driving a car in a straight line, and then cornering. He felt tugged from true.

It was weird, but undeniable. His whole body thrummed, his limbs trembled.

Slowly, like a blimp banking and drifting through the air, the sun moved.

'Galileo Galilei!' gasped Lebret. But there was no mistaking it – the sun was hauling itself away to the right. The water was desperately hot. Lebret squeezed his eyes shut – for an intense moment he wanted, more than anything in the world, to be able to pull off his face-mask, to rub his face with a towel. It itched almost unbearably. But he resisted the impulse to fiddle with his mask, and shortly the urge passed.

Slowly, very slowly, the sun swung about until it was away to his right. He knew he was still dropping through the water, but it was difficult to grasp the passage of time. Maybe he slept, or passed out, or something.

The next thing he knew was the flicker of movement below him. Somehow he had fallen past the sun – and that meant that he would soon fall back into the sphere occupied by the childranha.

But he felt a little more alert. The water was still hot, but less so. He looked down upon his own body, the diving suit ripped and torn in two dozen places. At least, he thought, I have descended further than de Chante managed, the poor fellow.

An idea occurred to him. He tucked his knife back into its little pocket, and used both hands to scoop air bubbles and smooth them over his skin. Little patches and pearls of air caught in the folds and rips of his suit and stayed there, glinting like silver. He worked carefully, like a cat grooming itself, and managed to spread a layer of air over most of his body. It was not a continuous covering, and it might prove useless in protecting him against the creatures – but perhaps it was better than nothing.

He brought out his knife again. For a while he amused himself by holding it down by his knees, letting go of the blade and watching it float up his body before grabbing it again. As if it were made of wood instead of iron! There must be some explanation for this mystery.

The motion below him was intermittent; no great swarms of the creatures moved below him – there being, he supposed, no great feast of dead leviathan flesh to draw them. Perhaps the bulk of the population of childranha has swum round and above, to where the food was. But there were still some down there. Lebret readied himself.

Time passed. The water began to cool. He could feel it.

A single fish lurched up at him, teeth flashing. He swept the knife in an arc in front of his chest, but the beast seemed to misjudge Lebret's location in the water, and swept past him. He twisted his head, his jaw complaining at the action. He could *hear* as well as see the scissory snip-snap of the thing's jaws in the water. It was biting at his blood, a scarf-life dissipating trail which was accompanying his descent. Why should his blood sink through the water faster than an iron knife-blade?

Lebret wriggled in the water, and rotated his position, to bring his blade to bear. But the fish was out of range, and seemed uninterested in him.

A line of three childranha snaked up at him from his left; he thrashed out with his boot and connected with one's snout – the odd little button protrusion in the middle of its circular face. It didn't like that, reeled away. But another swerved in and fixed its teeth in at the open wound in Lebret's calf. He swore, and slashed out with the knife.

The blade cut deep into the beast's back, severing its spine. This had the unfortunate effect of clamping the creature's teeth into Lebret's flesh in a death-rictus. He howled again, and tried to get the knife blade in to prise the jaws open. Other childranha were zeroing in on him, swimming up from the left and right.

One of the creatures swept up towards Lebret's face, but was forced away by the air. Three or four more went for his wounded leg and foot; but two of these bit into the body of the dead fish already attached there. They began worrying at the corpse, which shook Lebret's limbs and body painfully. The others darted off.

He slashed out again, and with two deep jabs he cut away the bulk of the body of the dead beast. The decapitated chunk slipped upwards past him, trailing black blood into the water, and the childranha all went after it. Only one remained, nipping at the diving-suit fabric, and Lebret was able to dislodge it.

Soon enough he was sinking into cooler, darker water, and the unwanted attentions of the childranha were behind him – or above him.

He pulled up his hurt left leg, tucked it into his stomach, the better to be able to work into the attached head of the fish with his knife blade. Trying to lever the teeth from their grip had little effect, apart, that is, from sending stabs of agony up and down his limb. He changed tack, and dug into the side of the creature's jaw, gouging out chunks of matter that slipped up past him. Soon enough he exposed the cartilaginous skull of the thing, and with a few quick stabs he broke open the hinge of the jaw. Then, stowing the knife carefully in its pouch, he prised the two portions apart, and pulled the teeth from their puncture wounds. It was unpleasant work, and sent sparkles of sharper pain shooting over the backdrop of more general agony.

Blood seeped from the leg. But there was nothing he could do about that, and the exsanguination was not too severe.

Lebret looked around him. Craning his head back, he could

see the suboceanic sun above him, and the glittery shimmer of its attendant life forms swirling and swimming. Below, though, was only darkness.

It occurred to Lebret that he had escaped two very unpleasant deaths – being torn to pieces and being boiled alive – only to encounter a third: asphyxiation. Eventually the air in his tank would run out, and he would choke. He could simply wait for that grim eventuality. Or he could simply pull the mask from his face and drown.

He smiled.

It was not possible to know how long he sank through those waters. It felt like days, but he doubted the three narrow tanks on his back contained so much air. Incrementally the water darkened around him, and chilled. There was a period when this was pleasant, after the scorching water above; but soon enough he was shivering. He was weak with thirst and prolonged pain, and presumably from blood-loss too; but he was also wholly and completely alone.

Down he went, eternally. His whole body was in pain. Soon enough the thirst grew so intense that he decided to risk removing his face mask.

He took a breath, pushed the mouthpiece out with his tongue and mask up just a little. The weird physics of this ocean meant that the air inside the mask did not bubble and gush away as he did this. In fact almost no water got inside the mask. Still holding his breath, Lebret gulped one, two, three mouthfuls of water. It was cold, and piqued pain from his hurt jaw, but it tasted clean, unsalty – even delicious. He was able to replace the mask and start breathing again without hiccough.

Assuaging his thirst provided only temporary respite, however. It allowed the many other aches and agonies of his battered body to press upon his consciousness. His jaw raged; his left leg was a string of separate little agonies; there were nicks and bruises all over his body.

It was darker still, and colder. Down, further down, and deeper…

Lebret dozed. He was not aware of falling asleep; and only knew that he had because he dreamt of monster-fish swarming up at him, and woke with a start to find himself scrabbling for his knife. But there were no fish, and he recognised the sensation – of sudden awakening – for what it was.

Soon enough his heart settled.

He pondered his situation. Was there any way he could work it exactly how much air he had? He tried wriggling to look over his own shoulder at the tanks, but the valves and dials were not accessible. He hung in the nothingness for a while, and a sensation of despondency stirred inside him. Surely it was demeaning merely to wait, passively, for his fate? But what else could he do?

His leg had stopped bleeding, at any rate. This was hard to see, for the light had dimmed almost to total black, but he could just about see detail in his own shadowy limbs. Tipping his head back, and ignoring the twinges the motion sent along his wounded jaw, he could make out the sub oceanic sun as a smudgy dot of brightness. But all around was murky. The dark material of the diving suit merged with the surrounding blackness, and his pale skin, visible through rents in the cloth, gleaming faintly, gave back the impression of a disconnected spread of oddly shaped items. As if his body had been metamorphosed into a shoal.

He thought back to the *Plongeur*, far above him now. How were they faring aboard that submarine? Billiard-Fanon had the pistol. He had probably shot Ghatwala by now, and possibly Jhutti too – poor, blameless Amanpreet Jhutti, who knew nothing about the message, or the real agenda behind Lebret and Ghatwala's involvement in the voyage. Still, everybody aboard that particular experimental French Naval Vessel would be dead soon, so their murders were almost inconsequential.

His mind drifted. Without sensory inputs he found his mind defocusing. Random memories spilled-in. A sensory deprivation tank – the KGB had showed him one of those, in Termez. They said: Moscow colleagues still favour the old Cossack brutalities: beatings and fingernail-wrenchings and the judicious application of electrical shocks. But – (Lebret could picture him now; a corpulent KGB officer called Seleznyov, with an oriental cast to his features, a fat black beard and bald brow with conch-like wrinkles curving upon it) – but, Seleznyov said, down here we have discovered that this simple box works better. Not for everyone. Mystics and Chinese are hardly touched by it. But Westerners (and here, Seleznyov eyed Lebret saucily) can't bear it. Left alone with nothing but their decadent thoughts! They break. After a couple of days, bring them back out of the box and they'll answer any question rather than go back inside.

Am I in such a box? Lebret wondered. The blackness was deeper now; the glimmers became fainter, and then were swallowed by the crow-coloured water. But sensory deprivation was impossible – the pain in his jaw, and to a slightly lesser extent in his left leg, kept agitating his mind, and refused to let him settle.

He was conscious, or not, or he was on some borderline between the two states of mind. It hardly mattered any more. He was sinking down and down. He fantasised about finally arriving at the ocean floor of this alien sea, and standing upon it. But there was no bottom. He would soon die, and then his corpse would sink forever through this infinite body of black water.

He thought about the native life forms. The disturbingly *human* quality they betrayed. A random chance, thrown up by a different evolutionary line? Uncanny, certainly. Were they terrestrial forms of life that had slipped through the same crack that had brought the *Plongeur* here? It was possible.

His mind wandered. He did not sleep, but hung for a long time conscious of nothing but the acid sensation of pain within his own body. He was grimly impressed by his own nervous system's persistence. He felt like crying out: 'Alright! You have made your point! I understand! Torn skin – broken bones – yes, yes, *I get it*! There is no need to go on so!' But the body does not listen to such entreaty.

The sun above him had become only a faint star, casting no illumination. Then he lost sight of it altogether. He was in perfect blackness.

Down and down and down.

How would he know that the air was going bad? Would he begin to hallucinate? Would he last long enough to drift into the ambit of a third sub oceanic sun, with who knows what horrific native fishy monsters circling it like planets in outer space? Surely not! He tried, for a while, breathing shallowly, to conserve such air supply as he had. But then he thought, what is the point in postponing the inevitable? Then he considered simply taking charge of his destiny, putting an end to his physical torment and committing suicide. But something held him back. A residual Catholicism? It hardly mattered. He did not believe that God was here, about to scoop him into his giant hand and press him to his tender breast. That could never be. Whether he acted or did not act was equally irrelevant.

Below him something was glimmering, very faint but definitely there. A monster of the deep? Lebret's heart began to thud in his breast. The shape loomed closer, acquired definition.

It was a gigantic hand, glowing faintly. It was a hundred metres long – *twice* a hundred metres, the fingers pressed together, reaching beneath him to catch.

Lebret felt a flash of panic. He couldn't have explained why – except the thought that a human form of titanic proportions (if that was his *hand*, then how big must the *whole body* be!) was somehow here, in this fantastically distant and alien sea – that this entity was reaching out to catch him, Alain Lebret, out of all the morsels falling through the water... Somehow this terrified him.

He began to wriggle, to struggle. It hurt to kick out with his left leg, but he thrashed with his right and crawled at the water with his arms. Perhaps he could swim so as to miss the giant hand.

He was closer to it now. Then, with a rush, he was level with it – it horizoned him, gleaming pink-white, and he landed *upon* it, actually touched down. The substance was hard, but not wholly unyielding; something dense and packed, like coral. Whatever it was, it was not flesh.

Lebret hit the surface like a parachutist reaching the ground. It jarred through his wounded foot, and sent a shock of pain up his spine; but he rolled with the blow and sprawled sideways upon it.

23

THE HAND

● ● ● ● ● ●

Fear had nested inside Lebret now. He was not acting rationally.
You might think he would be grateful to have found a platform –
somewhere to stand, instead of continuing to fall through infinite
water forever. But he was not thinking in any logical way about
his situation. He felt a grip of certainty that the hand was about
to fold over, to close into a fist with him in the middle – that it
was going to crush him. In that moment such a fate scared him
more profoundly than being burnt to death in a suboceanic sun,
or devoured by the childranha.

He got to his feet, and ran towards the edge of the hand. It was
that comical, slow-motion underwater running – yet, he *did* move,
his feet striking the platform below him and gaining a degree of
traction. It did not take him long to get to the edge, and then he
hurled himself free of the shape, to sink once again through the
infinite depths. Better that, than...

Than what?

He did not sink.

The glimmering shape of the gigantic, outstretched hand
hovered a couple of metres away and a metre above him. At first
he assumed it was falling with him; but the tug in his gut was
absent. More, the pain in his jaw was markedly less than it had
been.

He floated in the water for a little. Though there was very little
light, it was possible to see the underside of the hand. This was
enough to see that it wasn't a hand at all. It was, on the contrary,

a huge conch shell – improbably massive, but recognisably marine, nevertheless.

Cautiously kicking out with his good leg, Lebret swam up through the water. Once he was above the level of the giant spread-out scallop he felt the tug resume, and in a moment he was drawn back down onto the platform.

He stood up, feeling calmer. Regarding it now, he was surprised he had ever thought that this structure was a hand: its fan-shape and the broad, shallow flutes all leading towards its tapering end – all this said 'shell' very clearly. Yet it did not appear to be made of shell-stuff. Crouching down, Lebret poked at the substance with his bare fingers. It felt firm, with only a slightly spongy give to it, as if constructed of close-packed fibres. It had a consistency somewhere between stone and plastic.

He stood up again. He felt light-headed. Perhaps his air was finally running out. Perhaps all this was a hallucination – a dying man's vision. If so, Lebret thought, then I might as well explore it.

He made his way along the length of the gigantic scallop shape, towards its narrow end. The light grew a little brighter, and soon enough he saw why – in at the stem of the giant shell was a circle of light, a metre or so wide. Bending down, he looked into this.

It was a window.

On the far side was a circular corridor leading down, a clean white colour, lit with lamps inset into its walls. There was no ladder, and the corridor stretched many metres before opening out into – Lebret peered, trying to make out – a larger chamber.

He felt around the rim of this window with his fingers, and, as in a dream, found a catch. It pulled easily, and the window slid away. Lebret reached inside, through a wall of standing water and into air.

There seemed little point in delaying. Lebret thrust his head through the hole, out of water and into the air. The rest of his body followed and his sense of up-and-down deserted him. He was floating head down, except that it didn't feel that way. It felt as if the corridor had swung about. There was plenty of room to bring his legs about, and look back where he had come – the water was a membrane, bleeding spits and dribbles into the corridor, but otherwise not penetrating. There was a little red-button in by the rim. Lebret pushed this and the window slid back into place.

He pulled off his mask, and sniffed the air cautiously. It seemed breathable. Indeed, it tasted a good deal sweeter than the stuff in his tank.

The pain in his jaw was much reduced; although, as if following some pitiless cosmic logic of the balance of pain, the wounds in his leg and foot seemed sharper and more defined.

He wriggled free of the triple tank, and pressed his wet hair against his scalp. Droplets of water floated all around him.

'Hello?' he called, wincing as his jaw complained at the movement. 'Who is there?'

There was no reply. Well, there was no point in coming this far and then loitering in the corridor. Lebret put his palms on the smooth white sides, pressed with his good foot on the other side, and propelled himself along.

The corridor was longer than it had appeared from outside; but eventually Lebret came to the end, and passed through into a large, bulb-shaped chamber.

It was approximately the size of a two-storey house, without internal walls or divisions but with shelves, oriented variously, and with diverse items of mechanical or technological cast upon them. The space, like the corridor, was white-coloured and clean; and on the far side a large circular bulge shimmered dark-grey – water, Lebret assumed. But he took hardly any of this in, because the room's occupant so startled and alarmed him.

That occupant was a human head, three or four times the conventional proportions. So monstrous was this apparition, indeed, that Lebret stared for a long time before registering the entity's body at all – a regular-sized body, with a plump stomach, but with four legs in addition to the conventional two arms. At the end of each of the four legs was flat and broad appendage, more like a paddle than a human foot.

The being's face was unmistakably human: dark brown of skin, with a nose so large and pronouncedly aquiline it almost resembled a shark's fin. The eyes, though comparatively small in the broad face, were bright and alert. They were old eyes. There was no mistaking that about them. The forehead was smooth and broad, the black hair slicked back into a queue. The oddest thing about this individual – his size aside – was his beard. It looked like a regular beard, although unusually bushy and capacious, the strands of hair coiling and twisting in the zero-gravity of that strange place. But Lebret looked again and saw that the individual strands of the being's beard were not hair, but rather twisting tentacular filaments, moving not with any random action but purposefully, deliberately. The beard coiled and moved before the strange being's face.

This person (for I suppose we must call him a person) looked at Lebret. The beard shifted, opening a gap through which a wide mouth and little peg-like, wide-set teeth were visible.

'My dear fellow,' said the being, in flawless French. 'What on earth has happened to *you*?'

'Dakkar?' gasped Lebret, feeling woozy.

'Good gracious, your leg! And your face! What has happened to your face? And where – and where is everybody else?' He floated towards Lebret, accompanied by little squirting noises. The beard folded its myriad fronds about the mouth. Lebret, unable to prevent himself flinching away, noticed that the tentacles were all covered in tiny beads of water.

'I'm sorry, Monsieur,' said Lebret, tears springing in at his eyes. 'You are too – repulsive to – too repulsive to—'

'Come!' insisted Dakkar. His voice was high-pitched, even squeaky, and at odds with the over-sized head through which it emerged. 'You must have medical attention for your wounds!'

24

DAKKAR

🌑 🌑 🌑 🌑 🌑 🌑

Dakkar led him to the other side of the chamber, and dived into the bubble of water. Lebret was shuddering. There was something unpleasantly insectile about the fellow's motion – quite apart from his hideous appearance. The urge to flee was strong within him; but where would he go? Back onto the corridor to wear again the breathing apparatus (surely out of air, now) and into the black sea? His leg was raw with pain; at a dozen places his body ached and stung – most of all, he was exhausted.

Soon enough Dakkar reappeared. Shedding beads of water to float weightlessly in the air, his beard twisting monstrously, he scuttled over to where Lebret waited. 'Here,' he offered. 'It is the best I can offer by way of analgesic.'

He passed over a small, squishy object, like a marshmallow or a child's sweet. Lebret did not even pause. Why should he? He chewed the thing – it was sweet to taste – and then spoke. 'Can I have a drink?'

'The entire universe here is potable!' Dakkar replied. 'Surely you have discovered that? If you are thirsty, drink from the pool.' He gestured to the bulge of water through which he had recently emerged. Though Dakkar's arm was normal size, and the head disproportionate, the lack of any other visual clues kept tricking Lebret into seeing him as a normal man with a hideously wizened and shrunken body.

'In a moment,' Lebret gasped.

'What is your name?'

'Lebret.'

'Well, Monsieur Lebret. Let me examine you,' Dakkar said, bringing his enormous face close. His beard smelled strange; not excessively unpleasant, but unusual – an oily, or sour smell. Lebret was simultaneously fascinated and repelled by the ghastly motion of its component strands.

'You are Dakkar?' he asked.

'Call me that, by all means,' replied Dakkar. 'What happened to your mouth?'

'A man called Billiard-Fanon,' Lebret said, wincing at the plosives, 'shot me.'

'Shot you? With a gun?' Dakkar asked. Lebret nodded. 'Shot you with a gun *in the mouth*? Why then, you are a lucky individual! Such a thing should have been fatal.'

'Your beard,' Lebret gasped.

'It is strange to you,' Dakkar said, distractedly, angling his giant face left and right. 'Permit me?' He touched the outside of Lebret's wounded jaw with his hands – an old man's hands, wrinkled and spotted, not in keeping with the stretched, smooth appearance of the skin of his face. 'There is a crack in the bone of the jaw, I think,' he said. 'And several teeth have been knocked out. Well, well, I will heal it, as well as I can ... the crack, I mean. The teeth are gone. Not milk teeth either! They'll not grow back, on their own!'

'I did not think you a dentist,' Lebret muttered.

'Oh, don't misunderstand me – I *can* fix your teeth. But with a cartilaginous material, not with bone. It would be easy, but you might not like the results. From a cosmetic perspective, I mean.'

'I can live without a few teeth,' said Lebret, wondering what on earth Dakkar meant.

'Let me look at the leg. Please – take off this diving suit. It is so tattered and ripped it will fall apart soon, anyway.'

'I am,' said Lebret, pausing, 'reluctant.'

'This is no place for your pudeur!' declared Dakkar. 'Look at me! You think I care for appearances, or for bourgeois convention? Unless you mean to say that it is too cold in here?'

As a matter of fact, it was exactly the right temperature. Lebret said, 'It is not that. Only ...'

'Come! Think of me as a doctor.'

Slowly, Lebret began to peel off his shredded suit. Dakkar examined his leg. 'The flesh of the calf should present no problem; but there are some scraps gouged from the bones of your right foot.'

'It was – bitten.'

Dakkar smiled. The strands of his beard parted to reveal a satchel of some kind, slung across his chest. From this he brought out two oval shapes of a fabric Lebret did not recognise. He applied one to each of the two larger wounds on Lebret's leg. They felt slimier and more substantial than bandage cloth. He did not enquire more closely.

The pain was shrinking within him. 'Your analgesic is very effective,' he reported.

'Yes. You must not move your jaw unnecessarily, however. You will need to rest it, for the normal healing processes to work. It will take some time.'

Lebret stared at him. 'What happened,' he asked, 'to your head? You were not born so?'

At this Dakkar laughed aloud. 'Certainly not! I would have been displayed in every freak show from Abbottabad to Kerala! No, no, this has grown over the last several decades.'

'Why?'

'Partly to allow for the increased density and number of cellular connections, as is required by my greatly enhanced capacity for mentation. Although, partly, it is a function of other enhancements. You are fascinated by my beard?'

'Repelled,' groaned Lebret. 'But – yes, fascinated too.'

'The actual component tendrils are wired-in, if you permit the metaphor, to my frontal cortex – the nerve bundles run up here,' he touched his temples, beside his eyes, with both hands.

'Why?'

'It helps with both future planning and memory. When you get to my age, M'sieur, you need as much help as you can get! But the beard has other functions. It is a large surface area, which is easy to saturate with water, which in turn keeps my mouth and lungs moist when I am, as I now am, in air.'

'Air is no longer your natural element?'

'I am perfectly comfortable in air,' Dakkar insisted. 'But consider the nature of the universe we currently inhabit! Water is ubiquitous.'

'You undertook these … alterations yourself?'

'I have acquired many skills,' said Dakkar, evasively. 'Many skills. Although I am not so talented as to—' He trailed off.

'It is monstrous,' Lebret moaned, looking away.

'You'll soon get used to it. Now, tell me. Where is everybody else?'

'Everybody else?'

'You will not tell me,' insisted Dakkar, 'that you swam all the way down here in that raggedy diving suit?'

'The *Plongeur* you mean?'

'Is that the name you have given the submarine?'

'What do you know about the submarine?'

'I didn't know its name!' Dakkar laughed again. 'I could tell you its *mass* however, to the last gram.'

The pain had almost entirely gone from Lebret's face and leg, now. He was aware only very distantly of an achy tinge to the right side of jaw. He rubbed his eyes. 'I don't understand,' he confessed.

'You disappoint me,' said Dakkar, shaking his huge head slowly. He floated a little further off, and said. 'You must have known – all of you, inside the *Plongeur*, that you had passed beyond the limit of terrestrial oceans? You must have determined that you were inside a cosmos of water?'

'We,' said Lebret. 'Or I presumed so.'

'Well then! How was it that you still had weight? How was it that the *Plongeur* continued – plunging? Eh?'

'I don't know. We did not know.'

'It is a simple matter of deduction,' said Dakkar, rebukingly. 'Clearly something was drawing you onward. Down, if you wish to call it that.'

225

Lebret forced himself to look again at Dakkar's huge face. 'You,' he said.

'Indeed.'

Something was teeter-tottering inside Lebret's consciousness. He felt as if were about to swoon. 'How?' he asked.

'As to how,' said Dakkar, 'it is a little complicated. I fastened onto calcium with a draw of a certain force; and at the same time I fastened onto *iron* – in the vessel's hull and fittings – with a slightly lesser force. Take the latter away from the former and you have the simulated gravity that enabled you to walk about the decks of your submarine craft.'

'But,' Lebret said again. 'How?'

'Not with any *direct* connection, obviously,' said Dakkar. 'Not after the manner of a radio signal, or anything like that. When you first emerged here, you were many hundreds of thousands of kilometres away. Have you heard of infraspace?'

'No.'

'It may be a matter of terminology. Well, well. Things that happen in material space, the four dimensions we all inhabit – here, or back on earth. But equal-and-opposite things happen on the other side of the dividing line, in infraspace. It is dimensional, but configured according to a rather different logic. Anyway, anyway, let me not *lecture* you. The drawing-down force I applied to you operates via infraspace, at any rate. I isolated calcium on the one hand, since it is very rare in this place – except, of course, in *your* skeletons! Iron is rare too. I created traction and drew those elements to me. That would bring you soon enough down to me.'

'But why?'

'Why? My dear fellow! Without it, you'd have been drifting around aimlessly for immemorial ages! How would you have found me? Although –' Dakkar floated a little closer, and looked again at Lebret's jaw, '– it must have *tugged* most painfully upon your broken bone. I am sorry! I had no notion.'

'Calcium?'

'Yes, metals are rare here. The heavy elements, generally speaking, are rare. In the vacuum cosmos they are formed inside

226

supernovae, you know. But there is not an equivalent phenomenon here. Hence, iron too ... there's precious little of that.'

Lebret's temper sparked. 'You nearly *dragged* us into one of these strange sub oceanic suns!' he complained.

'Yes,' agreed Dakkar, nodding slowly. 'I am sorry about that. There were two stars between here and where you were – and though small, they both exerted a distorting effect within infraspace. Equal and opposite, you see. It means that the geometrical connection between the scallop shell and the metals it was tuned-to became ... a little twisted about. I hope you didn't become too overheated? There isn't a way of threading the connection entirely past the stars, I'm afraid.'

'We were attacked,' Lebret said. '*I* was attacked!'

'Ah, the life forms, the ecosystems, yes, I can well believe it. They did that to your leg and foot, I suppose? Yes, yes, I'm sorry. There's nothing I can, ah, *do* about them, I'm afraid. Even the Great Jewel has more or less abandoned them to themselves.'

'I do not understand,' Lebret complained.

'The lines of force of this suction ray tangled a little with the profiles of the two stars – the profiles in infraspace, I mean.'

'So you are drawing the crew – and the vessel itself – here?'

'To the platform outside. That's why I constructed it ... well, I *grew* it. A lot of the technology down here is grown.'

'When will it arrive?'

'More force was focused on the calcium – on you – to give you the experience of gravity within your vessel. When you left the craft, you accordingly "fell" more rapidly. But why did you leave the vessel? It was surely a very foolhardy thing to do!'

'I didn't know!' said Lebret. 'How could I?'

'But you must have realised that something like this was going on?'

'Something like *what?*' gasped Lebret.

'You must have understood that some force was being applied to your vessel!'

'Understand?' Lebret retorted, angrily. 'How could we possibly understand?'

But his irritation was matched, abruptly, by Dakkar's. 'You're *scientists*, aren't you? Couldn't you deduce it? What did you *think* was happening?'

'We,' Lebret snapped back, but with that syllable all his ersatz-anger vanished. Tiredness sloshed within him. 'We didn't know,' he concluded, feeling ashamed.

'It was only calcium that was being drawn down. Calcium and iron – the iron to a *measurably* lesser extent – was being drawn down. The rest of the materials inside your submarine must have floated – must have flown around! What did you think?'

'Some people,' Lebret confessed, 'suggested poltergeists.'

'Poltergeists!' Dakkar's huge face registered astonishment. 'Are you all idiots?'

'It was a chaotic time,' said Lebret, weakly.

'Poltergeists!' repeated Dakkar, disbelievingly. 'I was certain it would be scientists who responded to my message! Instead they have sent down a clutch of gullible mystics and table-rappers!' He sounded genuinely disgusted.

'The—the shock,' said Lebret. 'Of entering this place. The... strangeness of it.'

'Strangeness? Surely you were *expecting* strangeness?'

'The voyage was—' Lebret said. 'Look. Look, I must be honest with you.'

'Indeed you must!' said the gigantic head, in a thunderous voice, his tentacular beard writhing like a Medusa's tangle.

'The situation on, on *earth* is complicated.'

'You mean *politics*?' Dakkar spat the word, with immeasurable contempt.

'Indeed. Since you were there, events have – it is complicated.' Lebret ran the fingers of his right hand over his broken jaw. 'Your painkillers have worked extremely well, but presumably they will not work forever. And forming words is – difficult, with the swelling.'

'I can comprehend you very well,' Dakkar said.

'I am only saying, I must be brief. There was a world war. This would have been after you left – a cataclysmic war, dozens of millions were killed. It dealt a terrible blow to France, in particular.'

'There is always war,' said Dakkar, coldly. 'There will always *be* war, whilst empires oppress and distort human potential.'

Lebret leapt at this. 'Exactly! These are exactly my beliefs! This is why I have done what I have done. You see, out of that war, the First World War as history now calls it, came one great thing. A revolution, in Russia; the overthrow of the Czar and a new form of government based on principles of human co-operation and equality, inspired by the teachings of Karl Marx!'

'Marx,' said Dakkar. 'I met him, once.'

'You did?'

'He struck me as a conservative thinker.'

Lebret opened his eyes very wide. 'On the contrary!' he said. 'He is the most forward-looking of…'

'If he is forward-looking,' interrupted Dakkar, 'then why can he only conceptualise revolution in terms of the tools of *history*? I read his book. His plan was to replicate the uprising of Spartacus.'

'A mass rising, yes,' said Lebret. 'But their, I mean *our* populousness is the great weapon of the proletariat! As the Swedish poet Per Sitchelli wrote, *rise like lions after slumber, you are many, they are few.*'

'The future cannot be won with the weapons of the past,' insisted Dakkar. 'To rise up like Spartacus will only lead to millions of ordinary people being crucified, and the Caesars – and Czars – retaining an even tighter grip on power. No, no, the future must be won for justice and equality *with the weapons of the future.*'

'Ah!' said Lebret. 'Such as this suction ray, that can draw metals to it over immense distances?'

'That? That is nothing. One of the Jewel's precious *toys*, that is all. Of very limited use, down here, I might add, with metals so scarce.'

'You mentioned him before. Who is this Precious Jewel?'

But Dakkar only said, 'Please continue with your narrative.'

'My? My history of?' Lebret stroked his swollen jaw. 'Well, well. I'll say I am, Monsieur, I am *heartened* to discover that we share similar humanitarian aims – even if we can debate, pleasantly, the best means of achieving them ...'

'There's no debate on the matter,' interrupted Dakkar. 'I am right.'

Lebret waited, before continuing, 'As I say, I am heartened. Because you will perhaps be able to understand my particular situation. Because after the First World War there was a second, even more destructive ...'

'Yes, yes,' said Dakkar, impatiently. 'And after that no doubt a third, and a fourth and ...'

'There have only been two,' said Lebret.

'So far!'

'Well,' Lebret agreed. 'The point is that the Second World War was unprecedented in world history. Ostensibly it was fought between two mighty imperialist nations, on the one hand America-Britain, on the other Germany ...'

'Germany!' exclaimed Dakkar. 'Since when have they possessed an empire? They barely have a navy!'

'As I was saying,' Lebret explained, as patiently as he could. 'Things have changed since you ... since you *left*. And anyway, the war only appeared to be between these two imperial powers. In fact it was Russia who suffered the most – because the imperialists sought to destroy its revolution. This fact was proved by the way, as soon as Germany was defeated, the American powers attempted to press their advantage. The hot war, called Second, mutated into the First *Cold* War. Only with heroic effort has the Soviet Union kept the flame of revolution burning.'

'The ...?'

'Russia, I mean. This is my moment of honesty, M'sieur. If the others aboard the *Plongeur* discover what I am about to tell you, they will shoot me – plain and simple.'

'Shoot you again,' said Dakkar, 'I suppose you mean.'

'Well,' said Lebret. 'Yes. But you must understand. I am aboard the *Plongeur* as an agent of the French government. But whilst I am such an agent, I am also secretly an agent of the Soviet Union, a ...'

'A spy,' said Dakkar, looking bored. 'Yes. I see.'

Lebret gulped. 'I tell you this, I *confide* in you with this information, because—'

'Politics!' interrupted Dakkar. 'I am *entirely* uninterested in politics.'

'Please,' begged Lebret. 'Your message – it was intercepted by…'

'You adapted the vessel? You personally?'

'The *Nautilus* was refurbished, yes. Fitted out with an atomic pile – a new form of energy.'

'I am perfectly well acquainted,' said Dakkar, haughtily, 'with the principles of nuclear energy. How do you think the Jewel is able to bring such powerful energies to bear – the suction ray, for instance?'

'That was *him*? I thought—'

'The technology comes from him. I have merely utilised it here.'

'And who is the Great Jewel?'

'You do not want to have dealings with the Mighty Jewel,' said Dakkar, sternly. 'He is not well disposed to … your kind.'

'My kind?' repeated Lebret. 'If he is not my kind, then what is he? And are *you* not my kind, Monsieur?'

'Whatever I am, whatever I have become,' said Dakkar, with dignity. 'I have never been a spy.'

With a sinking sensation Lebret understood that, far from winning Dakkar's sympathy, he had actively alienated him. 'I wish the world were a different place,' he urged. 'I wish I did not have to act the traitor to my nation – and when world Communism has been achieved…'

'Monsieur,' said Dakkar, shaking his great head. His tentacular beard worked moisture in at his mouth as he spoke. 'Your politics, and the politics of your crew, are of no interest to me.'

'But—!'

'The game is larger than terrestrial politics!' boomed Dakkar. 'You don't understand!'

'I understand that *my* message was intercepted by a spy! But from what you say, it seems the crew of the official vessel have seen through your disguise. They attempted to execute you for your treason! Somehow you escaped, and stole a diving suit and came down here before them – but they are on their way!'

'It is vital,' Lebret urged, feeling the encounter slipping away from him, 'that the technological advances of which you spoke – that they do not fall into the hands of the Western Imperial forces! Let me take you back to Moscow! My superior officers refused to believe the veracity of your message, it is true; but if I bring you back then they *must* believe! And the technology capacities you possess can help win the world for Communism.' He put his hands together, pleading. 'You lived your life as an anti-Imperialist; don't abandon that principle now!'

'There is nothing trustworthy or honourable about you, Monsieur,' Dakkar announced. 'Nothing! I am Prince Dakkar! I choose to speak to the legitimate authorities. I shall wait for the arrival of the *Plongeur*, and address myself to its Captain.'

'The Soviet Union *is* a legitimate authority!'

'Yet you yourself concede,' Dakkar pressed, with a shrewd expression, 'that you took my message to them and they refused to believe you?'

'It,' sputtered Lebret, pressing a hand to the numb, spongy swollen jaw. 'It was complicated. My superior officers scoffed. It was hard for me to present the case without breaking my cover. I may not have done as good a job as I should. And there was a degree – I'm sorry to say it – a degree of *racism* in the reception of the news. You see, I had been based in India, and...'

'India?'

'I was supposed to be liaising with the British on behalf of the French. In fact I was working with the Soviets, with a view to destabilising Afghanistan, Pakistan, the Punjab. But the connection of your message with...'

'Enough!' boomed Dakkar. 'You tell me that you have betrayed your nation and failed your true masters. Why should I trust you?'

'But,' said Lebret, a feeling akin to despair swelling inside his chest, like ink poured into a vase of clear water. 'But – you don't understand the pressures...'

'You could not persuade the Russians, yet you persuaded the French?'

'We,' said Lebret, 'we came to them with your old submarine. The Indian authorities had discovered it – a museum piece. But a friend of mine had been involved in the Soviet nuclear programme; and he defected – or appeared to defect – to the West, and fitted it with an atomic pile...'

'This story wearies me,' Dakkar pronounced, his writhing beard jabbing accusingly at Lebret. 'All these betrayals and double-betrayals! What has happened to honour? I shall speak to your captain.'

'Captain Cloche is,' said Lebret, feeling sick in his stomach, 'dead; he is dead.'

'Dead?' With a squirting sound, like a child blowing a raspberry, Dakkar moved through the air towards Lebret, his huge head looming larger still and accusation in his eyes. 'Did *you* kill him?'

'He refused to bring the *Plongeur* down!' Lebret squealed, startled by the combination of hideousness and proximity. 'He was stubborn – but I didn't kill him,' he added, too late. 'He died in an accident. He, he.' Lebret was hypnotised by the snake-like wrigglings of Dakkar's beard. He could see detail in the mare's-nest of it – not just the coating of tiny water-bead, but myriad soft-looking thorns that lifted and laid themselves flat against each strand. And at the end of each individual tentacle was a miniature stoma, opening and closing as if breathing, or perhaps tasting the air.

'What? What?'

'He had an accident in his cabin,' Lebret concluded, weakly. 'His death was a tragic accident.'

Dakkar glared at him. 'You're lying,' he announced. 'A traitor, a liar *and* a murderer! Why should I have anything to do with you?'

The monstrous form reached out two of its legs, connected with the white walls and pushed off, spinning himself about. Then, darting like a fish, he shot straight towards the bulb of water.

'Wait!' Lebret cried. 'Don't leave me – what about the Jewel? What manner of being is he? Where is he from?'

Dakkar ducked his head into the water, and for a moment Lebret thought he was going to vanish entirely. But then, his four paddle-shaped feet planted on the side, he drew himself back into the air. 'The Pearl of Great Price,' he said, slowly, not looking at Lebret. 'The Multi-Faceted One.' He turned his huge head, and laid one eye on Lebret. 'I am Prince Dakkar, of a noble and honourable lineage. It is no arrogance in me to describe myself as a great man. But the Great Jewel is an entity incomparably greater than I.'

'Is he a man?' Lebret pressed. 'An alien? Was he born in this place, or did he come here – like you and I?'

'Do not,' Dakkar barked, 'juxtapose yourself and *myself* in any sentence your mouth may form!'

'Is he, you know, an actual crystalline life-form, a *sentient* jewel, or is he …'

But Dakkar dived into the bulge of water and vanished, leaving a scattering of droplets behind him to hang in the air.

25

THE PRODIGIOUS EMERALD

❥ ❥ ❥ ❥ ❥ ❥

Lebret emptied his lungs in a great sigh. 'Well,' he told himself. 'That didn't go so well.'

He looked about the chamber. The walls appeared to be made of a similar material to the gigantic scallop shell above – dense but yielding. There were a number of shelves and some items of what looked like advanced technology – a white cube with blue curving lines incised into it; a series of tubes that did not seem to open or otherwise respond to Lebret's investigations. There was a flat rectangular sheet fixed to the wall and a number of squirls like dry white pasta arranged in what might have been a pattern. None of this appeared to be of any immediate use to Lebret.

'Am I trapped here?' he wondered

He went back up into the corridor that led to the scallop shell and retrieved his air tanks. But fitting the mouthpiece and trying to breathe the contents made him cough. The air was almost exhausted. 'So I cannot use these to swim away,' he thought to himself. 'Unless I can somehow recharge them? But no – what would be the use? Where would I go?'

He floated back through to the main chamber, bringing the empty tanks with him. The thought of simply waiting, helplessly, for the *Plongeur* to arrive – to be denounced by the weird monster that Dakkar had become, and to face once again the violent animosity of Billiard-Fanon. The passivity of it was obnoxious to him. But what else could he do?

His ripped-up diving suit was floating where it had been

236

discarded. He pushed himself over to it and found the pocket with its knife. Looking at it in the bright light of that place he was surprised by how small it seemed: a small iron blade, a Bakelite handle. With so small a weapon had he truly fought off ocean monsters of nightmare?

Well, it felt better to be armed, even if armed with something so tiny. And the air tanks, even empty, were solid tubes of metal. He dragged them over to the bulb of water and left them there.

Floating about in his undergarments struck him as demeaning. He tried to cut a pair of make-shift shorts from the remnants of his diving suit, but the material was too tough for it. So instead he crossed his legs, floating in mid air about a metre from the bulb of water, and spent a half hour carefully sharpening the little blade against the metal of the empty air cylinder.

Tucking the knife into the elastic band at the top of his underpants, Lebret thrust his head into the bubble of water. Weightlessness gave his gesture the disorienting action of turning the world about – he pushed his head *down* into water, but it seemed to him his head was now poking *up* into a large watery space, illuminated with a string of bubble-lights stretching away into the murky distance. It was not immediately obvious whether this was open to the general ocean, or was a water-filled chamber of large dimensions. A number of shadowy shapes were visible in the middle-distance, but it was not possible to determine exactly what they were. If Dakkar was there, Lebret could not see him.

He withdrew his head and wiped away some of the water.

Always have a plan, Seleznyov had told him, once, long ago. 'It is better to have a bad plan than no plan at all. Always be thinking – how can I turn this situation to my advantage? What can I do to improve my odds?'

'A plan,' Lebret breathed. His thinking was hampered by not knowing how long it would be before the *Plongeur* arrived. But he could at least plan out possible scenarios.

If the submarine arrived before Dakkar returned... well, then, Lebret would have an advantage. Since young Capot had seen him, in the air-lock, after Billiard-Fanon had shot him, they must know that he was still alive. They would not be *too* surprised to see him there. The trick, then, would be talking down Billiard-Fanon's hostility – assuming the ensign was still in charge. But he could tell them anything he saw fit: tell them, for instance, that Dakkar was a monster. Get them on side. And when Dakkar returned, perhaps together they could kill him... repair the *Plongeur*, steal such of his technology as they could, and return to the surface...

It was far-fetched. He knew that. But Lebret consoled himself with the thought that just surviving this far had involved him superbly beating the odds. Fate must be preserving him for *something* – more than simply dying pointlessly in this distant pod.

So, to consider other possible futures. What if Dakkar returned before the *Plongeur* arrived? This, Lebret thought, was probable; he must have instrumentation that would inform him of the craft's approach. Well, then, Lebret might use the metal tanks as a crude club, or might deploy his newly sharpened diver's knife as a stabbing implement, and so end the creature's life. Would it be possible? His physical form was, evidently, much altered from what it had been before. But his skull, though hugely enlarged, must surely still be susceptible to blunt-force trauma. He must still have a beating heart that a knife could pierce.

What then? At least Dakkar would not then be able to denounce Lebret to the remaining crew of the *Plongeur*. He would have to think of some other explanation for events.

Better, perhaps, would be to *beat* Dakkar, to give him earnest of his intent, and force him somehow to help him – or help them all? But to enter into a fight with that monster... Lebret's heart quailed at the prospect. And even if he could force the creature to do his bidding, what would that bidding *be*?

To return home, of course. But to return home with more than just testimony that this strange ocean-universe existed. To bring back some technological marvel, something to prove to his masters in Moscow that he had been *right*...

His thoughts turned to the Great Jewel, the Many-Faceted One, of which Dakkar had spoken. Lebret, floating in that strange place, pondered what such a being might be. An aboriginal intelligence?

It did not seem unlikely to him that a water universe might give rise to crystalline intelligences. A great sapphire, its facets glinting in the dim light, and possessing within it enormous complexity. Was the Jewel to whom Dakkar clearly owed allegiance one such alien being? Were there many crystalline creatures? If there were one, presumably there were others.

Lebret thought – perhaps it would be best to speak directly to the Jewel creature? If menacing Dakkar compelled him to bring Lebret into the Jewel's presence, or to bring the crystalline being to *him*...

Exhausted, Lebret dozed.

He slept fitfully for a while, since the pain in his jaw had not entirely been removed. Then he sank deeper into slumber.

He dreamed.

He saw a giant emerald floating before him, a polyhedral structure of perfect proportion, symmetry and beauty, its glass-pure facets shining with an inner light. A perfect sea green crystal. 'Jewel,' he gasped. 'Perfection beyond human possibility!'

I am here, said the Jewel, speaking directly to Lebret's mind.

'You are a god!' Lebret wept, humbled and awed. Tears squeezed from his shut eyes to drift away as dots and blobs.

Belief in God is an intellectual opium, unworthy of you, said the Jewel. *I am the crystalline embodiment of dialectical materialism.*

'You,' Lebret gasped. 'You are a Communist?'

I am an advanced form of alien life, the Jewel communicated to him telepathically. *Naturally my kind are Communist, for it is the most advanced form of social organisation.*

'There are many of you?'

There were a million varieties of pure green glinting in the facets of the giant Jewel. *Naturally.*

'Yet Dakkar was hostile to Communism ... he dismissed all mundane political philosophies ...'

Dakkar is still in thrall to the prejudices of his kind. He is not enlightened, as I am enlightened.

'He called me,' Lebret said, crying again, 'murderer and traitor and ...'

He did not understand, the Jewel said, *that you acted according to the dictates of Necessity. Every true Communist understands Necessity. It is the logic of the universe.*

'Yes!' gasped Lebret, tears pouring from his eyes. 'Yes!'

When your metallic vessel arrives, I will compel the occupants to accept the rightness of your actions, said the Jewel. *We must repair your craft and use it to return to your world. And I shall come with you. You shall be greeted with adulation! You will be acclaimed a hero of the Soviet Union! With me at your side, and drawing on my superior technological and intellectual capacities we will establish global Communism on your world!* As if in ecstasy, the giant gemstone began to rotate about its vertical axis, slowly at first but then more rapidly. *I shall be the first of my kind to enter your world, but many more will follow.*

'I will be vindicated,' gasped Lebret. 'Everybody will see – I did what *had* to be done! All my sufferings … all my sufferings … will be *redeemed* in my triumph …'

The gigantic emerald was spinning so rapidly now that its facets had blurred into a symmetrical ovaloid. Light was pouring from it. There was a noise, too; a low level hum. But as soon as Lebret became aware of it suddenly increased in volume, and became a violent din. It was painfully loud. He clutched his ears. The certainty dashed in upon him that the Jewel was about to explode, killing Lebret and destroying the entire facility. He opened his mouth to cry, 'No!'

He was awake again, struggling weakly in mid-air and gasping. The chamber was empty.

There was a trembling in the walls. It began as a delicate tremor, and quickly grew into to an earthquake – an oceanquake, Lebret assumed. The strange thing was that he remained motionless, floating in zero-g in the middle of the room, whilst all around him the walls and shelves and Dakkar's strange equipment buzzed and vibrated.

Then, abruptly, it stopped.

26

SHAVING THE BEARD

♥ ♥ ♥ ♥ ♥ ♥

Sensation was beginning to return to Lebret's jaw; the distant intimation of pain. Still a little muzzy from sleep, and trying to separate out dream from reality, Lebret pulled himself across to the water. He put his own face forward to take a drink, and then pulled back, startled.

Dakkar's face was inside the bubble of water. His beard wriggled in its revolting fashion, the eyes glowered. But he did not break through into the air.

Lebret pulled himself back, pulling out his knife. The empty air cylinders were a few metres away. He was about to lunge for them, when Dakkar's gigantic head broke through in a spray of floating water-beads, and spoke.

'Shave me!' he boomed.

Lebret was taken aback. 'What?'

There was something violent, something hostile in Dakkar's eyes. But—no! Lebret looked again and saw a different emotion there: desperation. The monstrous figure was wrestling with himself.

'Shave me!' he cried, and this time there was no mistaking the tone of pleading. 'Quick – I know you have a knife … I know all your metal …'

'Shave you?' Lebret repeated.

'Be quick! The scallop is isolated from *him*, but it won't last long!'

Lebret hesitated. It was not that he expected a trap. Rather the sheer oddity of the request wrong-footed him. But Dakkar appeared to be in genuine distress.

'These tentacles,' he gasped. 'The Jewel did this to me! The beard... controls me. Please!'

Still Lebret hung back. 'You called me a traitor and a murderer,' he reminded him.

'*He* did that – the Jewel. I don't care what you are! Ah, ah, ah!' The whole giant face was convulsed with agony. 'I haven't seen another human being in decades! Please, I can't control my muscles to do it myself. But you – you can *shave me...*'

Lebret reached a decision. He swam through the air, and brought the knife blade down upon the hideous, wriggling mass of faux-beard.

'It's not a beard,' Dakkar was saying. 'The Jewel – *he* did it to me when he changed me – it's alive, sentient, and through it he controls me... aagh!' This last, a deafening scream, gave Lebret a terrible start and made him drop the knife.

'Don't stop!' Dakkar pleaded.

Lebret pushed away, and retrieved the knife. 'I hadn't even started – why did you scream?'

'The beard,' Dakkar replied, in a tight voice; 'it knows what you are about to do – it senses my disobedience. It is hurting me. Cut it off!'

'Won't that hurt you more?'

'Yes – but it must be done!'

The bizarre nature of the situation impressed itself upon Lebret's consciousness. But he had to accede. He pushed off with his feet against the wall and hooked his left arm around Dakkar's waist. The old man's frame felt puny, his skinny ribs pressed into Lebret's arm, thin and frail as breadsticks. He brought out the knife, laid the blade against Dakkar's oversize cheek, and sliced downward.

Dakkar howled and writhed, but in amongst the yelps of pain he was still trying to form words – 'Go on, do it, keep on!' Half a dozen tendrils floated free, the little mouths at the end opening and closing rapidly. 'Like spaghetti,' muttered Lebret, 'that has been possessed by the devil!'

'On!' urged Dakkar, through gritted teeth.

Lebret laid the blade again the fellow's cheek a second time, like a barber. But this time the beard reacted. As one, the tendrils bunched and curled at him. They enclosed his hand. 'Ugh!' he cried. He was able to yank himself free without difficulty – the tentacles evidently had very little strength in them. But as he brought the hand out, a dozen little mouths fastened on his skin and stung him.

'What did they do?' he cried. 'Your beard – bit me!'

'It is part of the Jewel's control methodology,' gasped Dakkar, his voice hoarse. 'The tendrils are directly plugged into my nerves and can administer terrible pain – as they are doing now! But they also manufacture within themselves a chemical agent, a neuro-... well, a neurotoxin, strictly speaking, which they periodically inject into me. It dilutes my capacity for free will and resistance.'

'What effect will it have on me?' Lebret demanded.

'Nothing! I told you, I have screened the scallop from ... *him*. Temporarily, at any rate. And without the implants, and the other body modifications he has performed upon me, the neurotoxin will be no worse than a nettle sting. But, please, you must hurry! Time is short and – the pain – is – very severe ...'

Dakkar shut his eyes tight. Lebret swam through the air to where his tattered diving suit lay and put his arm back in the sleeve, taking care to fold the end over his hand. Thus protected, he went back in for a third attempt at shaving the gigantic, sentient beard.

He got further this time. Whatever organic matter constituted the tendrils' stems was pliable and easily severed. Dakkar yelled and cried pitiably as his left cheek was cleared, and kicked his four legs like a bucking colt – although, floating in zero-gravity, these conniption jerks and motions served only to jiggle and rotate his body. Lebret held tight and began upon the gigantic chin. At some point during this procedure Dakkar passed out – from the pain, Lebret presumed. It became easier to shave him.

The tendrils jabbed and bit at the diving suit material, like malignant blind snakes, but they could not penetrate its thickness.

244

It occurred to Lebret to wrap his left hand in a fold of the stuff, and use it to pull out clumps of beard. The tendrils snapped easily enough, although it was a neater business scraping the knife blade over the skin.

The moustache was removed, and Lebret started up the right cheek. The skin that he revealed was a strange thing. Evidently stretched and distorted by being enlarged from Dakkar's original proportions, the pores were widened further by this monstrous self-aware beard. Finally he scraped Dakkar's neck clean, and floated back to admire his handiwork.

The air was filled with floating tendrils, most curling and twisting with repulsive motion, and winking their little mouths. But Dakkar's weirdly huge face was clean-shaven, now. In only a few places had Lebret nicked the skin.

The subject was still breathing, but his eyes were tight shut and he was unconscious. Lebret left him floating, and occupied a quarter of an hour moving around the chamber with the diving-suit, using it as a form of net to collect together as many of the still wriggling strands as he could. This was tricky, but he managed to bundle the majority into a parcel, and this he sealed by tying together the arms and legs into knots.

He was thirsty. The painkiller was beginning to wear off; he could feel the pain in his jaw looming back into consciousness, like jagged rocks appearing through fog. He stuck his head into the bulb of water, drank deeply and washed his face.

Then he waited. His hand was red and itchy where the tendrils had bit him, but he could still move it.

His thoughts went back to the strange dream he had experienced, immediately before Dakkar had re-entered the space. Had it been a dream, or a telepathic vision? Had the Jewel – whatever that evidently potent, alien entity *was* – actually been communicating with him? If so, perhaps it was not to be trusted.

Dakkar stirred, moaning a little. 'Your haircut is complete, M'sieur,' Lebret told him. 'I feel I should charge you a franc. How do you feel?'

'It is agony,' Dakkar groaned.

'Still? Even with the... the tendrils removed?'

'They were wired into my nervous system, beneath the skin; enough of them remain to cause me pain. Still – I thank you, Monsieur. You have done me a great service! My mind is clearer, despite the pain. And as for that... well, it is nothing more than I deserve.'

'Deserve? Surely not, M'sieur!' declared Lebret.

'I came down here with a crew of my own, Monsieur Lebret. I led them down here. The Jewel did this to me, but he did worse things to *them*.'

'What did he do?'

'He is fascinated by the prospect of our world,' said Dakkar, in a rasping voice. 'And naturally his mind runs to domination. It is his nature.'

'He wishes to invade our world? To conquer it?'

'I find myself almost incapable of condemning him for it! He can only think in those terms, he has no choice. But our world, our *reality*, presents him with a problem. Oxygen.'

'Oxygen?'

'It is a rare element down here.'

'But how can that be? Every molecule of water is one third oxygen!'

'True, of course,' Dakkar conceded, wheezing. 'But that oxygen is locked so tightly into its chemical bonds it takes prodigious energy to release it. No, the problem is *free* oxygen. At the beginning, the Jewel even refused to believe that there was such a thing – even though he had us, and could see that we breathed in the gas.'

'Why?'

'Why did he doubt it? Because oxygen is immensely reactive – stupendously so. What, after all, is fire but the aggressive oxidisation of whatever is burning? Think of it from his point of view. Imagine a creature came to you from a realm of fire, and reported that in amongst the brimstone hills and burning plains were lakes of pure petroleum. Wouldn't you doubt him – for surely the petroleum would all long since have been long ago burnt up by the surrounding fires? That is how the presence of so much free oxygen in our atmosphere appears to *him*. It ought long since to have been burnt up!'

'The oxygen is replenished by the action of photosynthesising plants,' Lebret said.

'Exactly. And in time he experimented with oxygen-producing algae. But even his best efforts were tepid compared to the naturally occurring flora of our terrestrial homes. His created algae serve as the ground for the various ecosystems he has established around the various stars near here, but they breed slowly and die out easily, and the higher organisms he designed live on the threshold of oxygen deprivation.'

'They seemed to go crazy for air when the *Plongeur* passed through them,' Lebret recalled.

'They would!' said Dakkar. 'Have you seen fish in a dying pond, gulping desperately at the surface? Poor things, they are trapped at their various stars – stray too far, away from the algae, and there is no free oxygen dissolved in this water at all. A fish would drown in this ocean as quickly as a man. But even close by the star there is precious little.'

'*He* made these beasts? The Jewel?'

Dakkar nodded. His skin had acquired a grey, exhausted tone to it; and his eyes seemed to be having trouble focusing. 'He took my crew – adapted them, cloned them, perverted their forms.'

'But why?'

'Isn't it obvious? He hoped to breed a new species capable of swimming through the oxygen rich oceans of the earth. He has many creatures, but none that could bear to swim such waters.'

'An invasion force!' murmured Lebret. 'Surely your crew would never agree to spearhead such an attack?'

'Oh, their humanity is long since gone, dissolved in the crucible of his *work*. I believe he intended them to retain *some* wit, some level of mental capacity. But they are born, live and die in such an oxygen-starved environment their brains are poisoned. They are blind knots of instinct. I brought them here, and such was their fate! You can see why I consider my pain deserved?'

'You cannot have known, Prince Dakkar!' urged Lebret. The

pain in his own jaw was growing now, and his leg was starting to tingle and sting. 'You cannot blame yourself!'

'You cannot conceive what it has been like,' said Dakkar, tears leaking from between his closed eyelids. 'The Jewel attached that – beard to my face, that entity to my brain. Since then I have lived a tormented existence.'

'Come!' said Lebret, uncertainly. 'I say, do you happen to have any more of those very effective painkillers on your person?'

Dakkar only groaned.

For a long time they were both silent. Lebret was beginning to feel hungry; and the ache in his jaw was increasing unpleasantly.

'I'm sorry about your teeth,' said Dakkar.

Lebret started. 'I thought you were asleep.'

'I am dying,' said Dakkar.

'Because I shaved your beard? But why did you permit me to do it, if it must kill you?'

'I am very old,' said Dakkar. 'What year is it, back in France?'

'1958.'

'Well! In that case I am a more than a hundred and fifty years old. The beard was keeping me alive. The Jewel was prolonging my life. He valued what I had in my head – my memories of earth, my ingenuity, and the thought that he could use me as a tool to help him invade the earth.'

'There must be something I can do!'

'You are the first fellow human I have seen in decades,' Dakkar said, mournfully. 'I could not have done this thing unaided – and so I thank you.' He appeared to fall asleep.

27

THE UNDERWATER GARDEN

● ● ● ● ● ●

Days passed, with Dakkar moving in and out of consciousness. The pain in Lebret's jaw grew fierce again, but it took coaxing to persuade Dakkar to fetch more painkillers. 'There is a garden attached to this facility,' the old man explained. 'For unlike the Jewels, I need organic sustenance to subsist, and that is where I grow my meals.'

'Jewels?' Lebret asked, sharply. 'Plural?'

'What?' replied Dakkar, vaguely.

'You said Jewels, as if there are many. Earlier you talked of one Jewel. Which is it?'

'I don't,' said Dakkar, 'I don't follow—'

'Never mind. You grow analgesics in this garden, as well as food?'

'At my age, aches and pains are a serious matter.'

'Can you fetch me some?' Lebret begged. 'The pain in my jaw is becoming hard to bear. And I feel hot – I feel feverish all over.' It was true; he was beginning to shudder with the onset of what felt like flu.

'I am too ill to go,' Dakkar insisted. 'And besides, without my beard how am I to breathe underwater?'

'The water in that space *is* oxygenated, then?'

'There is a small generator, drawing on infraspace for its power. It divides water to create the oxygen, both for the water in the chambers beyond the bubble, and in this space.'

'Well if you cannot swim down to this garden, I suppose I must,' said Lebret briskly, for his pain was making him impatient. 'Can you help me refill my air-tanks?'

'You mean your diving equipment?' Dakkar looked listlessly at the three tubes of tarnished metal. 'The air must be compressed,' he said. 'I would need to create a new machine, and I am sorry to say I do not have the energy.' He closed his huge eyes, wearily.

'How far is it? Could I swim there and back on a lungful of held breath?'

'Perhaps, if you were to hyperventilate a little – like the pearl fishers of Sumatra! Come, help me to the water and I will show you.'

Lebret guided Dakkar's floating body to the bulb of water. Wearily the old man pulled himself through to the other side; and Lebret pushed his own head through. Blinking, he saw Dakkar gesture listlessly towards the far end of the flooded space. When they both pulled themselves back into the air, the old man explained. 'Through that gateway, and you'll see. I grow food, medicines, various things. The difficulty for you will be that many of these items will be indistinguishable to you – they all look like white mallows, growing in racks. I know what they are, but you will have to harvest as wide a range as possible, and discover their particular virtues by experiment afterwards.'

'Very well.'

'It means,' gasped Dakkar, 'that you will certainly bring some food back as well. And I am hungry!'

'I'll do my best,' Lebret spent long minutes breathing in and out as deeply as he could, until he felt thoroughly dizzy. Then he slipped into the water like an acrobat through a circus hoop.

Swimming was not easy with his wounded left leg, but by dint of wriggling and paddling furiously with his hands, he made it to the end of the first watery chamber. Through the gate and he entered a brighter space – lamps shining on the grids and racks of genetically modified mallow-like growths. His breath was still good, so he took a moment to look around – it was another entirely enclosed chamber, filled with water, and with three sealed doors below, or along from, the lights. He quickly plucked as many as he could, and wriggled back to the chamber of air.

'There,' he said, releasing indistinguishable blobs of white from his arms to float through the air. Dakkar indicated one that had analgesic properties; and then the two of them ate several of the protein and vitamin morsels. They were flavourless.

Afterwards, Lebret asked more questions. Some of these Dakkar answered cogently enough; with others he appeared to drift off. He was paler now, and wrinkles were appearing around the edges of his face – as if his oversized head were actually beginning to shrink. The hair on the top of his head contained streaks of white that had not been there before.

'I am trying to understand,' Lebret said. 'This gemstone entity – he seeks to conquer our world?'

'Yes.'

'And to that end he created a number of sub oceanic suns! An entity with such powers could surely simply seize the earth – make a sun over New York to burn the city to ashes, say, and cow the rest of the globe with threats of similar terrors!'

'You do not grasp the nature of things here,' said Dakkar, croakily. 'This is his realm. It is his nature to have access here to the skein that separates infraspace from superspace – from the space we occupy and are in the habit of calling the universe. I do not doubt that one reason he hopes to break through into *our* world is to see whether he has similar control there. But as it stands, he knows very little about the earth.'

'He knows what was in your brain, I suppose?'

'Only if he thinks to ask me. He cannot simply flick through my thoughts, as the pages of a book. But he can ask me a question and compel me to answer truthfully. But then he needs to know which questions to ask! For example, he opened the portal—'

'*He* did that?'

'Of course! And he sent some of his creatures through. But the portal is, of course, into deep water, and on *earth*, unlike here, deep water is severely pressurised. His creatures were pulped to jelly! He has a prodigious intellect, but he simply hadn't thought through what conditions would be like in such a – to him – alien environment.'

'But the crack remained open?'

'He sealed it. A good thing too! The pressure differential would have resulted in earth's oceans decanting themselves wholly into this place in only a few years. Perhaps a hundred years passed before I came along in the *Nautilus 2*. I reopened it – how I wish I had not!'

'What happened to your vessel?'

'My vessel?' Dakkar sounded confused.

'The one in which you travelled here.'

'I scuttled it, blew it to shreds when I understood the danger the Great Jewel posed. But by then it was too late. He already had my crew – and myself.'

'So the portal has been open for … fifty years?'

'Not continuously. It is phased. But, in essence, yes.'

'Can it be permanently sealed? To lock him out.'

'Oh, he could open another, if he chose. He tried opening one in land, fifty years ago – in the wilds of Eastern Siberia. But that went wrong – catastrophically wrong. There was a huge explosion.'

'1908, Siberia …' Lebret muttered.

'He is competent with water as a medium; but solid rock is almost incomprehensible to him. Still, that doesn't mean he couldn't open another oceanic portal.'

Lebret shook his head. 'He has the powers of a god.'

'No, no,' wheezed Dakkar. 'He is powerful, but not supernaturally so.'

'Creating underwater suns!' Lebret countered. '*Fiat lux!*'

'They are not suns, not in the way familiar from our cosmos,' said Dakkar. 'Points of intense light, pushed up from infraspace, to enable the algae to photosynthesis, to make food and oxygen for the creatures. The cores are no more than a few metres across; although, obviously, they are surrounded by a much larger shell of roiling, superheated steam, and beyond that a layer of water tripping on the edge of boiling. Very complex flow patterns, actually.'

253

'And these are relatively *recent* inventions of his, I presume?' Lebret asked.

'Exactly!'

'If they were here long enough, I suppose they would eventually boil the water in the entire cosmos!'

Dakkar wheezily laughed. 'My contempt for your lack of scientific deductive powers was perhaps premature,' he said. 'You're right, of course. Eventually the entire cosmos would turn to steam. It would take a very long time, but it would eventually happen.'

'But if this cosmos is infinite in extent, as our universe is, then surely it would take an infinite amount of time to heat up?'

'The cosmos here is infinite in extent, as ours is; but that does not mean it is constituted by an infinite mass of water,' wheezed Dakkar.

'I—I don't follow...'

'The geometry of infinity folds space-time back on itself. And at any rate, the Jewel is, physically, trillions of kilometres away from where we are, here. It would take hundreds of thousands of years for the heat from these stars he had created to penetrate the medium and reach him.'

'Trillions?' gasped Lebret. 'How can he influence things *here*, when he is so very far away?'

'Trillions of kilometres describes the geometry of superspace. It is a different logic in infraspace, a dimension in which he has ... certain capacities.'

' "Infraspace",' Lebret repeated. ' "Superspace." If there is an *under*-space and we inhabit the over-space, then where is ... space?'

'A question as much philosophical as scientific,' was Dakkar's opinion. 'Personally, I incline to the opinion that space is actually a three-dimensional manifold, two spatial modes and one temporal mode of extension. Our four-dimensional bubbles, blown from the actual plane of existence, are anomalies in this larger scheme. But it hardly matters.'

He drifted off, and appeared to be asleep. Lebret ate a few more mallows, and took a drink from the bulb of water. He wondered, idly, what the toiletry arrangements were. A second, leisurely exploration of the space revealed nothing that looked as though it would serve. Presumably it would be possible to relieve oneself in the water – but as this was also the water he was drinking, he felt inhibited from doing so. In the end he compromised; floated back along the corridor and opened the lid onto the wide expanse of the shell-platform, lowered his body in up to the waist and relieved himself. It was all part of the larger ocean, of course, but this seemed somehow more hygienic.

Coming back below, rubbing beads of water off his naked legs, he found Dakkar awake and staring at him. 'I wonder,' he asked the old man, 'why you have a hatchway up there – but none for the entrance to your second chamber, there.' He pointed.

'Because that corridor opens into the ocean. If it had no doorway, like this bulb, why then – unpredictable flows and surges would force water through. This, however, leads through to a sealed chamber.'

Lebret came to sit beside the old man. His freakish dimensions no longer struck him as repulsive; indeed, there was considerable pathos in the pain and weariness of his eyes. 'I apologise; that was a trivial question. Let me ask a larger one.'

'Please do.'

'*Monsieur le prince*,' Lebret asked. 'Your … message, shall we call it?'

'Yes?'

'Did *you* send it? I mean – was it of your own volition? Or was it the Jewel, forcing you to lure human beings down here?'

Dakkar smiled thinly. 'You have started to demonstrate some impressive powers of scientific deduction. I am confident you can deduce the answer to that question for yourself. I am – tired. I am very tired.'

28

THE ARRIVAL OF THE *PLONGEUR*

❡ ❡ ❡ ❡ ❡ ❡

Lebret slept, and awoke thirsty. His eyeballs felt hot. '*Monsieur le prince,*' he said, as he pulled himself over to the water bubble to drink. 'I feel unwell. Hot – feverish.' The words did not form themselves very comprehensibly, and Dakkar, barely opening his right eye, gasped, 'What did you say?'

Lebret felt the side of his face; it had swollen further. 'Hot,' he said, making an effort to enunciate. 'Feel feverish.'

'It is likely, Monsieur,' croaked Dakkar, 'that the wound in your jaw has become infected. As, perhaps, was inevitable, without proper medical attention.'

The thought filled Lebret with hazy dread. 'What must I do?' he asked, as if through a mouthful of pebbles. 'What treatments do you have?'

'I cannot help you,' Dakkar gasped, and closed his eyes.

'Do you have penicillin?'

Dakkar did not reply.

As time passed, Lebret felt increasingly sluggish, hot and miserable. A trembling started up in his hands and head. 'I feel terrible,' he informed Dakkar. The latter did not reply. It was hard to see if he were even breathing.

More time passed – Lebret could not say how much. He felt increasingly unwell, and soon reached a state where all his sensations and thoughts were subordinated to the pressing misery of his physical discomfort. His face was sweltering, his eyes wincing and weeping. Shivers passed all over his body.

Hours passed. Perhaps it was days. The fever seemed to reach a point of maximum intensity, when agony in his jaw throbbed continually, and he sweated and wept and floated. The physical discomfort was compounded of a kind of existential bitterness – to have *survived* such ill fortunes as being shot in the face, and drowned in an infinite ocean, only to die of a stupid infection – it was insulting.

Then, very slowly, the fever drew itself back in, until Lebret's symptoms resembled a bout of regular flu, and he was able to move himself around with painful slowness. He drank a great draught of water, and then – uncaring – relieved himself into the same place.

The white blank screen was pulsing with pale light.

'Dakkar! Dakkar – what does it mean?'

Dakkar looked very near death. He roused himself, peered for a long time at the screen, and said, 'The submarine is here.'

'The *Plongeur*? Here?' gasped Lebret, shivering. 'Bring them inside! Open a corridor to the vessel's air-lock.' In his sickness he had lost the fear that Billiard-Fanon might take one look at him and shoot him dead. He craved company. Indeed, he craved being looked after; nursed, treated with the penicillin he knew existed within the vessel's First Aid Box.

But Dakkar shook his head. 'Not,' he said. 'Possible.'

'How are they to get in here, then?'

It took Dakkar an age and an age to answer. 'Swim.'

'But there are no more suits! Wait – can I speak to them?'

Without speaking, Dakkar crooked a finger at the screen. Trembling, feeling child-like again in the grip of his flu-symptoms, Lebret retrieved the technology. It unsnibbed easily from the wall. Waves of fever swept through Lebret's consciousness. He felt nauseous. His throat was tight. 'What do I do?'

Dakkar paddled one wizened finger against the shining board, and then fell back.

'What now?' Lebret wheezed. Despite the analgesic mallows, pulses of agony were radiating out from the side of his head. His brain was a monsoony, defocused, worn-out place. But Dakkar had fallen asleep, or lost consciousness, his gigantic head rolling backwards and the momentum of it causing his torso to swing round and rotate in mid-air.

'Hello?' said the shining board. It was Capot's voice.

Tears were dribbling from Lebret's eyes. It astonished him how relieved he was to hear the young sailor's voice. 'It's me! It's me!'

'Who? Who is that?' A second voiced chimed in. 'Where is that voice coming from?'

'Is that *you*, Pannier?' wheezed Lebret. 'God, it's good to hear you again, you old drunkard!'

'Who *is* that?'

'Don't you recognise my voice? I suppose I'm ill – my jaw is swollen, and I think my throat is constricted a little. I probably do sound different. It's me – it's Jean Lebret!'

There was a pause. Then Capot whimpered, 'Lebret.'

Pannier said, 'Can you hear this, Castor? It's not coming through on the radio – can you hear it?'

'I can hear it,' came Castor's voice. 'How is it broadcasting in here? Is it piggybacking the speakers – it's audible throughout the whole vessel!'

'I don't know how it works,' Lebret croaked. 'I am in a chamber, with – with somebody you will want to meet. There are various items of advanced technology here, one of which I am presently using, although I don't know how, to speak to ...'

'Lebret!' shrieked Capot, suddenly. 'Lebret – stop tormenting me! I never harmed you in life; why should you pursue me after your death ...?'

'I'm not dead,' Lebret began, but another voice – Billiard-Fanon's – came across the device. 'Lebret!'

'Listen, Billiard-Fanon – don't leap to any conclusions ...'

'I shall leap nowhere,' said Billiard-Fanon. 'I have received a vision from God Almighty! I *understand* the true nature of where we are.'

'You have come to a halt,' Lebret gasped. 'You know it! Go to the observation chamber, and take a look – you're resting upon a gigantic scallop shell. I know this to be true, because that's where I landed, a little while ago.'

'How did you ...?' Castor started to ask. But Pannier spoke across him. 'Are you dead?'

'No, not dead, though I am hurt,' said Lebret. 'You must come inside – you'll be amazed. I can explain everything.'

The low-key wailing sound was Capot moaning. '*How* did you survive?' Pannier pressed.

'You mean, after Billiard-Fanon shot me in the mouth?' Lebret replied.

'I am to be addressed as the Holy One,' boomed Billiard-Fanon. 'And my actions in shooting you were directed by God himself.'

'Is that so?' Lebret returned. His elation at being able to speak again to the *Plongeur* had pushed his feverishness to the back of his mind; but his hands were trembling nonetheless, and his head, jaw and throat burned and ached. 'Well in that case, I suppose my *survival* must have been directed by God himself too. It was certainly against the odds. And here I am, inside this chamber, speaking to you on a piece of technology that would make us all rich, if we could carry it back to France and sell it.'

'Are you alive?' Billiard-Fanon mused. 'Or are you a delusion – a devil, sent to trick us?'

'You're the Holy One,' Lebret creaked. '*You* should know.'

'You speak like a devil,' Billiard-Fanon announced.

The others seemed less persuaded by this quasi-religious explanation. 'What other kit is there, down there?' Castor asked. 'Anything interesting?'

'Come and see,' Lebret said. 'But bring the vessel's first-aid box with you. I have a fever, and need penicillin.'

'How are we to get to you?' Pannier asked. 'Some bastard stole the only remaining diving suit.'

'That was me – that was how I got here. Look – are you in the observation chamber? What can you see?'

'I'm there,' said Castor. 'I can see a faint light, and ... well, it certainly looks like a giant shell.'

'That's because it *is* a giant shell. Dakkar probably modelled it directly on Botticelli's *Birth of Venus*. It contains a device, or perhaps it only *focuses* the device's beam – and that has been drawing both us and the iron of the *Plongeur* down here. This is the end of the line, as the tram drivers say. Castor – can you see the source of the light?'

'A circle, I think.'

'Yes! That is a hatchway. Even without diving gear, if you take a deep breath you can swim easily to it; and through it is plenty of air – and food. Food!'

'And drink?' Pannier asked. 'A good Côte du Rhone? A little rum?'

'Listen,' said Lebret, tucking the communication slate under his arm and pulling his shivering body along the corridor. 'Look, I'm going to open the hatchway and put my head out.'

'And flood your compartment?' Castor asked.

'It's zero-g, it's a cosmos of water – it's a waterverse—' Lebret gabbled. It was hard to distinguish the sense of elation from the giddiness of fever. He felt as if his whole body were a helium balloon. 'Weightless, weightless. A little water spills in, but not – look here I am.'

He did not stop to consider whether the communication slate might or might not be waterproof; he simply opened the hatch and poked his head through.

It took a moment to adjust, of course, but even without goggles it was easy enough to see the *Plongeur*. Indeed, it could hardly be missed – a massive tube of metal lying on its side and filling most of the vast shell-shape. Lebret blinked, halfway along he could see the rip in the vessel's fabric – the mess room – and nearer the hatch was the oval porthole of the observation chamber. A pale shape, like a dab of white paint in the middle of a painter's nocturne, was Castor's face, pressed against the glass. Lebret waved, but as Castor lifted his arm to wave back Lebret had to pull himself back inside the corridor to breathe.

'I saw him!' Castor was saying. 'Lebret – I think it truly *was* him.'

'You *think*?' came Pannier's voice.

'His face is all swollen. But – I guess if he was *shot* in the face…'

'I have prayed!' boomed Billiard-Fanon, suddenly. 'And God has answered me. Bring out the heathen.'

'Who do you mean—?

'Jhutti!' snapped Billiard-Fanon. '*He* shall swim the waters. If he lives, as Lebret says he will, then perhaps we shall follow him. But we will watch from the observation chamber, and see whether this is all the devil's trickery.'

Lebret clutched the communication slate to his chest. He was shivering more violently now, and the fever was mounting in his head. The whole right-side of his head was pulsing and throbbing. It was intensely uncomfortable. 'Send Jhutti, by all means,' he said. 'But tell him to *bring some penicillin* with him!'

Presumably there was a delay whilst Jhutti was brought out from whatever cabin he had been held in, and forced or cajoled into the airlock; but time was becoming harder and harder for Lebret to grasp. The voices of the various members of the *Plongeur*'s crew mingled and jarred against one another. Only when somebody – Pannier, it sounded like – cried 'he's out!' and Billiard-Fanon demanded impatiently, 'Where? Where? Oh! I can see him!', did Lebret pull himself together.

He stuck his head back through the hatch and into the water. A shape was kicking and arm-stroking through the waters, like a man half-swimming, half-walking along the bottom of a swimming-pool: Jhutti! Lebret reached out one trembling arm, and the scientist seized it. It was a simple matter drawing him into the tube.

'It's true!' Jhutti gasped, as he sucked at the air. 'It's a structure – a corridor, and filled with air.'

'Is that you, Jhutti?' Billiard-Fanon demanded. 'Put your face back up, so we can see.'

Jhutti twisted about in the corridor, and thrust his upper portion back into the water. When he drew himself back into the corridor, Lebret grabbed him. 'Medicines, medicines!' he begged. 'Did you bring any?'

Jhutti shook his head, and tiny droplets of moisture left his beard to float away. 'They did not give me anything to bring,' he said. 'I am sorry.'

'Billiard-Fanon's shot wounded my jaw,' Lebret explained, muffling the words and shaking. 'I fear the wound has become infected. I must have medicine!'

'You do look ill,' Jhutti agreed. 'And I am sorry for it.'

Voices from the communication slate made it clear that the others were about to leave the airlock and swim across too.

'I am sure one of the others is bringing the first aid box,' Jhutti said, unconvincingly.

'I hope so,' shuddered Lebret. He took as deep a breath as his tightened airways would allow, and stuck his head back into the water.

Blink, blink, and he saw the whole scene in wavery but discernible fashion. Billiard-Fanon was in front, swimming with strong kicks of his leg and coming straight for the hatch. Behind him was Capot, and behind him Pannier. There was no sign of Castor.

Lebret, looking back at the *Plongeur*, saw what happened next before anybody; but there was nothing he could do to warn the others. From the rip in the metal flank of the submarine, a shape swam out; and it was followed by another, and then another. Childranha. Even in his feverish state, Lebret immediately understood what had happened. As the *Plongeur* passed by the second sub oceanic sun, some of the creatures must have gone inside the flooded mess hall. And why not? There was food in there, and Lebret had good cause to know how hungry the beasts were – for protein, and also for oxygen. As the vessel sank away from that sun, and oxygen levels in the surrounding ocean sank to nothing, the childranha would not have been able to leave that little cell of oxygenated water, even if they wanted to.

But they were leaving it now. Lebret tried to signal, waved his arm with the absurd slowness of all underwater motions. That, or the expression of evident terror on his swollen face, alerted the three sailors. They looked round, and saw the monsters speeding towards them. Each reacted in his own way.

Billiard-Fanon smiled. It was unmistakeable. He crossed himself, and resumed his swim. He did not even hurry his motions, as if perfectly confident that God would protect him.

Capot writhed and kicked, wasted energy and time in a panicky wrestle with empty water, and finally struck out as fast as he could for the hatchway. The leading childranha-fish overtook him easily, and sank its fangs into his shin. The young sailor opened his mouth and vomited out a perfect sphere of air; but where his foot had been was only a spreading mess of red liquid coiling through the clear water, and the first childranha was swimming left with a boot in its mouth. A second childranha darted in and bit into end of the severed leg.

Of all of them, Pannier's reaction was the most rational: he quickly assessed the threat, estimated the distance still to swim and balanced it against the distance back to the airlock, and immediately doubled back. He swum with large, strong thrusts of his legs and his arms and was back at the submarine before the childranha got to him. If he had been able to get the door smoothly open at first go he might have lived; but his fingers fumbled at the catch, and there was a flurry of childranha lurched at him, and then his arm was separate from his body and floating away to the side, trailing flossy strands of blood.

Billiard-Fanon was at the hatch. He pushed past Lebret, and ducked inside, disappearing with a wriggle.

Lebret looked back. Capot kicking and thrashing his arms, stirring up a cloud of dark around him – his own blood – as two childranha worried at his body. It was hard to make out exactly what was happening to Pannier, but certainly he had not made it back inside the submarine.

Somebody was tugging on Lebret's legs. In the zero-gravity this slight pressure was enough to drag his body down. He slid out of the water and into the air, gasping. 'Close the hatch, you idiot!' Billiard-Fanon was yelling. 'Close it!'

Lebret wanted to say: *we're safe in here, the air burns them.* But his throat was so tight with horror he could barely breathe. Jhutti pressed the button, and the hatch closed.

29

THE DEATH OF LEBRET

❛ ❛ ❛ ❛ ❛ ❛

'Both dead!' cried Jhutti. 'Devoured – both men devoured!'

'They were tested,' said Billiard-Fanon, in a strange voice. 'God tested them, and they were found wanting.'

'How can you say so?' demanded Jhutti. 'How can you possibly say that?'

'Do not raise your voice at *me*, M'sieur,' said Billiard-Fanon, placidly. 'Did I not *also* swim through the shoal of devils, like Daniel in the den, like Shadrach, Mesach and Abednego in the fiery furnace? And I am unharmed! I am unharmed!'

All three men were still inside the tunnel.

'I need penicillin,' Lebret gasped. A flush of terrible heat was washing through his body. His eyes were streaming, his muscles twitching and trembling. 'I fear that I have contracted blood poisoning.'

Billiard-Fanon took Lebret's face between his two hands and looked into his bleary eyes. 'I did *not* miss,' he said. 'I took aim at your face, right in the middle of your face, and I fired. Yet God has spared you!'

'I need first aid,' said Lebret. Helplessness almost overwhelmed him; tears of frustration and pain filled his eyes. As he blinked them away they had the effect of making Billiard-Fanon seem to shimmer and twitch, as if possessed by devils. 'I am dying,' he gasped. 'But penicillin will save me—'

'God spared you!' Billiard-Fanon cried. '*He* has a plan for you, my friend. Can you not see his light, glinting in my eyes?'

Lebret could see very little now. He was wheezing heavily, his whole body in a feverish agony. 'Penicillin,' he croaked.

'You *have no need* of medicine!' Billiard-Fanon declared, letting go of his face. 'God has spared you! He will not let you die. You were a wicked man, I know; a traitor and murderer. But God's grace is available even to the most wicked! If you have repented, in your heart. If you accept Christ. Your faith will cure you.'

Lebret did not have the energy to argue. He was aware of his surroundings only through a veil of pain and fever.

Jhutti carried him down the corridor and into the main chamber; and he heard Billiard-Fanon crying out about devils and monsters and instructed Satan to get behind him – which must have meant he had laid eyes upon Dakkar. Then Lebret slipped into a dream of being flayed, or of sinking into a bath of acid, or some nebulous but horrible Boschian experience of that nature.

Impossible to gauge the passing of time.

Consciousness returned, or a hazy approximation of it, once more; Lebret was aware of Jhutti pressing a soaking piece of cloth to his mouth, to enable him to drink.

'Monsieur Jhutti,' he croaked, in a faint voice.

'Monsieur Lebret,' returned the scientist. 'You are still alive, at any rate.'

'Not for long, I fear!' He coughed, and shivered, and then managed a smile. 'It seems stupid for me to survive all I have survived, only to die of a child's fever like this!'

'Can death ever be anything except stupid?' Jhutti wondered.

Lebret lay for a while. The white walls of the chamber hurt his eyes, so he closed them. 'How is Dakkar?'

'The monster-man? The hydrocephalic fellow?'

'He is human, Monsieur, and one of your countrymen too. But he has been ... altered.'

'Billiard-Fanon wanted to kill him,' Jhutti reported. 'I think I dissuaded him. He has gone mad, I'm afraid – the ensign, I mean. Religious mania. And anyway, we stand no chance of killing the large-head fellow, now; for I fear he is already dead. He is not breathing, at any rate.'

Lebret twitched and opened his eyes. 'Dead? A great shame. He was Prince Dakkar, once.'

'I have heard of him,' Jhutti said, wonderingly. 'Although I thought him a fictional creation.'

'Fictions *have* been written, based upon him,' Lebret said. 'But he is the authentic figure at those fictions' heart. Or – he was. Did he say nothing? Did he tell you nothing, before he passed?'

'He said a few things. Most of it was hard to follow. Billiard-Fanon baptised him! Crazy.'

'What did Dakkar say though? It may be important.'

'He told us to repair the *Plongeur*, and go back the way we came. He said we were in terrible danger from the Great Jewel. Whatever that means. Billiard-Fanon told him he was a devil. That was about the extent of our conversational exchange.'

Lebret was silent for a while. He could feel his own blood scraping along his arteries and veins. It was hard to breathe. 'Is Ghatwala…?' he asked.

'Dead, I'm afraid,' said Jhutti.

'And Boucher? What about Le Petomain?'

'Boucher is still alive; but his mind has gone. I don't know how long he will last aboard the *Plongeur*, unattended. As for Le Petomain…' Jhutti concluded the sentence with a shake of his head.

The two of them were silent for a while. In the corner, a gentle bee-buzz hummed louder, softer. It took Lebret's hot, muddle brain a while to realise that this noise was Billiard-Fanon snoring.

'I'm sorry, Amanpreet,' Lebret whispered, shortly. 'I'm sorry, truly I am. Ghatwala and I *did* conspire together. Perhaps we should have trusted you. Dilraj fitted a secondary system to the main machinery of the *Plongeur*, cunning camouflaged. We used it to direct the vessel down here, without the knowledge or consent of her captain or crew. We could not trust them. Perhaps we should have trusted you. We acted, as we thought, for the greater good.'

Jhutti was leaning as close to Lebret's mouth as he could. 'I'm afraid I can only understand some of what you say,' he said.

'Beware the Jewel,' Lebret said, and closed his eyes.

He did not open them again.

Billiard-Fanon woke, declared himself enormously refreshed by his nap, and plunged his head through the bubble of water. 'I am hungry,' he announced. 'Jhutti! Wake up Lebret, there. He promised us food! Let him tell us where the food is.'

'Monsieur Lebret will never wake again, I fear,' Jhutti reported.

'Oh!' Billiard-Fanon sounded surprised. 'So he *was* unworthy, after all! God's test is severe.'

'Indeed,' agreed Jhutti, distantly.

'Only we two remain. Of the entire crew!'

'You discount the lieutenant, aboard the *Plongeur*?'

'Poor mad Lieutenant Boucher!' laughed Billiard-Fanon. 'Shall we use the magic speaking slate to address him? But I cannot think he would welcome our conversation. What would we say? Tell him to swim to us? The devils would devour him.'

'They did not eat us,' Jhutti observed.

'Ah, but God has plans for *us*,' Billiard-Fanon said, in a conspiratorial voice. 'I suggest we search this place. Perhaps Lebret was lying about the food, but then again, perhaps there *are* hidden drawers and cupboards filled with cakes and ale, eh?'

The two men floated up and down the walls of the chamber. Jhutti moved the bodies of Dakkar and Lebret to one side, as respectfully as he could; Billiard-Fanon occupied himself with slapping and knocking the sides of the room.

'Nothing!' he said. 'What's this?' He picked up the tattered remains of Lebret's diving suit, and shook it. A clutch of grey-white strands spilled out and floated through the air. 'Snakes!' Billiard-Fanon yelped, throwing the suit from him. 'I shall crush their heads, lest they bruise my heel!'

Jhutti caught one of the filaments as it floated towards him, like limp spaghetti. 'These are no snakes,' he said, scornfully. 'I cannot tell *what* they are – some kind of seaweed, perhaps?'

'Edible?' asked Billiard-Fanon, eyeing the spread of spilled strands.

'Be my guest and try,' said Jhutti.

But Billiard-Fanon's attention had already moved on. He returned to the bulge of water, and thrust his head through it. After a while he came back for air.

'There is another chamber in there,' he announced. 'Flooded, of course, but perhaps containing food. You must dive into it, and have a look about.'

'And I say *you* must,' retorted Jhutti. 'At any rate, I choose not to.'

Lebret eyed him, but did not become angry. 'God has chosen we two,' he told him. 'I do not pretend to know why he chose you, a pagan. But though I *am* the Holy One, and exalted, even in these impossible depths, yet I do not presume to question His providence. But I do say this: *we must get along.*'

Jhutti did not reply.

'At any rate,' said Billiard-Fanon, having toured the room again. 'The water is potable. A body can live for a long time on water and no food – Christ managed forty days and forty nights. Perhaps God wishes us to fast, in imitation of Jesus.'

'I thought God spoke to you directly,' Jhutti said.

'He does,' Billiard-Fanon returned, immediately, his eyes flashing. 'But he has not communicated with me on *this* matter. Are they both dead? Lebret, and the big-head monster? I mean, not in a coma, or anything like that?'

'I'm afraid so,' Jhutti replied. He went over to the bodies, and felt for Lebret's pulse at his neck. 'Nothing.' Conquering his revulsion, he did the same with Dakkar's neck. 'Both dead.'

'Well we must dispose of them, or they shall go bad. Shall we carry the bodies up the corridor, and pitch them topside?'

'If we do,' Jhutti noted, 'then those terrible fish will devour them.'

Billiard-Fanon shook his head. 'Too terrible. They deserve better. Let us put them out of our sight, into the lower chamber.'

'But will that not poison our water supply?'

'We can draw water from above *or* below,' Billiard-Fanon noted.

'This way, although we must drink from above, we can at least ensure those devils do not desecrate their corpses.'

'What if,' Jhutti asked, 'the lower chamber connects directly to open water? What, then, is to stop the devil-fish from swimming round and devouring the corpses anyway?'

'I had not thought of that,' Billiard-Fanon conceded. 'Well, in that case it hardly matters *which* exit we use to dispose of the bodies. Come! Let us put them both below, and I shall say a prayer.'

The truth was that Jhutti cared little, either way. The succession of bizarre events had worn away his grip on reality as a solid quantity. He helped Billiard-Fanon push first Dakkar and then Lebret through, and kicked them both away. Then, for the sake of cleanness, he rounded up all the loose, dead strands of – of whatever they were. These also he thrust into the lower chamber.

'Now,' said Billiard-Fanon. 'We shall see how God intends to deliver us from this place.'

Jhutti looked at his companion. There was no trust in his look.

30

THE TETRAGRAMMATON

❦ ❦ ❦ ❦ ❦ ❦

Billiard-Fanon first prayed silently to himself; then he repeated the Lord's Prayer in a loud voice. Finally he insisted that Jhutti join him. Jhutti declined. 'My religious beliefs are not yours,' he noted, in a level voice.

'All that has been overturned!' Billiard-Fanon insisted. 'Surely, after all you have seen down here, having passed through this entire damnable dimension – surely after all that, you don't cling still to your paganism?'

'My religion is my own affair,' Jhutti repeated. 'But I will say that calling me *pagan* is offensive.'

'All offence is dissolved in the Lord Christ!' replied Billiard-Fanon, with a giggle. 'Come! I shall teach you the Lord's prayer, and in reciting it you will prise open your oyster heart.'

'No, thank you.'

'I insist!' said Billiard-Fanon. He reached inside his own shirt, and brought out a small oilcloth bag. 'Here!'

'Does that bag contain your prayer?' Jhutti asked.

'In a manner of speaking,' said Billiard-Fanon. Untying the end, he brought out a pistol. 'Here!' he cried, joyfully. 'The staff of Moses! Dry as a bone! Although is that not a strange idiom? For your bones, and mine, are never dry, washed continually by blood and lymph as they are!' He weighed in the weapon in his hand, and then pointed it at Jhutti.

Jhutti was almost too exhausted even to be scared. 'What now?' he asked. 'Will you shoot me too?'

'You know I will not hesitate,' Billiard-Fanon said, smiling strangely. 'You know I possess the strength of will to pull this trigger, and end your life?'

Jhutti nodded.

'Then, repeat after me: *Our Father, who art in heaven.*'

Jhutti looked at the barrel and then at Billiard-Fanon's gleaming face. He could repeat the words, of course; it would mean nothing. And defiance would serve no nobler purpose. But something in him refused to do as he was instructed. He shook his head.

Billiard-Fanon's expression hardened. 'Say the words,' he ordered. 'Say them, or displease me. You do not wish to see the displeasure of the Holy One!'

'I do not wish to see the Holy One at all,' said Jhutti.

For a moment Billiard-Fanon's look was that of a hurt child. He dropped the pistol to his side, as if rebuked. But then his eyes narrowed. 'I shall better be able to worship the almighty Tetragrammaton without you here,' he announced. 'JHWH has chosen me, and me alone. That much is clear.'

He raised the gun again, and pulled the trigger. There was a monstrous detonation, ear-hurting. Jhutti flinched. He couldn't help it. But the bullet did not strike him. There was a faint hum in the air, as if (perhaps) it had scudded close to his ear – although Billiard-Fanon had been aiming at his chest.

Jhutti opened his eyes. A huge shape, geometrically precise, sharp-edged, blue-green in colour, had interposed between himself and Billiard-Fanon. It was a moment before Jhutti understood that it had manifested just in time, and presumably therefore *in order*, to block the trajectory of the bullet.

'God, God, God, God!' howled Billiard-Fanon, throwing the weapon aside. 'You appear to me! I *am* the new Moses!'

The shape was a pyramid, comprising four equilateral triangles, each joined to all the others. A voice emerged from the jewel-shape, 'You are Amanpreet Jhutti?'

'No!' yelped Billiard-Fanon. 'Not him – *me*! I am the one elevated by your grace, even in the deepest of depths, in order to…'

'I have no interest in *you*,' said the Jewel. Its voice had a weird flatness of pronunciation, although it spoke French fluently enough. There was a distant, chime-like underlay to the sound. 'Amanpreet Jhutti, you are expert in the engineering of nuclear power?'

'Yes?' Jhutti replied, his heart suddenly running-on-the-spot inside his chest. 'What? What do you want?'

'Instruct me in the ways of nuclear fission,' said the Jewel.

The profound oddness of the moment kept sliding out of Jhutti's mind. As if it were a *reasonable* thing! – to have sunk to the bottom of the deepest ocean in the world in company of a madman only to be quizzed on his knowledge of nuclear physics by a giant geometrical shape. He said, 'You do not understand the principles of an atomic pile?'

'I do,' said the Jewel. 'Don't you?'

'Of course.'

Looking more closely, Jhutti could see that the bullet Billiard Fanon had fired was lodged *inside* the body of the structure. A line composed of dots – miniature bubbles – showed the trajectory it had taken before coming to a halt. Jhutti realised that though it *looked* crystalline – the word 'tetragrammaton' came into Jhutti's head, from whence he knew not – it was actually composed of some strange jelly-like substance. As to how it had suddenly manifested… Jhutti couldn't even guess. He almost reached out to touch it; but held himself back.

'Why ask me, if you already know the answer,' Jhutti said.

'It should, I think, be obvious why I am asking you,' replied the Jewel, with a note of asperity in his voice.

'God, God, God, God,' cried Billiard-Fanon again. 'Do not talk to *him*! He is a heathen. I am the chosen one!'

'Be quiet,' the Jewel instructed him.

'Restore gravity to this place, O God,' Billiard-Fanon pleaded, 'that we may kneel before you! That we may abase ourselves!'

'I am not here for *you*,' the shape said again, crossly. 'I am here for Amanpreet Jhutti, expert in the engineering of nuclear power.'

'But why?' Jhutti asked.

Billiard-Fanon howled, like a dog. 'My God-God-God-God,' he yelled. 'Why have you forsaken me? Or are you a devil? But that cannot be the case!' Jhutti could see him aiming his pistol once again, pointing it at the shape. 'I am the Holy One, and the truth is clear to me – the truth of the sacrifice of Jesus Christ. God must die, and I must kill him! God must die to be reborn again … *as me!*'

Billiard-Fanon discharged the pistol five times in quick succession. The noise was appalling, deafening, and Jhutti put his hands over his ears. Each of the bullets entered the body of the tetragrammaton, slowed and stopped.

The shape seemed to grow, to swell, and then – with a clonic jerk – it contracted. The six bullets were squeezed from its body like pips from an orange. All six converged back on their point of origin. Billiard-Fanon did not even have time to cry out. The impacts caused all four of his limbs to fly outwards, and sent his body karooming straight back to collide with the wall behind him.

'No!' shouted Jhutti.

'Be quick!' the tetragrammaton demanded. 'At this – *distance* – it is very hard for me – to maintain co – *herence*. Answer my question!'

'Are you God?' Jhutti gasped.

'No,' the answer rang out.

'Did you bring this submarine here so as,' Jhutti asked, stopping halfway through the question because it seemed too absurd. Shortly he finished: `…so as to speak to *me*?'

'Yes,' said the tetragrammaton. 'To ask you two questions! And you must answer them!'

'Very well,' said Jhutti, trembling a little. He looked past the shape at Billiard-Fanon's lifeless corpse.

'Do *you* understand the principle of nuclear fission?'

'After seven years of post-doctoral research, I should hope I do.'

'Do *you* understand the principle of nuclear fusion?'

'Fission? Yes, yes I do.'

'No! Do *you* understand the principle of nuclear *fusion*?'

'Ah, pardon me, I misheard. Fusion? I understand the principles,

I suppose. It is what happens in the heart of the sun. But as for making it happen on earth, inside a manmade reactor? We are a long way away from that, I'm afraid.'

And with that answer, the tetragrammaton vanished, de-appearing with a gust of air and a slight squelching noise. Jhutti was alone.

'Good gracious,' he said, pushing himself off to float over towards Billiard-Fanon's body and check for a pulse. 'Am I truly the last one alive? What to do now?'

31

THE JEWEL

● ● ● ● ● ●

To be weightless in air. To be weightless in water.

Lebret couldn't see anything. He wasn't breathing air into his lungs, and that fact disturbed him – felt wrong, awkward. He wasn't hot. He felt cold, he supposed; which is to say, he *must* feel cold, since he didn't feel hot. But actually, he didn't feel anything. He could not move his arms or legs.

He was not alone. He could not tell who was with him. He was dead. Was this how it was, being dead? He could not move the muscles that operated his eyelids; but he did not need to – his eyes were open. But he could not move the tiny ring of muscle inside his eye to bring the half-lit blurry mess of grey-green into focus. Was he dead? He considered this. It seemed to him an important question. Indeed, now that he came to think of it he wasn't sure it was possible to ask a *more* important one. He framed it in his mind. It was always there. It was the ocean bed underlying all our watery consciousness. He asked, 'Am I dead?'

'Just so,' said his companion.

Lebret did not move his lips or tongue; and he expelled no air with his diaphragm – indeed, he had no air to expel. Nonetheless he asked, 'Who are you?'

'I am the Jewel.'

This did not help. Lebret tried a different question, '*Where* are you?'

'Here.' As soon as this word appeared in Lebret's sluggish

brain, he could see – directly in front of his eyes. A crystalline tetrahedron. It rotated slowly, glinting greenly in the dimness.

'You are an emerald!' Lebret cried. But then he looked again, and it seemed to him that the shade was more blue than green. 'Or a sapphire?' And as he said this, it seemed to him that the gemstone darkened, became more richly green until it spilled into a deep, rich blue.

The faceted shape swung round, and Lebret caught a glimpse of himself in one of its triangular facets. His face was swollen and deformed, eyes glassy. But his eyes were evidently still operational, or how else could he see himself? Twice killed, and twice resurrected, he thought. Shot in the head; poisoned with sepsis; still alive. The strands of Dakkar's beard were fixed to his chin, and were swaying in the slight current.

'I thought them dead,' Lebret said. 'Those – whatever they are. Eels. Worms.'

'Water revived them. They were never truly alive, to die.'

'And you are connected to me – through them?'

'Yes,' said the Jewel, simply.

'So for that purpose – you must forgive me for reverting to this question, but it concerns me. *For* that purpose, does it not matter that I am – dead?'

'I have had some time to work with folk, such as you are. Yours is a strange substrate for consciousness – or so it seems to me. A soft and spongy brain, yet it retains all its neuronal connections, even after death. It is a simple matter to make it work.'

'Simple for *you*,' thought Lebret, bitterly.

'Yes,' agreed the Jewel.

'The substrate of *your* consciousness, then, is crystalline?'

'As you can see.'

'But, clearly, you are not physically present. Dakkar said that you were a trillion kilometres away.'

'Indeed. But I am bringing the shell *to* me. And you with it.'

'A trillion miles!' said Lebret. 'That will take ... hundreds of years!'

'It will indeed take some time, although not so long as that. But there is plenty of time.'

'Dakkar told me not to trust you,' said Lebret. 'He said you intended to conquer my world.'

'I do,' agreed the Jewel, readily. '*When* I have you, and your companion, here with me, *then* I shall move ahead with that project.'

'I shall not assist you!' Lebret declared fiercely. 'I shall resist.'

'I have learnt a good deal from the unexpected resistance of Dakkar,' the Jewel said. 'I shall apply what I have learned. I do not believe you will be able to resist.'

'But why?' cried Lebret. 'What good will it do you?'

'I have studied your cosmos, as best I can,' said the Jewel. 'It is a passing strange place. But each of the four universes is different from the other three, and each must seem strange to the inhabitants of the others, I suppose.'

'*Four* universes?'

'The tetraverse,' confirmed the Jewel. 'Did you think your vacuuverse the only cosmos? How could you believe such a bizarrely improbable thing?'

'It is the nature of consciousness to think itself unique, I suppose,' Lebret mused, mentally. Not a one of his muscles moved. He was neither hot nor cold. 'And therefore to gift its surroundings with uniqueness too. I thought my world the only one. Or I *did*, until we stumbled into this ... strange place. A waterverse! I could not believe an infinite space filled with water could exist. Is this cosmos infinite?'

'Geometrically, yes indeed; just as yours is. But it is of finite mass, as yours is. Indeed, all four iterations of the tetraverse manifest balance in terms of total mass.'

'What do you mean?'

The Jewel began to rotate more rapidly, spinning smoothly. Lebret saw his own drowned face flashing in each of the triangular facets in turn.

'I have studied the other three universes, as far as I have been able,' said the Jewel. 'Of course I have! Of *course* I have. *Your* universe is – I speak very approximately – a sphere with a radius of 10^{30} light years. Naturally, yours is a *vacuum* cosmos. Matter is spread in varying degrees of irregularity throughout it, but overall the constituent atoms are spread *extraordinarily* tenuously. When you look at the total picture – on average, the density of *your* cosmos is one hydrogen atom in every four cubic metres of volume. That is a medium whose density is about $10^{\wedge}30$ times less than water. And the *result* of this strange harmonious coincidence of numbers – which, of course, is no coincidence at all, but rather an expression of underlying geometric truths about the constraints on any existing universe – the result of this congruence is that the waterverse must be *one times ten-to-the-one-thirtieth* the size of the vacuuverse.'

'In other words,' said Lebret, working the sum in his head, 'it must be ... only *one* light-year across—'

'One light year *radius*. Two light years across. Approximately twenty trillion kilometres. If you wish a comparison, to help visualise the size – twenty trillion kilometres is the size of your own solar system.'

Lebret thought about this. 'I would have guessed that the orbit of Pluto would be considerably less than ...'

'Pluto? Nonsense! What is Pluto? Pluto is neither here nor there.' The Jewel was spinning more rapidly now, as if winding itself up with its own discourse. 'No, from the sun in the centre out to the edge of your sun's *heliopause*. The Oort cloud. You know the Oort cloud?'

'No,' conceded Lebret.

'Comets. Billions of comets. They fill a vast sphere, around your central matter-knot sun. Mostly they stay there, the comets, although occasionally they fall in and hurtle near the inner planets, trailing great fishy tails of steam behind them. But if you measure your system from its matter-knot centre out *to* its heliopause, it has a radius of about a light year. It is almost all vacuo, of course; but let us describe it as a single unity. Well, the waterverse is a similar size.'

'Though filled throughout by water,' Lebret said.

'Indeed.'

'But how does it not *collapse* upon itself?' Lebret pressed. 'I don't understand. Why does not gravity *compress* the water, over time?'

'A good question. Indeed, it is already starting to happen. But my waterverse has existed for only one-10^{30}th as long as your vacuuverse. A long time, measured by the days and years you use to measure the passing of time; but not long enough for the inexorable forces of gravity to create first whirlpools and tourbillions, and eventually gravitational densities strong enough to rip hydrogen and oxygen apart. That is in the future – the far future.'

'Are you seeking to escape? Is that what you are looking for, in my world?'

'That you ask such a question shows that you do not understand the larger structure,' rebuked the Jewel.

'You mean, the ... tetraverse?'

'Your ghostly vacuuverse, vast and tenuous. My waterverse. And the rest? There is also a cosmos consisting entire of matter.'

'A matterverse! Is it inhabited?'

'It is. Although its inhabitants are utterly other to what you would consider a life form.'

'Gas, liquid, solid. What, then, is the fourth? Surely those three exhaust the different ways in which atoms may be arranged?'

'The fourth is immensely smaller, by a large margin the smallest of all – an almost incomprehensibly dense cosmos. It is comprised of matter in a state of fusion-plasma.'

'Fire,' said Lebret, nodding slowly, and causing his hair to waft in the water. 'Universes of air, of water, of solid matter and – of fire!'

'Poetic, but imprecise.'

'So – you do not wish to conquer us? To rule our vacuum cosmos?'

'What is there *in* it to rule? To be king of nothingness? That is no ambition.'

'You wish to pass *through* our universe!' Lebret guessed. 'Your true aim is to reach the universe of rock – or perhaps the realm of fire!'

'Still you do not understand. The relationship between the four universes is a function of *infinite* geometries,' said the Jewel. 'Perhaps you are picturing these different cosmoses as strung out, like pearls on a thread – a very large sphere for the vacuuverse, much smaller ones for the waterverse, the matterverse and a miniature one for the fusionverse. If so, you are picturing them wrongly. Quite wrongly! When one infinite geometrical figure intersects another, they intersect *at all points simultaneously*. Or, to put it another way, if you put infinite geometrical figure A inside infinite geometrical figure B, you are at the same time placing infinite geometrical figure B inside infinite geometrical figure A. You cannot help but do this. Think of the tetraverse…'

'Hard to do!'

'Then you must exercise your intellect. As far as I have been able to determine, these four nesting universes are the sum total of absolute reality. But you interrupted me! Think of the tetraverse as four boxes, each inside each: the vacuuverse containing the waterverse containing the matterverse containing the fusionverse…'

'Russian dolls,' gasped Lebret.

'Well, that is not a bad way of conceptualising it. So long as you also understand that the order is reversed – the vacuuverse is simultaneously *inside* the waterverse, which is inside the matterverse, which is inside the fusionverse. And actually, we must factorial four to arrive at the full description of these hierarchies.'

'But why should there be four universes? Why not three – or five? Or a million?'

'Or an infinite number – yes, quite, quite. It is a good question. Perhaps because matter can only occur in four forms – gaseous, liquid, solid and atomically fused? We might as well ask why are there only four dimensions, length, breadth, height and time. Why not three, or five? Or an infinite number?'

The blue-green Jewel was spinning rapidly now, stirring the water and making Lebret's lifeless body wobble. The edges were blurring. 'You did not answer my question,' Lebret said. 'What *is* the nature of your designs upon my cosmos?'

'The balance of the tetraverse is a precarious thing. It is not a permanent structure. It is surrounded by a shell of pure fusion fire – and that fire is also *what is contained* within the structure, at the centre, and at every level – a flame that threatens to consume everything. The presence of your vacuuverse insulates the other realms from this destructive potential – because it is not only the outermost layer of the tetraverse, but also the hollow core of ultimate reality, and the intervening layer between all other cosmoses.'

'Like a thermos keeping heat and cold apart. Why should it have a special role?'

'Infinite geometries are complex. But the relative immensity of your cosmos is a relevant detail.'

'And?'

'And your planet, the world upon which you and your fellows live – though an infinitesimal *speck* within the larger whole – nevertheless, your world threatens the entire tetraverse. It is the weak link in the larger structure.'

'How?'

'It is a nexus, a world of land and oceans, blanketed with air and curled around a sphere of fiery magma. But populated – swarming with living beings.'

'My people.'

'You are ingenious, your kind. You do not understand the danger.'

'Of what?'

'If you are left to your own devices you will develop fusion energy. Already – as your iron-metal craft shows – you have developed simple nuclear power. But if you create fusion, not in the interior of vacuum moated stars, but upon your four-elemental world – in structures built upon land, beside the sea, open to the air – if you do this, then you will *break the seal*. You will breach the barrier that keeps the terrible power of the fusionverse, and give it and its inhabitants access to the other three universes. You are concerned as to what will happen if I invade your world – you should be more concerned as to what will happen if the fusionverse ever gains access to your cosmos. And through it, to mine.'

Lebret pondered these words for a long time. The Jewel was now spinning very rapidly, an ovoid blue-green blur. Something occurred to him, 'What if you are lying?'

'It makes no difference,' said the Jewel. 'I am drawing the structure you currently inhabit through the waterverse. It will take time, but eventually I will have direct access to you – and your companions. I do not need you to believe me.'

Lebret felt a painful twist of the awareness of his impotence, and the indigestible perspective of sudden cosmic perspectives he had been granted. But he could not close his eyes, or move any part of his body. His mind was awake.

'I will have your iron craft,' the Jewel said. 'I will have new examples of your kind, these *homo sapiens sapiens* who play such a dominant role in your world. I will have your nuclear-power engine. I have learnt a great deal since my last experimentations upon mankind. I will be able to control you, and I will have your device. It will be a simple matter, thereupon, to break through into your planet, and put a stop to your species and their meddling.'

Lebret's spirit quailed within him; but he existed in a state of perfect passivity. There was nothing he could do.

Years passed, or perhaps they did. Lebret had the sense of a great deal of time passing, but he had that perception, as it were, *from an external source*. It is difficult to explain how this felt for him. Ten trillion kilometres. Fifteen trillions kilometres. If his consciousness now only worked when the Jewel stimulated the quasi-crystalline pattern of neurones in his brain, how could he gauge the passing of time? Perhaps the Jewel switched him off (as it were) for decades at a time.

'Stop him,' somebody said.

Lebret could not be sure where this other voice originated, or who it was. It might have been Dakkar – although Dakkar was dead, and (unlike Lebret) beardless.

The Jewel was rotating so fast now it had lost its sharp-edged and pointed features, and resembled a blurry skull. Lebret might even fancy a face upon it.

'How can I stop him?'

'Name him,' said the other. Who was this other?

What name to utter?

And Lebret could not name him, because the entity was alien, and he did not know the name, and Lebret was altogether powerless. Dead, and, anyway – and anyway – what power did names have? Lebret did not know the name. There was no conceivable way that he could find out the name. He did not even know whether the Jewel had a name, beyond Jewel – whether his manner of life-form had any use for names. Names, Lebret thought, are a strange business, really. Animals don't need them – why should men and women? Yet we do; and names possess legal and religious and social and symbolic power. And then, with a little spurt of inspiration, the name arrived in Lebret's consciousness. He couldn't have told you from whence, but he sensed the rightness of it.

He had died twice; twice he had been brought back from death. He would die a third time. That was the potent death, that third. And the name was there. 'I understand,' he said.

'Understand what?' demanded the Jewel, suddenly, unaccountably furious.

'I know your name.'

'You *cannot* know my name! You *do* not know my name!' the Jewel shrieked, spinning so fast that the water around it was twisted into muscular flows and pulses. The edges were no longer visible – the Jewel was an elongated sphere, blurred at the edges.

'I know your name,' Lebret repeated.

This reiteration, oddly, appeared to calm the entity. The shrieking stopped; and for a while the structure simply span. 'And what *is* my name?' hummed the Jewel.

'Verne,' said Lebret. And everything went black.

32

TWENTY TRILLION
KILOMETRES UNDER THE SEA

❡ ❡ ❡ ❡ ❡ ❡

Fifty years had passed – *more* than fifty years. Closer to sixty. Back in his home, the calendar would be well into the twenty-first century by now. To be honest, Jhutti had long since lost track of the time. Mostly this was because of the sleeping – it was impossible to know what proportion of his life was swallowed by sleep, but it was evidently the majority. This, he had long since realised, was the Jewel's doing. It was clear that working at a distance, even through this 'infraspace' of which Lebret spoke, was limiting for the Jewel. He could do certain things: manifest a three-dimensional avatar of himself (although he had not done that since Lebret named him); draw the material substance of the base towards him, and even influence Jhutti's body chemistry, flooding it with narcotic hormones. If it were in any sense possible, Jhutti did not doubt that the Jewel would put him to sleep for the whole length of the journey – a coma. But he could not, of course – Jhutti would die of thirst and hunger. So, instead, the overwhelming wave of sleepiness swept over Jhutti's brain in a tide-like pattern; days and days in dreamless sleep, to wake – groggily, his head throbbing with migraine – for half an hour, just enough time to relieve himself, to drink like a dog at the hatch and nibble what food he could reach. Then the sleep would come like a wave, and he would slip under again.

Jhutti met this assault (for an assault is most assuredly what it *was*) with what defences he could. Pricking himself with sharp points only postponed the sleepiness for a short time. Immersing himself in water worked rather better, but only because he woke choking and coughing, and spent long minutes recovering, with burning lungs and thundering heart. After a time, Jhutti became more adept at holding off the sleepiness by sheer willpower, but these small victories lasted half an hour or more; and as he explored the space, and brought his considerable intellect to bear upon the various technical gee-gaws it contained, attempting to make them work – all the time he was having to fight off sleep. Eventually he always succumbed.

And then one day, Jhutti woke up. He could sense at once that something had changed; that the Jewel's power over him had diminished. And even, later, after he had been able briefly to communicate with his former shipmate it remained obscure to him why this naming had the effect it did. But he could not quarrel with the freedom it gave him.

He explored his space. The length of his own beard suggested that many years had passed since he had enjoyed uninterrupted periods of consciousness, but he could not be certain. That Lebret's body was entirely uncorrupted suggested that relatively little time had passed; but the other bodies – the corpses of Dakkar and Billiard-Fanon – had entirely disappeared. Jhutti pondered whether they had been in some sense transported away, or had rotted to nothing over many years. But in that case where were their skeletons? After going to the upper hatch and attempting to swim to the *Plongeur* he developed a new theory. Of the school of childranha only one remained – large, malignant looking, and lurking in the gashed side of the submarine. When Jhutti first poked his head through, it darted forth and rushed at him; he only managed to get his head back inside just in time.

Assuming that the lower chamber was open at some point to the larger ocean, a circumstance Jhutti thought likely (although he was unable to test it), it seemed that this one remaining beast had devoured both bodies, and also all its fellows. As to why it hadn't also eaten Lebret's body, Jhutti could not say; but he postulated that the tentacles embedded in Lebret's chin, which were evidently alive even though Lebret lacked pulse or breath, produced some chemical signal that kept the childranha away.

At any rate, Jhutti could not hope to cross to the submarine with that monster in the water. A thorough search of the space showed up a small knife, amongst other things, and Jhutti carefully sharpened this, and tied it to a pole with cut-up strips of wetsuit. As he did this, he thought of the book he had been reading immediately before embarking aboard the *Plongeur* – a short novel by the American writer Hemingway, concerning an old man and the sea. 'Man,' he said aloud, his voice croaky in the white space, 'is not made for defeat. A man can be destroyed but not defeated.' It heartened him.

He went up top with his makeshift lance, took a series of deep breaths, and put his head into the water. The fish came at him again straight away, and though Jhutti jabbed it several times in its devil-face, it did not back away. It occurred to Jhutti, thinking back on the encounter later, that it might be mad with hunger. Who knew how long it had lurked, with nothing to eat, waiting, like a pike in the mud of an immemorial pond?

Three times Jhutti pulled himself back into the safety of the air, gasping; and three times he pushed his head and torso back into the water. The creature never gave up, until a final stroke severed its spine, and it went limp.

After that Jhutti rested, ate, and readied himself. Swimming out upon the shell surface, he kicked the body of the last childranha away, and breast-stroked his way to the airlock. The mechanism was stiff, but still opened; and in minutes he was inside.

He was expecting a bad smell, but the air, though musty, was breathable. The engines were clearly still working, pumping oxygen about. He made his way about the deserted craft as if through a dream landscape. In Boucher's cabin he found the lieutenant's body, mummified and lying on its front. This, clearly, had taken a long time. But, miraculously, the atomic pile still hummed and functioned, unattended for however long.

Over the months that followed Jhutti returned to the *Plongeur* several times. The structural damage was beyond his power to repair, working alone; but he was at least able to swim through the flooded mess and retrieve food from the kitchens, and so vary his otherwise monotonous diet.

Back inside the white space, he tried every way he could think of to make the various technological gadgets operate. His only success, however, was with the communication slate. After a long period of fiddling, he opened a channel to Lebret. This in itself was so startling and unsettling a thing that he refused to believe it at first. It was made harder to believe, at least initially, by the incoherence of Lebret's communications – he spoke very slowly, with long pauses between words, and not everything he said made sense. But after several days of interaction, Jhutti came to the conclusion that it was truly him. 'Your body is in the next chamber,' he told the Frenchman. 'It is not breathing, your heart is not beating – how can there be brain activity?'

'The,' came Lebret's voice, croakily, from the white slate. 'Beard! Tentacles, tentacles, thinking fibres!'

'Can you be fully revived?'

'I – don't – know.'

'Do you wish me to try?'

Nothing. Half an hour of hiss. Then, so abruptly that it made Jhutti twitch, 'The Jewel!'

'What of him?'

'He is,' creaked Lebret. 'Drawing the structure. Towards him.'

'Why?'

Nothing.

'Are you still there? Lebret, I felt him in my head. He was forcing me to sleep – I don't know how. But he was managing it; keeping me effectively comatose until we reach the destination I suppose.'

'I – named – him.'

'You did what?'

'I named him – and reduced his power – and …'

'How?'

Nothing. Jhutti persevered for a while. 'What is his name? And what does he want with us? What does he want with *me*?' But there was no reply.

Jhutti waited. He became hungry, and so harvested some mallows and augmented the meal with a tin salvaged from the *Plongeur*. Then he slept, a short nap. Since the communications slate appeared to be waterproof, he took it with him and swam down to where Lebret's body was. Only the swaying motion of the tentacular beard, moving through the still waters, showed any signs of life. Jhutti debated with himself about dragging Lebret back into the air, but decided it would probably be best to leave him where he was.

Days passed. Jhutti returned several times to the *Plongeur*, like Robinson Crusoe salvaging what he could from the wreck of his ship. He rigged up a rudimentary exercise device with springs from the vessel, and initiated a regime to stretch and thus stress his muscles and bones. There was no way of knowing how long he would have to live in zero-g, but he was aware of the theories that predicted muscle wastage and bone loss for future astronauts. He would do what he could.

'The Jewel!' said Lebret, over the slate. His voice was weaker, more elderly-sounding.

Jhutti scrambled to the slate. 'Lebret? Lebret – are you alright?'

'He is the demiurge!' Lebret hissed. 'This is his world. But there are – rules. He must abide by his rules. Or break apart the whole thing!'

'Lebret, what are you talking about?'

'You can – defeat – him,' whispered Lebret

Jhutti had to put his ear to the slate. 'How? Tell me how?'

'Know – his – name—'

'What is it?'

There was a long pause. Then, gasping repeatedly as if saying the words caused him pain, Lebret said, 'His name is green, for he is the green man, and though we cut him down he will grow again! His name is glass, and his name is green, and he is the glass-green sea!'

'You're not making sense—' Jhutti said.

'He *is* the sea, he is its glass, he is its green, he is the emerald—'

'Is that his name? Emerald?'

'Enough!' cried Lebret, through the slate. 'Or – *too much.*'

There was, then, a period of two weeks or more (Jhutti was keeping a slate of sleep periods, but he suspected that his 'days' were several hours shorter than terrestrial days) when Lebret was silent. Indeed, Jhutti only had two further exchanges with him. In one he was fairly comprehensible, and talked about the Jewel's plans. 'Invasion!' Jhutti asked him. 'Are you sure? And why does he want *me*? What use to him can *I* be?'

'Atomic power,' Lebret said, haltingly. 'He understands fusion and fission, but only theoretically... this cosmos is not hospitable to it. No great stars, no heavy elements... but in ours – but in ours – but...'

'But the sub oceanic suns?'

'Mere fires, burning hot but not, hot but not an atomic torch... candles lit in infraspace...'

'What? What is that?'

'Never mind! The Jewel! Think of him!'

'And tell me about his *name*,' Jhutti pressed. 'You suggested that it had some form of talismanic power...'

Lebret's did not reply for a long time, and when he eventually spoke he sounded scared. 'His name? His name?'

'Yes – what *is* it?'

'I cannot!' shrieked Lebret. 'It *pains* me to try and think... to try and think of...'

He broke off, and did not speak for many days. Jhutti decided that, somehow, the Jewel was trying to block off Lebret's ability to articulate the name; perhaps triggering some sort of short-circuit whenever he tried to do so.

He made a series of trips to the *Plongeur*, and ran cables from its engine room through to the white space. Inside the submarine, he swam through the flooded mess and retrieved explosives from the armoury, setting these in selected locations about the pile. He could not hope to create a Hiroshima-style explosion, he knew; but he could create a fairly impressive bang. It remained to be seen whether he had the wherewithal to destroy the Jewel; but at least he could prevent the atomic pile – and himself – from falling into the entity's hands.

But should he? Suicide seemed an extreme action. Could he deduce the creature's Rumplestiltskin-style name? He ran through possibilities – a tyrant's name, a Caesar moniker? Or something angelic, God's right-hand? What had Lebret called the Jewel? A demiurge? Green, glass, water, sea, ocean, emerald. Was that it? Emerald?

And ice, mast-high, came floating by
As green as emerald…

'Monsieur,' croaked the communications tablet. 'Monsieur!'

'Lebret? Is that you?'

'We are deeper than thought. We are Prospero's books. We are Oort, Oort, Oort.'

'What? I don't understand!'

'You *cannot* destroy him,' Lebret hissed. 'You must destroy him! You cannot do it. But you can *name* him, and…'

That was the last thing Lebret said. Days passed in silence; and when Jhutti swam down to look again at his body the tendrils had all detached themselves from his face. Whither they had vanished he could not say; but they were gone. Over the following week, signs of physical decay began to manifest in the Frenchman's flesh, and Jhutti was forced to push his body through the chambers and out into the larger ocean, for fear that his corpse would poison his supply of drinking water.

The Jewel had removed whatever strange organic-machinery he had been using to keep Lebret's body from corruption, and to work the neural network of his brain. But why now?

Another week passed. There was a time when Jhutti slept, and dreamt that the *Plongeur* had exploded, silently but with a light brighter than a galaxy of suns.

He woke with a start. There *was* a light shining; it was beaming from the corridor that lead up to the hatch. Worrying that something was wrong with the submarine, Jhutti flew upwards, and poked his head through into the water.

There was a structure in the water – spherical, huge, much larger than the sub oceanic suns, though gleaming with so much lesser a light, that Jhutti was able to look directly at it. It was a million-faceted jewel – thousands of kilometres across; and it gleamed from some inner light source oceanic greens and blues.

Jhutti, his heart pounding, ducked back into the corridor to snatch a breath. When he put his head out again, the huge structure was even larger. They must be hurtling towards it with extraordinary celerity!

The voice clanged in his head, like a hammer blow. In French it boomed *I AM THAT I AM!* And then, with a less idiomatic expression it added *I GO NOT!*

Jhutti hauled himself back into the air. '*Je suis que je suis, je vais ne,*' he muttered to himself, wiping water from his beard and long hair. 'Can it be that the demiurge speaks French less fluently than an Indian?'

But the trigger was below him, in the white space, and panicking suddenly that he would be prevented from reaching it he pulled himself down the corridor and shot into the room like a cork from a pop-gun. Between himself and his makeshift trigger was a faintly gleaming dodecahedral jewel, three metres long, hanging in mid-air, and rotating very slowly. It cast sliding, glassy blue-green patches of colour upon the white walls. 'It's you!' Jhutti gasped. 'The demiurge himself!'

'You will not reach the trigger,' said the Jewel. 'You must accept the inevitability. You are mine. All of you were always mine.'

'If I might be permitted to correct you,' Jhutti said, looking around him to see if there were some projectile he could throw.

'You are looking for a weapon,' said the Jewel. 'Or you are hoping to throw something and set off the trigger. You see that I am able to manifest materially in your space. If you move towards anything, I shall manifest crystal pegs through your bones, and incapacitate you. I need what is in your mind. I do not need your consent to reach it.'

'If,' Jhutti repeated, letting his arms go slack, 'I may be permitted to correct you. It would be more correct to say *je ne vais pas…*'

'You think I cannot speak French,' said the Jewel in a monotone. And in that instant, Jhutti realised. The words appeared inside his mind, round and sweet as an apple. And at the same time Jhutti thought to himself, *Will he sense that I am about to say those words? Will he detect the motion of my diaphragm, the contraction of my vocal chords, and make appear a crystal splinter in my throat to choke me off? Dare I risk it?*

'There need be no unpleasantness,' said the Jewel. 'If you help me. What I want – it is the common good! This is *my* cosmos. I know what is right for it!'

Jhutti fixed his eyes on the slowly turning gem. The words were waiting to be spoken. But would he get them out in time? It would be, Jhutti thought, like an old Wild West movie, like a gunfight on the dusty main street. He would attempt to pull out his six-shooter – two words – and his adversary would attempt to pull out his weapon, and pin a crystal needle through Jhutti's windpipe.

His heart was pounding. He shut his eyes. He heard the Jewel say, 'What is your answer, Amanpreet Jhutti?'

He spoke.

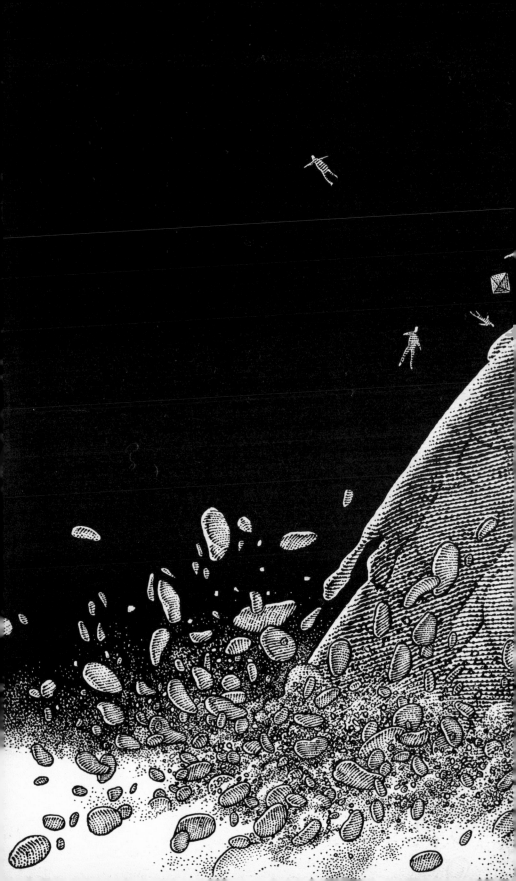

M·Singh

EPILOGUE

That the mind is in the world and at the same time the world is inside the mind. This is in the nature of infinite geometries, and these are the geometries with which we must deal. Take the example of a particular writer – say he lives in France. Say he carries the idea of France inside him. Each insulates each; and France exists within the world and is itself a world. And this world is subordinate to its more massive sun, which has captured it; and yet the world moves on its frictionless ellipses around and around, containing its sun in an invisible net of silk. The sun is part of a galaxy that surrounds a central black hole; and that black hole has broke the hymen of space-time itself and folded out, a point that is an infinite space in which the galaxy itself is nested. Thought and matter are each inside each other, and each flows without and within, and the principle of flow is the ocean.

You are dipped in this water, and it is with this water that you are baptised. Streaming, your head surfaces, like the head of somebody breaking the surface of an ocean of words. This ocean is glassy, and greeny, and we move towards it.

Jhutti opened his eyes. He felt as if he had been turned inside-out, or the reverse of that. 'Where am I?' he asked.